ANTONIA WHITE

was born in London in 1899, and educated at the Convent of the Sacred Heart, Roehampton and St Paul's Girls' School, London. she trained as an actress at the Royal Academy of Dramatic Art, working for her living as a freelance copywriter and contributing short stories to a variety of magazines. In 1924 she joined the staff of W. S. Crawford as a copywriter, became Assistant Editor of *Life and Letters* in 1928, theatre critic of *Time and Tide* in 1934, and was the Fashion Editor of the *Daily Mirror* and then the *Sunday Pictorial* until the outbreak of the Second World War. During the war Antonia White worked first in the BBC and then in the French Section of the Political Intelligence Department of the Foreign Office.

Antonia White published four novels: *Frost in May* (1933), *The Lost Traveller* (1950), *The Sugar House* (1952), and *Beyond the Glass* (1954). This quartet of novels was a major BBC TV serial in 1982. Her other published work includes a volume of short stories, *Strangers* (1954), and an autobiographical account of her reconversion to the Catholic faith, *The Hound and the Falcon* (1965). All these works and *As Once in May*, the early autobiography and other writings of Antonia White, are published by Virago Press.

Antonia White translated over thirty novels from the French, and was awarded the Clairouin Prize for her first one, Maupassant's *Une Vie*, in 1950. She also translated many of the works of Colette. Like Colette, Antonia White was devoted to cats and wrote two books about her own – *Minka and Curda* and *Living With Minka and Curdy*. She was married three times and had two daughters and four grandchildren. She lived most of her life in London and died in 1980 in Sussex, where her father and many generations of her family were born and bred.

ANTONIA WHITE

Beyond the Glass

New Introduction by Carmen Callil

Virago

To
KATHERINE GURLEY, M.D.
of Jersey City, whose friendship I value
so much and without whose encouragement
this book might never have been written

Published by VIRAGO PRESS Limited 1979
41 William IV Street,
London WC2N 4DB

Reprinted 1981, 1982, 1984

First published by Eyre & Spottiswoode 1954

British Library Cataloguing in Publication Data

White, Antonia
  Beyond the Glass.—(Virago modern
  classics)
  I. Title
  823'.914[F]   PR6045.H5634
  ISBN 0-86068-097-5

Printed and bound in Great Britain
by Hazell Watson & Viney Ltd
a member of BPCC

Introduction

It is unusual for the publisher of a book to provide its preface. Antonia White wanted to write a new introduction to the three books – *The Lost Traveller*, *The Sugar House* and *Beyond the Glass* – which complete the story she began in her famous novel *Frost in May*. Now eighty years of age, and a novelist whose small output reflects the virulent writer's block which has constantly interrupted her writing life, she preferred to talk to me. For though separated by age, country of birth and nationality, we share a Catholic upbringing which has been a dominant influence on both our lives. What follows is based on a long conversation I had with Antonia White in December 1978, and on the many times we've talked since Virago first re-published *Frost in May* earlier that year.

'Personal novels,' wrote Elizabeth Bowen in a review of Antonia White's work, 'those which are obviously based on life, have their own advantages and hazards. But we have one "personal" novelist who has brought it off infallibly.' Antonia White turned fact into fiction in a quartet of novels based on her life from the ages of nine to twenty-three. 'My life is the raw material for the novels, but writing an autobiography and writing fiction are very different things.' This transformation of real life into an imagined work of art is perhaps her greatest skill as a novelist.

Antonia White was the only child of Cecil Botting, Senior Classics Master at St Paul's School, who became a Catholic at the age of thirty-five taking with him into the Church his wife and seven-year-old daughter, fictionalised as 'Nanda' in *Frost in May*. This novel is a brilliant portrait of Nanda's experiences in the enclosed world of a Catholic convent. First published in 1933, it was immediately recognized as a classic. Antonia White wrote what was to become the first two chapters of *Frost in May* when she was only sixteen, completing it sixteen years later, in 1931. At the time she was married to Tom Hopkinson, writer, journalist and later editor of *Picture Post*.

'I'd written one or two short stories, but really I wrote nothing until my father's death in 1929. I'd worked in advertising all those years, as a copywriter, and I'd done articles for women's pages and all sorts of women's magazines, but I couldn't bring myself to write anything serious until after my father died. At the time I was doing a penitential stint in Harrods' Advertising Department...I'd been sacked from Crawfords in 1930 for not taking a passionate enough interest in advertising. One day I was looking through my desk and I came across this bundle of manuscript. Out of curiosity I began to read it and some of the things in it made me laugh. Tom asked me to read it to him, which I did, and then he said "You must finish it." Anyway Tom had appendicitis and we were very hard up, so I was working full time. But Tom insisted I finish a chapter every Saturday night. Somehow or other I managed to do it, and then Tom thought I should send it to the publisher – Cobden Sanderson – who'd liked my short stories. They wrote back saying it was too slight to be of interest to anyone. Several other people turned it down and then a woman I knew told me that Desmond Harmsworth had won some money in the Irish sweep and didn't know what to do with it . . . so he started a publishing business and in fact I think *Frost in May* was the only thing he ever published . . . it got wonderful reviews.'

Between 1933 and 1950 Antonia White wrote no more novels. She was divorced from Tom Hopkinson in 1938, worked in advertising, for newspapers, as a freelance journalist and then came the war. Throughout this period she suffered further attacks of the mental illness she first experienced in 1922. This madness Antonia White refers to as 'The Beast' – Henry James' 'Beast in the Jungle'. Its recurrence and a long period of psychoanalysis interrupted these years.

'I'd always wanted to write another novel, having done one, but then you see the 1930s were a very difficult time for me because I started going off my head again. After the war and the political work I did I was terribly hard up. Then Enid Starkey, whom I'd met during the war, suggested to Hamish Hamilton that I should have a shot at translating and they liked what I did. After that I got all these commissions and I was doing two or three a year but I was completely jammed up on anything of my own, though I kept on trying to write in spite of it. I always wanted to write another novel, and I wanted this time to do something more ambitious, what I thought would be a "proper" novel, not seen only through the eyes of one person as it is in *Frost in May*, but through the eyes of the father, the mother and even those old great aunts in the country. Then suddenly I could write again. The first one [*The Lost Traveller*] took the longest to write. I don't know how many years it took me, but I was amazed how I then managed to write the other two [*The Sugar House* and *Beyond the Glass*]. They came incredibly quickly.'

In 1950, seventeen years after the publication of *Frost in May*, *The Lost Traveller* was published. In it Antonia White changed the name of her heroine Nanda Grey to Clara Batchelor. 'Of course Clara is a continuation of Nanda. Nanda became Clara because my father had a great passion for Meredith and a particular passion for Clara Middleton (heroine of *The Egoist*). Everything that happened to Clara in *The Lost Traveller* is the sort of thing that happened to me, though many things are changed, many invented. I wanted *The Lost Traveller* to be a real novel – *Frost in May* was so much my own life. So I changed her name. . .' In every other respect this novel begins where *Frost in May* ends. It is a vivid account of adolescence, of the mutual relationships of father, mother and daughter as Clara grows to maturity and comes to grips with the adult world.

'When I finished *The Lost Traveller* I thought of it as just being one book, and then suddenly I felt I wanted to write another one about my first marriage. That was *The Sugar House*, which I think is much the best of the three. In it I see Clara's relationship with Archie (her husband) entirely through the eyes of one person, as in *Frost in May* – I think that suited me much better.'

The Sugar House was published in 1952 and takes Clara through her first love affair, work as an actress and a doomed first marriage. Unsentimental, often amusing, it is unusual for its moving description of a love between a man and a woman which is not sexual but which is nevertheless immensely strong.

Beyond the Glass, which completed the quartet in 1954, is technically the most ambitious of the four novels, dramatically using images of glass and mirrors to reflect Clara's growing mental instability. For Antonia White describes her first encounter with 'The Beast' in this novel, interweaving the story of Clara's new love affair with a vivid description of her descent into and recovery from madness. Antonia White remembers every moment of the ten months she spent in Bethlem Asylum (now the Imperial War Museum) in 1922–3. It is the extraordinary clarity of her recollection of that madness which makes this novel so convincing.

Antonia White's portrait of the life of a young Catholic girl in the first decades of this century is dominated by two themes – the heroine's intense relationship with her father, and the all-pervading influence of the Catholic faith. Antonia White's father centred everything on his only child, and Antonia was absolutely devoted to him. But to the end of his life he refused to discuss one of her earliest traumas – the expulsion from the convent she recorded so faithfully in *Frost in May* – and she has obviously felt that she disappointed him bitterly by going her own way in life. As a Catholic, her relationship with Catholic belief and practice has always been intense, a wrestling to live within its spiritual imperatives in a way which accorded with her own nature, clinging to her faith, as she says, 'by the skin of my teeth'. The struggle is brilliantly felt in this quartet, permeating everything that happens to Clara, affecting her adolescence, sexuality, her relationships with men.

To a modern reader these could be seen as experiences intimately connected with Clara's slow progress towards madness, but to Antonia White they were influences which were also profoundly enriching, in no way negative, part of an extraordinary life which she recalls with a mixture of astonishment and laughter, and which she recreates with consummate skill in these four novels.

*   *   *

When Antonia White completed *Beyond the Glass* her career as a novelist was over, but she always hoped to finish the story of Clara's life. 'I tried and tried because everybody wrote to me and said you can't leave Clara like this, and for years I tried, but only managed one chapter. Clara by this time is married again – to Clive – and has given up her religion and is living the sort of life her father doesn't approve of . . . going out to work and having a wonderful time. Her father is very upset because Clara has given up her religion and he feels she ought to have a child, because he wants a grandchild, but her mother doesn't disapprove at all, she thinks Clara has had such an awful time that it's time she had some fun. Clara gets on much better with her mother now. I finally finished what I still think is a very good chapter: Clara's father has retired and they're living in the Sussex cottage. Apart from his trouble with his daughter, he is having the most lovely time of his life ... they've extended the garden and he's at last got his great desire – a full-size croquet lawn where he spends all his time, playing out there in the blazing sun ...'

Carmen Callil, Virago, London, 1979

Antonia White died on 10th April, 1980

Part One

CHAPTER ONE

USUALLY, Claude Batchelor was so eager to get down to Sussex for his annual three weeks holiday that, the moment the prize-giving was over, he changed hurriedly into tweeds and was on his way within an hour. This year, for the first time, he had decided to take things more easily and go down the following day. Perhaps because, at fifty, he was feeling the strain of having consistently over-worked since he came down from Cambridge, he was wearier than he could remember ever having been in his life.

On the morning of the day he and his wife were to travel down to Paget's Fold he awoke with no joyful anticipation. On the contrary, his mood was curiously oppressed. A nightmare, whose details were already fogged, had left him with a confused sense of guilt and apprehension which he could not dispel. Normally, his dreams were rare, vivid and recountable. Of last night's he could remember nothing except that they had been of a kind he could have told no one and that they had concerned his daughter, Clara.

He had reason enough to be anxious about Clara. She had been married only a few months and it was obvious that things were not going well. Archie Hughes-Follett had begun to drink again and he suspected they were getting into debt. What troubled him far more was the swift and violent change in Clara herself. The last time he had seen her, there had been a defiance, even a coarseness in her looks and manner which had shocked him. Any real or fancied defect in his fiercely loved only child had always caused him such pain that his first reaction was to be angry with her. He had been so angry with her that day that, though several weeks had passed, he had felt none of his usual desire to placate her. He had deliberately tried to put her out of his mind and had almost convinced himself that, if she chose to ruin her life, it was no concern of his.

His disturbing dream had made him sharply conscious of her again. As he dressed, he remembered that his son-in-law had rung him up late

9

the night before, asking if Clara was there. At the time, he had been not worried but annoyed. It was one more black mark against Clara that her husband, drunk or sober, should not have found her at home when he returned. No doubt she had gone to some horrible Bohemian party. He had always disapproved of their living in Chelsea, a quarter about which he had lurid ideas. It was useless for his wife to assure him that it was Archie's drinking which had made Clara hard, insolent and slatternly. Since he was extremely found of Archie and had been strongly in favour of the marriage, he preferred to think that it was the deplorable effect of Chelsea on Clara that had driven his son-in-law back to the bars and drinking-clubs. Nevertheless, as he came downstairs, he found himself feeling vaguely guilty that he had not mentioned that telephone-call to Isabel. He would ring up after breakfast and make sure that Clara had come safely home.

In his anxious mood he had taken longer than usual to dress. His mother was waiting for him at the table where the bacon and eggs were already congealing on their dish. As usual, she had refused to help herself to so much as a cup of tea before his appearance. Breakfast was the one meal old Mrs. Batchelor really enjoyed. At all others she was cowed by her daughter-in-law's exasperated glances. This morning she had looked forward to a deliciously prolonged chat with Claude who would be able, for once, to eat without his eye on the clock. The prospect of his holiday would make him not only cheerful but extra attentive to her as he always was before a parting.

To her dismay, Claude looked sombre and preoccupied. She tried several openings with no more response than a polite "Yes, Mother" or "Really?" Finally, she risked mentioning her granddaughter. Even a rebuff would be better than indifference.

"What a pity Clara won't be going down to Paget's Fold with you this year. You'll miss her, won't you? You were always so happy together there. Summer after summer, ever since she was four years old."

Claude said, none too amiably:

"She wasn't there last year either."

"Dear me . . . fancy my forgetting. My memory's getting as bad as my hearing. Of course, *last* year she went off on that theatrical tour, didn't she? I daresay she little realised that by the next summer she'd be a married woman."

"Probably not." Claude's eye wandered furtively towards *The Times*. Mrs. Batchelor said in a suffering voice:

"If you want to read the paper, don't mind *me*, dear."

"No, no, of course not, Mother. I'm sorry."

"I thought you'd want to save it for the train. But if my chatting vexes you. . . ."

"Now, Mother, please. You know it doesn't. I'm afraid I'm a little absent-minded this morning."

"You're overtired," she purred. "I'm sure nobody at St. Mark's works as hard as you do. It must be bad for your health taking all those private pupils as well as all your other teaching. I wonder Isabel doesn't stop you."

"She couldn't if she tried. How often have I told you I *like* work."

"You overdrive yourself, Claude. You can't go on working day in, day out, even in the school holidays, and never taking a proper rest."

"My dear, good Mother. . . . I'm just about to take three whole weeks off."

"It's not enough. What's three weeks in a year? You're not as young as you were, dear. I don't like to say it, but you've aged quite a lot in the last few months."

"Thank you!"

"I only say it for your good, dear. I'm sure Clara would be upset if she saw how tired you look. She's so devoted to her Daddy."

"Hmm." His mouth tightened.

"Oh, but she *is*. . . . It's true she doesn't come over and see us as often as she did when she was first married. I know *I* haven't set eyes on her since she lunched here on her birthday."

"Neither have I."

Mrs. Batchelor's dull onyx eyes brightened with curiosity.

"Fancy! I made sure *you* had. Even though you hadn't mentioned it. Though *you* usually tell me things even if Isabel doesn't. And so often I don't hear when she does. She speaks so fast and she gets impatient if I ask her to repeat something. Yet I can always hear *you* quite plain, Claude. Well, you do surprise me! Not since her birthday! Why, that was in June."

"Yes."

"You don't think she's poorly? No, I'm sure Archie would have told you. Still I didn't think her looking at all well that day. In spite of her having got so much plumper since she married. Of course *I* think putting all that stuff on her face makes her look older. I'm sure anyone who didn't know would have taken her for more than twenty-two. It seems such a pity when you think of the lovely natural complexion she used to have."

"I entirely agree with you."

"I wonder you don't say something to her."

"It's no longer any business of mine. If Archie doesn't object. . . ."

"I can't see Archie objecting to anything Clara does. He's so very devoted, isn't he? By the way, I hope *he's* better."

Claude frowned and asked rather sharply:

"Better? I hadn't heard that he was ill."

"I was only thinking that he wasn't well on Clara's birthday and couldn't come to lunch."

Claude's face relaxed.

"Ah yes. I remember. Couldn't have been anything serious."

"A bilious attack, I daresay. He doesn't look as if he had a good digestion. He's so painfully thin and his nose is always rather red. They say that's a sign of chronic indigestion."

"Very unpleasant thing, dyspepsia."

"I wonder if Clara gives him proper food. She's not had much experience of cooking, has she? I could have taught her for I've had to cook all my life. Until I came to live with you and Isabel, that is. But I didn't want to interfere. Still, it's not Clara's fault that she's always expected to have servants to do everything."

"I'm sure Archie's extremely sorry that she hasn't. In a year or two they'll be able to afford as many servants as they like."

"When he comes into his father's money? Dear me, they'll be a very rich young couple then, won't they? I must say Archie's wonderfully unspoilt when you think he was brought up in luxury. I know Isabel has never cared for him but I've got a very soft spot for Archie. He's so jolly and unaffected. And always so very pleasant to his old granny-in-law."

"I'm very fond of him myself."

"I know you are. Though he's not clever like you. Anyhow Clara has enough brains for two, I always say. She looks rather discontented sometimes. I suppose it's because of all that bad luck Archie had about that Theatrical Club. I never did understand the rights of it all."

"There were no rights. The whole thing was a disastrous, foolhardy speculation. I wish to goodness Archie had never got interested in anything to do with the stage. However, I suppose now that he's got this acting job, it's better than nothing."

"I didn't know he *had* a job. A part in a play?"

"In some wretched musical comedy or other."

Mrs. Batchelor sniffed.

"I *do* think you might have told me, Claude. You might have known I'd be interested."

He said unguardedly:

"I didn't know myself till last night. Archie rang up."

His mother exclaimed eagerly:

"So it was *Archie* telephoning! Why, it was nearly midnight! I had my light on because I couldn't get to sleep and was having a little read. I thought 'Whoever could be ringing up so late ... how *very* inconsiderate!' Then I thought it must be one of those tiresome wrong numbers. Archie, well, fancy that! It must have given you quite a shock, him ringing up at that hour. I expect you thought at first something must be wrong."

He said stiffly:

"He apologised for ringing up so late. He had been rehearsing."

"I suppose he was so excited about getting the job. Still, you'd think he could have waited till the morning."

At that moment the telephone bell sounded from the study next door. Claude leapt to his feet.

"Did you ever?" said his mother. "Now whoever can it be this time? Surely not Archie again! Claude, there's no need for you to dash off like that. Why not let one of the servants answer?"

But Claude had already thrown down his napkin and hurried out of the dining-room. His unusual eagerness to answer the call made Mrs. Batchelor wonder whether he had been expecting it. All through breakfast he had seemed to have something on his mind. Was something going on about which, as so often, she had not been told? Could there be some mysterious and interesting trouble connected with Archie and Clara?

The minutes went by. Normally, Claude's telephone conversations were brief. Old Mrs. Batchelor's devouring passion, curiosity, had grown with her increasing deafness. More and more, the exciting scraps of gossip she longed to hear seemed to be deliberately muttered in an inaudible whisper. The telephone was in the adjoining room. In his hurry to answer it, Claude might have forgotten to shut the study door. On the pretext of looking for letters, she went out into the hall. To her annoyance, the study door was closed. Pausing outside, she listened. Her son was the one person whose words she could usually make out even when he did not raise his voice. All she could hear was an indistinct murmur, punctuated by long silences. Since he had only recently acquired a telephone, Claude tended to shout into it. This morning he was evidently keeping his voice deliberately low. Mrs. Batchelor's curiosity began to itch like chilblains before the fire. She had to use all her considerable will-power to move away from the door in the direction of the letter-box. She was only just in time. Barely had she reached the hall table when the study-door flew open and Claude emerged. She said, without looking at him:

"I just came out in case there were any letters. The postman's often late at this time of year. I'm getting so deaf I don't always hear his knock."

"The post came ages ago. Mother, for goodness' sake go and finish your breakfast." Claude's voice was so irritable that she wondered if he guessed she had been trying to eavesdrop. She peered up anxiously into his face. In the dim light, it looked not accusing but distraught. She said timidly:

"Something's upset you, Claude? Not bad news, I hope?"

"No, no Just some trouble about a pupil. I'll have to go out and deal with it at once."

"But, dear, you haven't even finished breakfast. . . ."

"I've had all I want."

He was already taking his bowler-hat from the peg on the hall-stand and picking up his chamois gloves. His mother was now quite certain that he was lying. The itch of her curiosity became unbearable.

"As urgent as all that? A *pupil*? Why, you're supposed to be away on holiday."

Claude did not answer. He was mechanically selecting a stick from the yellow drainpipe-like receptacle that stood just inside the front door.

"You're not going out without going up to say goodbye to Isabel? I've never known you do that all the years I've lived here!"

Claude was already opening the door. She went up to him quickly.

"Not even time to give your old mother a kiss?"

He stooped and kissed her flaccid cheek.

"I'll go up and tell Isabel you had to go out," she said importantly. "Have you any idea when you'll be back?"

"Long before lunch, probably. There's no need to tell Isabel."

The door slammed behind him. His mother decided to ignore the last words. She could always pretend she was too deaf to hear them or had misheard them as "Do tell Isabel". Since her own curiosity had been so cruelly frustrated, there would be a certain pleasure in arousing her daughter-in-law's. True, Isabel was not particularly inquisitive but she would be annoyed that Claude had gone out without saying goodbye. Old Mrs. Batchelor wondered whether she dared risk implying that she knew more than she did. Her mauve lips, with the mole on the upper one that so revolted her daughter-in-law, rehearsed soundlessly:

"I'm sure Claude will tell you all in good time, dear. I know you wouldn't wish me to break my promise."

Shaking her large head on which the dark wig, curled in an Alexandra fringe, sat slightly askew, letting a few wisps of her own white hair escape, she decided it was too dangerous. For a moment, she wondered if it was really worth climbing the six flights to Isabel's bedroom. She was heavily built and her short neck and tight stays made it necessary to pause and pant a great deal when going upstairs. The she remembered a remark she had not been intended to hear but which had pierced her capricious deafness.

"If you really want to know, dearest, why I insist on going on having my breakfast in bed, it's simply that I cannot face the sight of your mother before lunch."

The mauve lips tightened. Picking up her long, heavy black skirts with one hand and clutching the banisters with the other, old Mrs. Batchelor planted her velvet-slippered foot firmly on the first stair.

CHAPTER TWO

W HEN CLAUDE returned home some three hours later, his wife came quickly down the stairs as he opened the front door.

"I've been listening for your key. Wherever have you been all this time? I was getting anxious."

"I'll tell you in a moment," he said hurried. "Come into the study, Isabel. I must talk to you."

It had been too dim in the hall for her to see his face. When the light from the study window revealed it, she exclaimed:

"Dearest, whatever's the matter? You look ghastly. Are you ill?"

"No . . . no." He shook his head impatiently. "We'd better sit down. This is going to take some time."

He settled her in the big faded green armchair that had been in his rooms at Cambridge and, from force of habit, seated himself at his desk. Taking one of the fountain-pens from the bowl of shot in which he always stuck them, he began to screw and unscrew its cap, frowning as he did so. Well as Isabel knew his expressions, she could not decipher that frown. Did it mean anger or pain? He was silent for so long that she began to examine her conscience. If it were anger, it must be over something much graver than her latest filching from the housekeeping money. Only once or twice in their married life had she seen his face drained of its usual fresh colour to that ashy yellow. In the hard light of the window by the desk his few lines showed up as if they had been pencilled in. She began to be frightened. There was only one secret of hers whose discovery could possibly have made him look like that.

Unable to bear the suspense, she probed him gently:

"Your mother came up all those stairs to tell me you'd rushed out. She said something about an urgent 'phone call from a pupil. But her manner was so odd, I wondered if . . ."

"I told her a lie," he interrupted. "It was Clara who rang up. I've been over in Chelsea all this time."

"Clara!" Isabel was so relieved that she forgot to be surprised. Confidently, she raised her head and looked straight at him. He too had been avoiding her eyes but now he met them. The misery in his made her gasp:

"She's ill? . . . She's had an accident?"

"No, no. Not exactly ill."

"Is it that wretched Archie? Has he done something dreadful?"

He said sharply:

"You're always ready to think the worst of Archie, aren't you? In this case you're wrong."

"You don't mean it's Clara who's done something?"

"She proposes to do something that distresses me more than I can say."

Isabel's frightened face relaxed. She was almost smiling as she said:

"She's going to leave him? I'm not surprised. I only wonder she's stood it as long as she has."

Claude's blue eyes, which had gone so dull, snapped with some of their old brightness.

"Really, Isabel!" he exclaimed. "You *expect* your daughter to desert her husband after being married barely three months? Have you forgotten that they're both Catholics? And, incidentally, that we are?"

Isabel's large brown eyes opened wider under their almost invisible eyebrows.

"Why shout at me, Claude? Because I've guessed right?"

He dug the fountain pen viciously into the shot.

"It would be nothing to be complacent about if you had. As it happens, your guess is far from accurate. Even Clara is not quite as irresponsible as that. Isabel, this is a very serious matter indeed."

"I wish you'd tell me straight out what it is instead of lecturing me."

He stretched out a hand towards her but could not reach her across the desk. Withdrawing the hand again, he propped his head on it and said wearily:

"I'm sorry, my dear. I didn't mean to be angry. I'm rather tired and bewildered. It's not an easy thing to tell, even to you. Mind if I smoke?'

She waited while he went through the familiar movements of finding his pipe and stuffing it. It took longer than usual. The short white fingers were visibly shaking as they pressed the tobacco into the bowl.

"Poor dearest," she said. "Whatever it is, its obviously given you a terrible shock."

He nodded. Then he cleared his throat and said in a dry voice:

"I'd better begin at the beginning. After I'd spoken to Clara on the 'phone, I decided I'd better go over there at once. She was so incoherent, I couldn't really make out what she was trying to say. In fact I could hardly believe it was her voice—she sounded so strained and unlike her normal self."

Isabel muttered under her breath:

"She's been unlike her normal self ever since she married."

"Yes . . . yes, I daresay. I'm not denying that she's changed rather disturbingly in the last few months. But I've never seen her look as she looked this morning. If I hadn't known it was Clara who opened the door to me, for a moment I could have imagined it was some stranger twice her age."

"She's gone off quite alarmingly lately," sighed Isabel.

"I'm not referring merely to her looks. Though goodness knows she was slatternly and unkempt enough. No, it was something in her expression. A kind of distortion . . . rigidity. I can't describe it. Absurd, I know. I can only say it reminded me horribly of my father's face after that first stroke."

"Claude, you're frightening me. . . ."

He said quickly:

"I don't want to do that. I admit the most appalling ideas came into my mind. God knows the sort of thing that goes on in Chelsea at these parties one reads about. I wondered if she might have taken some horrible drug. She'd talked so wildly on the 'phone. But now her voice was perfectly clear and calm. We went into that little box of a sitting-room with those beastly yellow walls and gimcrack furniture and all those confounded mirrors. . . . Lord, how I loathe that house. . . ."

"I think it's very charming and artistic," Isabel murmured.

"I doubt if you'd have thought it either this morning. I can't pretend to describe the mess it was in. We sat down and she talked, as I say, quite calmly. From her eyes, I should say she'd been crying. She didn't shed a single tear in front of me. It would have been a relief if she had. There was something unnatural in the way she sat there talking in a

18

perfectly matter-of-fact voice as if she were discussing something quite impersonal."

"But that's how she always talks when she's terribly unhappy. Her self-control's frightening at times . . . just like yours. But what did she say?"

"In a nut-shell, that she and Archie were thinking of separating."

"And you told me I was wrong!"

"Wait. It's not just a question of leaving him for a time because things were difficult. Heaven knows I should have disapproved. But that would have been trivial compared to this."

"You mean she wants to get a divorce?"

"You know perfectly well the Church doesn't permit divorce."

"Haven't I always said the Church was inhuman? Oh, it's too cruel. Poor darling child. To be tied to a drunkard for life. I don't see how anyone could blame her if she . . ."

"My dear," he interrupted, "before abusing the Church, will you let me finish what I am trying to say?"

She sighed and closed her eyes.

"Very well. Go on."

"There *are* grounds on which the Church can annul a marriage. If Clara is right . . . and she seems to have gone into this very distressing subject very thoroughly . . . there are such grounds in their case."

Isabel's eyes flew open again.

"You mean there's a hope that she can get out of it?" she said eagerly. "Be really free . . . as if she'd never married at all? But that's the most wonderful news!"

He stared back at her.

"Wonderful news, you call it? I'm afraid I hardly agree."

"Why ever not, Claude? You've seen for yourself what a few months of this ghastly marriage have done to her. Now that some miraculous loophole has appeared . . ."

"You haven't heard the nature of the loophole."

"I don't care, as long as it exists. Oh, all right! What is it then?"

"To put it crudely, the marriage has never been consummated."

Her arched, slightly wrinkled eyelids fluttered.

"You mean Archie has never? . . ."

He averted his head and sucked nervously at his still unlit pipe.

"So I understand," he said stiffly.

There was a pause. Isabel gave one of her deep sighs. She said at last, as if talking to herself:

"What a relief! When I've tormented myself imagining what she might have gone through. *That* . . . with a man the worse for drink. Even if she's not as sensitive as I am . . ." She gave an expressive shudder and added in a stronger voice:

"The last time she came here, I was so terrified. Of course, I wasn't tactless enough to ask her."

"What do you mean, terrified? Terrified of what?"

"Why, that there might be a child on the way, of course. Her face, her figure, that nerviness . . . even *you* must have noticed them. It seemed the only reasonable explanation. And when you and she were closeted together in the study and it was obvious she'd said something that upset you, I naturally supposed it was *that*. Thank heaven, I was wrong!"

He stared at her as she sat there, a charming, incongruous figure in the sternly masculine room. She had got up late, as usual, and was still wearing a primrose silk kimono, feathered slippers and a boudoir cap. The lace lappets covered her hair and framed her face, emphasising the beauty of the full-lidded brown eyes and narrow, elegant nose while the ribbons tied under her chin hid the little loose fold that was beginning to form in spite of her careful massage. Fresh from her bath and newly powdered, she exhaled a sweet, troubling scent into the atmosphere of dusty books and stale tobacco. There was a mixture of disapproval and unwilling admiration in his gaze.

"For a Catholic, you say the most extraordinary things. Surely a child is precisely what you and I should have been hoping for."

"A child by a drunkard? *Our* grandchild. . . . *Thank* you," she said bitterly.

"You talk as if Archie were a chronic dipsomaniac. He only began to drink after his mother's death. When he and Clara were engaged, he practically gave it up."

"And took to it again as soon as they were married."

"He'd had another severe shock, losing practically everything in that wretched theatre club. To get that sort of news on one's honeymoon!"

"Excuses!" she broke in. "Always excuses for Archie! Haven't you any sympathy with your own daughter?"

"Most certainly I have. But there is such a thing as justice. There's also such a thing as a Catholic marriage for better or for worse. It's not something to be broken up lightly. A little patience and things might change."

"Of course, Archie's trying to persuade her to stay?"

"As it happens, you're wrong. According to Clara, he's the one who's so convinced that they ought to take this drastic step. For *her* sake. She says he's talked to a priest about it."

"That's the best thing I've heard of Archie yet. Naturally, *you* tried to argue him out of it?"

"I didn't have the opportunity. For the simple reason he wasn't there. He left last night."

"You mean he's *deserted* Clara?"

"Call it that if you like. It must have taken something like heroism on his part. Clara said she was quite incapable of making any decision. He thought, if he went away, it would make it easier for her to make up her mind to take action. . . . I think he acted far too impulsively. But it was an act of pure unselfishness."

Isabel said slowly:

"Yes. He *does* love her in his queer way. It's rather pathetic he should have been so faithfully devoted all these years. The moth and the star, I suppose. All the same, how Clara could *ever* . . ."

"Is it so surprising? After all, brains aren't everything. . . . Such absolute, faithful devotion for so many years. I fancy it's pretty rare in any young man. And in these days . . ."

"I can't think of Archie as a *man*. He's the same overgrown schoolboy he was four years ago. Except that now he's a dissipated and degenerate one. He looked more *like* a man *then*."

She glanced towards the black marble chimneypiece where the photograph of Archie stood among the ranks of photographs of other young men in uniform. Already they were beginning to look more dated than Isabel in her wedding-dress. Claude's eyes followed the direction of hers.

"Schoolboys, yes." He sighed. "Schoolboys, the whole lot of them."

"Dearest, it was all dreadfully tragic," she said, seeing an older cloud settle on his face. "But you mustn't let it become an obsession. At least Archie wasn't killed."

"He was wounded more than once. I wonder . . ." He paused and frowned, sucking at the pipe which he had eventually lit but which was drawing badly.

"What do you wonder?"

"Whether there might be some connection? . . . It's hardly a subject one can discuss with one's daughter. . . . Perhaps if Archie saw a doctor . . ."

"You seem determined this tragic farce should go on. Archie's being ten times more reasonable and humane than you are. Do you *want* to drive Clara to a nervous breakdown?"

He looked alarmed.

"You don't think that's a serious possibility?"

"Of course I do. Think of the way you described her this morning. *I* shouldn't have dared to leave her alone in such a state. Of course *I* wasn't even consulted. Not even so much as told my own daughter had rung up . . . so hysterical that even *you* were frightened."

"It was precisely because I was frightened that I didn't tell you. I didn't want to upset you till I'd discovered the facts. And I'm not quite such a heartless brute as you think. I suggested she should come down with us to Paget's Fold for a rest."

"She's coming?" Isabel asked eagerly.

"Yes. I sent the aunts a telegram on the way home. I told Clara to meet us at Victoria, not here. I don't want to have to enter on long explanations to Mother."

"Of course she guesses there's something up. You never saw anything so portentous as her manner when she came up to my room. Obviously she wanted to make me think she knew more than she said. *Does* she?"

"Certainly not. I'm afraid I didn't even tell her it was Clara who rang up."

"Thank goodness for that. Her curiosity is becoming a perfect mania."

"Could you criticise my mother another time? We're discussing Clara."

"I thought we'd finished with that. What more is there to discuss? If they've made up their minds . . ."

"Not finally, I hope."

"Dearest, that terrible conscience of yours! Why not leave well alone?"

"*Well*, you call it! When they've been married only a few months?"

"They should never have got married at all."

He said acidly:

"This time even you made no attempt to stop them."

"What would have been the use? This time she was determined to go through with it. The other time she was too dazed with shock after that little boy's death to realise what she was doing. Of course she was no more in love with Archie than before. Sorry for him, yes. Oh, all right . . . fond of him in a queer kind of way."

"I should have said she cared for him more genuinely than four years ago. This time, there was no money to dazzle her. Not in the immediate future, anyway."

"He'll run through it when he does come into it. No, you're the one who's more dazzled by all that than Clara. You've always been obsessed by the idea of her marrying Archie Hughes-Follett. Because it's an old Catholic family and so on. My family's just as old though they haven't got a penny. But thank goodness we Maules haven't degenerated through inbreeding."

"I don't deny his background appeals to me. Being a convert . . . and a lower middle-class one at that. . . ."

"Don't say that," she broke in. "*You're* not lower middle-class, whatever *some* of your family may be. . . ."

"Let's leave that old question, shall we, my dear? You don't have to remind me you married beneath you. . . ."

"You're saying it, not I . . ." she murmured.

"I don't deny," he went on, ignoring her, "that it was the background I'd dreamed of for Clara. Ever since I sent her to Mount Hilary."

"That *absurdly* expensive convent," she put in.

He continued steadily:

"I happen to like Archie for himself. His faults are obvious but they're all on the surface."

Isabel gave a faint yawn.

"Yes, dearest. So you're always saying. The point is, you wanted it so much that Clara knew she'd please *you*."

23

He swung round in his chair.

"If you're suggesting I influenced her . . ."

"Oh, not directly! But she hates it when you don't approve of her. . . ."

"That, my dear, is arrant nonsense. For some years Clara seems to have gone out of her way to do things of which I most thoroughly disapprove. Going on the stage, for example."

"Oh, she may *do* things you don't like. But she has fearful pangs of conscience after."

"Hmm," he said bitterly. "I can't say I've seen any signs of that. The last time she came here, she treated me with open contempt. And this morning, she refused even to consider any suggestion of *mine*. To suggest she renewed her engagement in order to please *me*. . . ."

"Don't be so angry. I never said it was the *only* reason. Obviously the main one was a rebound from some other shock."

"Shock?" he asked irritably. "What shock?"

"Oh, I can only guess. Clara's only really confided in me once in her life. *You've* always been the only parent who counted."

"Don't imagine I count *now*. . . . If I ever did! As to confiding . . . I can assure you my dear, there was no confiding, even this morning. She merely stated the facts and calmly informed me what she proposed to do. May I ask the nature of this supposed shock?"

"Ten to one, an unhappy love-affair."

"Really, Isabel . . . all these novels you read must have gone to your head. Unobservant as I am . . . I ask you . . . is it likely? Oh, there were plenty of young men around. But even you never suggested that any of the ones who came here . . ."

"I don't suppose he ever did come here." She paused and shook her head. "No, I'm sure it *wasn't* Clive Heron."

"My dear . . . these are wild speculations. Can't we come back to facts? At this moment, Clara is a Catholic wife married to a Catholic husband. . . ."

"Don't say it all again," Isabel burst out, putting her hands up to her lace-covered ears.

"Very well, my dear," he said in a hurt voice. "I suppose I should have known better than to expect you to see my point of view."

She rose and went over to him, laying her hands on his forehead.

"Poor dearest. How hot your head is. It's the fires of that remorseless conscience."

He dropped his dead pipe and put his hands up to cover hers.

"Am I being absurd?" he said wearily. "I only want to act as a Catholic father should."

"You seem to forget I'm a Catholic too. Oh, I know I'm nothing like such a good one as you. But I *do* believe, all the same. And *I* don't think God expects people to be tortured beyond what they can bear. And, in this case, the Church seems to agree with me. You say yourself the Church allows this . . . annulment . . . is that right?"

"Yes. Provided the authorities in Rome are satisfied with the evidence. I understand it's a very long, slow process."

"Then the sooner it starts, the better."

"You realise that it would be quite extraordinarily unpleasant for Clara herself? To begin with, it would go through the English civil courts. That means she would have to go into the witness-box and give the most embarrassing kind of evidence in public. These cases aren't, unfortunately, heard *in camera*."

"But it should be Archie, not Clara, who should have to do all these horrid things. After all it's *his* fault."

"Precisely because it's what you call 'his fault' Clara would be the plaintiff. He wouldn't have to appear since he doesn't propose to defend."

"But that's barbarous! *He* gets off scot free and *she* has to be dragged through the mud. As usual, it's the woman who pays. Still, *anything*'s better than letting this tragic farce trail on."

"You honestly don't think that, with a little patience . . . a fresh start . . . ?"

"Of course not. How *can* you be so blind? When even Archie. . . . It would be the cruellest cat and mouse game. Rest . . . then start the torture all over again like those poor suffragettes in prison. Don't you *realise* what would happen?"

"You really fear she might have a breakdown?"

"Yes. Or run off with another man."

He jerked violently away from her.

"Isabel! Of all the monstrous suggestions! Are you forgetting the child's a Catholic?"

"Don't Catholics ever give way to temptation? They aren't all such paragons of virtue as you, Claude."

He was silent for a moment, staring at the dusty cast of Pallas Athene on the bookshelf full of neatly labelled black files that stood against the far wall. Looking down at his face, Isabel saw a slow, patchy flush invade it.

"God knows *I'm* no paragon of virtue," he said at last. "But Clara . . . so young . . . and . . ." He paused again, painfully. "She's headstrong and self-willed . . . but one thing we definitely know . . . otherwise she wouldn't dare. . . ."

"Just *because* of that. Because she hasn't had any . . . any experience, she'd be all the more likely to do something she'd regret all her life. You know how impulsive she is when she's unhappy. Why, when little Charles was killed, her first idea was to become a nun."

He said with a wry smile:

"Hardly the same as committing adultery."

"Make me out a perfect fool as usual," she said angrily. "You don't *want* to see my point. When a woman's at the end of her tether : . . she'll do something she wouldn't *dream* of doing otherwise. Don't *men* ever . . ."

He made no reply. Instead, he glanced at the faded green armchair where she had been sitting and said mildly, as if he had not heard her:

"Will you go and sit down again, Isabel? I can't see you standing there behind me. I don't feel so utterly confused when I can look at you."

"Poor dearest," she said, kissing the bald patch in the middle of the brindled grey and gold hair.

She relaxed into the big chair again and, for some moments, neither of them spoke. Isabel said at last:

"It's terribly shabby but *so* comfortable. I don't wonder you can't bear to part with it."

For the first time that morning, he smiled naturally.

"The old Duke of Norfolk? Far too comfortable I used to find it at Cambridge. Larry said that was why he gave it me . . . as a temptation to idleness. I most certainly yielded to it."

"The only time in your life when you did. A very good thing too."

He shook his head, but the smile was still there.

"That chair's to blame for my getting a second. Well, partly to blame, anyhow. But I fear I'd be as bad if we had our time over again."

He glanced at one of the few non-military photographs on the mantelpiece. In thirty years it had faded so much that little could be seen beyond a pair of eyes that looked at once sad and amused, a thick, drooping moustache hiding a long upper lip and a pair of braided lapels in one of which was a white blot that had once been a gardenia.

"Larry O'Sullivan," she said softly, following his gaze. "No one ever took his place for you, did they?"

He shook his head. "No one."

"I remember him so well, after all these years. . . . However many is it now?"

"Nineteen, almost to a day."

"You're very faithful, aren't you? But I can understand. Once one's known that extraordinary Irish charm. . . ." She broke off, biting her lip.

"Yes, indeed. That Irishman who was a temporary master at the school during the war . . . Callaghan. . . . He reminded me just a trifle of Larry. You never met him. An odd fellow. Very intelligent but not very presentable. I'm afraid he drank. He went off to the front and was carried off by pneumonia."

Isabel was staring fixedly at the photographs. She said in a carefully neutral voice.

"Yes. I've heard you mention him."

Claude nodded.

She ran the tip of her tongue over her lower lip and said, more easily:

"He didn't sound very like Larry to me. I always remember Larry's exquisite manners."

"He admired you immensely, my dear," Claude added, with a certain restraint: "He worshipped beauty in any form."

"Strange that he never married."

Claude seemed about to say something then suddenly compressed his lips under the clipped, still golden moustache. When he did speak he merely observed:

"After all, he died at only thirty-three."

"I'd forgotten he was so young. Of course, it was before we became

Catholics. Strange that the reason he couldn't be Clara's godfather was because he was a Catholic and we weren't then. But it was you and he who insisted on her being called Clara because you both had such a passion for *The Egoist*. I wanted Cynthia."

"You don't still mind?" he asked.

"No, of course not." She sighed. "Poor pet, she's not awfully like Clara Middleton at the moment, is she? Don't look so miserable, darling. She'll blossom out again when this is all over."

He said sadly:

"Even for *that*. . . . God knows how much I'd like to see it. . . . But unless this is really the *right* thing for her to do. . . ."

"Claude . . . dearest. . . ." She twisted her hands together. "Oh, if only Larry were still alive. . . . He'd have agreed with me. *He* was the human, understanding kind of Catholic. Aren't converts *plus catholique que le pape?*"

"Perhaps . . . perhaps. . . . *He* took it easily . . . as he took everything in life. As I've never been able to do, except at moments. But don't get the idea he was lax when it came to fundamentals. Whatever he might say or do, the faith was in his bones. I've been surprised sometimes. . . ." He broke off again and added after a moment: "He made a good end. I've never doubted that."

"I'm sure he did. They do, that kind."

He looked at her with a puzzled expression.

"Odd," he said. "Something in your voice when you said that. . . . Quite suddenly I remembered another time you sat in that chair. It was years ago. . . . You looked very different. . . . So utterly worn out. You'd been walking about the streets in a bitter wind. Do you remember?"

"I . . . I think so," she said cautiously.

"It was my fault. I'd made you very unhappy."

"Had you?"

"It was you who were right that time. About Clara."

"Clara? Ah yes, Clara!" She added, with more certainty: "No, I haven't forgotten *that* morning."

"I'd behaved like a brute to you. But for you, I'd have behaved like a brute to *her*."

"Then, dearest, *dearest* . . ." she urged, suddenly alive and eager.

28

"Don't make things hard for her now. *Don't* interfere . . . leave it to her . . . all right, to *them*."

"You may be right . . . you may be right," he sighed and fell silent again. His eyes returned to the photographs until they came to rest on one. "Look at her *then*. . . . Only six years ago. . . . And to think of the face I saw this morning. . . ."

Isabel looked at the photograph of Clara at sixteen. Her fair hair was neatly tied back with a black bow and she wore a white, embroidered blouse with a V neck so modest that it barely revealed the base of her smooth neck. Her lips were pressed together in the effort to conceal their fullness of which she had always been rather ashamed; her eyes looked out, clear and unconfident.

"Poor pet . . . looking so desperately innocent. But much too serious. Still, she wasn't at her *best* at that age," said Isabel critically. "The photograph *I* love is that charming Elwin Neame of her at eighteen."

"I infinitely prefer this one," he said stubbornly.

"Clara loathes it herself. She says it has 'convent girl' written all over it."

"Perhaps that's why I like it."

"*And* she says," went on Isabel, "and I must say I agree—she looks as if she can't make up her mind whether to become a schoolmistress or a nun."

He said in voice half hurt, half angry:

"After all, there are worse alternatives."

CHAPTER THREE

WHEN HER father had gone, Clara Hughes-Follett stood at the window watching his stocky, upright figure retreat. She watched till, without once slackening his pace or glancing back, he vanished round the corner of Oakley Street. Then, with an effort, she turned to face the empty room.

All the time they had been talking, she had been aware of his eyes consciously avoiding the stains on the carpet, the littered cigarette butts, the pool on the painted table where Archie had slopped over his last glass of whisky. Clara knew how her father loathed the room even when it was tidy. During the last few weeks, she had come to loathe it herself along with all the other speciously gay little boxes with their fondant-coloured walls and brittle furniture. "A sugar house," she had said to herself only a few days ago, lying upstairs on the crumpled bed and staring at the pink distemper. "Hansel and Gretel's sugar house. And we're trapped in it."

Now that the trap had been sprung, she felt a perverse desire to remain in it. Instead of going upstairs to pack, she began to tidy the dishevelled room. She paused in front of the armchair where her father had sat so upright on the orange cushion which concealed its broken springs. There was a dent where Archie's untidy red head had rested, less than twelve hours ago. Hesitating to smooth it out, she found herself suddenly confronted with her image in one of the mirrors artfully disposed to make the room seem larger. She was as startled as if she had discovered a stranger spying on her.

Like herself, the other had fair, wildly disordered hair and wore a creased tussore dress but its face was almost unrecognisable. The eyes were dull and parched between the reddened lids; a pocket of shadow, dark as a bruise, lay under each. The features were rigid and distorted as if they had been melted down and reset in a coarser mould. She forced herself to smile, half-hoping the mask in the mirror would remain unchanged. But its pale swollen lips parted, grotesquely dinting one cheek with the dimple she hated.

Not since she was a child had she had this sense of another person staring back at her from the glass. In those days, she had often held long conversations with the reflection. Usually the other was friendly; a twin sister who thought and felt exactly like herself. Occasionally she became mocking, even menacing. Clara would smile placatingly and the other would return a sneering grin. Gradually the other would take charge, twisting its features into grimaces she was compelled to imitate. Clara would try to turn away but the tyrant in the looking-glass held her hypnotised. When, at last, she wrenched herself free, she was weak and giddy. For days after, she would hurry past mirrors with her eyes shut.

Now, staring at the other, she felt the old spell beginning to work. The dull stony eyes fixed her; the teeth bared slowly in a grin. In spite of herself, she felt the muscles of her own cheeks twitch and lift. As if something were pulling her over an invisible line, she took a reluctant step forward. Suddenly the telephone-bell shattered the silence like an alarm-clock. She broke off her tranced stare and picked up the receiver. Her mind was blank. If someone had asked "Who is that speaking?" she could not have replied. But at the sound of Archie's voice she recovered her identity.

"Clarita?"

"Archie! Oh, thank God!"

"I just had to ring up. I say, are you all right?"

"Well . . . I'm here. Where are *you?*"

"Call-box at the theatre. Only this minute got away from rehearsal."

"Where did you go? Where did you sleep?"

"Nowhere. Did *you* sleep?"

"A little, I expect. I don't really know."

"Darling, you sound all in."

"You must be too."

"Oh, I'll survive."

"Have you found somewhere to go tonight?"

"Yep. Maidie's fixed me up with a room. What about you?"

"I'm supposed to be going down to Paget's Fold this afternoon. With the family."

"Best thing you could possibly do. I've been worried sick in case you just hung on *there*."

"I'd much rather. I don't want to go *anywhere*."

"Darling old thing, you *must* go. I can't bear the thought of you there all alone. At least I've got the show to take my mind off things a bit."

"Yes."

"Darling, *don't*. You sound so utterly wretched. For two pins I'd chuck everything and come rushing round."

"I wish you would," she said frantically.

"Clarita . . . I'm trying like hell to be sensible."

"Sorry. I'll try to be too."

"You said 'with the family'. That means you've talked to your people?"

"Daddy's been here. He's only just gone."

"Did you tell him the whole thing?"

"I told him the brute facts."

"Must have been pretty bloody for you. Was he awfully cut up?"

"Yes."

"But he does see it's the only thing to do?"

"No. He says we oughtn't even to think of it yet."

"Well, for once he's wrong. Did you try and convince him?"

"Oh yes. I talked and talked. I don't remember what I said. It didn't seem to have any connection with *us*. He was shocked."

"Because of our being Catholics?"

"Mainly, I suppose. But. . . ."

"I can convince him about that. Or rather I'll put him on to someone who can."

"Archie, it wasn't just the Catholic thing. It was *me*."

"Darling, you're fancying things. Or you've got the wrong end of the stick. Hang it all, I'm the one to be shocked with. He could only have been bloody sorry for *you*."

"Oh . . . if I'd cried or something. But I didn't. I was as hard as nails. It was like someone else saying it all for me. Perhaps I *wanted* to shock him. You should have seen how he looked at me. Archie, I *frightened* him."

"Hold on, darling. You frighten *me* when your voice goes like that."

"He looked at me as if I were some kind of monster. Or *mad*."

"Clarita!"

With an effort she brought her voice down to normal pitch.

"You don't think he might be right?"

"Of *course* you're not a monster. *Or* off your head. Just dead beat."

"I meant right about our putting it off."

"Darling old thing, the longer we wait, the worse hell it'll be. Specially for you. We've *got* to go through with it."

Clara was struck by the firmness in his tone. She had been too relieved to hear his voice to pay much attention to what he said. Now she realised there was no hope. The thought of going on alone, of being forced to take action, filled her with a fury of panic. She almost screamed:

"Of course, if you're so anxious to get rid of me!"

"Shut *up*! That's bloody unfair and you know it. It's not what *I* think or *I* want. It's what's got to be done. That's what Sammy Sissons said this morning."

"This morning? You've been talking to Father Sissons this morning? You *said* you'd been rehearsing."

"So I have. Will you listen without snapping my head off? Honest, Clarita, I can't take much more at the moment."

"Neither can I."

"Rather I rang off?"

"No. . . . Don't, *don't*," she implored. "I'll be sensible. I swear I will. Tell me about seeing him."

"It's a long story. Rather queer, too."

"Begin at the beginning."

"Well, last night after we'd . . . well, after I'd gone off I just walked and walked. . . ."

She broke in plaintively:

"I kept *wondering* where you could be . . . all night I kept wondering. . . . Where *did* you go?"

"Don't ask *me*. Don't remember much except just walking and now and then sitting down on a doorstep. Anyway, somewhere about six I came to in the neighbourhood of Farm Street. I was bloody tired so I thought I'd go into the church and sit down. I suppose I dozed off for the next thing I remember was someone tapping me on the shoulder."

"Father Sissons?"

"No. But some old boy saying Father Sissons had seen me in the church and would I serve his Mass please? Well, I didn't like to refuse though I haven't served Mass more than two or three times since I left Beaumont. And I was so damn sleepy, I thought I'd make some ghastly muddle. Well, I went up and met Sammy coming out of the sacristy and just had the presence of mind to tell him not to give me Communion because I'd cut Mass last Sunday. Guess what he did."

"Asked if you'd like to go to Confession?"

"Dead right. He put everything down, took off his vestments and into the box we went. Hadn't been to Confession since Easter and there was a good bit to tell. I was so sleepy I probably left out half. When he'd given me absolution, he said, just as if it were quite *normal* for me to be at Mass on a weekday: 'Ten minutes for our thanksgiving and then you breakfast with me, my boy. And for goodness sake don't do your old trick of not leaving enough water over for the ablutions.' Fancy his remembering that from school . . . all those years ago."

She said, humbled:

"You went to Communion. And I didn't even *think* of going to Mass. With a church bang opposite."

"*I* didn't mean to. It just happened."

"Did it make things better?"

"I *feel* just as bloody about it all. But, in a way, yes. Can't explain *how*. Rather as if you were in the hell of panic on the way to an operation and knew somehow you'd just manage not to get off the trolley."

For the first time since they had parted, Clara gave a smile that was not a grimace.

"And I haven't the guts to get *on* the trolley."

"You will, darling. D'you know you said that just like *you*? Oh, Clarita!"

She asked hurriedly:

"What happened over breakfast with Father Sissons?"

"He made me come clean about everything from A to Z. Including the drink, naturally. Of course that had already come up in Confession I didn't mind talking about *me* so much. What I jibbed at was being made to talk about *you*. But he said he couldn't give any sensible advice unless he'd got the whole picture."

34

"What did you tell him about me?"

"Oh, that you'd put up a marvellous show but your nerves were getting all shot to pieces."

"I *haven't* put up a marvellous show. Nothing else?"

Archie said reluctantly:

"Well, about last night and that beastly painter."

"You might have spared me *that*."

"I tell you, he dragged it out of me."

"He'd no right to. It has no bearing *whatever*."

"Try not to be so furious. And, actually, it *has*. That was what clinched it for Sammy. I was beginning to hope he'd say 'Wait and see,' like your father. But when I told him that . . ."

"What did he say?"

"That you might have resisted temptation once but another time you mightn't. And I'd no right to go on exposing you to . . ."

She interrupted savagely:

"What does he think I am. A whore?"

"Clarita, be *reasonable*."

"I *am* reasonable. I wasn't tempted. I was revolted. . . . And you two have the impression . . ."

"Darling, we *haven't*," he said wearily. "Do try and understand. After all, you're a normal human being. Or *were* until I messed everything up for you."

"*You* didn't," she said, softening again. "I've messed things up for myself."

"I made you damned unhappy."

"It wasn't your fault. I've forgotten *how* to be happy. Oh, long before we got married. I can't even remember what it feels like."

"You'd be happy all right if. . . ." Archie stopped for a moment, then brought it out with an obvious effort, "if you married a real chap. Someone you could fall in love with."

"Archie, don't," she implored. "I don't *want* to marry. As to falling in love . . . I don't believe I could."

"Sammy's quite sure you will."

"How does *he* know? A priest!"

"He knows a damn lot. After all, you did once." Archie's voice sounded almost exhausted.

"So you even told him that," she said bitterly.

"Darling, he wanted to know everything."

"Oh, all right. Well, what did he say?"

"I didn't understand half of it. Anyway, it boiled down to the sooner the better. It's up to you now. Darling I *do* wish it was me that had to do all the beastly part. Sammy says he'll help you in any way he can. He'd awfully like to see you."

"Don't think I want to, thanks."

"Honestly I believe it might help. You don't know how terribly decent he was. I don't mind admitting I cracked up completely and made a bloody fool of myself. I told him I was an ass and a boozing swine but I truly did love you."

"Oh darling," said Clara wretchedly. "You're not . . . you're worth a million of me. I don't know why you . . ."

"Know what he said? 'I think she does too. Only not the sort of love for people to marry on'."

"Archie . . . I do. As much as I can *anyone*, I believe. But I suppose . . ."

He interrupted her again.

"And then he said: 'You don't have to stop loving her.' Funny, but that bucked me up more than anything else he said."

"Oh, Archie, *dear*. . . . Now you're making *me*. . . . Well, what else *did* he say?"

"Oh, a lot of stuff right above my head. Holy talk, you know. Must have fogotten who I was and thought he was talking to some budding J. in the novitiate."

"What sort of holy talk?"

"Oh, all about acceptance and loving another person's good even if it happens to be the opposite of what *you* want. Then he suddenly remembered it was *me* and came down to earth. Said we were a couple of young fools. . . . I mean *I* was . . . and you were lucky to have a hope of getting rid of me with the approval of Holy Church. Also that you'd better hurry up because the law's delays were greased lightning compared to Rome's."

"Hearty Catholic humour," said Clara. "Afraid I've never appreciated it."

"He had to make me laugh or I'd have maundered off again. Then he gave me a whisky, just one but a good stiff one, and packed me off to rehearsal."

"And you got through all right?"

"Not too bad. Thank God I didn't have to sing. I'm as hoarse as a crow. I say, darling, I'll have to ring off in a minute. There's another chap in the company who's been waiting ages to make a call. He's beginning to bang on the window."

" We'd better say goodbye then."

"Not goodbye, please. It sounds so beastly final. He can wait another minute. Just tell me you're all right."

"I'm all right," she said obediently.

"Promise?"

"Yes."

"And you'll go away and get a good rest?"

"Yes."

"I'll be so much less worried about you if I can think of you down in the country with your people tonight. Just clear out and leave everything. I'll fix things with the Woods. I'll come over some time and collect my stuff. Oh . . . one other thing . . ."

"Yes?"

"The railway. It's yours you know. Absolutely and entirely yours."

"Archie, *please*. I'd feel awful. . . . Every time I looked at it. . . . No, *please*. . . ." She was almost in tears.

"Same here. All right, darling. Shall we give it to Sammy for his ruddy boys' club?"

"Yes, do."

"Well, good luck, my darling old thing."

"Good luck, dear, *dear* Archie." She mastered her rising tears. "Your first night. . . . Just think of nothing but your first night. . . . It's *got* to be a success."

"Bless you."

"Bless *you*."

He muttered almost inaudibly: "Pray for us" and rang off.

She paused a moment before hanging up the receiver. Talking to Archie had half brought her back to reality. Nevertheless she still could not bring herself to take any action. She slumped down in a chair and fished out a flattened packet of cigarettes that protruded from the crevice where Archie must have thrust it last night. As she stared help-lessly round the matches, the Angelus began to clang from the church opposite. Dropping the yellow packet, she stood up and joined her hands. For the first time for many years, she said the Angelus aloud and slowly, as she used to do at school, making a careful genuflection instead of her usual hurried bob at "The Word was made flesh". After the bell had stopped she stood a few moments longer, with her hands still clasped, making a silent, confused petition for Archie.

Saying the Angelus calmed her and gave her just enough strength to face doing what had to be done. Its bell, announcing it was already mid-day, had restored her sense of time. She wound up her watch, reckoning that she must leave the house in less than three hours. With one of her sudden switches from listlessness to activity, she ran down to the kitchen. She had eaten nothing since about six the day before. She stared at the cup, at the oilcloth spotted with burns from Archie's cigarettes. It was unimaginable that it was only yesterday she had made that cup of tea. She clutched the table, looking fixedly at her own hands, trying to convince herself that they belonged to the same person who on a sudden, excited impulse had gone to see this painter whom she barely knew. If she had not yielded to that impulse, she and Archie would still be together. She had had no time to reflect on that strange, violent evening. It was all there, in her mind, with every detail vivid; the hiss of the broken gas-fire, the shadow of the brushes on the ceiling, the weight of the man's body on hers, the suffocating panic, his ironic kindness after her rebuff. But it was there unconnected with real life; a scene she had once acted in a play. She shifted her stare back to the tea-cup, frowning with the effort to think. It had not been a scene in a play. It belonged to the same realm as the dregs in the cup and the jug half-full of sour milk. It was because of something Gundry had said that the situation between herself and Archie had flared up to its crisis. When she had made that cup of tea, when she had yielded to that impulse to go to Gundry, she had lit the fuse which had exploded the Sugar House and all it stood for. Feeling suddenly weak and sick, she sat down at the kitchen table and drank up the cold, scummy dregs. She found that she was shaking all over with a slight, but uncontrollable tremor All at once, though she was still exhausted and trembling, she was invaded by a kind of ruthless energy. She rushed upstairs, flung

38

open cupboards and drawers and began to pack. As she did so, she had the odd impression that it was not she who was stripping hangers and throwing armfuls of clothes into suitcases but some callous, efficient stranger. She herself was lying on the unmade bed, staring blankly at the cracks in the sugar-pink ceiling.

CHAPTER FOUR

IN TWO years, nothing seemed to have changed at Paget's Fold. The old aunts were wearing the same clothes and looked as Clara remembered them from her childhood. Aunt Leah's silver hair fell in the same soft fringe above her narrow, dead-white face: Aunt Sophy's, which must have been as golden as her own in youth, was still the same indeterminate brown and pinned up in the same thin coil, from which soft, damp wisps were always escaping. Her face was still like a plump, shrivelled yellow apple with streaks of pink below her faded pansy-blue eyes. Clara had always thought of her great-aunt Leah, whose stiff manner matched her thin, bleached appearance, as an old lady; Aunt Sophy, only two years younger, had never seemed to her like a real grown-up. She was so short that she looked like a plump, prematurely-aged child and she still had a child's impulsiveness and soon-forgotten spurts of temper.

The rooms were the same in their odd medley of furniture which ranged from plain, solid, worm-eaten pieces made by village carpenters a century and more ago, through Victorian horsehair and mahogany to throw-outs from Valetta Road and objects ingeniously constructed by the aunts themselves out of tea-chests and packing cases. The Misses Sayers had never resented their poverty or been crushed by it. Paget's Fold was a monument to their diligence and independence. Everything that could be done by human hand they had done to their house, from covering its oak beams with whitewash and its ancient wood and plaster walls with layer on layer of sprigged wallpaper to making it cushions from Isabel's old silk dresses and curtains from Clara's discarded muslins.

As a child, she had never considered the effect quaint, pathetic or ugly. She admired every button-trimmed hair-tidy and wool mat. The 'real' furniture at Paget's Fold interested her no more than that at Valetta Road: what fascinated her were the aunts' wonderful contrivances that made Paget's Fold like a large home-made doll's house.

She loved the red blinds, with their crochet lace edging, that had to be rolled up with infinite care for their pulleys were only cotton-reels; she loved the dadoes and picture-frames of varnished corrugated paper; the pillows stuffed with goose-feathers collected from the green outside; the little stools and sofas and dressing-tables, which, when you lifted their chintz skirts, revealed a skeleton of old trunks or hatboxes. Most of all, she loved to trace some forgotten, once-familiar object magically transformed and given a new life: scraps of an evening dress of her mother's inlaid in a patchwork quilt; a hair-ribbon of her own tying back a curtain; a child's bead necklace unstrung and patiently stitched, bead by bead, into the initials I.B. on Isabel's state pincushion.

Everything was the same, but she could not recover the old blissful security. Her parents tried hard to keep up the illusion, both for her and for themselves, that this was just one more family holiday, no different from innumerable others. But sudden silences would fall at mealtimes and Clara was often aware of puzzled, hastily averted glances. Claude's decision that the aunts must, on no account, be told the real reason for her being there created an atmosphere of constraint.

The aunts, incapable of the most innocent deceit, had swallowed the story unquestioningly. Clara was tired from the unusually hot summer in London and, as Archie was rehearsing for the next three weeks, what more natural than that she should take a holiday with her parents? Had they suspected anything was wrong, they would have said nothing. As it was, they were always making innocent comments until keeping up the pretence became a nervous strain, especially as Isabel, who could see no need for pretending, was always on the point of giving the secret away.

Aunt Leah, though delighted to see Clara, was a trifle shocked and wondered how poor Archie would manage with no one to get his meals. One of those awkward silences fell when she hesitantly suggested that he might like to come down at week-ends. It was easier to deal with Aunt Leah's faint censoriousness than with Aunt Sophy's constant desire to send Archie boxes of fruit and vegetables. One morning she came in so triumphantly with an apronful of the second crop of peas she had nursed for Claude and Isabel that Clara felt she could hardly bear to discourage her. She turned red and stammered:

"You see, Aunt Sophy, he gets all his meals out. It would be a shame to waste them."

"Yes, dear. I forgot. Of course a man wouldn't cook for himself. Suppose Leah made him one of her fruit cakes you always enjoy so much?"

"No, *please* don't bother. They're such a trouble to make. And well . . . he hardly ever *eats* cake, you know."

Two days later Aunt Sophy appeared at breakfast with a basket of plums, her face pink with pleasure and exertion.

"There, I've got the very thing. They don't have to be cooked and everyone finds fruit refreshing in this weather. I've picked them just at the right moment, with the dew on them. I'll wipe them and pack each one in tissue paper. Then they'll travel perfectly."

Clara was searching for some new excuse when she caught a frantic signal from her father's eye. She said hastily:

"I'm sure he'd love them, Aunt Sophy. I'll help you pack them, shall I?"

"No, no, my dear. I'll do them myself. I've got my own little fads about packing fruit . . . not that I'm sure you wouldn't do it beautifully. Besides, I'd like them to be a little present from his old great-aunt-in-law whom he's never seen. We were so very disappointed that we couldn't come to your wedding."

"*You* could perfectly well have gone, Sophy," said Miss Leah. "You know that I urged you to do so."

"And leave you here alone with that dreadful attack of bronchitis?"

"I could have managed very well. Clara, your Aunt Sophy is just making excuses. The fact is she was too shy to go without me."

"Stuff and nonsense, Leah. I don't deny I should have been shy with or without you. Clara's wedding was such a grand affair. But, if Clara wanted me there, I wouldn't have minded how queer and old-fashioned I looked. London scares me but I'd have gone to Timbuctoo to see her married. No, Leah, you're being very wrong, trying to put it on me. How could I have left you . . . my own sister . . . gasping for breath and no more fit to look after yourself than a baby?"

"Really, Sophy. I trust I have a little common-sense."

"Not when it comes to managing oil-stoves and creosote kettles. And you forget how often that cough used to make you sick."

Aunt Leah said with dignity:

"*Please*, Sophy. I'm sure no one wishes to hear people's ailments discussed at table. Let's talk of something else. I've so often wondered what can be the origin of that expression 'go to Timbuctoo'. No doubt you can tell us, Claude."

"I'm afraid not, Aunt."

"What about you, Clara? You were at school more recently than any of us."

Clara shook her head regretfully. She knew how Aunt Leah treasured miscellaneous scraps of information.

Isabel, always irritated when Aunt Leah scolded or patronised her favourite Aunt Sophy, said mischievously:

> "I wish I were a cassowary
> On the plains of Timbuctoo
> I would eat a Missionary
> Prayer book, bible, hymnbook too."

Aunt Sophy gave a delighted giggle but Aunt Leah looked genuinely hurt. She said quietly:

"I may seem very old-fashioned, my dear. I hope I can enjoy a joke as much as anyone. But when one thinks of the heroism of our missionaries and the dreadful things they had to suffer. . . . It seems a little unkind . . . perhaps almost irreverent. . . ."

Claude frowned at his wife. There was a painful silence during which all three of the Batchelors remembered that Aunt Leah's secret, passionate wish had been to be a missionary. Aunt Sophy broke the silence with her usual kindliness:

"There, there, Leah. You know Isabel meant no harm. And if there's any joke you *can* enjoy, I've yet to hear it. I don't count those old riddle-me-rees and conundrums you get out of *Beeton's Annual* and *Enquire Within*. They're too clever for me. Now I must go and see about Archie's parcel."

"It's too kind of you, Aunt," said Claude miserably. "You shouldn't take so much trouble." He hated deception at any time. Deceiving the aunts, who had such boundless trust in him, made him feel as if he were committing a sin. He added, with a forced heartiness which could hardly have convinced the most guileless:

"How delighted Archie will be. Won't he, Clara?"

"Oh, yes. He *adores* plums."

Aunt Sophy's faded blue eyes brightened.

"Now isn't that lucky? They don't agree with some people. And isn't it lucky we always save boxes? That one you sent us at Christmas, Claude, with those beautiful biscuits in it, will be just the thing."

She bustled off happily. Her tiny cottage-loaf figure was so short that she had to stand on tiptoe to reach the string latch of the door to the stairs. On the same impulse, Clara and her father stood up from the table.

Aunt Leah exclaimed anxiously:

"But you've eaten hardly any breakfast, either of you. Isn't the bacon done to your liking?"

"It's delicious, like all your cooking, Aunt. I'm just not very hungry. And the garden looks so extraordinarily tempting this morning."

"Your appetite isn't as good as usual this year, Claude. Sophy and I have both noticed it."

Isabel said calmly:

"Mine is. You give us such lovely food that I get quite reckless about my figure. Even the garden isn't going to tempt *me* from your home-made marmalade." She picked up the yellow rose by her plate and smelt it. "Darling Aunt Sophy. She's put a flower there for me every morning ever since we first started coming down here. I daren't think *how* many years ago now." She helped herself to butter and marmalade and looked mischievously at her husband and daughter standing there, mute and stiff.

"If you're going, why don't you *go?* I hate being stared at while I eat. I'll come out when I feel like it."

There was nothing for Clara to do but to leave the room with her father. Unlike the old days, she was furious with her mother for not accompanying them. Ever since they had come down to the cottage, she had done her best to avoid being alone with either of her parents, particularly with her father.

They walked in silence along the tangled, dew-wet paths, making instinctively for somewhere out of earshot of the house. In the orchard, where the grass was so long that they stumbled nearly knee-deep in it, they came to a standstill. Clara looked unhappily at a tree whose

44

branches were nearly breaking under the weight of fast ripening plums.

"Daddy, we can't let her send them. Why didn't you let me stop her?"

"We can't hurt her feelings again. As a matter of fact, I'm going up to London tomorrow. I'll take the plums myself."

"Going to London? But you *never* do that in the holidays! Well, then why ever didn't you tell Aunt Sophy?"

"Because, I haven't had a chance to tell your mother yet. I met the postman on the green and took the letters. There was one for me from Archie."

Clara frowned. It was the first time he had spoken of Archie except in the aunts' presence. She had not been consciously trying to forget Archie but each day at Paget's Fold, without restoring the past, had successively deadened her sense of the present. Now it was as if the real Archie, not the lay-figure they referred to in public, had suddenly intruded into this orchard he had never seen.

She asked nervously:

"What did he say?"

"It was a very touching letter. He wants very much to see me. I shall wire him that I'll come up tomorrow."

"Does he mention me at all?" she said, with an absurd pang of resentment that he should have written to her father and not to herself.

"Most certainly he does. In the most pathetically affectionate way." Claude sighed. "Poor boy, poor boy. What a tragedy it all is. I believe you're very fond of him yourself, in spite of everything. . . . If only . . ."

Clara broke in: "It's no good, Daddy. Of course I'm fond of him. But I can't explain. I couldn't begin to explain to you or anyone about me and Archie. But we can't go on. Not either of us. . . ."

He looked at her with a kindly puzzled expression.

"My dear . . . I do realise you've suffered very much. . . . Perhaps I see life too much in terms of rules. This is something where I'm out of my depth." It was still an effort for him to smile but he managed to do so. "Anyhow, it seems the rules are in your favour. Do you know this Jesuit Archie speaks of . . . Father Sissons, I think?"

"I've never met him. He was one of his masters at Beaumont."

"He wants me to talk to him too. It seems I'm in a minority of one. If this priest thinks it's for the best, as well as Archie and yourself and your mother . . . I suppose I'd hoped that, now you've had a little time to think things over . . ."

All Clara could think of at the moment was what Archie or Father Sissons might say about her. Suppose they were to mention Stephen Tye or the fact that she had gone to Gundry's studio? Her old terror of her father's disapproval revived sharply. It was in this very orchard, years ago, on the day of her grandfather's funeral that he had abused her so bitterly for having let a distant cousin, a shy young farmer, kiss her. She said desperately:

"Daddy, why *need* you waste a whole precious day in London? Why not just write to Archie? The thing's decided. We've got to tell the aunts sooner or later. Why not get it over now and stop all these beastly deceptions?"

"I hate them as much as you do. But nothing will stop me going to London tomorrow, quite apart from the question of the plums. I very much want to *see* Archie."

She sighed.

"Oh, well, if you've made up your mind. . . . But *can't* we tell the aunts the truth?"

"My dear child, it's unthinkable. Can you imagine attempting to explain such a thing to them? Even if they understood, it would come as the most appalling shock."

"Claude, how *absurdly* you exaggerate."

They started at hearing Isabel's voice. She was walking slowly up the overgrown path between the flower beds and the vegetable plot, picking her way delicately through the wet grass and twirling a rose-coloured sunshade over her shoulder.

Claude put his finger to his mouth. As she came up to them, he asked in a low voice:

"Was I talking very loud?"

"You forget I have ears like a cat's." Isabel smiled. "How guilty you both look. Like two conspirators. Well, *have* you conspired something about poor Aunt Sophy's plums?"

Claude told her about Archie's letter, adding:

"Of course I shall have to make some excuse to the aunts about going to London tomorrow. A pupil or something. . . ."

"All these complicated fibs. What's the *point* of them? I'm sure the

46

aunts would much rather be told straight out than find out some day that you've been deceiving them. Oh, I know how prim and proper Aunt Leah is. But if *you* think it's right, she'll accept it. She won't understand what you're talking about but she'll be too proud to admit it. As for darling little Sophy, all *she*'ll care about is that Clara's going to be happy again."

"Happy!" said Clara rather bitterly. "Really, Mother, it's not quite as simple as that."

"Darling, I didn't mean all at once. But till you're free, you haven't even a chance of being happy."

"I'm afraid I haven't any rosy dreams about the future. I haven't even thought about it."

"My child, you're probably wise," Claude sighed. "In any case, is happiness so *very* important in this life?"

"Really, Claude!" said Isabel. "All right, *you* don't think happiness is important. But I don't see that's any reason to make other people miserable."

"Certainly not. But have I done so? And, if so, whom?"

"The aunts, of course. They see something's wrong and, being the aunts, they think it's *their* fault. They imagine they've offended you or aren't looking after us as well as usual or some such rubbish."

"Good heavens, Isabel, you don't seriously suggest that?"

"I'm not *suggesting* it. I'm saying what is perfectly obvious. Clara knows it as well as I do."

He looked stricken.

"But this is appalling."

"It's my fault," said Clara wretchedly. "I've ruined your holiday by coming down here. I'd better go to London with Daddy tomorrow and stay there."

"No, no, darling. That's the last thing we want. Isn't it, Claude?"

"God knows it is. You're looking a different person . . . almost like your old self . . . already. Isabel, is there nothing I can do?"

"Either tell them straight out or behave, both of you, as you used to do. If *I* can make silly jokes and over-eat so as not to hurt their feelings, why can't you?"

"Your mother's right, Clara. But when one has a guilty secret . . ."

"One should swallow one's own smoke. It's part of the penalty of having a guilty secret. What you're doing is keeping the secret and making *them* feel the guilt. . . . And if you won't tell them . . ."

"No. There I stand firm. Otherwise, you're perfectly right, my dear. You have the natural human approach in these things. Why is it the more I try not to hurt people, the more I seem to do so?"

"I'm just the same," put in Clara. For the first time for months, she slipped her arm through his.

Isabel took a step back and surveyed them both, smiling and twirling her sunshade.

"How like each other you look at the moment," she said.

Claude looked at the rosy reflections playing over her pale oval face and her scarcely marred neck and smiled.

"You're unflattering to Clara. She should look like *you*."

"One beauty in a family's enough. Anyway, I've lost interest in my looks," said Clara.

"That's a silly thing for any woman to say. Especially my clever daughter. What you mean is, you're afraid of being foolish and frivolous like your poor *Maman*."

"You make me sound the most revolting prig. Am I a prig?"

"Only in spots, darling." Isabel slowly furled her pink sunshade.

"The sun's gone in. Do either of you feel frivolous enough to play a game of croquet?"

"Why, certainly, my dear," said Claude with alacrity.

"Good. Then I'll go in and ask the aunts if they'd like to come and watch. Of course they'll say they're too busy but they adore to be asked."

"You would think of that," he said admiringly. "And, if you *are* going in, Isabel . . ."

"Yes?"

"I wondered if. . . . You don't think perhaps it might be better if *you* told Aunt Sophy about my going to London tomorrow."

She laughed and tapped him with the ferrule of her sunshade.

"Oh, dearest, you'd go to the stake for truth in the abstract, wouldn't you? But if a fib's *got* to be told . . . and *your* fib too . . . let a woman tell it. I believe you're a Mahomedan at heart and think women have no souls."

He laughed too.

"And I'd say I was a moral coward, as all men have been since Adam."

48

"A moral coward is the last thing you are, Daddy," said Clara hotly.

When Isabel had gone, Claude turned to Clara.

"I wish you appreciated your mother more. I'd give a great deal to have some of her intuition . . . that simple, impulsive way of dealing with things."

"I prefer you as you are," said Clara. For the first time for months she gave him a quick, spontaneous kiss. He looked almost startled as he muttered "Thank you . . . thank you, my dear."

CHAPTER FIVE

THE NEXT morning, after her father had left for London, Clara invented every possible pretext to avoid being alone with her mother. But when, after lunch, Isabel insisted on going for a walk instead of dozing as usual in the hammock, she could hardly refuse to accompany her. As Clara had expected, the walk was a short one. No sooner had they crossed two or three fields than her mother sat down under a hedge and patted the parched grass beside her.

"It's too hot to be energetic," she said.

Reluctantly, Clara sat down too. For a time, neither of them spoke. Clara fidgetted and stared moodily across the fields which sloped gently down to the disused canal which wound like a narrow river between pastures that still showed green though the higher meadows were baked almost to the colour of stubble. No barges had come up it for a century and its surface was almost solid with weed and lilies. On the farther bank was an old pink brick, slate-roofed farmhouse flanked by a poplar on either side. That farmhouse, whose poplars never seemed to be stirred by the wind, always had a peculiar magic for Clara. Though so near, she had never visited it and it seemed part of an eternal landscape which never varied, year after year. Other fields and farms changed with the summers; pasture would be ploughed up, clover be planted instead of corn, a harsh blue-white corrugated roof replace the mellow thatch on a barn. But this farm – it was called Hollow Land and was associated in her mind with a poem of William Morris's which she had loved as a child – never altered. The poplars were always the same bluish green, the single hayrick beside them the same faded gold, as if they were painted in a picture and impervious to change. The sight of Hollow Land, more still and dreamlike than ever on this golden August afternoon, softened her sullen mood.

"How lovely and peaceful it is," said Isabel. "Why can't life be like that exquisite landscape instead of being so sad and complicated?"

Clara said nothing and her mother went on:

"When I was a girl, I really used to believe that the future would *be* like that. I suppose I was hopelessly romantic."

"Aren't you still?" asked Clara, patronising but indulgent.

"Perhaps. You always try to make out that you're so cynical and disillusioned. I don't believe you are really."

"I'm not sentimental, that's all." Honesty compelled her to add: "At least, I hope not."

Her mother sighed.

"You hate admitting you have *any* feelings, don't you? At any rate to me."

Clara flushed angrily. She could hardly tell her mother that she had a dread of being like her; emotional, impulsive and greedy for praise and affection. The dread was all the more acute because, however sternly she tried to repress or disown it, one side of her was constantly betraying her into behaving exactly like Isabel. At moments she could hear the echoes of her mother's high, straying tones in her own. Pitching her voice deliberately low, she said coldly:

"We can't all be the emotional type."

"Still, with two such emotional parents . . ."

"*Daddy*'s not emotional," Clara cut in.

"Really, darling! Considering how clever you are, you do say the most absurd things. I've known very few men with such violent feelings as Daddy."

"Well, at least he controls them. He thinks everything out logically."

"Not when he's angry or upset. I can assure you there have been plenty of times when it's your silly, illogical mother who's stopped him from doing something he would have regretted afterwards."

Clara said fiercely:

"Why don't you come to the point and say 'I told you so'? I've been waiting for that ever since we came down here. Well, now's your chance. Say it and have done with it. I'd rather be crowed over than pitied."

"My darling child, the last thing I want is to crow over you."

"You've every right. I always wondered why you didn't try and stop me the second time."

"From marrying Archie? You know perfectly well you wouldn't have listened to me."

"No. But I'm surprised you didn't try. After all, you brought it off the first time."

"That's a very unfair way of putting it. You know that you were longing to get out of it yourself, only you couldn't face disappointing Daddy and all the rest of the fuss. You were grateful enough at the time. And it was I who had to do all the horrid part, explaining to Archie's mother and sending back the presents."

"Yes. I admit you were very good about all that," said Clara, grudgingly.

"I'd have done anything for your happiness. I always would. You don't know how many battles I've fought on your behalf. Yes, with Daddy. He adores you but he can be terribly hard and unreasonable just *because* he adores you."

Clara was perfectly aware that her father could be violent to the point of cruelty when she did anything of which he disapproved. But nothing would induce her to admit the least imperfection in him to her mother. She said drily:

"Let's get back to the point. I'd simply like to know – out of pure curiosity – why you didn't try and stop me this time."

"Because things were different. *You* were different. Oh, not just that you were older. Or because you didn't confide in me. I don't believe you ever *have* confided in me except that once when you were seventeen. If you knew how wonderful that was for me! But you'll never understand that, unless some day you have a daughter of your own."

"That's rather improbable, isn't it?" said Clara with a grimace.

"Of course it isn't. Some day, when this horrible business is over, you'll marry again and have children."

Clara shook her head.

"You're quite wrong there. If there's one thing I'm certain of, I shall never, never get married again."

Her mother smiled.

"That shows how young you still are. You think your life's come to an end because you've had a terrible experience."

"You exaggerate. I've survived one or two quite ... well ... uncomfortable experiences. I'm surviving this one. In fact I'm beginning to wonder what all the fuss is about." She tugged out another grass stalk. "Oh, I admit I worked myself up into rather a hysterical state. I'm disgusted when I think of it. Thank goodness, I'm perfectly reasonable now. Just rather flat and bored, if you want to know. I assure you it's a great relief not to have any feelings. I'm certainly not going to risk getting involved with anyone again. In any case, it's unimaginable."

"Is it, my poor pet? And what *do* you propose to do with your life?"

"I haven't the remotest idea," said Clara, contriving a yawn.

Isabel sighed. After a moment, she said hesitantly:

"You won't believe me. But *I* think you're just numb from shock. You were the same after that time when . . . when that dreadful thing happened up in Worcestershire."

"When Charles was killed? You needn't be so awfully delicate. I've quite got over that. Thank goodness, Archie and I can talk about Charles quite naturally now." She added, less cocksurely. . . ."Could, I mean." -

"It was so understandable your wanting to marry Archie *then*," said her mother. "He stood by you so splendidly at that terrible time. Of course *I* knew you weren't to blame for the poor child's jumping off the wall and breaking his neck. But you had the morbid idea that you were. And that nurse was so shockingly jealous and told such dreadful lies about you at the inquest. You even tried to convince Daddy it was your fault. In fact you did convince him. I only just stopped him from writing you the most cruel, unjust letter."

"*You* did? I thought it was Patsy Cohen. I must have written *her* a crazy letter. I knew she went round to see him. She said she didn't know he *could* be so angry."

"She did come round. I never approved of your little Jewish friend, as you know, but I thought it was nice of her to try and plead for you. But I can assure you, darling, it wasn't Patsy who made Daddy see reason. It was your poor foolish mother."

"It's all ancient history, isn't it? I expect no one remembers exactly what happened."

"I remember very exactly indeed," said Isabel. She compressed her lips. "I've good reason to remember every detail of that morning."

Clara said carelessly:

"I've quite lost sight of Patsy. I wonder what's happened to her."

"Married, let's hope," said Isabel tartly. "If I'd had a daughter as . . .

well, flirtatious is putting it kindly . . . as that . . . my mind wouldn't be at rest till she was safely married."

"Really, mother!" Clara laughed for the first time. "I don't think she could help it. She was so soft-hearted. And so desperately attractive to men."

"I suppose so. I've never admired that flashy sort of prettiness. And her methods were so obvious. Always rolling those enormous eyes . . . beautiful eyes, I admit but so *empty* . . . at any man in sight. . . ."

"I believe you're jealous."

"Jealous! Of a chit of a girl with ugly hands and no profile?"

"I didn't mean of her looks. But she adored Daddy. She told me once that, if only he were free, she'd like to marry him."

Isabel smiled.

"Then she has better taste than I supposed."

"All right, you win. Anyway, you know you're safe. I believe Daddy would be just as moral even if he weren't a Catholic. If Patsy had *really* made up her mind . . . even for fun. . . ."

"Daddy has plenty of experience in fending off young women," said Isabel. "I know several of his girl pupils have fallen in love with him."

Clara looked surprised, even shocked.

"How extraordinary. Well, I suppose, for a *man* he's not so old." Her expression became thoughtful. "I wonder how they *dared*."

"You can't stop yourself falling in love. People fall in love against all reason and commonsense. At *any* age." Isabel's expression, too, was thoughtful.

"Of course, Patsy was only joking," said Clara hastily. "But she did admire him enormously. And he disapproved of her much less than you did." Her faint smile gave way to a slightly puzzled look. "Funny. I've just remembered something."

"What's that?" asked Isabel.

"Oh, nothing. Just that whenever I saw Patsy after that, she never mentioned Daddy. Before that, she was always talking about him and asking after him."

"Perhaps he was cross with her for trying to interfere on your behalf. He was cross enough with *me*."

"Yes, I daresay," said Clara. "People usually are when other people butt in, even with the best intentions. I don't blame them."

"I'm sure *you* were cross enough," said her mother reminiscently. "You said the most dreadful things to me when I 'butted in' as you call it."

"About my marrying Archie that other time? Did I? I don't remember after all these years. Was *that* why you didn't risk it again?"

"No. Because this time nothing would have stopped you. And I think I know why. That other man must have hurt you very much."

Clara was so startled that she said, without thinking:

"How could *you* know? I'll swear *Archie* never. . . ."

"No one told me. But I'm right?"

"Oh, very well," said Clara sullenly. "But it was utterly and completely over. By the time I got married, I'd practically forgotten his existence."

"Were you very much in love with him at the time?" Isabel asked in her dreamiest voice.

"Oh, I thought so, of course," said Clara contemptuously. "Yes, I had all the symptoms you read about in your Mudie novels. Now I can't even remember what it felt like. So much for grand romantic passion." She turned her head away to avoid her mother's scrutiny.

"Poor darling. You needn't pretend with me. I'm sure it went very deep."

"I assure you I'm not pretending. Sorry to disillusion you if you think I'm nursing a secret sorrow or keeping a stiff upper lip. What's more I can prove it. Before I married Archie, I deliberately went to see the man *and* his wife, just to make sure I *didn't* still feel anything. And I didn't. Nor a tremor."

"Ah, so he was married!" said Isabel. "I daresay that came as a terrible shock to you. Men are so unscrupulous when they're attracted to a young girl."

"You're wrong again. For one thing he was unattached when I met him. For another, he wasn't in the least a wicked seducer. On the contrary, it was all 'I'd never forgive myself' and 'You're only a child.' *That* line."

"He sounds like a philanderer," said Isabel thoughtfully. "I believe they're the most dangerous of all. My poor darling. When they marry, it's usually for money."

55

"Very sensible. Actually, it was someone who could give him good parts."

Isabel said after a pause:

"Do you think you'll ever go back to the stage?"

Clara shook her head.

"I'd never be more than third-rate. That's one thing I found out by going on tour."

"You were very good in one of those student shows . . . no, two. Not in all of them, I agree. A little stiff and self-conscious. And your voice is like mine . . . too light to carry far."

"Which two?" asked Clara in spite of herself.

"Such very different ones. Mélisande . . . and that little French princess in Henry V."

Furious with herself for having fished for praise, especially from her mother, Clara said rudely:

"Any idiot can drift about the stage in a long wig, saying '*Je ne suis pas heureuse*'."

"Not as you did," said Isabel romantically. "You made me think of Undine . . . *wasn't* it Undine . . . the water-nymph searching for a soul?"

"I've no idea," said Clara.

"*Je ne suis pas heureuse*," murmured Isabel. "You brought tears to my eyes. Perhaps I felt it was an omen. Oh dear, how pathetically it's been fulfilled. And the other little princess showed how gay and charming you were *meant* to be. Let's hope *that* will come true one day."

"Kate didn't take any acting either. It was just a question of playing up to Stephen. *He* carried the whole scene." To her dismay, Clara felt her skin tingle. She averted her head in case she was visibly flushing.

"He was the one, wasn't he?" said her mother softly.

"Let's drop the subject, shall we? Unless you want to discuss him as an actor. He's going to be quite astonishingly good. His Richard II for example . . . particularly the deposition scene. . . ."

"Of course I've always thought *your* real gift was writing."

"Writing! Mother, please. Please don't be funny!"

"What is there funny about it? I'm not talking about your advertisements and clever little stories . . . though they're very good of their kind. Lots of people would be only too glad to be able to do them as well. But that other story . . . the one in the *Saturday Westminster* . . . 'The Hill of Summer' . . . why, it was quite exquisite."

"Fluke," said Clara furiously. She clawed a pebble out of the dry grass and threw it viciously and aimlessly. "If there's one thing I *do* know, it's that I'll never be able to produce anything but slick nonsense. If you knew how I loathed the very *mention* of writing. Can't we talk about something else? I'd rather discuss even love-affairs than *that*."

Her mother sighed.

"I wonder if you're as fierce and defiant with *anyone* but me."

"Oh, I expect so. Do *you* like being probed about your private life?"

"It depends who does the probing. Of course, if it's no concern of theirs and they're just doing it out of curiosity. . . . But I suppose *you* think a mother has no right . . . even with her only child. . . ."

Isabel sounded so unhappy that Clara felt a little ashamed.

"Sorry, Mother. I'm afraid I'm an awful failure as a daughter. Bad luck for you none of the others survived. They'd probably have been much nicer." It was the first time for years that she had mentioned or even thought of those three younger sisters who had died at birth. She waited apprehensively for Isabel's outburst of melancholy reminiscence. To her surprise, it did not come. Instead, her mother said:

"I don't grieve about them any more. After all, they're in paradise, aren't they? And I never *knew* them. No, darling, it's the *real* daughter I care about. And if I could have them back, all three . . . as model little angels of daughters . . . I wouldn't, if it meant losing my one real one. Even if she *is* rather difficult sometimes."

Clara felt guilty. She wished she were capable of making some sweet, impulsive gesture. All she could do was to mutter:

"I don't *mean* to be beastly to you. It's something in *me*, not you. I really admire you in lots of ways."

"No one's fonder of admiration than I am," said Isabel. "It's my besetting sin. Yet I'd almost rather be plain if you could. . . ."

"I should hate you to be plain," Clara cut in. "I expect the truth is I'm jealous of your looks."

"Nonsense. You're very attractive yourself when you're well and happy. Anyway, mine won't last much longer. Perhaps it's just as well."

Clara accepted the topic eagerly. She was most at ease with her mother when she could tease her about her fatal beauty.

"You've always been a menace, haven't you? All those men who used to follow you in the streets and slip notes into your hand at church. Really, I wonder Daddy didn't keep you under lock and key."

Isabel smiled thoughtfully.

"Yes, peculiar things used to happen. It's very naughty of me . . . but I'm afraid I *did* enjoy it a little."

"Used to," mocked Clara. "You know perfectly well they still do. . . ."

"Perhaps. But I don't enjoy it any more. Oh, not that I'm not as vain as ever. . . ."

"When did you suddenly become so virtuously detached?"

"I don't know about virtuously," said Isabel slowly. "Oh, several years ago."

"Was it about the time I was first engaged to Archie? I remember you suddenly had a tremendous burst of piety. You took to going to the Oratory every afternoon."

It was Isabel's turn to avert her head. Her pale skin never flushed but tiny broken veins were suddenly visible under the powder.

"Yes . . . about that time . . . yes."

"Sorry, mother. I only meant it as a joke. You sound as if I'd really upset you."

"No . . . .no . . . It's just that I've tried not to think about it."

"Why, was it something horrible?"

"No . . . no. . . . Not horrible at all. . . . A little frightening, per-haps."

Clara suddenly recalled the evening in Marcus Gundry's studio. She said sympathetically, almost as if Isabel were a contemporary.

"*I* know how frightening a man can be. Even someone you like very much."

Her mother looked at her curiously.

"I wonder how much you *do* know. . . . No, there's something more frightening still. Discovering feelings in yourself . . . violent feelings you never even suspected you had. . . . Feelings that would make you throw up everything . . . yes, even your religion . . . just to be with a particular person. . . ."

"You mean *you've* felt that. . . . Only a few years ago?"

Isabel said with agitation:

"Nothing wrong happened. I swear it didn't. Call it a tremendous temptation. I've never told Daddy. I never meant to tell *anyone*."

Clara frowned, but said nothing.

"Now you'll despise and condemn me. Oh, why was I such a fool as to tell you of all people? As if you weren't critical enough of me already! As if you could possibly understand! Now, all your life you'll have something against me."

"Why rush to these wild conclusions? I haven't uttered a word."

"But that frown . . ."

"It's not a thing you can take in all at once. One doesn't somehow imagine one's own *mother*. . . . I've always supposed you loved Daddy. . . ."

"But I do . . . I do . . ." said Isabel vehemently. "Only just for the time this blotted everything else out. Call it a fever . . . call it insanity. . . ."

"Well, at least you got over it. . . . That's one good thing."

"Getting over it's hardly the word. I tore it out of myself. Oh, I'm not a good Catholic, like Daddy. But for those weeks I was. . . . I *had* to be. . . . I couldn't have done it if I hadn't prayed and prayed . . . for *him* too."

Clara was embarrassed by her mother's mention of religion. In spite of herself, she was shocked though she could not tell exactly why. She was convinced that her mother was speaking the truth; that she had, indeed, behaved almost heroically. Nevertheless she felt an unreasoning resentment which she could not entirely control. . . . She wanted simultaneously to forget what she had heard and to press for every detail. She stared ahead at the landscape which seemed no longer peaceful but sinister; a dream on the edge of becoming a nightmare.

"This man. Did Daddy know him?"

"Yes. But he didn't know that I did."

"You used to meet him secretly?" Clara's voice hardened. She was glad of the excuse for righteous disapproval.

"I only met him twice. The first time was pure accident. Then I avoided him. I wouldn't see him. I wouldn't answer letters. . . ."

"Very correct," said Clara drily. "All the same you did see him again."

"Once, yes. And even that wasn't deliberate. It was that awful morning your letter came about the little boy being killed."

59

Clara pounced on it.

"You said just now you remembered every detail of that morning. I was conceited enough to think it was because of *me*. . . . Well, one lives and learns."

"And it *was* because of you. All the things were connected up together. . . . You . . . and Daddy being so terribly angry with you. . . . Oh, darling, it would be hopeless to try and make you understand. . . . I'm sorry I spoke of it at all."

Clara remembered something.

"That night you came into my room . . . about the Archie thing . . . after we'd run into each other in the Oratory. Was that what you meant? When you said there was something you might tell me some day."

"Did I? Well, now I've told you."

Clara said nothing for some moments. Then she muttered:

"And I supposed it would be something wonderful and mysterious. So it was nothing but a love-affair."

"How contemptuously you say it. Wait till something of that kind happens to you."

"I shall take jolly good care it doesn't. Do you know what became of him?"

"He's dead," said Isabel quietly. "He joined up. He didn't have to."

"And got killed at the front?"

"He got pneumonia in those dreadful trenches. He'd been drinking too much for years. He didn't have a chance. He died in a few days. I wouldn't have known if Daddy hadn't told me. I had to pretend to be just conventionally sorry."

"He *drank?*" said Clara, astonished. "But you've always pretended to have such a horror of men who drink. Look how you've always raged about Archie's drinking. And you've never let us forget about that one solitary time Daddy came home tight. You still harp on it though it was before I was born. Mother, I simply don't understand you."

"It's not pretence. I loathe the sight of a drunken man. I don't understand myself. I can only say that even that wouldn't have mattered."

Clara stared at her mother. Though puzzled and shocked, she was conscious of a reluctant admiration. In the sunlight Isabel's face seemed suddenly to have aged. It was as if the carefully preserved bloom had withered, showing another face with a still, haggard beauty of a different order. Isabel seemed unconscious of her daughter's eyes. Her own were almost closed. With a strange pang, Clara thought "She'll look like that when she's dead."

Abruptly, she stood up and gave herself a violent shake as if throwing off something heavy and clinging.

"I'm afraid all this is rather out of my depth," she said. "Let's go back, shall we? It must be getting on for teatime."

Shortly before dinner, her father arrived back, looking extremely tired. However, during the meal, he roused himself enough to give a convincing account of his day and to dwell elaborately on Archie's gratitude for Aunt Sophy's plums.

"He'll be writing to thank you, in a day or two."

"I'm sure I wouldn't wish him to go to all that trouble," said Aunt Sophy, obviously delighted. "And you shouldn't call them my plums, since everything here is yours, Claude. All I did was pick them."

"Now, Aunt dear," Claude insisted. "How many more times am I to remind you both that you're to look on this place as yours?"

"We know how kindly you mean," said Aunt Leah. "But you know we shall never do that. It wouldn't be right."

"I warn you. . . . One of these days, if you aren't careful, I shall make it over to you legally, lock, stock and barrel."

"Oh please, Claude," said Aunt Leah in genuine distress. "Of course, you know we wouldn't accept it. But I don't like your so much as suggesting it. Your mother deprived herself of it to make it over to you as a twenty-first birthday gift."

"A present is hardly a present if you can't do what you like with it," said Isabel. "If Claude wants to . . ."

Aunt Leah's eyes filled with tears.

"Isabel. . . . I beg you. . . . Oh, pray don't refer to it again. We are so happy as things are. . . . Please, never so much as mention such an idea."

"Now Leah, don't make such a fuss . . ." said Aunt Sophy briskly. "Of course it was just one of Claude's jokes. . . . You never could take a joke, you know. . . . As if he weren't worn out with his tiring day! You must have a glass of my parsnip wine, Claude."

When he had finished eating and had drunk some of the home-made wine, strong as a liqueur, which the aunts never touched except in illness, Claude suggested that Isabel and Clara should take a turn with him out-of-doors. Normally, however lovely the night, they sat with the aunts round the lamplit table while Aunt Sophy mended and gossiped and Aunt Leah tried to give the conversation a more serious turn. Luckily, the aunts saw nothing strange in this break from the ritual routine.

"I was just going to suggest that myself," said Aunt Sophy. "I'm sure you need a breath of air, poor boy, after being up in that nasty, dusty London all day."

As the three of them strolled up the road almost in silence, Claude told them in a resigned voice of his interviews with Archie and Father Sissons.

"There is really no point in further discussion, I suppose," he ended. "Father Sissons seems quite convinced that Clara should begin proceedings as soon as we get back to London. Actually, he used some of the arguments you used yourself, Isabel."

"And, because he was a man, you listened to them," said Isabel.

"Not because he was a man, because he was a priest. Frankly . . . I had hardly expected some of the things he said. . . . Well, obviously his knowledge of human nature is far more extensive than mine."

"What sort of things?" asked Isabel.

"Oh well . . . we needn't go into them. The less we talk about this painful subject the better. I'm sure Clara will agree."

"Yes," said Clara vehemently. She could guess all too clearly the line Father Sissons would have taken. To her relief, there seemed no sign of disapproval of *her* in her father's voice, only the flat, tired tones of a man too weary to fight any more.

"Amazingly competent, the Jesuits," he said after a pause. "He had got it all worked out for you, Clara. He even put me on to an excellent solicitor . . . not a Catholic . . . to handle the civil side. Ramsden, I think the name is. The ecclesiastical side can run concurrently but, of course, you will need separate evidence. Also they have to get permission from Rome before the Church proceedings over here can even begin."

"What appalling complications and red tape," said Isabel. "When you think how easy it is to *get* married."

But she, too, sounded weary and did not pursue the subject. Clara listened abstractedly while her father talked on about technical details. Once he said rather sharply:

"After all, this concerns *you* Clara. You hardly seem to be listening."

"I'm sorry. Yes, I heard. But I can't *do* anything till we get back, can I?"

Gradually, all three fell silent. Clara found herself thinking of what her mother had said that afternoon. The darkness, the steady beat of their steps on the road produced a hypnotic effect. It was as if the three of them were walking in a dream. It began to get on her nerves. She had an insane desire to shatter the trance by screaming out: "I know something about her that you don't know." The impulse was so strong that she had to press her lips together. The small effort restored her to reality. She relaxed her lips and let out a quick breath as if she had only just avoided some imminent danger. To her relief, Isabel spoke.

"It's been such a worrying day for you, dearest. But what a heavenly night it is. It seems a shame to go in."

He said, as if startled from a dream of his own:

"What's that? I had almost forgotten where we were. . . . Yes . . . we must get back. . . ."

They turned about and, relapsing once more into silence, retraced the road to Paget's Fold. The smell of wild peppermint in the ditches gave place to the smell of camomile as they crushed the flowers on the green underfoot, climbing the gentle slope up to the house. They paused at the gate to take a last breath of the soft night air. Over the house the walnut tree stood like a rounded black cloud against a sky full of stars.

"A bat," said Isabel, almost in a whisper. She always heard the high squeak a moment before Clara. Claude could never hear it at all.

The aunts had left the curtains of the living-room undrawn so that the light should shine out on the uneven brick path where tufts of musk grew in the cracks. Clara and her parents had approached so quietly that the two old faces bent towards the lamp did not look up. Aunt Sophy was sewing; Aunt Leah reading her bible. Clara forgot everything in the absorption of watching them. This was their real life, night after night, when the Batchelors were not there: Aunt Sophy still making those dresses for farmers' wives, as carefully and hardly less elaborately than when Clara was a child; Aunt Leah reading her daily chapter of scripture before she allowed herself to pass on to anything secular. The sewing would be whisked out of sight as soon as the Batchelors entered for Aunt Sophy feared that, if Claude knew that they needed the money, he would increase their yearly present. The bible would be slipped under the table on to Aunt Leah's lap, not because she was ashamed of her devotion to scripture but because she felt they might be embarrassed. One of the notions most firmly lodged in Aunt Leah's head was that Roman Catholics were not allowed to read the bible: she felt it might wound them to be reminded of their loss.

Clara waited in terror for her parents to spoil a moment which, for her, was becoming enchanted. But they stood as silent as herself, not unfastening the gate, the click of whose rusty latch would have instantly disturbed the calm of the two old, intent faces. The night scent of stocks and nicotine came up intoxicatingly from the bed under the lighted window; it was so still that she could hear the whirr of the moths' wings round the lamp. It was the smell of all the summer holiday nights of her childhood. Something in her blank, stony heart melted as it had not melted for a long time: it felt swollen, yet lightened as if it had expanded to take in sorrow and joy, others' as well as her own. She was aware of her father and mother having moved imperceptibly away from her and standing close together. She did not resent it. She wanted to savour this sense of being apart from these two pairs of human beings; each pair so dissimilar, yet so deeply united. For a moment she felt neither old nor young, as if some part of herself were as unchangeable as the rest was amorphous and unpredictable. That part seemed to have no other desire than to stand outside, watching, observing, registering every shift of shadow on the two old women's faces, every sound and scent in the clear darkness outside. Then, all at once, without warning, the smell of stocks and nicotine and trodden grass awakened an overpowering longing in her . . . a longing not to be alone but to be loved, to share her whole life, her whole being with someone else. It was so overwhelming, so violent that she would have burst into tears had she not broken the spell by flinging open the gate and stumbling up the path to tap on the window.

In the one moment of fright on the old ladies' faces before they realised who was tapping, she experienced a third sensation . . . a touch of pure panic. She had an instantaneous vision of herself as someone forever outside, forever looking in through glass at the bright human world which had no place for her and where the mere sight of her produced terror.

Part Two

CHAPTER ONE

IT WAS the first time Clara had been in a solicitor's office. While the youngish man on the other side of the desk slowly wrote her answers to his questions on thick blue foolscap with a quill pen whose squeak set her teeth on edge, she stared round the dreary room.

Behind Mr. Ramsden the wall was lined with black japanned boxes lettered in white "Estate of Mr. X" or "Executors of Mrs. Y". Depressed as she was already, the place had such a mortuary air that she could almost believe the boxes contained the ashes of the people commemorated on them. Mr. Ramsden's appearance and manner increased the funereal atmosphere. Not only did his black coat and tie suggest an undertaker's but he asked his questions in a hushed, considerate voice as if in the presence of the corpse.

"Your husband's name is Archibald James Hughes-Follett – is that correct?"

"Yes."

Only once before had Clara heard Archie referred to as Archibald James. She glanced aside through the grimy window at the plane trees shedding their leaves in the courtyard of Grays' Inn. It seemed impossible to connect the present moment with a morning, only last April, when she had stood before the candle-lit altar and accepted him "till death do us part".

"Now residing at?" urged Mr. Ramsden gently.

She recalled herself with an effort and told him. As he carefully formed the letters on the blue paper with the squeaking quill, she absently traced her old initials C.B. in the dust on the mahogany desk.

To her dismay, Mr. Ramsden noticed the gesture.

"I must apologise for the really disgraceful state of my office. It is not a very attractive place for a lady at the best of times but, with our cleaner away ill, I fear it is quite shocking. I do trust you have not soiled your glove beyond repair."

Clara flushed and shook her head. She tucked the wandering hand into her muff and clutched it firmly with the other to restrain it. She was finding it extraordinarily difficult to control her thoughts as well as her movements. At one minute her mind was an utter blank; the next it was off on some irrelevant, even frivolous tangent. At that very moment she had an absurd desire to ask Mr. Ramsden how, in that room where dust lay thick on everything, he himself remained as immaculate as if wrapped in invisible cellophane. His black hair shone with the same discreet lustre as his black boots; his black coat seemed to have been newly sponged and pressed; his stiff collar gleamed so startlingly white that it made the handsome teeth he bared in that restrained, commiserating smile seem dingy by contrast.

"Your marriage took place at the Brompton Oratory in April of this year 1921?"

"Yes."

Mr. Ramsden's smile became a trifle more relaxed.

"I'm sure a lady as young as yourself will not mind telling me her age."

"I'm twenty-two."

For a moment, the solicitor looked ever so faintly incredulous. Then, looking at her with quite human curiosity, he said:

"Really! As young as all that!"

Clara smiled for the first time.

"I know I look much older. But I honestly was twenty-two last June."

"Please, please Mrs. Hughes-Follett, do not think I would doubt your word for one moment. Now that you are smiling, one could well believe you were even younger," said Mr. Ramsden gallantly. "It is only natural that the severe nervous strain of your . . . ahem . . . peculiarly distressing marriage should have left some temporary traces. I am sure they are *purely* temporary. Once this ordeal is over . . ."

"How long is it going to take?" Clara interrupted.

Mr. Ramsden laid down his quill, pressed the tips of his well shaped, well-groomed fingers together and looked at her through his shining glasses. The brown eyes behind the glasses looked in such excellent condition that Clara could not help wondering if Mr. Ramsden's spectacles were merely part of his professional make-up. Or were they simply a protective device, like the glass in front of a book-case, to preserve those handsome eyes, so correctly drawn and coloured yet so uninteresting, from dimming or fading?

"We-ell, it is not possible to say exactly. I am afraid you will have to exercise a certain amount of patience. The law's delays, you know. I doubt if there is any hope of our getting your case into the present session – the lists are very full. But say . . . mind you, I am not committing myself . . . say February or March. Presuming we get a favourable decision and allowing six months for the decree to be made absolute . . . then there is a reasonable possibility of your being a free woman in slightly less than one year from now."

"It seems a long time," sighed Clara.

"At your age, I am sure it does," said Mr. Ramsden. "At my considerably more advanced one, I assure you a year seems negligible. Forgive my asking, but are you by any chance entertaining another matrimonial project?"

"Oh dear, no," said Clara emphatically. "I'm quite certain I shall never marry again."

"There, let us hope, you are mistaken. But, in the present circumstances, I am glad of your assurance. You understand, Mrs. Hughes-Follett, that in the case of a petition for nullity, it is desirable that the plaintiff should be most particularly . . . ahem . . . discreet in his or her behaviour. I understand you have returned to live under your parents' roof."

"Yes. . . . The day after we . . . separated."

She frowned. 'Separated' did not seem the right word. It suggested something quiet and painless. But she could not visualise Mr. Ramsden writing anything as violent as 'tore apart'.

"Very proper. Very proper indeed," said Mr. Ramsden, squeaking off another sentence on the blue foolscap. "And have you seen Mr. Hughes-Follett on any subsequent occasion?"

"Only once. He came back to Tithe Place to collect his things and I was there packing up mine."

Clara clenched her hands together inside her muff and stared at the black deed-boxes, trying to fight down a memory that had suddenly become vivid. The dusty office, the law books, Mr. Ramsden squeaking away with his quill pen were the reality now. At all costs she must forget that afternoon in the Chelsea house when Archie had walked in as she was miserably tidying up. In spite of herself, Archie's dishevelled red head, the flushed unhappy face above the collar rimmed with grease-paint obtruded itself between her and the impeccably neat, flawlessly respectable person of Mr. Ramsden.

The solicitor looked up. She forced herself to see those brown eyes, that looked as if they were as meticulously cleaned and polished as their protecting glasses, instead of a pair of blue ones, bloodshot with drink and weeping.

"On that occasion, did Mr. Hughes-Follett try to force you to continue living with him as his wife?"

Clara said in a flat voice:

"He would never force anyone. He did want it, yes."

She could hear Archie's tormented voice. "I know it's just bloody weakness, Clarita. But the last weeks have been such hell. Worse than the first days even. Couldn't you give me one more chance? I swear I wouldn't have asked you. . . . But actually finding you here . . ."

"And you very properly refused?" asked Mr. Ramsden.

Clara looked down at her muff. It was a recent gift from her father and Archie had never seen it.

"I said no. I don't know about 'very properly'. I felt an utter beast. I still do."

"Your sentiments do you credit, Mrs. Hughes-Follett. The fact remains that you have undoubtedly taken the wisest possible course in seeking to annul this exceedingly unfortunate, one might almost say disastrous marriage."

"I suppose so," Clara said almost inaudibly. At that moment she wanted nothing but to bolt from that room and never set eyes on Mr. Ramsden again. As if he guessed her feelings, he addressed her almost sharply.

"Come, come, Mrs. Hughes-Follett. You should allow yourself to be guided by those who have your best interests at heart. Still, you are a free agent. If you do not wish me to proceed with the preparation of your petition . . ."

"I'm sorry," said Clara wretchedly. "I know I'm being tiresome. I realise I've got to go through with it."

Mr. Ramsden awarded her the commiserating smile.

"My dear young lady, pray do not think I am unsympathetic. I fully realise the extremely painful nature of your ordeal. As your legal adviser, I warn you that I shall have to ask you questions of an exceedingly delicate, even distressing nature. But you must regard me as a surgeon, who is forced to inflict pain for the ultimate benefit of his patient."

"Yes, I see that."

"You are looking somewhat overwrought. Perhaps you would like to defer further questioning to another interview."

"I'd rather go on now and get it over."

"Excellent."

Mr. Ramsden beamed at her through his glasses, drew in his breath and grasped the quill pen with renewed vigour.

"We will proceed then. And pray remember that these questions, which must seem to you so embarrassingly personal are utterly *impersonal* to me. In my profession, we learn to be strictly detached."

The questions proceeded. They were far more searching, far more intimate than anything Clara could have imagined. Mr. Ramsden's hushed voice and tactful circumlocutions embarrassed her more than any brutal frankness. There was nothing to do but harden herself and reply coldly and candidly. There were moments when she realised that her composure was slightly shocking to Mr. Ramsden. It was he who occasionally cast down his eyes and faltered while her own face and voice remained stiff and aloof. Her detachment was not entirely assumed. It was impossible to connect these questions with those two living human beings, who had once laughed and quarrelled and wept together. The questions concerned two puppets A and B and had only one object: to discover whether those puppets had or had not performed a particular mechanical gesture.

"Had you any reason, Mrs. Hughes-Follett, during the period of your engagement, to suppose that your future husband was incapable of . . . er . . . consummating the marriage?"

"No. It's hardly the sort of thing one discusses, is it?"

Mr. Ramsden's dark lashes drooped modestly behind his glasses.

"Pray forgive me. . . . But in these days when young people are often so remarkably frank. . . . Let me pass on. . . . May I enquire, had you known of such a disability, would you have refused to marry Mr. Hughes-Follett?"

For the first time, Clara felt herself flush. Her reasons for marrying Archie had been too complex for the question to have any relevance. She could only stammer foolishly:

"I don't know."

"Yet I take it you were willing yourself to have the . . . er . . . normal conjugal relations?"

She could not say "I don't know" again. She could not admit that, in the abstract, the idea terrified her. How could she explain that something which would have seemed quite natural with Stephen seemed unnatural with Archie? She would have submitted, she would have tried to play fair, but she could not conceal from herself that it was a relief that the demand had never been made.

Misinterpreting her blush and her silence, Mr. Ramsden said kindly:

"Let me put it in a way which is perhaps less embarrassing for a lady to answer. You hoped that there would be children as a result of the marriage?"

"Yes. Oh, yes." She was surprised how emphatically she said it. That was another odd thing. She did not want children in the abstract yet she would have liked to have had Archie's. If she had married Stephen, she would not have wanted them. He would have found them a bore and she herself had wanted nothing but Stephen.

Mr. Ramsden looked relieved. He permitted himself an almost sly smile.

"Ah, that is better. For legal purposes we can assume: *Qui veut la fin veut les moyens*, as the French say."

He wrote a long sentence with the quill pen. As he did so, Clara thought the aphorism was not true in her case. Mr. Ramsden's writing was so clear that she was able to read it upside down.

"The Petitioner was at all times ready and willing to consummate the marriage and expressed herself keenly desirous of having offspring. The frustration of her natural hopes, through no fault of her own, caused the Petitioner such grievous distress and such damage to her nervous health that, on her parents' advice, she decided to seek the annulment of her marriage."

Clara had to bite her lip to avoid smiling. She wondered what Mr. Ramsden would say if he knew that not only the advice but the very knowledge that a Catholic marriage could be annulled had come from a middle-aged painter who had tried to seduce her?

When the solicitor read the statement over to her and said: "I think that puts the case correctly, does it not?" she answered vaguely:

"Oh yes. I expect so."

He looked slightly hurt.

"Of course, if there is anything you feel could be added or more strongly put? I am open to suggestions . . . though I fancy that, from the legal point of view, no alteration is necessary."

It occurred to her that he wanted her to praise his style. She said politely:

"Oh no. I'm sure it's most impressively put."

Mr. Ramsden brightened again.

"There is a little touch of . . . what shall we say? . . . that one likes to give even to these dry-as-dust formalities. I understand you are a young lady of some literary ability."

"Whoever told you that nonsense?" Clara asked rudely.

"Nonsense?" Mr. Ramsden looked pained. "My dear Mrs. Hughes-Follett, Father Samuel Sissons is one of the last people who talk nonsense. He mentioned something of yours that had impressed him in some periodical." He gave a slightly rueful smile. "Perhaps you think we dried-up lawyers take no interest in our clients as human beings?"

Clara felt ashamed. It was obvious that Mr. Ramsden really meant to be kind.

"I'm sorry," she said. "I always seem to be rude when people mention writing. Guilt, I suppose."

Mr. Ramsden looked quite humanly surprised.

"Guilt? How very remarkable. In connection with such a very innocent, one might say benevolent occupation. I must say I have often been tempted myself to take up the pen in my spare time. We dried-up lawyers see some curious aspects of human nature, you know. We even have to be something of psychologists in our humble way."

"I'm sure you do," Clara agreed.

"Guilt," mused Mr. Ramsden, laying down his quill. "You know . . . guilt is quite one of the rarest things we come across. It is surprising how many people are genuinely convinced of their innocence, even when the facts are most decidedly against them. Unshakably convinced, you might say."

"Yes?" said Clara, feeling none too unshakably convinced of her own.

Mr. Ramsden twitched his shoulders and reassumed his professional smile.

"Which makes it all the more pleasant," he said with unction, "when one is convinced oneself, as one undoubtedly is in *this* particular case."

He stood up.

"I don't think I need bother you with anything further today. We shall have to have some more interviews later on. The next proceeding will be for me to arrange an appointment for you with the court doctors so that I can obtain their evidence."

"Doctors?" said Clara, aghast.

"I am afraid so. I wish I could have spared you, but the law is adamant. There has to be an examination by two independent doctors appointed by the court."

Mr. Ramsden looked tactfully out of the window.

"I see. Yes," said Clara faintly.

He turned and gave her a sharp glance.

"You have nothing to fear. . . . Even if there were anything, you understand me, previous to your marriage, which you could not quite bring yourself to disclose to me. . . . It might make our case more difficult to establish, that is all. . . ."

"No. Nothing."

"Excellent. You will forgive me. In my profession we have to be prepared for every eventuality."

"Yes. Is there any other awful thing I have to do?"

"No, no," he smiled reassuringly. "Just one other small formality. One of these days, we shall have to get Mr. Hughes-Follett up here so that you can identify him in my presence."

She had risen herself but her knees began to tremble so much that she had to sit down again.

"See Archie, here?"

"Yes. But only *see*. You won't have to speak to him. In fact you will not be able to. You see that glass door leading to the inner office?"

"Yes."

"He will be behind that. All you have to do is to tell me that the person there is indeed your husband."

She made a great effort and stood up again.

"Behind that glass door? I'm to look at Archie through a glass door."

"You are looking very pale. Would you like me to get you a glass of water?"

"No . . . no . . . I'm perfectly all right." Her voice was out of control, high-pitched and shaky.

"Is there anyone with you? Or calling for you?"

She shook her head.

"Shall I get my clerk to ring for a taxi?" He sounded genuinely concerned.

"No . . . no, thank you." Her one desire was to get away as quickly as possible without any more fuss.

"But you look positively ill. I am afraid this has been a terrible ordeal for you. You were so self-possessed . . . I did not realise. . . . Try and put the doctors out of your mind."

He took her hand and gave it a reassuring pressure, as if he were a doctor himself.

"Yes. I'll try."

It was not the thought of the doctors that she found so hard to put out of her mind, as, blessedly alone at last, she walked shakily down the stone stairs. It was the idea of seeing Archie there behind that glass door, glaring at him speechlessly like a fish in an aquarium, 'identifying' him like an object in a shop window to Mr. Ramsden. Her imagination went off on one of its crazy tangents. She saw herself beating both fists on that glass door, breaking its dusty panels, crying to Archie:

"Darling . . . it's all a mistake. . . . Let's stop it."

But as the chill wind struck her face outside, blowing the early-falling plane leaves round her ankles, she knew that they could not stop it now. They were no longer Archie and Clara. The squeaking of Mr. Ramsden's quill had inexorably transformed them into plaintiff and respondent in an undefended suit of nullity.

CHAPTER TWO

Clara was rather shocked at the ease with which she had slid back into the household at Valetta Road. Once they had returned from Paget's Fold and she had put away her things in her old bedroom, it was almost as if she had never left home. It was strange to be living in her parents' house with nothing to take her away from it and no work that had to be done. Before, there had been school, a wartime office job and lastly the Garrick Academy to occupy her. Now she had not even the distraction of writing free-lance advertisements. There was no immediate incentive to look for work. Father Sissons had induced Archie's uncle, Lord Fairholm, to pay Archie's debts so as to give him a clear start. He had moved into cheap furnished rooms with another man in the *My Girl Billie* company and, now that the play had opened, he insisted on sending Clara a little money for herself so that she should not be entirely dependent on her father. She was too listless to have any ambition either to earn more or to use her fitful, unreliable talent for something better than sales copy or slick magazine stories. The necessity of appearing punctually at meals, doing errands for her mother, washing her hair, and mending her clothes carried her through each uneventful day and prevented her from falling into the drifting apathy of her last weeks with Archie in Tithe Place.

She was neither happy nor unhappy, merely indifferent. If she was now unusually compliant about going up to gossip with her grandmother in the stuffy bedroom which she had always done her utmost to avoid, if she was willing to spend hours with Isabel reviewing her mother's wardrobe or discussing the merits of various shades of powder, it was from no desire to give pleasure. Any occupation, however trivial, helped to fill up the day. Better still, it prevented her from having to think or to make any decision. She seemed, indeed, to have become incapable of thought. Her father, delighted to have her home again now that he had accepted the situation, sometimes tried to lure her into a discussion. In the old days she had enjoyed talking to him about subjects in which Isabel took not the faintest interest. Now her mind dissolved at the mere threat of having to form any opinion. She could barely manage to take in what he was saying, let alone make an intelligible reply. Sometimes a phrase would lodge in her brain and go on repeating itself like a record when the needle sticks, distracting her from hearing what followed. Sometimes a word such as 'Consequences' 'Unemployment' or 'Inflation' would slowly write itself on the air as if traced in smoke and her eyes would follow each stroke, intent only on the shaping of each letter. Occasionally she caught her father staring at her with a half-angry, half-anxious expression. Then her mother would say: "Don't bother Clara with your old politics and things. Can't you see she's worn out with all she's been through?"

Clara was not grateful for her mother's solicitude. She realised that she was supposed to have gone through a great ordeal in the few months of her marriage. Now it was over, she could no longer recapture the misery and despair. Sometimes, when she opened the black notebook in which she had recorded her feelings at the time, she could hardly believe that she ever felt anything so violently. One thing she was quite sure of: she would never feel violently again. Then she had been passionately anxious about so many things . . . about herself, about Archie, about what possible use could ever be made of the rest of a life which had been nothing but a series of false starts. She had had moods of exaltation as well as despair: a poem, a picture, the sight of a face in the street could suddenly rouse her to an excitement which made her long to communicate it to someone else. Since her return to Valetta Road she had experienced neither. She could no longer read anything but newspapers and magazines. The poets and novelists she had once loved now seemed to be writing of a totally artificial world of emotion and experience; a world she had no desire to enter.

There were, of course, moments when she was disquieted by her lack of desire for anything at all. Since she had always been restless and impatient, always longing to hurry on the future, this mood of mild indifference seemed unnatural. She avoided her old friends, not from sensitiveness, but simply because she could not be bothered to make any move. When she thought of Archie, it was with none of the old pity and affection, but with a faint envy. It was probably better to be able to feel violently as Archie did, to want something passionately even if you

79

lost it as soon as you had found it. In any case, if Archie had lost her, he was doing what he had always longed to do. He was making a success of it. Tiny as his part was, several notices had mentioned him by name and praised him.

Nearly six weeks passed during which there was nothing Clara was forced to do but go up to Gray's Inn for an occasional interview with Mr. Ramsden. Once or twice these momentarily disturbed her indifference but she learnt to master a fit of trembling or a sudden threat of tears. But the day when he said:

"Mrs. Hughes-Follett, your husband is in the office for purposes of identification," she suddenly turned faint. At first she would not so much as open her eyes when Mr. Ramsden led her to the glass-topped door and whispered: "You need only take one glance."

She forced them open and there was Archie, mute and staring like herself, on the other side of the glass. He looked different. His untidy red hair was sleeked down: he was wearing an overcoat she did not recognise. Her automatic control returned. She looked at Archie as if he were a photograph and said: "Yes, that is my husband." Then Mr. Ramsden led her back to his own office and kept her in idle chat for a few moments. She heard her own voice saying words with the right intonation but had no idea what they were. The clerk called her a taxi. When she got into it she found she was icy cold and that her right temple was throbbing in a sickening, painful rhythm. The hammer strokes fell faster and harder till, when she paid off the driver at Valetta Road, black zigzags were dancing in front of her right eye and she thought she was going to vomit. All the next day she lay in bed in a darkened room. Unaccustomed to physical pain, she was surprised that the body could feel so violently when the other sensibilities were numb.

She had another of these headaches after being examined by the two court doctors. During the examination she managed to detach herself so completely from what was going on that her body seemed to have no connection with her. She even felt an insane desire to laugh at the doctors' elaborate precautions, as if it were their modesty and not hers which had to be safeguarded. But afterwards she found that she was shaking all over and, by the time she got home, her right temple was throbbing like a dynamo. She lay for hours aware only of the terrible, insistent beat to which the words "Virgo Intacta" fitted themselves as if to the pounding rhythm of train wheels.

Some days after this, Mr. Ramsden announced triumphantly that there was a hope that her case might be squeezed into the current session and heard before Christmas. Clara felt no elation, merely a relief that, for the time being, there would be no more interviews with the solicitors and she would have to take no action of any kind. Mr. Ramsden had suggested that she might like to begin preliminary inquiries with the ecclesiastical authorities. But since proceedings could not be officially begun until she had obtained the civil decree, she thankfully put it off.

When she had been at Valetta Road for over two months, she noticed that her parents were becoming a trifle restive. Her father began to hint that, now she was looking so much better, it might be a good idea for her to find work of some kind. Clara was immediately on the defensive. "What kind of work?" she asked. "I don't imagine you want me to go back to the stage, do you? Anyhow, I shouldn't have the remotest hope of getting a part in London. And I can't go on tour because of the case."

"Good heavens, no, my dear. Anything but that! What about your advertisements and so on?"

"I've lost the knack. Besides you always disapproved of that too."

He could not deny it and suggested hesitantly that, as her French was good, she might be able to coach some of his younger pupils. This suggestion alarmed her so much that, for the first time, she burst into tears. She could not tell him why the idea of giving a boy a few French lessons caused such panic. The real reason was that it revived the idea of being a schoolmistress which her father had cherished for her all his life. Home, instead of a refuge, suddenly appeared to Clara as a trap. She would never escape again. At twenty-two she was going to be condemned for life to what she had spent years trying to avoid ... a career of teaching. Not even in a school but as her father's junior assistant. She saw herself twenty years hence, a dry spinster with pince-nez. "Mr. Batchelor's daughter. Such a help to him. A pity she never took her degree of course." "Wasn't she on the stage once? I even believe she got married!" "My *dear* ... people will say anything. You've only to look at Miss Batchelor to know neither of those absurd rumours could possibly be true."

Her father, though disturbed by this sudden burst of crying, was inclined to press his point, though gently. Luckily her mother came to her rescue with a suggestion that silenced him.

"Claude, how *can* you be so tactless? Just when she was beginning to get over things . . . to bring up the subject of teaching boys. Charles Cressett . . . you *can't* have forgotten Archie's connection with all that tragedy?"

It was easy after that to escape to her bedroom and bathe her stinging eyes. As she did so, she was aware of a sensation she had never expected to feel again. She felt she must get out of the house, do something, above all, see someone who did not belong to her family. Feverishly she did up her face, changed her dress and ran softly down the stairs, hoping to be out of the house before the meal was finished. She was too late: her mother was already coming upstairs for her ritual afternoon rest.

"Going out, darling? What a good idea! It's so bad for you staying indoors so much."

On an impulse, Clara drew her mother into her bedroom and shut the door.

"Mother . . . would it matter if I were out to dinner tonight?"

"Of course not, darling. Have you got an invitation? I'm so glad if you have. You haven't seen any of your old friends since you came home."

"No. Nothing definite. I just feel I want to get away from Valetta Road. Do you understand?"

Isabel kissed her.

"Of course, darling. You don't know how often I wish *I* could. The minute dinner's over, Daddy disappears into the study and there's nothing for me to do but read or strum the piano or go to bed." She added hastily: "I mean there *was*, until you came home. You can't think how lovely it is having you back again."

"I'm pretty rotten company I'm afraid," said Clara, pulling down her eye-veil to avoid another kiss. She was grateful to her mother for her intervention at lunch but she was in no mood for demonstrations.

"What a charming hat," said Isabel. "I'd forgotten it."

She stepped back and looked critically at Clara.

"Why, you suddenly look more like your old self. Your face always had so much life in it. All these weeks its looked like a house with the blinds down. And now . . ."

This time there was no avoiding the kiss.

"Go and enjoy yourself, pet. I'll make some excuse to Daddy."

Once she was out in the street, Clara's flatness returned. Where, after all, could she go? Whom could she see? Honour demanded that, once out of the house, she must stay out till considerably after dinner time. She ran through a list of the old friends she had shockingly neglected since her marriage but not one of them appealed to her. She could not face curiosity, excited sympathy, tactfully veiled triumph. It was a sunny late October day with a wind sharp enough to make her eyes, still sore from crying, water behind the eye-veil. She pulled the fur collar of her coat almost up to her nose and began to walk fast and aimlessly. After a while, finding she was automatically walking south, she deliberately took the streets that led to Chelsea.

Chelsea seemed so remote from her present life that she could almost fancy it did not exist except in her imagination. When she found herself once more in the King's Road, though recognising every shop and tree, she still could not believe that, only a few months earlier, it had been her daily thoroughfare. Not till she stood on the corner by the Catholic church, staring across at the 'Sugar House' did she recover any sense of connection. The orange curtains were drawn and the windows shut. She crossed the road and walked down the side street, peering guiltily through the flap of the letterbox into the shed which their landlords had called a 'studio'. She could make out a faint glitter of metal in one corner. Archie must have left some of the sleepers when he dismantled the model railway. Someone – was it Archie himself? – had piled them up anyhow against the wall. She was suddenly seized with the mad idea that it was not her life here that had been an unreal dream but her present life in West Kensington. She had an insane desire to get into the house, barricade herself in and never return to Valetta Road again. Suddenly she remembered that she still had the key to the house in her handbag. Recklessly, she retraced her steps and was just going to turn the corner to approach the front of the house when she heard the street door open. She flattened herself against the wall, her heart beating violently. A woman came out. Clara could only see her from the back but she recognised the brassy hair of Mrs. Woods, the owner. Mrs.

Woods hesitated for a moment, then, mercifully, took the other direction.

Clara had always disliked their landlady. The idea that Mrs. Woods might have found her, not merely spying through the letter-box of the shed but actually breaking into the house, made the sweat start out on her forehead. She turned and walked, as fast as her shaking knees would let her, through the back streets that led to the embankment. Leaning on the parapet to recover her breath, she took the key of the Sugar House out of her bag and threw it in the river.

The action cleared her head. For the first time she realised, however dimly, that her standing there, staring at the dancing coins of light on the dark water, was part of a continuous stream of life. Since her marriage she had had an increasing sense of unreality, as if her existence had been broken off like the reel of a film. Nothing that had happened to her seemed to have had a connection with any past or to be leading to any future. Now she perceived, though she could not yet feel it, that her life could not, in the nature of things, remain in this state of tranced immobility. However sluggishly, it would go on like the river and the mere going on must produce some changes for better or worse. Whether she liked it or not, she could not go back to the Sugar House. A startling idea occurred to her. She could not yet imagine summoning up the will to do so but, like a revelation, she saw that it might be possible for her one day to leave her parents' house again.

Excited by the mere possibility, she went into the 'Blue Cockatoo' and sat there drinking coffee and smoking for nearly an hour. Her thoughts took no practical turn: she merely let herself drift on a tide of vague, slightly guilty pleasure. On the wall was a poster of the London Group's autumn exhibition. One of the painters exhibiting was Marcus Gundry. That strange episode in his studio the night that she and Archie had parted was now the most unreal of all. It was not that she did not remember it: it was simply isolated in her own consciousness like a vivid dream. Staring at his printed name, a simple, yet astonishing fact presented itself. Marcus Gundry was a real person. In order to have his name printed on that poster, he had bought materials, stretched canvases, painted pictures, sent them to a Committee. She became aware of an even more astonishing fact – a discovery so startling that she caught her breath with excitement. What had happened to her that evening had happened also to him. He too had lived through those hours, evidently with very different feelings, but they had been part of his experience as of hers. For her the experience had been disturbing, even shocking, yet, as she sat alone in the arty little restaurant, aware of the sulky glances of the waitress who was a Chelsea 'character' and obviously regarded her as an intruder, it suddenly acquired a new importance. Marcus Gundry had had no preconceived ideas about her: he had simply accepted her as another human being. And she had felt another human being in a more special sense. It was true she had behaved in the most extraordinary way; relaxed and happy one moment, hysterical with terror the next. But, throughout that evening, for one of the few times in her life she had been completely natural. She had said exactly what came into her mind; she had asked questions she had never dared to ask before; she had made an utter fool of herself and she had not minded. All that seemed important now was the extraordinary sense of being alive after months of deadness that she had had that evening. An impulse came over her, as strong as her impulse to let herself into the Sugar House. She stubbed out her half-smoked cigarette and stood up, hardly able to control her impatience at the slowness of the sullen waitress. Out in the street again, she realised that her sudden longing to see Gundry was as crazy as the other. But to want anything again was so intoxicating that she could no more control the want than she had been able, all these months, to force her will into any channel. As she hurried along, so eager to be there that, if a taxi had passed, she would have hailed it, what was left of her reason kept saying "This is absurd. You know it's absurd. It won't even work. You know perfectly well that Gundry is only interested in you as a possible mistress. You haven't the slightest intention of becoming his mistress. It won't even be like the last time. You will be in a perfectly ridiculous situation. He'll be furious. . . . He'll be bored." She was scolding herself so vehemently that her lips moved as she almost ran along. Not looking where she was going, she muttered quite audibly "Stop it, you idiot!" At that moment, someone blocked her way. A hand fell on her arm.

"Stop *what?*" inquired a mild, amused voice.

She looked up, dazed, and found herself staring into a face she knew.

"Clive Heron!" she gasped. "Of all people!" She added with perfect sincerity: "You can't *think* how glad I am to see you."

"Don't tell me you were thinking of me at that very moment because I certainly shan't believe you," he said, turning and falling into step beside her.

"And you would be right. You couldn't have been farther from my thoughts," Clara said, with the gaiety which the appearance of Clive Heron always induced. His appearances had always been rare and unpredictable. In the interval, Clara was apt to forget all about him yet, whenever she ran into him again, she was always aware of this sudden lightheartedness.

"I am always right," said Clive Heron. He clutched the hat which always looked far too large and heavy above the small, delicately featured face which seemed too frail to support even the weight of his pince-nez. "*Must* we walk in the teeth of this appalling gale? I was deliberately keeping my back to it."

"We could turn round and walk up Oakley Street. Unless you're going anywhere special?"

"No. I'm merely taking my Saturday afternoon constitutional. The direction is *entirely* determined by avoiding these icy blasts. What about you?"

"I'm not going anywhere special either. At least, not now. I've changed my mind."

"Stopped it, in fact?"

"Yes. Thanks to you."

They turned into Oakley Street and Clara tried to lengthen her step to keep up with Heron's strides.

"You can't do it," he observed. "Better tittup along in your usual ridiculous fashion."

Obediently she returned to her usual short step.

"May one inquire stop *what?*" he asked, after a moment. "From the way you were dashing along, muttering to yourself, you seemed to be fairly far gone. Suicide?"

"Not quite as final. I was trying to stop myself from going to see the very last person I *ought* to see."

"Hmm. Do you *want* to be restrained?"

"Yes."

"What do you expect me to do? Escort you back to your own door-step?"

"No. I've said I'm not going to be home till after dinner and nothing will induce me to go back to West Kensington for hours and hours and hours."

"West Kensington? I thought you were living in Tithe Place."

"I was. But I'm not now."

"Dear, dear, how very confusing. I wish people wouldn't gad about so. I had just got it into my consciousness that you were living round the corner from me. In another month or two, I might even have brought myself to the point of ringing you up. Now I've got to absorb an entirely new set of referenda. Really, my dear girl, it's intolerable. What *have* you been up to?"

"Too complicated to tell you in the street."

"Well, at least you have some grains of sense left. Oh God, now we've got to turn into this infernal wind again. What do you want to *do?*" he asked in an exasperated voice.

"I haven't the least idea."

"For heaven's sake . . . don't expect *me* to make any decision. You know I'm *perfectly* incapable. *Suggest* something."

She said bravely.

"I'll accompany you to *your* doorstep. If it's still the same one."

"Of *course* it's the same one. The mere contemplation of moving would drive me into a frenzy. Come *along.* I warn you, I shan't open my lips till we're out of this howling gale."

Only when they were outside the house in Paultons Square where Heron had rooms, did he relax his expression of tortured endurance. He carefully removed his pince-nez, wiped his watering eyes and actually smiled at Clara. Looking up at him, she realised it was the first time she had seen him without his glasses. His eyes were childishly blue and the area of protected skin round them so white that it made the rest of his pale face seem almost tanned. Without his pince-nez, which had worn a permanent groove either side of his nose, an entirely different Clive was revealed. The small features which had always seemed as impersonal as if Clive had simply selected them for their unobtrusive elegance like a shirt or tie, suddenly composed into a real face. This face seemed to belong to someone whom Clara did not know at all . . . a vulnerable creature with an odd beauty, neither masculine nor feminine. He had removed his hat along with the pince-nez and a sudden gust of wind caught his red-gold hair and tossed it up in a crest above the high white forehead, giving him a momentary resemblance to a Blake angel.

He gave a little shriek:

"My God . . . my *hair*! For mercy's sake, come *inside*."

CHAPTER THREE

"VERY PECULIAR. *Most* extraordinary." Clive Heron leant back in his chair, carefully adjusted one long leg over the other and fitted a fresh cigarette into his holder with slow precision.

They had spent all the afternoon in his rooms and had just finished the dinner sent up by his landlady. It was not till they had settled down to their meal that Clara had been invited to 'explain her situation'. During the afternoon, Clive had devoted a long time playing gramophone records. Next he had demanded 'the *precise* implication' of certain theological terms in a book he was reading and had noted Clara's replies in his small, exquisite writing on the blank page at the end. Finally, they had discussed from every possible angle, but without reaching a conclusion the desirability of Clive's adopting a kitten.

Clara, who was far more intuitive about cats than about human beings, had long ago decided to treat Clive Heron as if he were a cat. It had worked surprisingly well. Now, by patiently allowing him to go through the rituals which surrounded all his actions, whether the placing a chair at the exact distance from the gramophone to ensure the best sound effect or the careful uncorking of a bottle of sherry, she proved that she was aware of the enormous concession of being allowed to enter his rooms. Hitherto they had always met in public places; occasionally, by pre-arrangement, for a dinner, theatre or concert; more often, by chance, in the street. Even in the street, he did not always acknowledge her. Sometimes he would walk past her, affecting an absent-minded stare which he knew perfectly well did not deceive her. Sometimes, when she saw him approaching and rashly waved to him, he would go so far as to bolt up a turning which he had obviously never intended to take. Only once had she induced him to enter her own home, since he disliked going into his friends' houses almost as much as inviting them into his. With infinite prevarications, he had 'provisionally' accepted an invitation to her twenty-first birthday party at Valetta Road. She had been quite prepared for him not to turn up. He had, however, been, not only the first to arrive and the last to go, but the success of the evening. Clara was used to her friends being enthusiastic about her father who was always at his best as a host. Clive, with his usual unexpectedness, had taken a violent fancy to Isabel. Since then he had rarely run into Clara without inquiring after "your *marvellous* mother" or "that *incredible* woman whom you haven't the wits to appreciate."

The fact that he had invited her in was remarkable. His insisting on her staying to dinner was more remarkable still. He was obviously pleased with himself and with her that the rash experiment was, so far, turning out well. Nevertheless, Clara knew that she must leave all control to him. She had been fretting to talk about her 'situation', but she could see him holding her off with deliberate mischievousness. Now, with frequent interruptions from him at points where she wanted to get quickly on with her narrative and blank silences when she paused, expecting comment or even sympathy, she had at last been allowed to tell him as much as he was interested to hear.

"It sounds more peculiar than ever when I say it in this room," she said.

"Why?"

"Because it's such an eminently reasonable, civilised room." She glanced round at the cream-panelled walls, the orderly rows of books, the two table-lamps whose shades had just been adjusted to their present angle after much deliberation on Clive's part and groans of "Why *can't* people leave things *alone?*" The few pieces of furniture, obviously carefully chosen for elegance or comfort, were maintained at the highest level of polish and repair. "It suits you extraordinarily well. Did you acquire all these things bit by bit or in one grand sweep?"

"I didn't acquire them at all. They're furnished rooms. Nothing belongs to me but the gramophone and the books. I loathe possessions."

"I didn't know you were so austere."

"I'm not in the least austere. I should like to have the best of everything. It's simply that I don't like owning things. Once you own things you're a slave to them. You have, in fact, to *do* something about them. Look at all these objects. Very agreeable. I can enjoy them but I'm not responsible for them. If, heaven forbid, I had to move somewhere else, I could leave them without the slightest pang. Whereas, if I possessed them, I should have to take all sorts of appalling *action* . . . get them stored or removed or whatever people *do* with objects. The mere idea paralyses me. You look ruminative. Are you attached to possessions?"

"I don't know, because I haven't had many. I'm afraid I could get attached to them all right. I can imagine thoroughly enjoying having a beautiful house of my own and quantities of good clothes and all that sort of thing. No, what I was ruminating about was something else. Something that's just struck me as odd."

"*What?*"

"That you've got something in common with Archie, though no two people could be more wildly unlike in other ways. He hated possessions, too."

"Hmm. Yet, if you'd stuck it for a year or two, apparently you could have had everything in that way you wanted. I'm rather surprised you chucked it so soon. After all, from the money point of view, you were on to a remarkably good thing."

"I thought you didn't approve of riches."

"Inaccurate, as usual. In the first place I don't approve or disapprove of anything in that sense. In the second, though I happen to dislike possessions, I don't in the least dislike money. On the contrary: 'Put money in thy purse'. The more the merrier. Not *keep* it there, of course. Get rid of it as quickly and agreeably as possible. Otherwise it becomes a possession."

"That's obviously how Archie felt. Only he got rid of what wasn't there."

"Well, it would have been there if you'd held on a little longer. Haven't you been slightly impetuous? He sounds an amiable enough chap. I know plenty of women who'd be rather relieved to be let off the usual concomitants of marriage."

"I was relieved," Clara admitted. "But it wasn't as simple as all that."

"No doubt, no doubt," he said equably. "I can see the situation bristles with formidable possibilities. Now, tell me what *really* interests me. What line does your Church take about it all?"

She told him what she knew of the complex process of annulling a Catholic marriage. He nodded approvingly.

"Perfectly logical. Just as I supposed. Marriage, as such indissoluble. Query, what constitutes a marriage? When in fact is a marriage not a marriage? Onus on you to prove certain conditions have not been fulfilled and proofs independent of civil law required. Am I correct?"

Clara nodded.

"Good. I always suspected it was a fallacy that they'd trump up a case for you provided you could pour enough cash into the Vatican coffers. But I like to get things straight from the horse's mouth."

"I *hope* I've got it right," Clara said anxiously. "Anyway there's certainly no hanky-panky. Rome grinds slow and grinds exceedingly small. I'll probably be reduced to powder by the time it gets through."

"You oughtn't to complain if you are. After all, for you it's the mills of God, isn't it? Don't you *expect* to be dust and ashes in this vale of tears? I appreciate the Catholic Church *far* more than you do."

"Not quite enough to become a Catholic though," said Clara maliciously.

He waved his cigarette, threw back his head and emitted the half-amused, half-exasperated "Ah" with which he savoured any characteristic 'nonsense' of Clara's.

"My *dear* girl! What a barbarian you are! I appreciate the Catholic Church ... probably considerably more than most Catholics ... precisely because I'm *not* involved in it. In any case, I don't believe it's possible for anyone to *become* a Catholic. If one's born into that tradition, one should accept it precisely as one accepts one's nationality. I don't approve of conversions ... or de-conversions for that matter. One should remain in one's situation."

"Then you should disapprove of me. It's true I was only seven when it happened but I *am* a convert."

"Rubbish. You had no control over that any more than if you'd been baptised as a baby. Besides you were properly brought up in the whole thing ... it comes natural to you. I count *you* as a real Catholic. The person I disapprove of ... in so far as I disapprove of *anyone* ... is your father. A man *soaked* in the Greeks too. A *deplorable* lapse."

"I think it was rather magnificent," said Clara hotly. "He must have gone through awful struggles. Look at what he gave up. He became one at thirty-five ... just when at any moment he might have become a headmaster. Well, that finished *that*. He'll be an overworked, underpaid assistant master for the rest of his life now. I doubt very much if I'd have had the guts to give up so much if *I'd* been in his situation.

Anyway, as regards the Greeks, he said it was Plato and Aristotle that first put him on the way to it."

"Which shows he totally misunderstood both of them. As I've always suspected."

"Weren't they looking for truth? And if Daddy became convinced that Catholicism *was* true, wasn't he absolutely right to accept it, even if it involved giving up things? Of course *you'd* say it wasn't true so he just made a ghastly mistake."

"There you go again," he groaned. "Have I ever said it *wasn't* true?"

"You can't mean *you* think it's true."

"Of *course*, it's true. But *poetically* true, not literally true. That's the trouble with your father. He's too literal."

"Then I am too."

"Can't you *really* see the difference between literal truth and poetic truth. Come, come, I know you're not an idiot."

"I think I'm rapidly becoming one – Still you can try and explain."

"It's *perfectly* simple. There are different realms of truth. Take a Cézanne picture . . . even any typical good old apples and crumpled nappies. You know perfectly well you are beholding a portion of eternal truth when you gaze at it. Poetic truth in fact. Now take the actual objects he painted . . . the physical apples and crumplers . . . verifiable, existing objects. Literal truths, in fact."

"Yes, I see *that* difference. And in a sense the Cézanne is *more* true . . . because it is *poetic* truth . . . just as Raskolnikov's murder or Othello's is truer than a literal account of a murder in the *Daily Mail*."

"I should prefer to say it belonged to a different realm of truth . . . to the realm of essence rather than to the realm of existence. But you've got the rough idea."

Clara frowned. . . .

"It's funny . . . I seem to understand dimly when people use analogies from art. I haven't the most rudimentary sense of philosophy and never will have. But surely religion's something beyond *all* categories . . . art, philosophy . . . everything?"

"Why? Why shouldn't it be simply another realm to be explored, another activity of the human spirit?"

"Because . . . oh, because it involves *everything* in a person. I can't argue with you. I get all muddled. Once you're convinced there is a

God and that your whole life here and hereafter depends on your relation to that God . . . that truth surely transcends all others. . . . Or aren't you convinced there *is* a God?"

"No. In my opinion . . . and in that of vast numbers of people infinitely more competent than I am . . . God is an unnecessary hypothesis. No . . . no . . . don't try and come it over me with those official proofs. Any logician could dispose of them in five minutes. They're simply respectable rationalisations after the event . . . cooked up by people who already *were* convinced."

Clara's head seemed to be filled with a whirling fog.

"If only I had a *mind*," she sighed.

"You do very well without one," he said with his sudden delightful smile. "Don't think I object to people believing in God. If that's your natural approach to things, you should accept it and enjoy it. It's entirely a matter of temperament."

"I suppose you'll say that weak-minded people need some sort of prop and religion gives it them and strong-minded people can do without it," Clara said rather angrily.

"Now, now . . . I'm not such a fool as to suggest anything of the kind. There are thousands of strong-minded theists and thousands of weak-minded atheists. Nor do I suppose, as people so often do, that there is anything particularly consoling about believing in God. On the contrary, I can quite see it can put one in the most agonising predicament. 'It is a fearful thing to fall into the hands of the living God'. Yes, indeed."

"You don't talk like the stock atheist."

"Of course I don't. I'm not a stock anything. I'm unique. In fact, I often have a sinister suspicion that I *am* God."

Clara laughed.

"It's no laughing matter, I assure you. It might be the most appalling thing to be God. Because no one could save Him from *His* agonising predicament." He added gaily: "*No one* has any idea what I suffer. I'm mad, you see."

She perceived obscurely that he did suffer and said slowly:

"Am I mad too? Honestly, there've been times lately when I've wondered whether I wasn't going out of my mind . . . if I hadn't actually *gone*, in fact."

"Very probably," he said cheerfully. "Definitely mad in spots. Which is why I've always had such a fancy for you. But you're quite different from me. With your amazing literalness, your passion for translating everything into immediate, violent action, I shouldn't be surprised if one day you went right over the edge and landed yourself in a strait-jacket."

"Thank you."

"Don't mistake me. I'm not saying you *will*. Merely that it's an interesting possibility. Because, of course, you'd recover and feel marvellous. My situation is far more deplorable, because I'm permanently in the strait-jacket. I shall never technically 'go out of my mind' and I shall never be cured."

"Cured of what?"

"My particular neurosis. My invincible horror of taking action of any kind or making any decision. Which wouldn't matter in the least if it weren't coupled with the most appalling anxiety and guilt about *not* taking action. Your Archie is impotent in one way and I'm impotent in another."

Clara said sympathetically:

"I know about that sort of impotence. For months . . . all the time I was with Archie . . . it was like a sort of creeping paralysis. Its been the same ever since I went back to live with my family. When I look back, I can't imagine how I ever *wanted* to do anything, let alone attempted to do it. Not only things like going on the stage or writing advertisements, but even writing a letter or reading a book."

"Don't *mention* writing letters," he said with a sympathetic shudder. "Or ringing people up . . . I *know*."

"At one point it got so bad . . . that was in the Archie days . . . that I couldn't be bothered to get dressed properly or even comb my hair. I just slouched and mooched about all day in a kind of stupor."

Clive's pince-nez glittered at her.

"Dear me! Most interesting. Evidently you're quite One of Us. Not so far gone as me, of course. Otherwise you wouldn't dare relax for one moment. With me, if once the hair weren't accurately combed, the shoes properly laced, every object exactly placed, the same bus caught every morning, *The Times* always carried under the *left* arm, the entire structure would collapse. The deluge, in fact."

95

Clara murmured:

> "But I beneath another sea
> And whelmed in deeper gulfs than he."

"*Precisely*," he said. "You've got it."

They were silent for some minutes, smoking companionably. Clara was careful to drop her ashes neatly in the tray which Clive had already emptied several times.

He said at last, with that sudden radiant smile which revealed his unusually white and even teeth:

"Astonishing, how much I like you. I did, the first time I set eyes on you, you know. *When* women are all right I actually prefer them to men, though no one would believe it."

He had moved his head slightly so that his eyes were clearly visible behind his glasses. There was a questioning expression in them which did not match the cheerfully confident assertion. For some reason Clara felt suddenly out of her depth and could think of nothing to say. After a pause, he asked:

"By the way, have you quite got over our old friend, Stephen Tye?"

She nodded. "I'm rather shocked at myself for having got over it so completely. And so quickly. Months before I married Archie. Yet I really and truly thought I was in love. I was completely obsessed by him for well over a year. Now I can't even remember what it felt like. I must be disgustingly shallow."

"Not necessarily. When the fever goes, thank heaven it *goes*. But I'm surprised you can't remember the symptoms. Thank goodness, I'm sane at the moment and have been relatively free since my last Object left me. But there's not a quiver of the Object's eyelashes, not a tremor of my own knees, not one shade of the tortures of suspense and jealousy I can't recall in the minutest detail."

Clara said stupidly:

"You mean you've been in love?"

He said impatiently:

"Of *course* I've been in love. What do you take me for? Over and over again. I've doted upon and been doted upon. Once or twice it's even been simultaneous. I assure you there's nothing I don't know about all *that*."

This was such a surprise . . . and, for some reason, not altogether an agreeable one . . . that Clara could only say feebly:

"Of course, I don't know you very well, do I?"

"Rubbish. You know me considerably better than most people. I just happen not to have mentioned all that side of my life. I only mention it now to assure you that it does exist. Or rather, shall we say, did exist. I've certainly been immune since this last set-to. . . . Possibly I'm cured forever. *What* a relief!"

"I suppose I must be, then. Yet I don't feel anything as definite as relief. Perhaps you don't appreciate being cured if you've forgotten what it felt like to be ill. You make me almost wish . . ."

"Wish *what?*"

"That I *could* fall in love again . . ."

"You will, Oscar, you will."

She shook her head.

"No. Honestly, I don't think I could. I can't imagine doing anything positive ever again."

"You seemed positive enough about *not* doing something when you cannoned into me this afternoon. What *was* all that about?"

"There, you see. I'd already forgotten about it. Yet, at that moment, I felt absolutely *compelled* to go and see a particular person. And I knew it was an insane thing to do."

"Why more insane than coming here with me?"

"Too complicated to go into. Anyway, it's done me worlds more good talking to you. Even if he'd *let* me talk.

"*Do* be more explicit. If *who* had let you talk?"

"Oh . . . a painter called Marcus Gundry. . . . If you knew him, you'd realise it was crazy of me."

Clive raised his faint eyebrows and tucked in his small chin as he did when he was, or affected to be, startled. This time, she thought he really must be startled for the cigarette dropped from his holder.

"*That* old Turk! Well, well, well!"

"So you know him?"

"Oh . . . vaguely." He bent down anxiously to recover his cigarette. "Intact, thank goodness," he said with relief. "They call him the Ram of Derbyshire. *Rather* a good painter, though. I bought a picture of his once but I've never been able to decide *exactly* where it ought to hang.

So it's still reposing in a cupboard . . . I haven't even got so far as removing its integuments." He frowned and fitted the cigarette delicately into the ivory holder. "Gundry! Of all the unsuitable confidants for a young woman in your situation! Are you in the habit of going to see him?"

"I've been precisely once."

"Ah, I think I see your point. You'd be lucky if you survived twice. I imagine you're very much his type."

"He was extraordinarily kind. He let me off. But he made it very clear he didn't want me there again just to have a nice, cosy chat. Yet *that* was the part *I* found so exciting – It was the only time I've felt human for months and months. Except today." She paused and frowned. "Yet even this isn't *quite* the same . . ."

"Obviously," said Clive. "No risk. Hence no excitement. One of your few flaws is that you have a craving for dramatic situations in ordinary life."

"Have I? What a genius you have for deflating me."

"I prefer to call it disintoxicating."

"All right. I'm sure it's very salutary. I even like it. But when I talked to Gundry. . . ." She broke off. "No, I can't explain the difference. If I tried, it might sound rude."

"Come *on*, you absurd creature. Don't you know I adore hearing anything about myself . . . however unpleasant? I feel I've really pulled it off when someone talks as if I actually *existed*."

"Don't *you* feel you exist? I don't either. I believe this afternoon . . . in the 'Blue Cockatoo' of all places . . . I suddenly realised, for the first time, that . . ."

"We are talking about Me . . ." said Clive firmly. "Kindly stick to the point. *What* is the difference between a cosy chat with Marcus Gundry and a cosy chat with me?"

"Well . . . you're obviously a much more remarkable *person*. And I couldn't enjoy being with anyone more. I always have enjoyed it. Whatever we talk about, whatever we do. It's like a sort of enchantment. You appear and disappear like some creature from another world. . . ."

"I disappear," he murmured. "*Quite*."

"Yes. It wouldn't be crazy to rush off frantically to look for you. It would simply be unthinkable. You wouldn't be *there*. I believe you really could become invisible when you don't want to be seen. But, given certain conditions, you suddenly materialise like a rainbow. And you produce exactly the same sort of pleasure. Whatever mood I'm in, I suddenly feel absurdly gay and irresponsible."

"Very flattering. You said just now I deflated you."

"That comes later. You make me realise I'm a complete nitwit. I even feel I ought to do something about it. But I don't, because when you vanish, you vanish completely. I don't even think 'How nice – or how improving – it would be to see Clive Heron.' I don't think about you at all."

"Then surely we've achieved the ideal human relationship? We enjoy each other's society without impinging on each other's consciousness."

She laughed.

"Ideal, perhaps. But not exactly human. You see, I can't think of you as an ordinary human being."

"There you are! *You* can't . . . and I can't. Sometimes I can put it across on the Objects. Especially if they're perfectly simple, straight-forward creatures as they frequently are. The more 'ordinary', the more madly attractive I find them. But I *long* to be an ordinary human being. I should *adore* to be a great hearty extrovert with a moustache and a pipe, playing golf every week-end and bellowing with laughter at stock-exchange stories."

"You *wouldn't?*"

"I'm perfectly serious. However, like most ideals, it's unattainable. So I merely *contemplate* it, which is the proper way to treat ideals. My only quarrel with Catholics is that *occasionally* they make the fatal mistake of attempting to realise theirs in the realm of existence instead of leaving them where they belong, in the realm of essence. However, we'll let that pass since it obviously disturbs you. Gundry, of course, *is* an extrovert. Most painters are, lucky dogs. Is that why you prefer his conversation?"

"I didn't say I preferred it. All I'm trying to say is that it has a different effect on me."

"Explain yourself."

"I'm trying to. You are *extraordinarily* like the Caterpillar in Alice. . . . Well . . . when I talked to Gundry . . . and I have only talked to

99

him once properly . . . I positively felt as if one day, heaven knows how, I might conceivably be able to *do* something. Whereas with you, though everything seems marvellously exciting or amusing . . . you make me giddy talking about things I don't understand . . . or we listen to music and you make me *listen*, not just vaguely hear a pleasant background buzz while I wonder whether or not to wash my hair tomorrow. . . ."

"Put it off," he interposed. "One should *always* put things off. . . ."

"*But*," Clara continued firmly, "I go away with the feeling that all one's got to do is to look on . . . enjoy, criticise . . . but not participate. Is that nonsense?"

"Not at all. But why this lust for action and participation and so on? The spectacle's *there* to be contemplated. Why not be a civilised spectator? I assure you there are none too many of them. They have enormous value. Gundry paints a picture. I have acquired the wits to see that it is quite a good picture and I buy it. The result is Gundry can live for a few weeks and paint another picture. *You* seem to think it would be better if I spent the money on canvases and paints and produced some inefficient daub of my own."

"Of course not. But haven't you ever wanted to produce anything?"

"Not unless I was assured beforehand it was going to be absolute perfection. Why clutter up the world with a lot more mediocrity?"

"Stephen said some of the poems you wrote at Oxford were extraordinarily good."

"Nonsense. They were exactly like the poems *everyone* writes at Oxford. I had the sense to know when to stop. For God's sake don't rouse my guilt about writing. There's a conspiracy among the Panjandrums to force me to write. If they knew the agonies I go through at the mere thought of putting pen to paper, even to write a letter. The mere idea of *pens* and *paper* causes such appalling anxiety that I never keep either in the house. If I have to write a letter, I go to my club."

"Don't you have to write at the Home Office."

"By a merciful dispensation, no. Once my secretary was ill and I thought I should have to *resign*. My job is mainly criticising what other people write. At which, of course, I am *admirable*."

"Yes, I'm sure. If I ever wrote anything, I should be terrified of your seeing it."

"What nonsense! I used to adore those advertisements of yours. *Gems*, my dear! They would have been works of art if only they hadn't incited to action instead of contemplation. *Most* insidious. I once *actually* bought a bottle of hair lotion because I couldn't resist your blandishments. I'm sure you could make a fortune if only you'd put your mind to it. What are you looking so glum about?"

"Because I suppose that's all I'm fit for. And I'm too stupid to do even that now."

"Well, what the hell do you want to do? I suppose eventually you'll have to do something owing to the brute necessity of earning a living. Now that you've flung away the prospect of living in idle luxury. Can't you eventually get vast alimony out of this chap?"

"I wouldn't take it if I could."

"There you go," he said affectionately. "*Quite* mad. Still, oddly enough, I see your point. D'you want to go back to the stage?"

She shook her head.

"No. I'll never make anything but a fifth-rate actress."

"I'm inclined to agree. Old Stephen's going on all right, isn't he? I saw his Antony. Not as good as his Richard but bloody good in some ways. He's a real actor. Not interested in anything *but* acting. I must say I should adore to have been an actor. The trouble is, I'm too intelligent. So, incidentally, are you. I admit you seldom give any obvious signs of it. But I'd give all my poor old wits to have been Irving."

"I used to think Stephen was very intelligent. I let him bully me like anything."

"Only because you were bemused. You know as well as I do that Stephen wasn't intelligent about anything but acting. Very proper, too, He had a few stock remarks which, being a good actor, he delivered with the right intonation."

It was so true that Clara had to laugh.

"Yes. Even when I was most bemused, I used to think he said things as if he were trying out a new way of putting across a line. Even those charming, spontaneous gestures . . . you couldn't help feeling they'd come in handy later on when he'd worked them up to look even *more* spontaneous. Do you think all good actors are insincere? Because I believe Archie's going to be quite a good actor though he's the sincerest person I know. Anyhow, he's got awfully good notices in this one tiny part. His first on the *real* stage."

"Fluke, probably. Though I admit he wasn't at all bad."

Clara gasped.

"You mean you've *seen* him? Why ever didn't you tell me?"

"Why should I? I can't diagnose his case history as a husband. But his case as an actor rather interests me."

"I didn't know you ever went to musical comedies."

"Of course I do. Especially when Sherry Blane's in them. *There's* acting for you. Pure comic genius. I wish to God I'd seen Dan Leno. Blane's obviously got something of the same thing."

"What about Archie?"

"Oh *well* . . . all right in that particular *thing*. It was brilliant of Sherry Blane to pick him. Your great gangling gawk of a husband couldn't be a better foil to his incredible smallness and neatness. He even brought it off extremely well . . . as amateurs often do. But he hadn't the faintest idea *why* he brought it off. That's why I said 'fluke', I very much doubt if he's got the real right thing. What he *has* got, of course, is an amazingly beautiful voice. My dear, I haven't heard anything like it for years. Even in that staggering rubbish he sang, it positively melted the fibres of the heart. Why on *earth* doesn't he get it properly trained and become a concert singer?"

"It *is* a heavenly voice." Clara had almost forgotten its extraordinary beauty. Recalling it, she felt such a pang that she did not answer Clive's question. He went on talking but she was no longer listening. Suddenly she heard him ask angrily "*Why?*"

"Oh, sorry," she said hastily . . . "Because Archie only cares about the theatre. Also because he absolutely loathes what's called good music."

"You're woolgathering," he said. "Or didn't you want to hear what I said?"

"Weren't you asking about Archie? I suddenly began to think about him."

"Now, no . . . none of these hankerings and regrets. Archie is *foutu*. I was making some inquiries about *you?*"

"Me?"

"*Yes* . . ." he shouted. "I was asking why the hell you didn't do something about writing. You could, you know."

"Advertisements?"

"*Not* advertisements. That piece of yours in the *Saturday Westminster*. Not half bad."

"Fancy your having read it."

"I read everything."

"You never mentioned it at the time."

"No. I *almost* brought myself to the point of writing to you. But the *effort* of coming to grips with pen and paper plus the appalling necessity of having to buy *The Stage* to find which provincial town you were appearing in at that moment. . . . Well, I'm mentioning it now."

"You mean you *liked* it?" said Clara, puffed up with irrational joy.

"Certainly." He added in his mock-Bloomsbury voice: "*Very* remarkable. *Quite por-ten-tous*."

"Obviously a fluke like Archie's." She tried to sound careless.

"Not obviously. But conceivably." he maddeningly agreed. He stood up, carefully picked up their two ashtrays and emptied them. Clara did not dare to renew the subject. A card on the mantelpiece caught his eye. "Oh, Lord, I suppose I shall have to do something about *that*."

"About what?"

"Nell Crayshaw."

"I know that name. . . . I've seen it in *Vogue* or somewhere. . . . I remember now . . . photographs."

"That's right. She's a remarkably good photographer. The *only* person who's ever managed to capture my elusive phiz. I wish she'd stick to taking photographs and not invite me to parties."

"Do you hate parties?"

"Not invariably. But how can I possibly know beforehand whether I can face a party on a particular day?"

Clara said rather wistfully:

"I can't remember when I last went to a party."

"Does that mean you want to go to this one? It would be perfectly all right with Nell. The more, the merrier."

"The point is, do *you* want to go?"

"I never *want* to do anything. I might consider the possibility if you came and backed me up."

"I'm rather tempted. It's such ages since I've done anything like that. Yet . . . I don't know. I feel terrified at the prospect of meeting new people. I've got so used to just mouldering away with my family . . . doing nothing, seeing no one."

His eyes glinted mischievously behind his pince-nez.

"Well, it's probably time you were forced into the social whirl. You do look slightly mildewed now I come to think of it. So I presume I shall have to sacrifice myself."

"Oh, no," she insisted. "I'm not going to add to your torments. Let's forget about Nell Crayshaw and her party."

"*Actually* of course, I enjoy suffering. Anyhow we needn't commit ourselves yet, need we? If I rang you up . . . perhaps better if *you* rang me up – on the morning of this jamboree . . . we might go into the matter. We'll leave it like that, shall we?"

"Very well."

"Wonderful. We've positively made a decision. Really you have the most *salubrious* effect on me."

"You mean I've persuaded you to do what you meant to do all along."

"Exactly. But by ordering me to do it, you've removed the appalling load of guilt. It's an immense relief to be forced to do something."

"I should have thought you loathed being made to do things."

"Ah, that's just where you're wrong. That's why I was so exquisitely happy in the army. Happiest days of my life."

"It's difficult to imagine you in the army."

"Of course I went through *agonies* of indecision before joining up. Not the usual ones because, oddly enough, I'm not alarmed by cataclysms in the outside world. They're *far* easier to cope with than the stresses and strains in the poor old psyche. As for death . . . what *could* be more desirable? No, it was the *small* things . . . the idea of having to sleep in a tent with other people and the *horrifying* possibility of having my hair cut by an army barber. But once I'd crossed the Rubicon, it was a miraculous relief. I was a dazzling success. Yes, my dear, actually mentioned in despatches! I had no sense of self-preservation at all. It was after two years at the front that I was afraid I was *just* beginning to crack. The noise, you know. That infernal din began to get on my nerves. And just at that *precise* moment . . . I should almost *certainly* have run away if I'd had to endure one second longer . . . my daimon arranged for me to receive a beautiful, knock-out wound and I was invalided out."

"I didn't know you'd been wounded. Is that why you look so ethereal?"

"I've always looked ethereal. Actually I'm exceedingly robust. It was distinctly unpleasant at the time but now it doesn't cause me even a modicum of discomfort. I've lost one kidney and if I happened to lose the other that would finish me. The net result is that I receive the maximum disability pension. Very agreeable."

"I still can't picture you in uniform. Did you have a moustache?"

"Certainly not. I even got away with that since Nature, for once, was on my side. I've got a photo of myself somewhere."

He rummaged carefully in a drawer and produced it. Clara examined it with interest.

"Did Nell Crayshaw take this?"

"No. I didn't know her in those days. Just some hack. My mother blackmailed me into having it done."

Clive's face had been a little plumper but it still looked extraordinarily small and frail above the stiff lapels of the tunic. The fine hair (it had been thicker then), though severely brushed, still showed a childish tendency to curl: the eyes looked out through the pince-nez with an unusually earnest expression.

"Fascinating," she said. "Did you really look so saintly?"

"I presume so. After all, I was only twenty-two. Seven years less contagion of the world's slow stain."

"I'm only twenty-two now," Clara sighed. "I feel thirty at least. And look it."

"You exaggerate. I admit you don't look as you did when I first met you. A little dimmed . . . and, by your own absurd standards . . . a little over-inflated. Don't think *I* object. . . . I think women ought to look like Renoirs or even Rubenses."

"So did Gundry," said Clara crossly.

"Of course. All painters like women to be fat. There, there, don't look so enraged. You're not all *that* fat. But I agree, the bloom should be recovered. And no doubt will."

"What does it matter whether it's recovered or not?" said Clara with sudden gloom. "Truly, Clive, I *do* feel my life's over."

"All right, it's over then. It's your own fault for getting into such ridiculous situations."

"I expect so," she said meekly.

"The fact is my dear, you're probably a poor old neurotic like myself. You're in the dust and ashes state. . . . Pestilent congregation of vapours and all that . . . *I* know."

"I believe you do."

"Of course, I do. I very seldom emerge from the pestilent congregation. Yet, a little while ago, you observed I was like a rainbow. Let's have a good cry, shall we?"

"And smile bravely through our tears? I've lost the habit."

"So have I unfortunately. *Sunt lacrimae rerum* . . . yes, *yess*. One registers the fact but the tears don't well up. Fortunately, perhaps. If they did, one wouldn't be able to turn them off.

> 'He weeps by the side of the ocean
> He weeps on the top of the hill
> He purchases pancakes and lotion
> And chocolate shrimps from the mill.'

What could be more exquisite?"

"Yes, indeed. And you *did* purchase lotion."

"*Yess*" he said solemnly. "I purchased lotion."

Clara was suddenly aware of the time.

"It's frightfully late. I must go."

"Nonsense, it's Sunday tomorrow."

"That's just why. Daddy likes me to go to early Mass with him and thunders on my door at seven."

"Of course, if you insist on your superstitious practices . . . all right. But before you go, I *must* show you something."

He took another photograph from the drawer and handed it to her. "This is one of Nell's. She didn't want to part with it but I insisted."

Clara was studying the photograph of a tall young man in uniform, wearing the tartan trews of the K.O.S.B.

"Is he a friend of yours?"

'Never set eyes on him. He's one of Nell's innumerable younger brothers."

"He's extraordinarily good-looking," Clara admitted, staring at the young officer's face. The eyes, under thick straight black brows, were unusually beautiful, evidently light in colour – grey, she guessed. The camera had caught what was obviously a typical expression, a one-sided smile and a confident, slightly mischievous look. As she studied it, the young man's face seemed so extraordinarily alive, unlike the usual strained composure or uneasy grin of a photograph, that he seemed to be smiling at her with a peculiar intimacy.

"Did you ever see such a perfection of the type?" Clive urged. "I mean, Brushwood Boy, and all that. My God . . . if *only* I could have looked like that."

She remembered the stiff little photo of Clive in uniform; the pince-nez, the small pale face with that remote, unworldly look. Nothing would have been more unlike all the subalterns in her father's study. With a sudden pang, she asked:

"Was *he* killed in the war?"

"Gracious, no. Though I admit he looks the kind that invariably did get killed. Luckily, he was just too young. He's in the regulars. Coping with the Irish troubles at the moment, I believe . . . I see he's got you, too."

"Well, it's a marvellous photo of a marvellous young man.

"Quite dispassionate?"

"Oh yes. . . . That is, I mean, one can't help being moved by any-thing . . . well, so perfect of its type, as you say. One can't quite believe he's real. Yet the odd thing is, I feel as if I'd seen him before."

"In your dreams, probably. He's obviously an Archetype. Probably a crashing bore in real life."

"Yes, probably."

"I suppose there's a remote chance he might be at this ghastly party. However, if we knew he were going to be present, we'd be wiser not to go. Then we could preserve our illusions. Don't you agree?"

Clara said, not quite truthfully:

"I'm completely neutral."

He studied her face:

"Man delights not me; no, nor woman neither."

She gave him back the photograph, half with relief, half with reluctance. The young man's picture had begun to give her an uneasy feeling. She could not be sure whether it was pleasurable or frightening. Then she smiled at Clive Heron. . . .

"Not in general. But *you* delight me."

He smiled back rather sadly.

"*Quite*. But you see, my dear, I'm not a *man*."

CHAPTER FOUR

I<small>T WAS</small> nearly midnight when Clara got home. She let herself in with a feeling of guilt, and was relieved to find that her father had gone to bed. In vain she told herself that she was grown-up and free to come and go. The fact remained that she had not told her father that she meant to go out.

She was cowardly enough to hope that she might sleep through his knocking on her door to tell her it was time to get up for Mass. They had a pact that, if she did not answer his first knock, he assumed she must be asleep and did not persist. So far, she had never cheated. But tonight, the prospect of the long walk to church alone with him alarmed her and she was tempted to avoid it. It was some time before she got to sleep and her dreams were uneasy. Perhaps because she and Clive Heron had been talking about Stephen Tye, she dreamt about him for the first time for many months. In the dream, she recaptured some of her old feelings about him. At first, aware that she was dreaming, she was surprised at having even the illusion of love. She seemed to hear Clive Heron whispering: "There you see, my dear. *That* was what it felt like. Merely a question of disinterring it." Soon she lost consciousness of dreaming. She was sitting in the study and Stephen, in one of his rare, gentle moods, was reading her poems from *A Shropshire Lad*. She was frightened that her father might come in and find them together. Then Stephen vanished and she was all alone on an empty stage reciting "Summertime on Bredon". The auditorium was so dark that she could not see if there were anyone in it. Nevertheless, she recited each verse very carefully, pitching her voice as if declaiming to a large audience and trying to get the right intonation for each line. It seemed to her she was reciting very well. Not only was her voice completely under control but it had a range and variety she had never suspected. She listened to it with interest, enjoying this unusual sense of power and freedom. By the time she came to the last stanzas, she was convinced she was reciting to a vast, if invisible audience. The reason for their utter silence was that they were spellbound by the beauty of her speaking. She was launching splendidly on the last of all . . .

> "The bells they sound on Bredon
> And still the steeples hum
> Come all to church, good people. . . ."

. . . when there was a noise like a clap of thunder from the auditorium. Was it a burst of applause? Or a furious stamping of feet to drown her? She broke off, disconcerted, frantically trying to remember the next lines. Then the auditorium melted away like a mist: she found herself no longer standing, but lying down. She was in her own bed and her father was knocking urgently on the door. Still half-asleep, she called out automatically:

"I hear you. I will come."

As soon as they were in the street, she glanced anxiously at him to read his mood. His face was neither smiling nor stern. Anxious to know how she stood, she decided to be brave and introduce the subject herself.

"Mother did explain I'd be out to dinner last night?"

"Yes. She said she thought it would do you good to get out of the house. I hope you had a pleasant evening, wherever you went."

"Yes, lovely," she said volubly. "Who do you think I ran into? Clive Heron . . . do you remember him? That man in the Home Office who came to my twenty-first birthday party. You and mother both liked him.

"Heron?" he frowned. "Oh yes. Tall thin man with reddish hair and pince-nez. Very good company. Intelligent, I imagine."

"Yes, awfully. I met him by chance and we dined together."

"I trust he gave you a good dinner. I remember he was very knowledgeable about wine. Did he take you to Soho or somewhere more impressive?"

Clara sensed danger but, not wanting to lie, said, far too lightly:

"Actually we had dinner in his rooms. His landlady is a marvellous cook. He kept saying . . ."

Her father stopped dead on the pavement.

"You dined *alone* in a man's rooms? . . ."

Clara was so terrified by his voice that she lost her head.

"Oh no," she gabbled. "There were two other people there. Awfully nice . . . I'd never met them before though he's often talked about them and wanted me to meet them. . . ." She searched wildly for a convincing name. "Crayshaw . . . Nell Crayshaw . . . she's a quite famous photographer. Years older than me . . . older than Clive Heron. . . . And a brother of hers in the army . . . on leave from Ireland. . . ." She paused, desperately trying to think of a Christian name for the brother. . . instinctively rejecting 'Stephen' the first that came into her mind.

"I see," said her father less fiercely. He was appeased enough to begin walking again.

Relieved, she walked on too. There was silence during which she had time to decide on 'Richard' for Nell Crayshaw's brother.

She said with a nervous giggle:

"Sorry to have frightened you, Daddy. I do realize I've got to be discreet. Mr. Ramsden's always impressing on me I have to be awfully careful about appearances. Not to be alone with a man and so on."

She was horrified at her voice. Nothing could have sounded falser and more frivolous. Even if he did not at once guess that she was lying, she was talking in the way that most exasperated him.

He said angrily:

"Really, my dear! Quite apart from your . . . er . . . situation, I should hardly have thought it was necessary for Ramsden to warn you. A young married woman . . . for *you* are still married, you know. . . . You sound almost as if you were in the habit of being alone with men other than your husband."

"Well, I'm not," she said sullenly. But she pulled up her coat collar and averted her face: she could feel that she was blushing.

They walked almost the length of a street in uneasy silence. Clara was miserably inventing material to back up her lie. She decided she would talk about the army. Her father always responded eagerly to any talk of the war. She would tell him that Clive Heron had been mentioned in despatches. What could she think of to make the unknown Crayshaws sound convincing? The regular officer's point of view compared to the temporary officer's? Very tricky. Nell would be safer. Clive had been *so* kind . . . thinking that a professional photographer who worked for the papers might be able to suggest ideas to

111

Clara for an article. There was nearly half a mile still to be spun out before they reached the church.

Suddenly, her father spoke. From the altered tone of his voice, she realised with relief that she could stop cudgelling her imagination.

"My dear, you must forgive me. When I'm worried, I often speak more sharply than I mean to. And when one spends so much of one's life ticking boys off. . . . And, well, I can't help worrying about you. Your mother says I forget you are grown-up now, and that conventions have changed since the war – but I couldn't bear you to do anything people might misunderstand. I care so immensely about your reputation."

"It's very sweet of you."

He took her arm in sign of reconciliation.

"I'm glad you had an amusing evening. I realise what a dull time you've been having lately. Would you care to ask your friends to dinner one night? I could find something tolerable for them to drink."

"That's awfully kind of you," she said quickly. "Clive's still talking about that Château Yquem. Actually Nell Crayshaw has asked Clive to bring me to a party of hers next week."

She felt his arm stiffen in hers.

"Not one of these Chelsea parties I hope – Of course, I daresay the newspapers exaggerate . . ."

"Darling Daddy, I've no idea. Because I've never been to what's called a Chelsea party. Archie and I never met anyone who gave them. Nell Crayshaw lives in Chelsea . . . so does Clive for that matter, but I assure you she's *eminently* respectable.

His arm relaxed. He said penitently:

"Why do I always leap to the worst conclusions about you on no evidence? I ought to be ashamed of myself."

During Mass, her mind was nibbled all the time by distractions as it had been, Sunday after Sunday, for the past few months. This morning, tired from a late night and with scraps of her talk with Clive Heron buzzing through her head, she hardly even tried to concentrate. Up to the time of her marriage, however her thoughts might stray, the Mass had always been a living reality to her. She had never had to keep reminding herself "This is the most important thing that happens in the entire world." Lack of conscious fervour did not worry her unduly.

She had been trained not to attach much significance to devotional feelings. The essential thing was to assent to this reality with her mind and will. Now, as she tried to affirm it, she half-wondered whether she truly believed it any more. Suppose, as Clive Heron said, God were an unnecessary hypothesis? That idea was too monstrous. To entertain it would be a sin against faith. She drove it away, saying inwardly, "Lord, I believe. Help Thou mine unbelief." She glanced at her father's absorbed profile, so like some Roman Emperor's. "He is a Roman," she thought. "He likes everything clear-cut and definite. Once he has made up his mind, he'll stick to it, no matter what it costs him. Inconceivable that *he* should ever have any doubts about faith. Why, why can't I be like him?"

He was so utterly unaware of her that she could safely keep up her sidelong scrutiny. There he knelt, following each prayer, faintly moving his lips as he did so, in the Latin missal he had since the day he was received. It was getting battered now. She counted up . . . nearly fifteen years he had had it. There were dark marks at the bottom of the pages of the Canon where his thumbs pressed, always in the same place. She moved imperceptibly closer to him as if his intentness and conviction could communicate themselves to her uncertain, straying mind. The warning bell rang for the Elevation. Instinctively, she shifted away again to leave room for the movement he invariably made. As usual, he bent forward, placed the open missal on the seat of the pew in front, slid his elbows along the rail and bowed his head into his hands. As usual, he spread his fingers so that, looking down through them, he could read the actual words of Consecration. Looking down sideways into his missal, she too read *Hoc est Corpus Meum*. For a second, she seemed to hear Clive Heron's "*Poetical* truth . . . my dear . . . not literal truth." She shut her eyes and was aware of the extraordinary hush that falls on the most fidgeting, coughing crowd during the interval between the two Consecrations. The bell shrilled again. On the second stroke, like nearly all the rest she raised her head and stared at the uplifted Chalice. "No . . . *every* kind of truth," she thought. "Forgive me, Lord."

But no sooner had the third bell rung and she saw the heads come up raggedly and heard the first tentative sighs and rustles of relief after tension, than her mind began to flutter again. She was oddly touched by the way her father always kept his head down instead of raising it at the second bell of each elevation as nearly everyone else did. It was one of the 'Catholic ways', those family gestures she had acquired at her convent school which were second nature to her now and which he, as a convert in middle life, had never picked up. He had a pathetic admiration for her ease among such superficial things; the accent, as it were, with which she spoke the Catholic language as if it were her mother tongue. How superficial it was, she thought, compared with his solid, unwavering piety. There was no sacrifice, she was sure, that he would not make either for his faith or to carry out what that faith enjoined. How shallow was her own religion, alternating between fervour and a cold observance that amounted almost to indifference. Was it merely part of her general numbness that religion could arouse neither her paralysed mind nor her paralysed heart? She could come to life for a moment, as she had done with Gundry and Clive Heron. But, once alone again, the stimulus faded and she was left with the same blank inertia. Was it her own fault? A terrifying text slipped into her mind. 'The lukewarm He shall spew out of His mouth.'

She saw her father turn back the pages of his missal, as he always did at a particular moment, to the prayer of St. Thomas Aquinas, which he used as a preparation for Communion. The *Domine, non sum dignus* was approaching; she realised she had not made the slightest attempt to prepare herself, either by trying seriously to take part in the Mass or by any other method. Dared she go up to Communion at all? Could this deadness of hers, she thought in sudden panic, be deadness of the soul? Was she in a state of mortal sin? Her lie, on the way to church, had been cowardly, but no more than venial. She searched her mind for some definite lapse since her last Confession which conformed to the canons of 'grave matter, full knowledge, full consent' and could find none. There was nothing concrete; only the diffused general state of weariness and apathy; this sense that something in her had died and already exhaled a faint odour of corruption. She glanced across at the thumb-marked page her father was reading. She followed a sentence or two, translating the Latin of the familiar prayer into the English version she knew better: "as sick to my physician, as blind to the light of eternal brightness, as poor and needy to the Lord of heaven and earth." Who was sicker and blinder than herself? Who needed the Physician more, even if she did not deserve to be cured? She put all the sincerity she could into the '*Domine, non sum dignus*' and went up to the rail with the others.

Afterwards, she felt no warmth of devotion, no sense of the presence of Christ of which, when she was a child, she had occasionally been vividly aware. Neither did she feel guilt or terror, as if she might have made a sacrilegious Communion. But for some minutes her restless distracted flittings of the imagination were stilled. Her mind was enclosed in a silent, but not menacing darkness. When she tried to formulate some remembered prayers of thanksgiving, it was almost as if an invisible hand were gently laid on her mouth, forbidding her to attempt to speak. Then the ban seemed to be lifted. She made incoherent petitions . . . "Please show me where I have gone wrong. . . . Please let me come alive again. . . ." She went on to vague, childish petitions for others . . . for Archie, for her parents, for friends long neglected . . . then, oddly and suddenly, for Marcus Gundry and Clive Heron.

For the first time for many weeks, it was her father who waited for her. As they walked home together, she was more than usually conscious of the change in his mood that followed his weekly Communion. On the way back he was always relaxed and gay, ready to make small jokes, especially against himself.

"I hope I'm not walking too fast for you, my dear. The fact is I am shockingly hungry for my breakfast. I'm afraid I should never make a fasting friar."

She quickened her pace to keep up with that quick marching step of his.

"Good for me to take a little exercise. Mother keeps worrying about my having got so much fatter."

"Ah, well, it's nothing serious at your age. Though heaven forbid you should ever acquire *my* figure." Claude Batchelor, though far from lean, was not really a fat man. It was his full face, broad shoulders and rather short legs that gave him the stocky look about which he was secretly sensitive. "That friend of yours . . . Heron . . . you were talking about just now. I can't tell you how much I envy *his*. Tall, without being too tall, and so amazingly slim and elegant."

Clara laughed.

"Yet only last night Clive was saying he'd give anything to be much more solid. He loathes looking so ethereal."

"What perversity. I suppose *you'd* like to be one of these female lamp-posts that are unfortunately becoming so fashionable."

"Of course I would. I should also like to have smooth black hair, a dead-white face and enormous, mysterious green eyes."

"Thank heavens you can't have your wish. Why, your golden hair has always been one of your greatest charms, my dear." He smiled at her. "Look as you looked only a few months ago and you needn't envy any young woman. And, thank goodness, you're beginning to."

"Clive said I was looking dusty and . . . oh yes . . . mildewed."

"Infernal cheek. Well . . . perhaps the old sparkle hasn't quite come back yet. But you've lost that terrible air of strain. At least these quiet weeks have done your nerves good."

"Oh yes. I'm a perfect cabbage nowadays."

"I'm glad you're beginning to want to see people again. It's bad for you to lose all interest in the outside world."

"I don't awfully want to see people, you know. Yesterday it just happened." She added in a burst of confidence. "When I went out – it sounds horrid when you're all so sweet to me – it wasn't with the idea of seeing anyone. I just felt I wanted to be out of the house and on my own for a bit."

"So your mother told me. I admit I was a little distressed at first. But she said it was perfectly natural. And then she suddenly turned the tables on me."

"How?"

"She insisted that *I* ought to get out on my own sometimes. She said I was getting into a groove, doing the same things day after day. School, pupils, writing my text books . . . one night of bridge a week, usually with the same couple. If we go out to dinner or have some people here as we do occasionally, it's all arranged beforehand. No element of the unexpected."

"She's quite right. Well, had she any suggestions?"

"A very definite one. Of course, at first I said it was preposterous. Then I suddenly realised it was something I'd secretly longed for for years."

"It sounds most exciting."

"When I tell you, I'm afraid you'll find it more ridiculous than exciting. . . . Simply that one evening a week I should go out on my own. No one, not even your mother should know where I was going. No one was to ask where or how I'd spent those hours. On that evening, no one . . . family, friends, parent, pupil . . . would know where to get hold of me . . . even in a crisis."

"It's not ridiculous. But it's certainly revolutionary." Clara said slowly. It was so revolutionary that she could hardly take it in. The idea of her father making such a violent change in his habits was faintly shocking.

"Probably it will never be more than a wild idea. There are dozens of reasons against it. . . . Still, as a notion to toy with . . ."

She saw that he wanted her encouragement. Surely, if anyone deserved a few unaccounted-for hours of escape, it was her father. Why then did she feel vaguely annoyed? Did she resent the mere possibility of change in someone she thought unchangeable? Or did she think he had no right to put himself, even for a few hours, deliberately out of her reach?

"My first reaction, of course, was that I simply couldn't afford to" he went on. "To give up a whole evening of pupils . . . especially at the moment . . ."

The wistfulness in his voice reproached her. She took his arm and said eagerly:

"You *must* do it, Daddy. You can't go on wearing yourself out at the grindstone. Perhaps you'll have marvellous adventures. Remember the days when you used to long for the knock on the door and the appearance of the mysterious agents of the Foreign Power?"

He laughed.

"No, my dear. I don't crave for fantastic adventures any more. Absurd, though, how long those schoolboy fancies *did* last. I still embark on them in my dreams. But they . . . and my annual Oppenheim . . . indulge the old cravings enough. You forget I've turned fifty."

"Well, that's not awfully old for a man."

"Old enough for the batteries to begin to run down. I admit I feel a trifle tired sometimes these days."

With a sudden stab of fear she asked:

"You're not *ill*, Daddy?"

"Good heavens, no. This temptation to a night off is pure laziness."

"What nonsense. The more I think of it, the more I'm sure you ought to do it. As to giving up an evening of pupils ... you take some of them for nothing. Be firm from now on. No deadheads. No reductions for hard cases."

He shook his head.

"I couldn't do that. There are parents who just can't afford the fees. And their boys are often the brightest. I'd never forgive myself if some boy with a real gift for Classics couldn't go to the University because I wouldn't give him a few hours coaching for a scholarship. How could I have ever hoped to go to Cambridge without one?"

"*You* didn't have any private coaching."

"Well, I was lucky. And I doubt if competition was so fierce in my day. But that's one thing neither you nor your mother will argue me out of. My dreams of being a great classical scholar were over long ago. But if there were the remotest chance of my helping a boy with it in him ... I'd rather take a dozen geese for nothing than miss a possible swan."

"Don't you *ever* think of yourself? I thought for once you were going to."

"I assure you I'm thinking quite impenitently about myself. There is a possible solution. Your mother is heroically prepared to agree."

"What is it?"

"Well, for some time, a young Indian law-student – his uncle's a Rajah and an old pupil of mine – has been wanting to come as a P.G. ..."

"But that's one thing you swore you'd *never* do," said Clara, aghast.

"I know, my dear. However things are a little difficult for me at the moment. One way and another, it has been an expensive year."

Clara said guiltily:

"That's my fault. You were so terribly generous, giving me that wedding. And now, having me back on your hands ..."

He squeezed her arm.

"Forget all that, my dear. No, no, I've always been a bad manager of money. ... I do fairly well on paper but there are always unexpected demands. ..."

"You help too many people ..." she muttered uneasily. In her apathetic self-absorption she had not thought, till now, that she was one of them. It had never occurred to her to offer him any of the small sums

Archie sent her towards her keep. "Daddy, I ought to be contributing something . . ."

"I wouldn't hear of it," he said. "If my only child can't live under my roof. . . . This P.G. idea . . . it would only be for a time. I know how your mother hates the notion. But she says she'll agree on two conditions."

"Namely?"

"That I don't take on any more extra work. And that I *do* take this weekly evening off. I haven't asked *you* whether you have any objection to Ullah's coming."

"Of course not." She was, in fact, dismayed by the idea. But something had begun to dismay her far more.

"Daddy," she said. "Tell me the truth. You *are* quite all right, aren't you? You're still looking terribly tired though you've had your holiday."

"Nothing whatever to worry about," he smiled. "Very well, your Mother did insist on my seeing a doctor. Just as I expected. Nothing organically wrong. Slight fatigue or nervous exhaustion or whatever they call it. Anno Domini, in fact."

"But you're not *old*," she said wretchedly.

"Well, perhaps I've been a little hard on the old machinery. Still I'd infinitely prefer to wear out than rust out."

She clutched his arm.

"Don't even *talk* of either. Oh do please take care of yourself. When can you take your first evening off?"

"Well . . . we'll think it over. So I have your *Nihil Obstat* . . . Indian student and all?"

"Of course, Daddy."

"Then perhaps we'll add the *Imprimatur*. Let's hope nothing happens to make any of us regret it."

CHAPTER FIVE

THAT SUNDAY afternoon Clara retired to her bedroom and took out a shiny black notebook she had not opened since she left Tithe Place. She had begun it originally, in the first weeks of her marriage, as a sop to her conscience. It had been intended as a kind of sketchbook in which she put down anything that struck her while the impression was still fresh. She had hoped to sharpen her eye and ear so that, though incapable of producing even the smallest piece of finished work, she could tell herself she was 'practising'. Unfortunately, the notebook had soon degenerated into mere maunderings of self-analysis and self-pity.

Talking to Clive Heron had roused her just sufficiently to think of using the notebook for its original purpose. However, her faint impulse carried no further than turning over to a fresh page and writing the date very neatly at the top. She decided to begin by reading all her former entries. By the time she had read them through twice, she was so disgusted with the spectacle she presented that her one desire was to destroy the notebook.

Honesty, however, forbade this. It would be good for her vanity to preserve this repulsive record. For one thing it would puncture the recurring illusion that she might some day become a real writer. For another it would remind her of the depths to which she could sink when her emotions were out of control. Some of the entries were almost illegible. When deciphered, they were so incoherent that they might have been written by a lunatic. One whole page, which she had no recollection of writing, was even written the wrong way round so that she had to hold it up to a looking-glass to read it. During those last weeks with Archie, had she really been, as some people had hinted, on the verge of a mental breakdown?

She felt almost grateful for her present indolence and apathy. Presumably they were signs of sanity. Evidently it was an advantage not to suffer, to have no ambitions or desires, if these things produced such shaming outbursts. At least she could now behave like a civilised person.

She was astonished, as well as disgusted, to find how violent her feelings had been. Could she really have felt such passions of absurd misery, bitterness, frustration and even more absurd hope? The creature . . . she could hardly bear even to think of it as 'Clara' . . . who had written some of those pages had had a short memory too. Over and over again, some state of mind was described in almost identical words as if it were being experienced for the first time. On her second reading she could discern a rhythm in these recurring entries. It was like watching someone hurling themselves repeatedly against a wall until they fell back, exhausted and battered. The creature kept rising up again, full of absurd hope and good resolutions, only to go through the hurling and battering all over again, sometimes in a passage written at one stretch.

She shut the notebook and thrust it well out of sight at the back of a drawer. As she did so, she had a curious pang, as if she were burying something. The creature, heaving and wallowing in its morass of misery, had at least been alive. But, if that was what it meant to be alive, nullity was better. Her mind, tired by even that much attempt at consecutive thought, slipped out of gear and spun round on the word 'nullity'. A decree of nullity would be merely the outward confirmation of the inward fact. It was she herself who was null and void. Nullity had charms. It was sober and decent. There would be no more struggles, no more of those ludicrous or tragic catastrophes which result from trying to do things. Above all, there would be no more violent feelings, either of pleasure or pain. Null and void. Null and void. She sat staring at the roses on her bedroom wall-paper, saying the words over and over again till she was half-hypnotised. The mirror on her dressing-table was in her line of vision. Her eyes shifted unconsciously from the wall-paper to the square of glass. Her own face stared back at her, rigid and vacant, wearing a peculiar little smile.

For the next few days she walked, as it were, on tiptoe. She concentrated intently on each small thing she did, whether brushing her hair or changing her mother's library book. How simple life was, after all. One did the next thing and then the next. No need to think or fuss, above all to feel. It was restful, even pleasant, like doing row after row of plain knitting. Her father took the first of his secret evenings off. She felt a kind of amused pity that, at his age, he should be afflicted with this craving for change. She wondered whether she ought to tell him how much more satisfactory it was to be passive and detached. No, Clive was the only person who might conceivably understand. She was almost tempted to ring him up and tell him: "My dear, I've discovered the *only* way to make existence tolerable." But her new code of behaviour forbade initiating any action. True to it, she was neither surprised nor curious when one morning the maid knocked on the door and said that a Mr. Heron wanted to speak to her on the telephone.

She went downstairs without haste. She felt superior because her own inaction had driven Clive to the astonishing length of ringing her up. It was another proof of her detachment that she had genuinely forgotten all about Nell Crayshaw's party. She was completely indifferent now as to whether she went or not, but the new code demanded passive acceptance of anything that offered.

Clive, for once, was surprisingly definite. He was in the mood to go to a party and he wanted her company. He sounded, indeed, almost enthusiastic. She said languidly:

"All right. If you're really keen on going. . . . Yes, yes. I've said I'll come. Paultons' Square is on the way? Very well. I'll pick you up. Ring up if you change your mind."

She went through the motions of dressing for the party with the same slow care she had taken to using for everything. It was the first time she had dressed for a party with neither excitement nor apprehension. Always before, she had been keyed up, anxious how she would look and what impression she would make. Until Stephen's time there had been the secret hope of meeting some new and interesting man. When she had gone to parties with Stephen there had been the secret fear of his meeting some more attractive woman. Probably because she had dressed without the usual nervous fuss, she noted ironically that she looked prettier than she had done for months. Her hair had recovered some of its old lustre. It was in a biddable mood and had fallen easily into soft, loose waves. Her skin had lost its parched look and the black velvet dress, which disguised the weight she had unaccountably put on since her marriage, showed up the whiteness of her arms and shoulders. The dress recalled the first black velvet she had ever possessed. She had been fifteen then and still at her convent school. Her father had disapproved of it as too old and sophisticated but her mother had backed her up. She remembered how excited she had been when she had first tried it on, how grown-up it had made her feel, almost as if it transformed her into a different person. But, almost at once, she had taken an equally violent dislike to it. It was not because of grief over her grandfather that she could hardly bear to wear it again after his funeral. It was because of the terrible things her father had said when Blaze Hoadley had kissed her in the orchard at Paget's Fold. The kiss had been her first and could hardly have been more innocent but he had turned on her with such savage bitterness that she had been too paralysed to attempt any defence. She could no longer remember his words, but she could still recall her own humiliation and the feeling, which had lasted for days, that she must, in some way, be corrupt.

She stared critically at her reflection, wondering how much her face had changed in seven years. Then she gave a small, cynical smile.

"What a fool you were then. And what a fool you've made of yourself ever since," she thought. "Well, let's hope you've learnt a little sense at last."

To test this, she deliberately tried to summon up the face of the young officer in the photograph. Clive had said it was just possible he might be at the party. She was surprised to find how clearly his features came up in her mind. Normally she had a confused memory of faces, even those she knew well. But she could see this stranger's as vividly as if she were looking again at his photograph. She could even see details she had not consciously noticed; one eyebrow was a trifle ragged; the nose swerved a little from the straight; the smile revealed a gap between the front teeth. The slight flaws emphasised, rather than marred, the young man's striking good looks. Clara mentally examined his image, admiring it in a detached way, as she might have admired the picture of some splendid animal. Certainly she had never encountered a man as attractive as this. Yet, even in the days when she had been capable of feelings, she was not sure that he would have aroused them. His attraction was so obvious that it seemed to put him out of reach. She would have taken it for granted that she could not interest him. Now, she was delighted to find, she was not even curious enough to want to see him in the flesh. She was genuinely indifferent as to whether he went to the party or whether she went herself. Had Clive rung her up at that moment to say he could not, after all, face it, she would have taken off her party dress and gone to bed with perfect equanimity.

Part Three

CHAPTER ONE

THEY ARRIVED rather late at the party. Clive had insisted on Clara's coming up to his rooms for a fortifying drink. By the time they had found a taxi and directed it to Nell Crayshaw's studio, which was one of a group of four tucked away in a cul-de-sac by the river, the room was smoky and crowded. Except for a few candles on a shelf above the piano, it was in darkness and everyone was listening intently to the young man who was playing. Scarcely a head turned as they lowered themselves cautiously on to cushions on the floor.

"Op. 78. *What* luck!" whispered Clive. Clara nodded vaguely. She guessed it was a Beethoven sonata but could not recognise it. However, she did recognise the pianist whose face was only visible in the dimness. Avery Cass had been the most brilliant of the music students who regularly attended the Cohens' Sunday parties. The sight of him reminded her of her neglect of Patsy. She hoped Cass would not recognise her. Though she was sure he could not see her, she fidgeted on her cushion, trying to draw back still farther into the darkness. Clive hissed at her below his breath. After this rebuke, she sat rigidly still. Her eyes were growing used to the dimness; she could make out pale blots of faces. Then a theme recurred, so exquisite that she could not help attending. As it vanished in a complex labyrinth of harmonies through which her ear was not good enough to follow it, she became aware of a new distraction. She felt that someone was trying to attract her attention. None of the indistinguishable faces on the far side on the piano seemed to be turned towards her. Yet she was convinced that the person was not sitting anywhere near. She did her best to ignore this plucking at her attention but it continued with a gentle, teasing persistence. Then she tried another technique. She spoke silently to the unseen intruder: "Stop it. I don't *want* to be disturbed." It was almost as if she heard the reply. "I know you don't. All right. See if you *can* stop me." It developed into a kind of game. She forgot all about the music in concentrating against the intruder. It was like wrestling with a friendly

127

antagonist. Sometimes she thought she had won and the other had given up. But, as soon as her mind was left blank again, she realised she had been enjoying this odd game and missed the invisible attack. The next moment, the amused inner voice (she knew by now that it was a man's) would come clearer than ever "You may as well give in. My will's stronger than yours."

When the sonata was finished, there was a moment's silence, followed by clapping and subdued, appreciative mutterings. Clive turned to Clara with a happy sigh. "There's glory for you! I don't wonder it was the old boy's own favourite. And, my God, that chap can play it." Clara, aware that she had heard barely a note of the last movement, guiltily murmured "Marvellous."

"If we had *any* sense," Clive whispered, "we'd go now."

By her new code, Clara should have agreed at once. But the thought of going had suddenly become unendurable. She said:

"I think he's going to play again."

Cass had stood up but Nell Crayshaw had darted over to the piano and forced him down on to the stool again. People began to call out suggestions for what he should play next. But Cass smiled, shook his head and plunged into a dance tune. Soon people were on their feet, pushing back what little furniture there was and beginning to dance. Couple by couple joined in until Clive and Clara were among the few still sitting huddled on the floor against the wall. He said irritably:

"Oh, hell. You don't want to dance, do you? Nothing will induce *me* to."

"I'm quite happy to watch," said Clara. "Anyway, even if I could *see* anyone, I'm sure I wouldn't know a soul, but you and Avery Cass."

"Avery Cass?"

"The man who's playing the piano."

"You *know* that phenomenal creature?"

"I used to slightly. He was a friend of some people I used to know awfully well. I don't suppose he'd remember me. Frankly I rather hope he won't."

"Why? Is he a frightful bore?"

"Far from it. It's only that he might put these people on my track. Not that I didn't like them. I just don't want to be involved again."

"*Quite*," said Clive approvingly. "One should never be involved. Still less re-involved."

"Still, if you desperately want to meet him. . . ."

"I've heard him. That's all that's really necessary." He hummed a phrase from the sonata with perfect accuracy. "I'll have a word with him on my own, if I feel like it. At the moment, the only thing I want *desperately* is a drink. How about you?"

"All right, yes," said Clara. She did not in the least want a drink.

"I *think* I can make out the bar through the inspissated gloom. I'll battle my way through the shuffling horde and get us both one."

"Sure you feel strong enough?"

"I shall definitely collapse if I *don't* have a drink. Thank goodness, dear Nellie never spares the booze."

He unfolded his long legs with agility and began to thread his way through the dancers. Clara noticed how precisely he timed each step, as if he were dancing himself, so that he slid slowly and deftly through the shifting crowd, neither jostling nor being jostled. No head turned, no couple stepped aside as he passed. He was like a ghost; moving invisible and intangible in his own dimension. It would be impossible to imagine Clive deliberately impinging on her mind as the unknown man had done.

Though she was concentrating on Clive, she was perfectly aware that the other was approaching her. It was no surprise to feel a hand beneath each elbow, firmly pulling her up to her feet from behind. Turning round, she recognised him at once though he was not wearing uniform and it was too dim to see his face properly.

She said, without thinking:

"So it was *you*."

"Did you mind? I couldn't resist trying it on. You put up an awfully good show to keep me out."

Someone turned on a subdued lamp. Though the room was still very dim, she could make out the small gap between his front teeth as he smiled down at her. Then he stopped smiling.

"What made you say 'It was *you*' like that? You can't have seen me before. I'd know."

"I've seen your photograph."

"Good Lord, where? Not in a shop-window, I hope. Or some beastly advertisement? Nell's capable of anything."

"You needn't worry. A friend of mine begged it from your sister."

"She's no right to give my photo to girls I don't know."

"It wasn't a girl, it was a man."

"Why the hell should a man want my photo?"

"He's interested in types. He thought you were the perfect subaltern."

"I doubt if my C.O. would agree. Who *is* this man, anyway?"

"The man I came with. Clive Heron."

"The one sitting beside you? Pale, red hair, pince-nez, mole under the left eye?"

"How could you see all that in the dark?"

"I've got cat's eyes. How else do you think I saw *you*?"

"Mental cat's eyes too, apparently. Do you often do this . . . telepathy or whatever it is?"

"Only with my own family up to now. But we know each other so well it hardly counts. I just tried it with you for fun. I was pretty astonished when it worked."

"Not as astonished as I was," said Clara. "Such a thing's never happened to me before. However well I knew people."

"All the better. Let's dance." He put his arm round her. Before taking her hand, he said in a changed voice:

"Tell me something."

"Yes?"

"That chap you came with. You're not seriously tied up with him? I don't approve of butting in."

"You're not butting in."

"Good." Yet still he hesitated. Something seemed to have overcast his gay confidence. Then he smiled again. "After all, I'm only asking for a dance."

Clara did not answer. Standing there in the circle of his arm which enclosed her firmly but without pressure, she was aware of the strangest sensation. It was as if the whole of her past self had suddenly dropped away and she were a perfectly simple, perfectly free creature. She put her left hand on his shoulder. He glanced down at it and said:

"You're wearing a wedding ring. I didn't see it before. What does that mean?"

"I can't explain now."

He frowned and asked in a muffled voice:

"Is it all right?"

"All right? What do you mean?"

"Blest if I know what I *do* mean. Even if I did . . . I'm no earthly good at talking. I'm getting out of my depth. When you put your hand on my shoulder, I had a very queer feeling."

"I had too," she said softly. "I suddenly felt absurdly happy."

"So did I. But at the same time. . . . You know that prickling they call 'someone walking over your grave'?"

Conscious of nothing but this delicious irresponsible sense of confidence, Clara smiled.

"You're being morbid. I tell you it's all *right*."

As he took her other hand, she noticed that he too was wearing a ring: a ring that did not look quite right on a man's finger. It was a gold band mounted with a small white enamel shield bearing a red cross. They danced in complete silence. An extraordinary feeling of lightness possessed her; a lightness she had known hitherto only in those pleasant dreams where she floated down flights of stairs, hardly touching the ground. She felt as if she were simultaneously asleep and awake. Far from being unaware of what was going on round her, her senses were more alert than usual. Even in the dimness of the smoky, crowded room, she noticed details of faces and dresses with a peculiar sharpness. Scraps of conversation came to her clearly through the general soft babel; she found she could follow several threads of disjointed talk at the same time, just as she could distinguish the separate layers of scent, tobacco smoke, hot wax, alcohol and human flesh which made up the smell of the room. She was almost more conscious of all these small, vivid new experiences than of the man she was dancing with. Yet she knew that they came to her only through him. If she lost contact with him, this miraculous enhancement of life would vanish. Though she was so acutely aware of what was going on around her, the two of them seemed to be moving invisibly in another dimension, just as she had fancied Clive Heron doing when he had woven his way through the dancers.

From her new world, she watched Clive weave his way back again, a drink held carefully in each hand. At first he was no more than any other strand in this web of heightened perceptions. She observed with impersonal interest the unusual length of his thumbs, clasped at full stretch round the two large tumblers. But when she saw his pince-nez peer round till they found her, a pin-point of light from a candle coming and going in each lens as they followed her movements, she missed a step in the dance. For a moment, like a sleeping top just beginning to falter, the tranced tension slackened. Cautiously, as if realising the risk she was taking, she freed her right hand and waved to Clive over Crayshaw's shoulder. But though the pince-nez were steadily fixed on her, Clive made not the faintest acknowledgement. She felt Crayshaw's arm tighten a shade against her spine, drawing her back into the perfect rhythm of his steps. The faltering top recovered its balance and spun into its trance again. But now she was aware only of her partner.

The music stopped. They found themselves standing at the edge of the floor. For a moment, they stood motionless, still embraced. They looked at each other, blinking and vaguely smiling, as if awakened from sleep.

Crayshaw recovered himself first. He took her arm and hustled her through the crowd into a corner that was momentarily empty.

"What's happened to us? Have we both gone mad? Or is it only me?"

"Me, too," she said.

"I simply don't understand."

"Neither do I."

She looked into his eyes. As she had supposed, they were grey. The thick black eyebrows were drawn together, giving his face with its aquiline, slightly crooked nose a fierce expression. She smiled.

"How angry you look."

His eyebrows relaxed but he did not smile back.

"It's no joke," he said. "I started it as one and it's turned into something else – It's beyond me."

"Beyond me too."

Suddenly he laughed.

"Well, we can't just stand here glaring at each other and saying 'I don't understand'. Let's get out of this beastly atmosphere. Perhaps some fresh air will bring us to our senses."

"I can't just go off like that. . . . There's Clive . . . the man I came with. . . ."

"You needn't worry about him. . . . He's gone off himself."

She said with a faint qualm. "He can't have. He was there just now while we were dancing."

"Do you realise we were dancing for well over half an hour?"

"Oh – that's not possible."

"I'd have said the same. I've usually a pretty good sense of time. But I happened to look at my watch before and after."

"You're *sure* he's gone?"

"Absolutely sure. I saw him with his coat on, saying goodbye to Nell. Go and get *your* coat. Is it a decently warm one? I've got some rugs but it's an open two-seater."

"Warm enough." As she moved away, her extraordinary light-heartedness returned. She turned back towards him, laughing.

"I can't say goodbye to your sister because I don't know which she is. It was too dark to see her face when we came in."

"Don't worry. You'll meet Nell soon enough. Thank God, I've got a month's leave and this is only my first day."

He added, smiling:

"Anyway, I couldn't introduce you now if I wanted to. I don't even know your name. Hurry and get that coat."

"All right, Richard," she said, without thinking.

"Good Lord. . . . So you *do* know mine."

"I didn't know I did, I guessed right, then?"

"You really didn't know?"

"No. But I remember now. Something too silly to explain. My father was cross with me about something. I told him a lie. I said I'd met your sister . . . and you . . . somewhere. I had to give you a Christian name. The one that came into my head was Richard."

"Odd," he said. "Coming events? All the same . . . damn, I can't guess yours. . . ."

"Clara."

"All the same, Clara." He paused. "You'll think me the most ghastly prig. Girls fib, I know. But don't to me. I won't to you, either. I feel it's rather important. Do you feel that too?"

She said soberly:

"Yes. I do."

CHAPTER TWO

As they walked arm in arm across the courtyard round which the four studios were built, Richard halted.

"Listen. Can you hear the river?"

The air was chilly on Clara's face after the hot, crowded room. She listened and, through the noise of the piano and the laughter inside, she could hear a rhythmical sluck, sluck, that sounded only a few feet away. She shivered and moved nearer to him.

"How close it sounds," she said.

"Much too close. I tell Nell she's crazy to live so near. If ever there were a flood, she'd stand a good chance of being drowned. There's a passage that runs down a slope between those two studios opposite. Nothing but a few iron posts at the end of it. At high tide the water comes up well beyond them. You could walk slap into it. It's always slippery, down at the end. If you went down there in the dark, even at low tide, you could easily lose your footing and fall in."

"You sound as if you were warning me."

"I am warning you. You strike me as being a trifle absent-minded. You're never to walk down that passage without me."

"Very well. You talk as if we . . ."

He cut in: "I think we'll be about this place a good deal during the next few weeks. Nell has two of these studios. She and her man. . . . I'll explain all that later . . . live in the one where the party's going on. She's turned the other – the one she uses for work – over to me for my leave. We could go there now. But I don't want us to be indoors any more for the moment."

"I don't either." It seemed natural that he should make all the decisions.

"Shall we go down that passage to the river before we set off in the car? It's rather eery down there. Like the end of the world. You'll be perfectly safe with me."

"Yes."

They moved slowly along the passage which ran, dark as a tunnel, between the two unlit buildings. At every yard, the rhythmic slucking sounded louder and the dank breath of the river came stronger. One of the things of which Clara had an irrational terror was the sound of water lapping over stone in the dark. She was terrified, too, of walking, even by daylight, on any slippery surface. But, though the path was slimy under her thin high-heeled shoes, holding Richard's arm she trod as surely as on a carpet. She knew with absolute certainty that, as long as she was with him, nothing could ever frighten her again.

They passed through the posts. The tide was out. They stood together on what seemed a lonely shore. She could hear the river but it was invisible in a pearly mist. Above, the sky was half-veiled, half clear, with silvered clouds round the moon. A tug hooted in the distance. They stood for some moments inhabiting this world of water and sky and luminous vapours before they kissed. It was a deep, unhurried kiss more like the recognition of old lovers, long parted, than the fierceness of sudden passion. They kissed only once, then stood for a while enfolded, saying nothing, not even each other's names. Her head was buried in the hollow of his shoulder and his cheek pressed so close against her own that she could feel the movement of bone and muscle as he muttered:

"Let's go back."

They walked in silence up through the dark passage into the courtyard again. The piano and the laughter sounded brutally loud to Clara after the quiet. But the noise of Richard starting up his car did not disturb her. Like the hoot of the tug down there by the river, it belonged to their private world. He said, above the coughing of the engine:

"If you'll be cold, I'll put the hood up."

"I shan't be cold."

"Good."

They drove for some miles and she watched him as he talked in short bursts, his eyes intent on the road. He handled the car easily, with the minimum of effort. She remembered that Archie had driven a car with the same careless skill. It was the first time she had thought of Archie since that evening with Clive Heron. At that moment, Richard asked:

"Will you tell me now? About your husband and everything?"

The story did not take her long to tell. At first she spoke reluctantly, not because she found it difficult but because she did not want to be reminded that she had once had another life. He listened without comment till she had finished. Then he said in a low voice.

"Lord, that man must have been through hell. He sounds a good chap, too."

She said eagerly:

"Oh, I'm glad you see that. People don't always. My mother, for example. She never understood him."

"I don't believe any woman could understand what he must have felt like. Not even you. I could imagine killing myself if my body wouldn't do exactly what I wanted it to do. It would be as good as being dead already."

"You're tremendously good at physical things, aren't you?"

"Games and all that? Pretty fair, yes. I'm not sports mad, if that's what you mean. No, it's more that it's the thing that makes me feel alive . . . exercising it, making it do something it couldn't do yesterday. Hardly matters what . . . handling a boat, picking out one bird's song among a dozen others, judging the wind when I'm shooting . . . it makes me . . . this sounds awfully pompous . . . but I can't think of another word . . . *exult*."

"According to you, I'm half-dead already. I'm hopeless at using my body."

"You shouldn't be. Not from the way you dance."

"Oh, dancing. . . . Even that I do shockingly badly most of the time. I've no control over it. Sometimes it comes right with one particular person . . . just for an evening. The next time, even with them, it's just as likely to go wrong."

"It will always be all right with *me*," he said confidently. "I could teach you all sorts of other things. I *know* I could. All that's the matter with you is that you're a trifle absent-minded, as I said before. You've got to be absolutely inside yourself . . . really *there* in your bones and muscles and all the rest. Then you just leave it to *them*. They know by instinct what to do, if you'll let them."

"How simple you make it sound. But, now I'm with you, everything seems simple."

"I always thought everything *was* simple. This last hour or so, I'm not so sure."

136

They drove on for a time in silence. Then Richard began to talk about himself. He told her a little about his life with the regiment in Ireland and a good deal about his family and his home in Wiltshire.

"I suppose we're absurdly clannish. We children are three-quarter Scots. Maybe that accounts for it. Anyway, we care awfully what happens to each other. When something goes wrong with one, it affects us all. Even Nell feels it, though she's least typical Crayshaw of the eight of us. She hates having to upset our father and mother over all this business. Not that they've ever said a word or ever will. It hurts them all the same."

"What is it that hurts them?"

"It's a long story. But I want you to know. Well, she got married . . . years ago now . . . to a terribly nice chap. Naturally he joined up and went off to the front."

"Was he killed?"

"Better if he had been. No, he got a bad head wound. Now, he's in an asylum and permanently insane. He may live for years but he'll never get better."

"Oh, how dreadful for Nell. I can't think of anything worse if one loved someone."

"Neither can I. Nell's tough but there was a time when she nearly went to pieces herself. Up to a couple of years ago, she used to go and see him, though he didn't recognise her. Then things got worse still. He recognised her but he hated the sight of her."

"Mad people are supposed to do that, aren't they? Turn against the people they're fondest of? Oh, it must be almost worse to go mad than to go blind."

"Pretty little to choose between them, I should say. I'd rather be dead than either. They had to stop her going to see him in the end. It brought on violent attacks. . . . They had to put him in a padded cell. I say, you've gone awfully white. I oughtn't to have told you."

"If just hearing about it . . . oh, how did Nell endure it? And how can *he* feel?"

"John? God knows, poor devil. I suppose you don't actually suffer when your mind's gone. Nell's got her work. She's frightfully keen on this photography and damn good at it. And, for the last year, there's been this man Gerald Moreton."

"I remember now. You said 'Nell and her man' . . ."

"That's the one. It's a shame they can't get married. Nell's well on in her thirties. She'd like to have children. But she doesn't think it would be fair on them. And you can't get a divorce for insanity. Even if it's a hopeless case."

"It's tragic. Does she love this man as much as . . ."

"She'll never forget John, as he was. It's just as if he were dead. And she couldn't feel the same about anyone else. But she's very fond of Gerald and she'll stick to him. And he's crazy about her. He can't bear to remember she ever had a husband. That's why she's gone back to her old name."

"Poor thing. . . . You can't blame them for living together. . . . After all, it's not as if they were Catholics . . ."

"I'd forgotten, for the moment, *you* were a Catholic." He added, as if to himself, "Funny you should be, too."

"Why? Is Gerald Moreton one?"

"Quite the reverse. Long before he met Nell, he was going to be a C. of E. parson. Then he decided he didn't believe in it all and that the only honest thing to do was to chuck it. Now he's just an agnostic or whatever you call it. So's Nell."

"And you?"

"Oh, C. of E. like my parents and all the rest of us. I've never thought much about religion. Just taken it for granted it was a good thing. But I'm rather impressed by Roman Catholics. They're so awfully in earnest about it. They let it interfere with their ordinary lives."

"Do you know many Catholics then?"

He did not answer at once. She glanced up at his profile and saw he was frowning. After a moment, he said:

"Oh well. After a couple of years in Dublin, one's bound to have met a good few."

Again they fell silent. They had driven fast but Clara had no idea in which direction. At last he turned the car up a deserted side street and stopped under a tree. She supposed they must be in some suburb on the outskirts of London. But to her the tree above them and the privet hedge on which the headlights glimmered looked like the margin of an enchanted forest. He dropped his hands from the steering wheel and she turned towards him, waiting breathlessly for him to take her in his arms. He looked at her with an odd, strained smile that was almost a grimace and said:

"Not till I've told you something."

He pulled the leather glove from his left hand and she once more noticed the curious little ring with the red cross on the white shield. Clara felt suddenly cold. She asked:

"Something to do with that ring?"

He nodded.

"A girl in Ireland gave it to me. I didn't exactly want her to. But I took it. What's more, I promised to wear it."

Clara glanced at the privet hedge and saw it for what it was: a privet hedge in a suburban garden.

"You're engaged to her?"

"No. But things looked rather like going that way. I like her very much. And she. . . ." He broke off and looked straight ahead again.

"She wants to marry you?" Clara just managed to keep her voice steady.

"It sounds rather awful put that way. As if I were the hell of a conceited chap. Perhaps I am."

She said, trying to sound careless:

"It's quite natural women should fall in love with you. You should be used to it by now."

"Don't be sarcastic. Still, I asked for it, I suppose. Of course there's a certain amount of fluttering round any garrison. But very few hearts get seriously damaged. There's always a chap with an extra pip or a more glamorous mess-kit to come along and mend them. But this girl's different."

"What do you feel about her?"

He hesitated.

"At this moment, I don't know. Almost as if I couldn't remember. Yet it was all clear enough when I walked into Nell's party."

"How did you feel then?"

"Awfully fond of her. Not absolutely ready to settle down straight away. But when the time came, I thought I'd made as good a go of it with Kathleen as with anyone."

"How prudent you sound."

"We Crayshaws . . . the boys anyway . . . are canny when it comes to marriage. Though we tend to marry young and like it. Once we're roped, we make reasonably good husbands and fathers. I've got two nephews and a niece already. We usually seem to run a bit wild and then let some nice girl pick us and get on with the job. And our own jobs tend to take most of our energy and keep us steady."

"Did you always mean to go into the army?"

He considered for a moment.

"I couldn't be anything else but some kind of soldier. Not in the modern world. I'd like to have lived when one didn't have to have a profession and just rode off and fended for oneself. But I'm getting pretty fed up hanging around in Ireland doing nothing. It's not my idea of soldiering getting my N.C.O.s to make up to servant girls to find out if there are any arms hidden about the place. I'm jolly tempted to try and get transferred to the Flying Corps."

Clara said, involuntarily:

"Don't."

He stared at her:

"Why did you say that so frightfully definitely?"

"I don't know myself. It just slipped out."

"No fibs," he said sternly. "You saw something, didn't you?"

She could not answer. Out of nowhere it had suddenly flashed into her mind, with perfect clarity, that some day, perhaps soon, perhaps years hence, Richard would be killed in a flying accident.

"Rather not say?" he asked, more gently.

She nodded. After a moment, she said:

"I seem to be a little crazy tonight. That game of yours . . . I'm out of my depth. I don't know what's real and what isn't."

"Think I'm not out of my depth, too?" He gripped her by both shoulders and turned her so that she had to look straight into his eyes. "You and I. . . . This is real. . . . It's got to be, hasn't it? . . . Don't ask me why. It's just a fact."

She said softly:

"How wild your eyes look."

"You can't see yours."

"Richard . . . what's happened to us? Are we bewitched?"

"Would you live on a desert island with me?"

"Yes."

"Or in one of the beastly little villas in this road?"

"Yes."

They were both laughing but their eyes were fiercely intent. Then Richard frowned and said soberly:

"There's no risk I wouldn't take. Just for a second I was worried about *you*."

"Why?"

"I don't know. I tell you I'm absolutely in the dark. I only know it's all or nothing for us."

"Yes."

"Would you risk it?"

"Yes."

His face remained clouded.

"We might have to wait years."

"Because of what I told you?"

"About this case and so on? That . . . and maybe something else."

"What do you mean?"

"Don't ask me. Just a hunch. Something to do with you. I've no idea *what*. Let's call it nonsense and forget it."

She said happily:

"Yes, forget it."

His face relaxed.

"Good. I'm asking you to trust me. Because all I know is its got to happen. And I can't see further ahead than the next few weeks. But I'll give you a sign."

He took his hands from her shoulders and stripped the little red and white ring from his finger.

"Oh, no," she cried in sudden terror. "Too soon."

"Too late," he said almost harshly. His aim and throw had been so swift that the ring had already dropped in the middle of the privet hedge.

Something in her seemed to wail, "Remember where it fell." Whether she said it aloud or not, he ignored it. He heaved his shoulders and gave a sharp, hissing sigh before he drew her into his arms and she forgot everything but that they had found each other.

CHAPTER THREE

URING the next three weeks, it seemed to Clara that everyone and everything about her was in a conspiracy to make her happy. This happiness was of a different order from anything she had known or even imagined. It was almost like the acquisition of some magical power that transformed, not merely herself but every person she met, everything she saw and heard and touched.

She spent the greater part of her time with Richard. Often they parted without planning when or where their next meeting should be. She had become so expert at 'the game' that he had only to will her and she went instinctively to the right place at the right time. The strange sense of heightened perception she had felt when she danced with him had now become her permanent state even when they were apart. While she was with him it made everything they did or said or saw together register at the time with astonishing sharpness. Afterwards the details were apt to vanish in a vague golden haze.

She realised that, until now, she had never even begun to know what it meant to be alive. Not only everything she did with Richard but the most trivial words and objects seemed to be charged with extraordinary significance as if she were living in a fairy-tale where everything had its own language and conveyed a secret meaning. At first she had moments of doubt that the spell might break and she would find herself back in the old dull world. But soon each day not only confirmed but increased her sense that everything had become flawlessly, effortlessly right. No activity, physical or mental any longer presented any difficulty. The flesh she had put on during those months with Archie disappeared so quickly that every morning she arose with a lighter body. Soon her clothes hung loose on her but she did not trouble to take them in. She knew that, whenever she wanted to, she could discard all her present ones and become possessed of delightful new ones, perfect to the last detail, as effortlessly as a snake sloughing its skin. Her mind worked with astonishing speed and clarity. She was full of plans and projects to be worked out when Richard had returned to his regiment. She did not tell him that soon she would be making a great deal of money. For one thing, she wanted it to be a surprise: for another, she did not yet know exactly how she was going to make her fortune. That would be revealed to her when the time came. She was also convinced that, in due course, she would write a very wonderful book. She had only to convey this dazzling new intensity of vision to make it unlike any book written before.

This new clarity of perception affected her relations with other people. She was able to understand and adapt herself to strangers, even at a first meeting. Richard introduced her to one of his married brothers and she felt at once that she had known Angus and Cecily all her life. It was delightful how they had accepted her as if she and Richard were already married. Cecily had taken it for granted that she would like to come and help bath the baby and, though she had never handled a baby before, her new physical expertness had made it quite easy. Richard had come in when she was drying the little creature and their eyes had met above its damp, ruffled head. As they smiled at each other, she was surprised to find how natural and inevitable it seemed that she should bear his children. Something which had once been clouded with fears and anxieties now appeared as a new delight. In that quick exchange of looks she mentally accepted all the pain that it had once terrified her even to imagine. She thought, "It would be for him. Our children must be completely alive as he is. I'll refuse an anaesthetic. Nothing must take the edge off it. He'll lend me his strength."

She was equally at home with Nell and her lover, Gerald Moreton. This was all the more gratifying since Richard had warned her that Nell did not always 'take to' people. And, indeed, there was a bluntness, at times a roughness about Nell that the old Clara would have found intimidating. But the new Clara easily pierced this slightly forbidding shell and recognised Nell's honesty and generosity. Nor was she affronted, as she would once have been, by Gerald Moreton's rather provocative teasing. Though he dared not do so in front of Richard, he could not be alone with her even for a few minutes without gibing at Catholics. He liked to insist that her nullity suit was a "put-up job" and typical of the way "you R.C.s can slither out of anything if you know the ropes." Normally she would have been hurt and insulted.

143

But she took it in good part and teased him back because she perceived that, beneath his rather aggressive 'cheeriness', he was an unhappy man, obscurely disturbed by his own loss of faith and bitterly resenting the fact that Nell could not get free from her insane husband. But it was not only with those whom she already thought of as her new 'family' that the charm worked. People in shops, bus conductors, waiters, all seemed to feel it too. They smiled at her in a special way as if they knew her secret and were grateful to her for being so happy.

Though she knew that Richard was the cause of this wonderful new access of life, her happiness was not dependent on being with him. It was like a sparkling fountain inside herself that overflowed into every detail of her daily life, even into brushing her hair or talking to her grandmother. She brimmed over with affection for everyone; she would have liked to stop strangers in the street and tell them she loved them. She found herself planning wild schemes of benevolence, not only for her father and the aunts at Paget's Fold but for people she had almost forgotten. It was difficult sometimes not to burst out singing or laughing from sheer ecstatic joy. Sometimes it seemed to her that she could savour the ecstasy even more fully when she was alone than when she was with Richard. Not long after their first meeting she discovered something so obvious that she wondered she had not discovered it before. Sleep was a sheer waste of time if one were really alive. Night after night she would lie awake, neither restless nor impatient for the next day; content simply to feel this high pulse of life throbbing through her. She would get up and dress, as refreshed and clear-eyed as if she had had nine hours deep sleep. She also began to discover that it was hardly necessary to eat. Her appetite had almost vanished yet everyone was saying how amazingly well she looked. She wondered if she ought to tell someone about these remarkable discoveries. Supposing she had hit on the secret of life? Perhaps she ought to test it out a little longer so as to prove her theory scientifically. In any case, with the infinite prospect of time before her, she could afford to wait.

This patience was one of the things that surprised her most, for all her life she had been violently impatient. It bore no resemblance to that dull, artificial detachment she had achieved for a week or two before she met Richard. She could laugh at that now along with all the other illusions and follies and miseries of the past. Her present patience was something entirely different; it grew naturally out of her certainty that nothing could ever go wrong again. It was Richard who became impatient sometimes and wondered how long it would be before the case was settled and she was free. She felt so much married to him already that sometimes she forgot there still had to be a barrier between them. Sometimes, in his arms, her whole being seemed to dissolve into one magnetic current flowing towards him. It was he who would remind her, gently as a rule, but now and then sternly, not to try him too hard.

One thing, though reassuring, did strike her as remarkable. This was the extraordinary change in her father. In the first few days, when Richard had said he wanted to meet her parents, she had been hesitant about bringing him to the house. However casually she and Richard might behave, she knew very well there was no hiding the intensity of the bond between them. Her father would be shocked and apprehensive: she dreaded the inquisition which would follow when they were alone. Yet, when the two did meet, her father seemed to accept Richard almost as naturally and inevitably as she had herself. It was as if the magic had worked on him too. She had never known him so affectionate and so genial. She caught him looking at her sometimes with such radiant kindliness that she was impelled to go over to him and kiss him. It was as if he had forgotten all about her situation and saw her as she could not help feeling herself to be, an unmarried girl who had found her true love. Occasionally he said something which showed he had not forgotten but he said it with a gentle compassion quite unlike his old anxious severity.

On one of the few evenings she had spent entirely at home, the after-dinner pupil rang up to say that he would be half an hour late. Her father suggested that Clara and her mother should take their coffee with him in the study. He sat down in his usual place at the desk while her mother took the big green armchair and Clara a small one by the mantlepiece with its load of photographs. As she drank her coffee, she found her attention strangely drawn to these young men, most of them mere names to her, who had been soldiers like Richard. Though she knew so many of them were dead, they all seemed suddenly like living people. They seemed to be looking at her and smiling at her as if they were glad to know she was going to marry a soldier. Some of them had an urgent, almost pleading look as if there were something important they wanted to tell her.

Her father said with his new, happy look.

"It must be years since we were last able to do this. It has almost the charm of forbidden fruit."

Her mother laughed.

"You're acquiring a taste for forbidden fruit, Claude. It must be the effect of your mysterious Monday evenings."

"I assure you they're very innocuous evenings, my dear. But I admit that the mere fact of their being secret does give me an absurd pleasure."

"They're doing you all the good in the world. He looks a different person these days, doesn't he Clara?"

Clara tore herself away from the compelling faces on the mantelpiece and said gaily:

"Of course he does. Darling Daddy!"

Isabel smiled at her.

"As to *you*, Clara. . . . You can't think what a relief it is to see you happy again. It's as if you'd been under some kind of curse and the bad spell had suddenly been removed. She's never looked so gay and pretty in her whole life, has she Claude? Why, she's more than pretty, she's almost lovely. . . ."

"She's certainly never looked better," her father said. He added, with the faintest touch of anxiety, "It's almost bewildering . . . this extraordinary change."

"Nonsense, Claude," said Isabel. "She's been through the most appalling experience and thought the whole of her life was ruined. Now, thank Heavens, she's met the right man and everything is going to be different."

"Don't leap too far ahead, my dear. Remember there is a very long way for Clara to go before she can make any definite plans. Clara, believe me, there's nothing I want more than to see you happy. And, personally, I've seldom seen a young man I liked more than Richard Crayshaw. When I see you together, I'm apt to forget how things are. Perhaps I ought to be more of a heavy father. Somehow it's hard to deny what obviously gives you so much happiness. . . . What do you think, Isabel?"

"I can't see what possible harm there can be in their seeing each other," her mother said. "After all, it's only for another week or two. Then Richard has to go back to his regiment. They obviously fell in love at first sight. It's like an exquisite fairy-tale. Clara, darling, you're saying nothing. Does it hurt you to hear us talking so prosaically about you and Richard?"

Clara smiled.

"Oh no. I don't mind at all. I'm glad you see without my having to explain."

"Of course," said her mother, "you can't exactly get engaged just yet, can you. . . ?"

"Really . . . Isabel . . ." her father began in mild rebuke.

"We don't need to be engaged," Clara broke in. "There's nothing complicated about it. We just know."

"You mean that if, and when it becomes possible, you hope to marry?"

"It's not a question of hoping – only of waiting."

"Dear child . . . there are so many bridges to cross. And it's all so sudden. . . . Can either of you be sure so soon that . . . ?"

"Don't worry her," Isabel interrupted. "Can't you just let her be happy?"

Clara said suddenly:

"Isn't it strange, Daddy, that, after all, I should be going to marry a soldier?"

"Why strange, darling?" Isabel asked. "And why, after all?"

Clara went on in an eager rush, talking directly to her father.

"You remember when I was little, how I loved everything to do with the army. How I hated dolls and always played with soldiers. I wanted to be a colonel of Hussars when I grew up. That Hussar cap I'm wearing in that awful photo of me at seven on the mantelpiece. I used to sleep with it on my pillow. It all comes back now when I talk to Richard. He's surprised to find how much I know about all the regiments and their battles and so on. I've told him about all those army games I used to invent for Charles Cressett." She was aware of a sudden interchange of glances between her parents. "Oh, don't be frightened. I often talk about Charles to him. You see nothing upsets me when I talk about it to Richard. He's very fond of children. We might even call our first son Charles. But it was about soldiers you wanted to know, wasn't it? This is the strange thing. During the war

147

you know, I couldn't get *into* it. I mean, I somehow couldn't feel any connection with it. Perhaps because I was just too young to have anyone I very specially cared for out at the front. Oh, I used to write to people's brothers and all that and sometimes an officer on leave would take me out to tea. But I didn't keep imagining all the time what was happening to them. Not as you did, Daddy. Even when they were killed ... ones I knew ... I didn't really feel it. I've often felt guilty about that."

She saw that both her parents' eyes were intent on her face and felt a sense of triumph to see how absorbed they were by her words even if they did not quite understand them. Often there were things she was only on the verge of understanding; she could not expect them to know more than she did. When she herself understood more, there were so many things she would be able to tell them. Aware that she had fallen silent and that they were waiting thirstily for her next words, she went on:

"Well, I don't any more. And, quite suddenly tonight, while I've been sitting here with you, I know why." She swept up her arm and pointed to the photographs. "You see, they've forgiven me. They've told me so. They're so very happy that I'm going to marry a soldier."

The door-bell rang. Her father, looking a little pale, as was natural enough after the wonderful news she had just given him, said:

"Forgive me, my dears ... my pupil. Clara, dare I suggest you have an early night for once? You've had some rather late ones."

She saw that, even if there had been time, this would not have been the right moment to tell him that sleep was quite unnecessary. Instead she ran over to him and kissed him, saying ...

"I'll go to bed this minute if that's what you'd like."

Her mother smiled a little uncertainly.

"What a biddable child you are these days. But perhaps bed *would* be a good idea. Your eyes are so bright and your cheeks are so flushed. And you hardly touched your dinner."

She passed her hand over Clara's hair.

"Why, it's all electric like a cat's fur. Darling, you mustn't get over-excited ... you'll burn yourself out."

Clara laughed softly.

"I can't burn out," she said.

Only one thing had very faintly disturbed the radiant delight of those three weeks. This was the intrusion of the young Indian student into Valetta Road. He had arrived within a few days of her meeting Richard and she could not get used to his permanent presence in the house. It was not an intrusive presence for she rarely saw him except at mealtimes. Yet she was always being reminded of him, if only by the almost noiseless footsteps passing her door or the sight of the wrought silver vessels which he kept in the bathroom for his religious ablutions. She did not actively dislike Wajid Ullah but the glowing affection she now felt for everyone with whom she came in contact refused to extend itself to him. His face, with its dark eyes and splendid teeth would have been handsome had it not been heavily pitted with the smallpox which had also slightly coarsened his delicate features. She could not say what it was about Ullah that gave her a faint feeling of uneasiness; whether it was his scarred face, his exaggerated courtesy that seemed to have a touch of mockery or a way he had of staring at her with those dark eyes whose whites were tinged with yellow and then suddenly averting his head. She often saw him staring at her mother in the same way and occasionally covertly glancing from one to the other as if comparing them. When he did this, a curious little smile sometimes twitched his mauvish lips. Wajid Ullah slept on the top floor in the room next to her parents. Her own bedroom was on the first floor. Sometimes she fancied that those singularly quiet footsteps paused for a minute or two as he passed her door on his way upstairs. Once he annoyed her by asking her, with his polite but insatiable curiosity about all English customs:

"Excuse, but you are young married lady and yet you live under your father's roof?"

"Yes."

"In my country that would be thought very strange. For how many months then, is it custom for a bride to remain under her father's roof before husband fetches her away? With us it is only in case of very young child-bride. My sister at home is such child-bride. The young man of such fine appearance who visits this house is, of course, your husband?"

She was on the verge of saying "Yes" when she caught that look in his dark eyes she had seen before, a look of courteous insolence, almost of veiled desire. Suddenly she was seized with such a passion of rage that she could have struck him. He said meekly, with a deprecating smile on his mauve lips.

"Excuse. . . . No offence meant. . . . I ask only from interest in customs of country. Pray do not trouble to answer. I never wish to displease you."

CHAPTER FOUR

RICHARD'S leave was drawing to its end. Clara made no attempt to dissuade him from spending the last week of it with his parents in Wiltshire. He was to go down to Peacocks on the Saturday and she was to join him there on the following one for his final week-end before he returned to Ireland.

On one of his last few days in London, he said:

"I suppose there's no hope of your being able to come over to Dublin? It may be a hell of a time before we can see each other again."

She shook her head, smiling.

"I can wait."

"We're supposed to be posted back to England soon. But, in the army, you can never be sure of anything."

Clara said:

"I don't even feel apart from you."

"Nor do I. All the same, I wish we could get married straight away without any fuss and I could take you back with me. I'm beginning to feel I want us safely tied up. Oh, I know it's impossible. I'm not complaining really . . ."

"What are you frightened of? Don't you know everything *must* come right for us? *Aren't* we tied up? I couldn't feel more married to you than I do.

"I didn't say I was frightened. It's just that ever since we met, it's been like living in some extraordinary other world. I want to see you safe and solid in *my* world. See?"

"But our world's the same. How could these extraordinary things happen between us otherwise? How could we possibly play our game? I've never been able to do that with anyone else. Have you?"

"Not in the least like this. Only somehow, I'm beginning to feel more and more out of my depth. In every other way, I'm the most ordinary of ordinary chaps. I love you most terribly . . . absolutely beyond anything I thought possible. . . ."

"Ah, so do I you . . . so do I you," she said softly.

He caught both her hands and clutched them with the palms against his cheekbones.

"I belong to you," he said.

She looked into his face, more familiar to her these days than her own. She never looked in a mirror now except for the most cursory glance. But she knew every modulation of his, not only its structure which no expression could distort, but every slight flaw of skin or feature which made it Richard's face and not the almost ludicrous perfection of a type. Her look travelled up from the firm, mobile mouth with the small moustache which did not hide the groove of the upper lip to the grey eyes with their thick black brows and lashes. On the upper lids the straight lashes grew so close together that they looked like a crow's quill. Then she saw that the eyes themselves, usually bright as an animal's, were slightly clouded. She said quickly:

"You're worried about something. What is it?"

He shook his head between her cupping hands.

"Nothing definite. Let's take the car and go off into the country, shall we? We've hung around London rather a lot the last few days."

"Yes, let's."

She tried gently to withdraw her hands but he kept them clutched against his face.

"How awfully hot your hands are. In the old days they were always cold till I'd warmed them. You're not feverish or anything, are you?"

She laughed.

"Of course not. I've never felt better in my life."

"All very well to laugh, my girl. But I've noticed that lately you hardly do more than pretend to eat. And you're getting thinner every day."

"So much the better."

"Hmm. I'm not sure I approve. Anyway I'm jolly glad you're coming down to Peacocks for the last week-end. Even you won't be able to resist my mother's cooking. In any case, if you're going to be one of the Crayshaw family, she won't let you off, any more than the rest of us."

Clara said happily:

"One of the Crayshaw family. I love to hear you say that."

He kissed the palms of her two hands and laid them gently back in her lap.

"I think you'll like my mother. People do."

"Will she like me?"

"Of course. She would, in any case. And I'll be spending a lot of next week talking about you."

"I wonder what you'll say."

"So do I. Sometimes I wonder if it wouldn't be better just to spring you on her without preparing the ground. Of course the moment she sees me, she'll know without my telling her that something's happened to *me*. She won't ask me any questions. The minute she sees *you*, she'll understand."

"You *are* worried about something," Clara insisted.

"All right. Just a bit, yes."

"Something to do with the . . . with Kathleen?"

He nodded.

"She's met her. She's very fond of her. Oh, she knew perfectly well there was nothing definite. But I could see she rather liked the prospect. . . ."

"And she mightn't like this prospect so much?"

"She'll like it far better. Once she's seen you and seen me. She'll realise we're so absolutely . . . well, that it's just inevitable. I meant to write and tell her. But I'm hopeless at putting things into words on paper. Only I had a letter from her this morning, asking me to give her love to Kathleen when I wrote. Of course she'd posted it before I 'phoned her last night to say you were coming down for my last weekend. But it brought it home to me that I've been rather a swine. I *ought* to have written to Kay. But how can you say these things in a letter?"

"Has she written to you?"

"Every week. She always does. I've just skimmed through them. I can't remember a thing that was in them."

"If you didn't answer . . . won't she guess?"

He shook his head.

"I hardly ever do answer. I've told you I'm no hand at writing letters. No, I'll just have to tell her straight when I see her. She'll understand. But I hate hurting people. I wish I'd got it over."

"You're very fond of her, aren't you?"

"Yes," he said frankly. "I always will be. Once I like people, I go on liking them. But you and me . . . it's something entirely different. I could easily imagine being much more attracted by some other girl than Kathleen. But us . . . that's something I couldn't have imagined if I tried."

"Do you think *I* could have?"

"More easily than I could, maybe. There's something about you I can't quite follow. I don't know what it is. But every now and then I feel it. Especially lately."

"Can't you try and tell me?"

He frowned.

"I can *try*. Give me your hand," he took it and said again, "Burning hot. It's as if you were on fire inside. I look at you sometimes and it's as if you were melting away. Sometimes when we're together . . . even when I have you in my arms . . . it's almost as if you suddenly weren't there. Usually, it's only for a split second . . . and then you're back again and everything's real."

"It *is* real . . . it's all real," she said passionately. "Perhaps neither of us knew what was real before."

"I never knew anything like this. But at first we both seemed to be in the dark . . . sort of bewildered. . . . Now it's as if you'd got cat's eyes in the dark . . . and I hadn't. Sometimes I almost feel as if you weren't a girl at all. . . ."

"What am I then?"

"The Lord knows." He looked down at her hand. "I picked up a paper in Nellie's studio the other day. There was a poem in it. I don't often read poetry. But something about this made me think of you. Some of it actually stuck in my head."

"Tell me."

He muttered, still staring at her hands.

> "Alone in wet Berehaven, ere Whitsuntide came in
> I met a faery woman and she was white of skin
> She laid her white hand on me, my own was coarse and brown
> And in my veins I felt the tide of life go up and down."

He broke off. "Can't remember any more."

"I believe you can," she urged.

"Only vaguely. It was all very sad and *we're* not sad. It's one of the things I love most about you, the way you enjoy everything so tremendously. This faery female left *her* man waiting hopelessly forever in the rain."

Clara laughed.

"You can trust me not to do that. Anyway it's you that's leaving me."

He straightened his shoulders and laughed too.

"Thank goodness, we *can* laugh. I remember the last line . . . rhyming with 'rain' of course . . . 'I'm weary with the waiting but she never comes again'."

"Dear, dearer, dearest Richard," she said happily and kissed him. "Where shall we go in the country?"

Looking up into his eyes, she saw that they were bright again.

"That's what we need," he said. "Get out and blow all these morbid notions away. It's not like me to be morbid. Let's go somewhere *you* know well. I keep taking you to places and to see people I like. You don't know how I'm longing to take you to Peacocks. When I'm back in Ireland, I want to be able to think of you in places and among people I know. So as to banish the Banshee woman for good and all. I've seen you in your own home . . . good. I've seen your father and a nicer man there couldn't be. But isn't there somewhere in the country, somewhere you've known all your life . . . that's your equivalent of Peacocks?"

She said excitedly.

"There's Paget's Fold. Oh, Richard, I can't imagine anything more wonderful than seeing you at Paget's Fold. Why did I never think of it before?"

Just as they were setting out, Clara said on a sudden impulse:

"Do you mind if we stop at Westminster Cathedral? I'd like to go in for a moment."

"I'll come in with you," Richard said.

He followed her up the aisle and went into the bench behind her. Clara knelt for some minutes with her face buried in her hands. She was conscious of nothing but an immense overflowing of gratitude for all this new joy. Then her thoughts became more coherent. She asked God to bless Richard and herself. For the first time in weeks, the wild tension of happiness slackened to something sober, almost sad. She found herself praying: "Keep us safe, whatever happens. Give me grace to accept whatever Your will is for both of us."

As they came out on to the steps of the porch, Richard looked at her with an expression that was strange to her: a gravity that made his face seem for a moment older, almost careworn.

"I'm glad you did that," he said. "I liked seeing you in there. You looked so much at home. It means a lot to you, doesn't it?"

The sobriety still lingered in her mind, as if a cloud had passed over its brilliant, heightened illumination.

"Yes," she answered quietly. "But not as much as it should mean. Nothing like as much."

He said, with the same unusual gravity:

"It might to me one day. I can't tell. Meanwhile, you don't have to worry, Clara. I know what it means, marrying a Catholic. I'm prepared to accept all the conditions."

She said gently:

"Kathleen's a Catholic too?"

He nodded, then said hesitantly:

"I didn't quite know what to do in there. I found myself sort of mentioning her as well as you. You don't mind?"

"Mind?" Clara said with a sudden pang of self-reproach. "Oh, Richard . . . how could I mind? It's what I should have done myself. But I forget that anyone in the world matters but *us*. Is being happy making me frightfully selfish?"

He caught her arm.

"Of course not. Perhaps just a trifle absent-minded, now and then. Come along, let's get going."

On the drive down to Paget's Fold, her dazzling joy not only returned but soared up to a new peak of exultation. It was a brilliant November day. Leaves and bare stems, stubble and dying grass, glowed with soft fires of crimson, amber and rosy brown. To Clara it seemed that it was she and Richard who kindled all these fires as they raced through the countryside like a torch, scattering sparks of light to left and right, leaving a trail of glory. It was difficult not to sing aloud as they sped along, her hair streaming in the wind. She wanted to cry out, "We are life. We are joy. We set the world on fire as we pass." But she had to keep her wild exhilaration secret. Richard, his face growing happier as each mile took them deeper into the country, was in a mood to talk. He was constantly drawing her attention to a bird or a late flower, speculating what fish might be in a stream or game in a covert. Moreover he wanted Clara to tell him everything about Paget's Fold and her two old great-aunts. At one point, he slackened speed and asked:

"I say, do you think we ought to descend on them like this, unannounced? Oughtn't we to stop somewhere and telephone them?"

Clara pealed with laughter.

"A *telephone* at Paget's Fold. You can't think how funny that is. Wait till you've seen it. You might as well expect the aunts to have an aeroplane."

Richard laughed, but not uproariously.

"Of course, after what you've told me. But those old darlings . . . mightn't they be a bit flustered? They might think they ought to produce one of those marvellous meals for us and be upset because we hadn't given them any warning."

Clara was momentarily sobered.

"You're quite right, Richard. I never thought of anything but wanting to show *you* the place. I've never in my life burst in on them without warning. But I'm sure they'll be delighted to see us."

Richard said firmly:

"We'll stop in Horsham and have lunch. Then at least they won't have to worry about feeding us."

"I'm not hungry," Clara assured him.

"Well, I am," he smiled. "Hungry as a hunter. What's more, I'm jolly well going to see *you* eat a decent meal for once."

She swallowed some food obediently and they set off again. Soon they began to pass landmarks she recognised, the church three miles from Paget's Fold where she and her parents heard Mass on Sundays, the steep hill with the monument to the cyclist who had been killed at its foot, the ruined windmill at Owlbridge, the last village before Bellhurst. Now, as every tree and pond and gate became familiar, Clara's mood changed. Her happy exultance remained but it took on something of the quality of a dream. She could not believe that she was really here, with Richard, in these old beloved surroundings. It was almost more than she could bear. She half wished she could wake up before the dream took them to the house itself. But the next moment they were on the road that divided the two great sweeps of the green and she saw Paget's Fold. It looked so different that she only stopped Richard just in time. Looking out for the great walnut, she had seen not a green but a golden tree; the sumach by the gate was flaming crimson; a dozen details she could not immediately take in made it appear strange, almost disconcerting. At first, all this seemed to confirm that she was dreaming; then she realised that she had never before seen Paget's Fold in November.

As they stepped out of the car, Richard stood for a moment, stretching his limbs and drawing in deep breaths.

"What terrific air. You can smell the sea in it. It can't be far away, the sea."

"Only a few miles."

"When we've seen your aunts, shall we drive on to the sea? Do you know somewhere where it's not all built up and beastly?"

"I don't know," she said vaguely. "Beyond Rottingdean, there might be."

"I'll find somewhere," he said. "Look, there's someone coming out of the house."

It was Aunt Sophy, making her way down the brick path to the gate and peering uncertainly at the car and their two figures. The house might look different but Aunt Sophy was the same as ever. She wore her old black gardening-skirt, green with age, and the purple crochet shawl she pulled over her blouse on chilly days.

"Aunt Sophy, isn't it?" Richard whispered. "She's just as you described her."

Clara ran up to the gate and flung her arms round Aunt Sophy over the iron rail. The old woman stared at her, half-smiling, half-bewildered.

"Clara . . . is it really you? Well . . . this *is* a surprise . . . Oh dear . . . what will you think of us? But we never got your letter. . . ."

"There wasn't a letter. We came as a surprise."

"And that must be Archie with you . . . Oh, dear . . . I'm sure it's a great pleasure to see you both. . . . But it's *such* a surprise. . . . I can't quite take it in, dear. I'd better go and tell Leah."

Clara felt as if the dream were turning into a nightmare. She had almost forgotten Archie's existence. Now, for a moment, she remembered all the past and realised that the aunts had still been told nothing. She clutched Aunt Sophy's tiny sloping shoulders through the purple shawl and whispered. "Darling Aunt Sophy, I can't explain now. This isn't Archie. It's Richard . . . Richard Crayshaw. I so much wanted him to see you both. And Paget's Fold."

Aunt Sophy said with a kind of helpless obstinacy:

"I'm sorry, dear. I don't quite understand. We're not used to meeting strangers. And the house isn't looking as we would wish. Let me go and tell your aunt. She'll want to change her dress."

"No, please. I want Richard to see you just as you are. Come and be introduced."

Richard had remained tactfully in the background, pretending to do things to his car. Aunt Sophy advanced with such shy reluctance in the grip of Clara's arm that she almost had to be dragged along. But when she looked up into Richard's face, her puzzled, anxious expression relaxed into a faint smile. She said gallantly:

"I'm sure you're very welcome. Clara should have warned us she was bringing a friend to see us. Then we could have made a little preparation."

"It was my fault," Richard said. "It was such a marvellous day and I had my car. I was dying for some country air. I practically forced your niece to let me drive her down here. Will you forgive us?"

"Yes . . . yes, of course," said Aunt Sophy with more confidence. "I'm sure anyone would be tempted by the country on such a beautiful day. Clara dear, I can see the drive has done you good. You look very much better than when I saw you last. Except that you seem to have got very thin." The anxious look returned. "Oh dear, you must be very hungry after all that motoring. I wonder what I can find. . . ."

"*Please*," said Richard. "We've just eaten an enormous lunch in Horsham. . . ."

"That's just as well." To Clara's relief, Aunt Sophy actually smiled at him. "You see . . . being two old ladies living on our own . . . we don't always bother much about food."

"You're as bad as my mother," Richard smiled back at her. "When my father and the rest of us are away, she lives on tea and buns and hardboiled eggs."

"Are you one of a large family?"

159

"There are eight of us. Six boys. Two girls."

"Indeed. That's very large for nowadays. More like the families there used to be when I was young."

Clara watched Aunt Sophy with astonishment. As a rule she was too shy to talk to anyone until she had met them a great many times. Now she was talking quite naturally to Richard and almost ignoring her own presence. But suddenly the worried look appeared again.

"I mustn't stand here chattering like this. My elder sister doesn't even know you're here. Your Aunt Leah is up in her room, Clara. If you don't mind, I'll just go up and have a word with her. Perhaps you'd care to show your friend the garden, dear. Though I'm afraid it's looking far from its best."

Richard said:

"My mother would envy you those zinnias. She's a pretty good gardener but she's failed with zinnias year after year."

"They're very troublesome," Aunt Sophy agreed. "I can't tell you how many failures I've had with them myself. And you know, this year, I'd got so tired of pampering them I practically said, 'Come up if you want to and don't if you don't. I wash my hands of you, you nasty spoilt little things.' And look at them. They've been flowering away since September." She pointed to the bright clumps of crimson and orange, ochre and magenta.

"He knows about flowers," said Clara fondly. "I didn't even know those were zinnias till this moment."

"Your mother would," said Aunt Sophy. "It's a wonder to me how well Isabel knows all the flowers. And yet your father, who's country-bred, can't tell an aster from a Michaelmas daisy. . . ." She glanced hopefully at Richard. "Do you know our nephew – Mr. Claude Batchelor? Perhaps you're one of his old pupils?"

"Not an old pupil. But Mr. and Mrs. Batchelor have been frightfully good to me."

"That doesn't surprise me. We think the world of them. Have you known them long?"

"Only since I came on leave. I've been in Ireland for the last two years and I'm going back very soon."

"Ah well, it's natural you should want to see as much of England as you can. Now you must excuse me."

Though Aunt Sophy's face looked slightly puzzled, it was considerably happier as she trotted off into the house.

Looking back afterwards, though she remembered innumerable details of that day, Clara had no clear recollection of the time she and Richard spent inside the house. She did however remember standing in the orchard with Richard. Alone with him again, her faint uneasiness had vanished. She was back in her enchanted world where there was nothing surprising in his being there with her, his head outlined against the lichened branches of an apple tree where a few bright globes still hung. He said: "If I sent your Aunt Sophy a young tree to replace this old Elliston that's dying off, would she think it cheek? We've got some nice little Ellistons coming on in the plantation at Peacocks. Or perhaps she'd rather have a larch. A larch would look fine in that space at the end. I like the idea of something from Peacocks being planted here."

"Oh, so do I," she said eagerly. "And I know she'd love it. But please let it be a larch. That's a tree I do know. I've always longed to have one here."

"Right. A larch it shall be. For *you*. That's a solemn promise."

Suddenly the air was filled with the whirr of wings. He swept his arm up:

"Look. Skylarks. A whole flock of them!"

She stared up into the clear, faint blue. The birds were tumbling and flying in a wild, mazy pattern. Then for a moment, Clara saw them hang absolutely still against the sky. She saw, too, that the dark specks of their bodies were arranged in a curious way: some singly, some in clusters of two and three. She cried out . . .

"Richard . . . it's a message. . . . They're writing music in the sky. . . . Music for us. . . . Oh, if only I could make it out!"

But the next moment, the birds had resumed their mazy dance and the pattern had dissolved before she had had time to decipher it. Almost immediately, Aunt Sophy had come out to summon them.

She supposed they must have spent quite a time talking to the aunts inside the house for, when they drove away, it was beginning to get dark. She had an odd impression that the aunts had been much more at ease with Richard than with herself. This puzzled her because, even with Aunt Leah, she had been gayer and livelier than ever before in her life. She had even made her laugh a great deal. Yet, if that was so, why had she a persistent image of Aunt Leah's pale face looking more pinched than usual, not with disapproval, of course, since that was impossible, but with something almost like fear? No, she was sure they had all been very gay. She herself most certainly had. Except during the very last moments before she and Richard left when she had suddenly stopped talking and laughing. Forgetting even Richard's existence, she had had a flash of intense awareness of all the poverty, all the bravely born frustration of the two old women's lives. Soon she would be able to make up to them for all the hardships. But first there was something she must do herself. She thought how often she must have hurt them, how selfishly she had taken all their kindness for granted. Aunt Sophy was standing at the bamboo table, looking out of the window. Clara jumped up from her chair and flung herself on her knees at Aunt Sophy's feet.

"Darling Aunt Sophy," she cried. "Forgive me. Forgive me for everything."

Aunt Sophy's face looked down at her in bewilderment, two pink stains blotting her plump, finely-wrinkled cheeks.

"Forgive you, Clara? Now, dear, what's this nonsense? Get up at once or you'll spoil your nice skirt."

But Clara would not get up. Somebody lifted her gently from behind. She heard Aunt Leah say:

"There, there Sophy. It was just one of Clara's little jokes."

As she and Richard stepped into the car and turned to wave goodbye to the two small figures standing very close together by the gate, the sun was going down behind the house and a mist was rising from the green. She felt a momentary sadness and said to him:

"I wonder when we shall be there together again."

"I wonder, too," he said, almost with sigh. Then he turned to her and asked briskly:

"Still want to go on to the sea? Looks as if there might be fog coming up later. I'm game to risk it if you are. Or would you rather we went straight back to London?"

"Oh, let's go on to the sea."

"Right. The sea it is."

He started the car with an unwonted jerk. The next moment the tall screen of elms by the pond had hidden Paget's Fold completely from their sight.

They drove on towards the wall of the downs. The fast-waning light turned the western hills to pale yellow-green velvet. To the right Chanctonbury's wood lay like a dark wreath on a vast mounded grave. Neither of them spoke for some time. Clara was feeling a little drowsy with the strong air and the even speed of the car. At last Richard said:

"What dears those two are. I loved their house. It fits them as perfectly as a bird's nest fits a bird." He paused, then said hesitantly: "I say, darling . . ."

"Yes?" She glanced at him and saw that he was frowning. "What's the matter, Richard?"

"Oh, nothing really," he answered, his profile intent on the road. "Just that . . . well, you did overwhelm them a bit, didn't you?"

"Overwhelm them? How? I don't understand."

"Oh well, if you don't understand, it's no good my trying to explain." He changed gear rather abruptly.

She said in panic:

"Richard, you're not angry with me? Have I done something awful?"

He put one hand on her knee.

"No . . . no . . . of course not. You just had me puzzled a bit at one time, that's all."

She pressed her fingers to her temples.

"I don't remember this afternoon very well. But I thought we were all so happy."

"Well . . . yes," he said slowly. "Somehow, I didn't feel *they* were."

"But I so wanted them to be," she wailed.

He said comfortingly:

"Of course. I expect it was just that. I do the same sort of thing sometimes when I feel a situation's a bit sticky."

"What sort of thing?"

"Oh . . . you know . . . play up a bit . . . overdo the cheerfulness. It's just that I've never seen you like that. You're usually so marvellously natural with people. . . . Sorry, I can't explain. Let's forget it."

Clara said nothing. A mist seemed to be rising in her head like the mist that hung over the ditches. Her eyes suddenly smarted and turned wet. She stared ahead at the blurred, dancing road. Then she felt the car slow down and heard Richard say . . .

"Clara, why, you're crying."

The next moment the car had stopped and she was held close in his arms. . . .

"My love, my love," he whispered. "Don't do that. I can't bear it."

She lay a minute or two against his shoulder in an ecstasy of relief. Her eyes were closed. She could feel his lips moving gently round their sockets, kissing away the tears that oozed under the lids. Then she recovered herself, sat upright again and managed to smile.

"Sorry, Richard. I can't think why I did that."

"*I* can," he said ruefully. "You know, just for a second, I came as near being angry with you as I hope I'm ever likely to be. Whereas any fool could see this afternoon was a frightful strain on you. And it was all my fault. I shouldn't have been such a blundering ass."

"You . . . how?"

"Well . . . practically forcing you to take me down there. Hang it all, you'd told me what they were like. They were shocked to death, poor lambs, seeing you turn up with a totally strange chap when they obviously think of you as still married to Archie. I doubt if they even know you've started these proceedings."

"It's quite likely Daddy hasn't told them," she said, trying to keep her head clear. "He wouldn't in the summer. He probably wants to wait till it's all over."

"Exactly. And I made you barge in on them unexpectedly. Which is something you say you've never done in your life. I could hardly have created a more beastly artificial situation if I'd sat down and worked it out, could I? And I expect *you* to be as natural as a kid staying with them for the summer holidays. Richard Crayshaw, you're an ass."

She asked hesitantly:

"Was I *so* unnatural?"

He kissed her quickly.

"Just a bit wrought up. Forgive and forget?"

"Of course."

He started up the car again.

"On to the sea, then. Absolutely nothing's going to spoil our last two days, is it?"

"Nothing," she said happily. But she gave a little shiver.

"Cold, my sweet? There's a rug in the dicky."

"No. . . . Just your saying 'last two days'."

"Silly girl. You know perfectly well I only meant till I go down to Peacocks."

"Yes. But I suddenly realised next week is almost here. It's going to be awfully strange without you."

"Even for a week? Who said only this morning she could wait for months? So you *are* going to miss me after all?"

"It's just that as if next week were something I simply couldn't imagine."

"Then you must start busily imagining the week-end."

She moved a little closer to him.

"Tell me again about Peacocks," she said.

She drew him on to talk about the place he loved. As he did so, all the uneasiness vanished from his face. She loved to hear him talk of Peacock's but, as the dusk gathered, her strange drowsy feeling increased. Without losing consciousness, there were stretches when she was aware only of the sound of his voice but not of what he was saying. But there were no more moments of terror or unhappiness. She lay back in her seat in a gentle bliss, content that she should drive on and on with him forever.

She supposed they must have stopped somewhere on the coast and left the car for the next thing she remembered clearly was walking on the shore in the darkness with Richard and hearing the noise of the sea.

She heard him say:

"We can get up on to that ledge of rock. It's a bit slippery. Hold my hand tight."

Then they were standing together on a narrow shelf with their backs against rock. It was so dark that the sea was only visible as crawling, broken arcs of white. It roared in their ears and flung up bursts of unseen spray in their faces. When he turned and took her in his arms so that she no longer felt the solid rock behind her, it was as if the two of them were alone in the middle of a wild dark ocean that surged and thundered round them on all sides. They clung desperately together like two drowning creatures: his invisible face was wet against hers and she could taste the salt on his lips. His voice sounded strangely, so close in her ear that it was like a voice in her own head:

"I wish we need never go back. Shall we stay and be washed away?"

She did not know if she answered aloud. Her whole self, straining so close to him that they seemed a single being was concentrated into one desperate appeal: "Never let me go."

The next thing she remembered was hearing his voice saying urgently:

"Wake up, darling. Sorry, but you'll have to help me."

She opened her eyes, bewildered. They were in the car and standing still. All round them was a dense fog. Had she been asleep? She had no recollection of having got into the car. She blinked her smarting eyes and asked:

"Richard . . . where are we?"

"Dashed if I know," he said. "I've never seen a worse fog than this. I'd have let you sleep on otherwise. I think we're on the right road but I can't see a yard ahead. If I give you a torch, think you could walk in front and guide me? It mayn't be so bad farther on."

Suddenly her head cleared. She felt confident and efficient. She said gaily:

"Right. Just give me the torch."

She walked slowly ahead for a mile or more. The fog was so thick that Richard's head was only a blurred shape behind the windscreen. The car followed her, nosing along like a blind animal. She began to feel a sense of elation, feeling him dependent on her guidance. At last the fog grew less dense and he called her back into the car.

"Good girl," he said approvingly. "Lots of girls wouldn't have done that without making the hell of a fuss. I like feeling one can depend on you in a crisis."

She said happily:

"When you're there, nothing *seems* like a crisis. I could do *much* more difficult things."

He tucked the rug round her, looking down at her. His eyes were reddened and his face grimed with fog: drops of moisture beaded his eyelashes and moustache. She felt a rush of warm, comradely affection for the tired, almost battered face he presented.

He said:

166

"You must go on feeling like that when I'm not there. Otherwise I'll worry about you."

"What is there to worry about?"

"Oh . . . nothing, really. Just that I want you to be awfully sensible and look after yourself next week. I feel I've been making you overdo things a bit. You're looking tired."

"It's the fog," she said. "You're looking tired yourself."

"I am a bit at the moment. It's a strain having to creep along, not seeing where you're going. But there's no need for you to keep awake. Get on with that sleep I interrupted."

She must have dozed off again for the next thing she remembered was Richard shaking her and saying:

"Come on darling. We've arrived."

She opened her eyes and said stupidly:

"Why, we're in Valetta Road."

"Yes, thank heaven," he said. "There were times when I wondered if we'd make it. Luckily it got much better after Horsham. Even so, we've been over three hours on the road."

She stretched her stiff limbs and got out of the car.

"Come in for a moment. I'll get you a drink. Daddy has some whisky in the dining-room."

"Darling, it's frightfully late. Better not, don't you think?"

"Just for a moment," she pleaded.

They tiptoed into the dining-room and Clara switched on the light. He said:

"Don't bother about a drink. I'll just say goodnight and go. It's high time you were tucked up in bed."

She was standing by the mantelpiece, half intending to do something to the dead fire, when she caught sight of her face reflected in the big mahogany-framed mirror above it.

"Richard . . . how frightful I look!"

She stared in dismay at her pale, grimy face with its reddened eyes and the tangled wisps of hair round it. It reminded her of something: she could not remember what.

"We're neither of us looking our best at the moment," Richard laughed. "Hardly surprising, after what we've been through."

His face appeared over her shoulder in the mirror. It looked strange to her: almost sinister. It was not merely the tiredness and the smudges of dirt from the fog that seemed to distort it. He grinned, revealing the little gap between his front teeth. She said with sudden anger . . .

"Don't laugh at me."

"I'm not laughing at *you*, idiot," he said. "Just at my own filthy mug. I look like a coalheaver."

"Richard . . . do you think those two people in the glass really are us?" she asked anxiously. "When I was little I used to think it was another *person* I saw there. She frightened me sometimes. I thought she wanted to pull me through into her world. Looking-glass Land, you know. Where everything's the wrong way round."

He pulled her almost roughly back from the glass and turned her so that she faced him.

"Stop it, darling. In a moment you'll be having morbid fancies. . . . I'm going to kiss you goodnight and leave you. Just let's fix up where to meet tomorrow."

"You can send me a message, can't you?"

He frowned.

"I'd rather not. I think maybe we've been overdoing the game a bit. It's probably a bit of a strain for you. Even for me, maybe. Let's just be two perfectly normal people tomorrow shall we, for our last night before I go down to Peacocks?"

"Oh, very well," she said with a touch of sullenness. "What do you want us to do?"

"I've got to do some shopping before I go back to Ireland. Better not come along. It would be rather a bore for you. Could you bear to come and have supper with Nell and Gerald? I half-promised we would, my last night. We can get off on our own after."

She controlled a wild, helpless feeling that had suddenly invaded her mind and said meekly.

"Very well. What time shall I go to the studio?"

"About seven?"

She nodded.

He put his arms round her. Suddenly the helpless feeling flared up all over her body into a blind, panic-stricken rage. She struck out at him so fiercely that he stepped back, staring at her with his mouth open.

"Clara . . . what on earth . . . ?"

His face looked so comical, gaping at her, half-affronted, half-frightened, that her rage vanished and she began to laugh.

"You absurd Richard! You really thought I meant it. It was just a joke."

His face relaxed but it looked guarded and uneasy.

"I really took you in," she said, still laughing, but more quietly. "You really did think I was angry."

She put her arms round his neck and kissed him. He yielded, but with a certain stiffness.

"You took me in all right," he said. "But don't do that again without warning."

She released him and stood silent, her head bowed. In that moment she took in what life could be without him. What insane impulse had driven her to try and shatter their perfect world? She could not plead with him. If she had killed his love, nothing could revive it. She waited, almost longing for him to go, to leave her alone in her misery.

Then she felt his arms close round her, gently but securely. His face was against her hair, but he did not kiss her. He said:

"You can't get rid of me so easily. It's just that, these days, I can't follow all your moods."

They drew apart and looked sadly and searchingly into each other's eyes. She knew from his how haggard were her own.

"Oh, Richard. Neither can I. . . . Neither can I. . . ."

CHAPTER FIVE

THE FOLLOWING morning when Claude went up as usual to say goodbye to Isabel before setting off to St. Mark's, his face was overcast. Propped up against her pillows, she smiled up at him over her breakfast-tray and asked:

"Is something the matter? You look very gloomy."

"I'm rather worried," he said, sitting down at the other end of the bed. "Have you seen Clara this morning?"

"No. She hardly ever comes up till after you've gone to school. Why? Haven't *you* seen her then?"

"Oh yes, I've seen her," he said heavily.

"What's wrong then? For a moment, I thought you were going to say she didn't come in last night."

"Oh, she came in. Though goodness knows at what unearthly hour."

"She was out with Richard, of course. Well, she's often come in late. Isn't it rather absurd to start being a heavy father now, dearest? After all, he's going away tomorrow."

Claude sighed.

"I suppose I ought to have been a heavy father before. But seeing the child so happy, I hadn't the heart to say anything."

"Why this sudden attack of conscience?" She smiled up at him but, seeing no change in his troubled expression, said more seriously:

"Claude, I'm sure there's nothing to worry about. I'm perfectly certain you can trust that boy."

"As far as one can trust any young man in love, yes. I like young Crayshaw as much as you do. But Clara seems to have forgotten that her position is a very delicate one. To do him justice, I think he is far more aware of it than she is. He had the grace to ring me up just now and apologise for bringing her back so late. They were motoring and got caught in a fog."

"Then what *are* you fussing about?"

"My dear, do you know what Clara calmly announced to me at breakfast, as if it were the most natural thing in the world?"

"That she was engaged to Richard? She'd only be saying what's obvious to us all. Don't look so angry.... I know there's all this wretched legal business to be got through first...."

"Actually, that was not what she said. Even Clara must realise that they cannot possibly consider themselves engaged even if they hope, all being well, to be married some day. But I could hardly believe my ears when she told me where the two of them went yesterday."

"Well, where for goodness' sake?" Isabel asked impatiently.

"Of all places – to Paget's Fold."

Isabel laughed.

"They could hardly have gone anywhere more innocent."

"But Isabel . . . imagine what the aunts must have thought. They only know that she's married. And she suddenly bursts in on them a young man who's not her husband."

"Well, I daresay they were rather surprised. But I'm sure they were charmed with Richard."

"Richard's charm is hardly the point. They have no idea that Clara hopes to have her first marriage annulled."

"You don't mean you still haven't told them?"

"There seemed no point in disturbing them till it was all over and settled. And that, alas, may not be for a very long time."

"I always said you should have told them when we were down there in the summer."

"Perhaps, I should. Clara's forced my hand. I shall have to tell them now."

"Dearest, I can't see anything very serious in all this."

"Can't you? I know you think I'm hopelessly hidebound and conventional. I wish to heaven it hadn't happened."

"I hope you haven't been scolding Clara. I think it's very touching she should want Richard to see the place she loves so much. She never took Archie there. It's a proof that she's really and truly in love this time."

His face relaxed a little.

"Poor child. She's most certainly in love."

"Why 'poor child'? It's the most wonderful thing that's ever happened to her. She's a different person in every way these last few weeks. It's like seeing a rosebud you almost thought might never open suddenly burst into a rose." She leant forward and seized his hand. "Claude. . . . You haven't tried to spoil it for them?"

"You needn't worry, my dear. I could hardly say anything in front of my mother and Ullah. I am sure Clara had not the least idea what I was thinking. The only hint I could give her was to try and change the subject. But she kept returning to it. My mother looked a little disturbed but wisely said nothing."

"That's one thing to be grateful for. I must say your mother has shown remarkable restraint about Clara and Richard. Though she's obviously devoured with curiosity."

"She has a perfect right to be interested," said Claude rather sharply. "But I wish Clara would be a little more discreet in front of Ullah. He looked at her in a way I didn't altogether like just now. Obviously I can't take him into my confidence about our family affairs. But he knows that Clara is a married woman. I'm afraid he may be getting an altogether wrong impression of her."

"How terribly you worry about what people think? What *does* it matter? Oh, how I hate all these prying eyes and petty, unimaginative minds! Clara and Richard . . . it's all so exquisite and fresh . . . like Romeo and Juliet. . . . You've felt the spell of it yourself. You've reminded me of the Claude I knew . . . let's forget how many years ago. That young man who thought nothing of walking six miles in the rain on the off-chance of seeing a foolish young girl called Isabel Maule. Now suddenly you go and turn into that severe schoolmaster who *dared* to say happiness wasn't important."

He sighed, glanced at his watch and sprang to his feet.

"I can't make you see my point. And the severe schoolmaster must be off to his school. Otherwise he'll be late."

When he had kissed her, she detained his hand on her shoulder for a moment and looked up into his face.

"Claude . . . I believe something else is worrying you?"

He said, after a moment:

"Perhaps, my dear. I don't know. If so, it's something too vague to give it a name. . . . When you said just now Romeo and Juliet . . ." He broke off.

"Our Romeo and Juliet are going to have a happy ending," Isabel assured him, laying her lace-draped cheek against his hand. She was wearing the little ribboned cap she had worn that morning in the study when Claude came back from Tithe Place. "Oh, Claude, they *must*. It would be too cruel if anything went wrong."

"I sincerely hope it won't," he said soberly.

"You're not suggesting anything *has?*" Her voice was anxious now. "You said Richard telephoned this morning. Did he speak to *her?*"

"No. She wasn't down. In any case, he didn't ask to. But he asked me how she was."

"As if he were worried, do you mean?"

"It struck me he sounded rather uneasy. He said more than once he should have brought her straight back from Paget's Fold. Apparently they drove on to the coast afterwards. He said he should have realised she was overtired already."

"Is *that* all? That just shows what a nice, considerate young man he is. For one awful moment, I thought you were going to suggest there might have been some hint of a quarrel. I daresay she *is* a little tired. Though she's been looking so radiant, one would never guess it."

"She was decidedly pale this morning."

"Not depressed?"

"Not in the least."

"Well, she's a whole week to rest in before she goes down to meet his people."

"She doesn't seem to be thinking of resting. She talked of spending the day working."

"Richard's last day in London . . . *Working?*"

"She's not meeting him till tonight at his sister's place. But she had a letter from those advertising people she used to work for. They want some stuff from her and are prepared to pay her twenty-five pounds if she can do it quickly."

"Poor pet . . . if she's tired. : . . But it's a tempting offer. Twenty-five pounds is a big fee, isn't it?"

"I should certainly have thought so. It represents nearly fifty hours of pupils to me. But Clara's only comment was . . . 'I'll do it for twenty-five *this* time. Next time they'll have to pay two hundred and fifty'."

"Well, that was obviously a joke. Why look so disapproving?"

"Because I got a distinct impression she didn't mean it as a joke. She said it with extraordinary conviction. And there was a very odd look in her eyes."

"Claude," said Isabel firmly. "It strikes me that you're the person who's overtired. You seem determined to find something to upset you this morning. If poor Clara can't go and have tea with her old great-aunts or make a little joke about money, it's high time you took one of your famous nights off."

His face relaxed at last.

"You really think I'm being morbid and fanciful?"

"Of course you are. Stop worrying and start looking forward to Monday night. It's Friday today so the worst of the week's over."

"Absurd how I do look forward to those Mondays. Goodbye, my dear. If I don't go this moment, I *shall* be late. Then I shall get the sack and no more Monday nights."

She kissed him.

"There. That's the first smile I've seen this morning. Goodbye, you male Cassandra."

But when he had gone, the gaiety left her own face. She sat, with her hands clasped round her knees under the bedclothes, staring into space trying to remember something. She wanted to recall some lines of Juliet's but the ones she was searching for did not come. Try as she would to find them, thinking back to an amateur performance in her youth when she had played Juliet to some dim, nameless Romeo, the words she wanted would not return. Instead, with such insistence that she began to whisper them under her breath, there came ones that she had forgotten:

> "It is too rash, too unadvised, too sudden
> Too like the lightning which doth cease to be
> Ere one can say: It lightens."

CHAPTER SIX

CLARA WAS glad to have an interval to herself before meeting
Richard that night. Yesterday things had slipped out of focus
and she wanted to recover the bright, sharp image before seeing
him again. At all costs they must part tonight in perfect harmony and
serenity. There was a film of drowsiness over her mind. She felt she
wanted to tiptoe through the day, holding herself carefully, until the
turbulence of last night had subsided, leaving her calm and radiant
once more. She decided to put off doing the advertising campaign till
Richard had left London. A glance at the agent's letter had shown her
that it would present no difficulties. Without conscious effort, headline
and slogans came into her head as she moved about her room, perform-
ing small tasks with deliberate slowness. She was not displeased at
having some work, however trivial, in prospect. There had been
moments yesterday when the crystal sphere of security in which she
was enclosed had nearly cracked and she had been giddily aware of a
whirling darkness outside. This small sign from the everyday world was
a reassuring token that it, too, recognised her as destined to succeed in
everything she undertook. It was significant that they had offered her
double her usual fee. That was only the beginning. Soon money would
begin to flow to her in larger and larger quantities, not only for her
own and Richard's needs, but for all those others whom it would be
her delight to help. Tomorrow or the next day she would sit down to
this, the first of an endless series of commissions which would come
unasked and be fulfilled with expert ease.

Today, for the first time since she had met Richard, she felt the need
to think, even to analyse. In the middle of lazily tidying a cupboard,
she broke off and went to the drawer where she kept the black notebook. Sitting down, she opened it and decided to make an entry. As
she sat frowning and biting her pen, trying to find what she wanted to
say, she remembered the last time she had looked at that notebook,
intending to write in it. Since the night of Nell's party, she had not

given Clive Heron a thought. Now she felt a touch of guilt. If it had not been for Clive, she would never have met Richard. The least she could do was to let him know the amazing thing he had done for her. Perhaps next week, when she was on her own, she would ring him up. Since she had seen him last, she had had experiences beyond anything Clive could imagine. She might be able to convey some hint of them to him. At least she could show him the miraculous effects in her own person. If only such a miracle could happen to him! Then her mind reverted to Richard and the dim ghost of Clive Heron vanished. After a little thought, she slowly wrote a few sentences in the notebook. She wrote slowly, not only because the words did not come easily, but because she could not control a faint, persistent tremor in her hand.

"I begin to feel there must be a space between us, however one we are. We are like two spinning planets magnetised in harmony. But it is essential each should keep to his own orbit and not be drawn into the other's. If one should waver ever so slightly. . . . What am I frightened of? Some fearful psychic collision? How foolish that sounds. But I nearly lost *my* balance last night. Something overwhelmed me. For a second I wanted to destroy everything. I struck out at him blindly. Was it that this happiness is almost too much to bear? This is morbid. We cannot . . . we must not be destroyed. It is just that I must be a little careful, for both our sakes."

She arrived at Nell's studio a little before the arranged time. Remembering her wild, dishevelled reflection in the glass last night, she had dressed, for the first time for weeks, with conscious care. For the first time, too, she had looked long enough at her face to notice the changes in it. Like her body, it had grown thinner so that the shape of the bones was just discernible under the fair skin, so unusually pale tonight that for a moment she thought of using rouge. She decided against it. This pallor, along with the narrowed contours which made her eyes seem much larger gave her face a look of her mother's. She had always been convinced that she had inherited none of Isabel's beauty; her features were mainly softened versions of her father's and her notable fairness the replica of his. But, tonight, in spite of the difference in colouring, the woman who looked back at her from the glass was unmistakably Isabel's daughter.

When she reached the studio, Nell was busy in the kitchen and her lover, Gerald Moreton, was sitting in front of the fire, reading. He closed his book and gave her a teasing smile.

"Hullo, Clara. All alone? Where's the faithful Richard?"

"I'm early, I expect. He said he'd be here at seven."

"Running before the clock, eh? Looks almost unnatural, seeing you by yourself. However, I suppose you've been in each other's pockets all day as usual. Especially with the prospect of an entire week's separation."

Nellie came in with a tray of plates and cutlery.

"Stop teasing the child, Gerald," she said in her slightly harsh but pleasant voice. "You know perfectly well Richard was helping me in the dark-room this afternoon. And that he's round saying goodbye to Angus and Cecily now. Clara's got more sense than to want to be with him every second."

Clara looked up at her gratefully. She had a great affection for this handsome, slightly masculine woman. Nell was nearly as tall as Richard, with the same flat back, square shoulders and long legs. Her hips were so slim that her corduroy trousers, stained with chemicals, looked natural and workmanlike on her. Her hair, black as his, was cut in a straight fringe above the same marked brows but her eyes were green, not grey and her features blunter.

"Shall I lay the table for you, Nell?"

"All right . . . if you're feeling energetic." When Nell smiled, sharp creases appeared about her mouth and eyes and one saw that the firm flesh was beginning to lose its elasticity. "Richard seemed a bit apprehensive in case you might be tired. Apparently you two young idiots got lost in a fog and got home at some unearthly hour."

"He might have thought of a more original excuse," said Gerald Moreton, grinning. "Clara, I hope you and Richard haven't been up to anything Holy Mother Church doesn't approve of. She's rather pale, now I come to look at her. And do I see dark circles under those bright eyes?"

Clara began to lay the table. She saw that Gerald was in his most provoking mood and was determined not to rise.

"Leave the girl alone," said Nell. She screwed up her eyes at Clara. "I rather like you pale – Gives one a chance to see your face, not just that schoolgirl complexion – Richard's always nagging me to do a portrait of you. You look more photogenic than I've ever seen you. Pity we can't get down to it tonight."

"Put your mind back on your cooking" said Gerald. "I'm sure I can smell something burning."

Nell hurried into the kitchen and Clara went on laying the table. Moreton watched her without offering to help. In repose, his bony head was rather fine. When he smiled, the face lost its distinction and took on the faintest tinge of vulgarity.

"It amuses me to see you doing something so down to earth as laying a table" he said. "You're not really the domesticated type, are you?"

"What type am I, then?"

"Lord knows. Bit of a highbrow, I should say. You've quite a good brain if it weren't cluttered up with all this Catholic nonsense. Still one doesn't expect women to be logical. All the same, I'm surprised you should have fallen so heavily for young Richard. Triumph of matter over mind, I suppose."

"What do you mean?"

"Case of nature redressing the balance. Your first husband was a dud. And Richard's obviously the answer to any maiden's prayer . . . physically. You needn't look so shocked. I'm not trying to be offensive. There's nothing to be ashamed of in a good, healthy sexual attraction. Quite the reverse. Of course, as a Catholic, you're bound to have appalling guilt about sex."

Clara managed to control herself and said lightly:

"There's nothing you don't know about Catholics, is there, Gerald?"

"I know they can't possibly believe all they pretend to. No rational person could in the modern world. The C. of E.'s bad enough. But even they don't seriously expect you to believe in the Immaculate Conception and all that."

Clara laughed.

"I never supposed they did. It's only been an article of faith for Catholics since 1854."

"Come off it. You're not seriously suggesting they didn't have to believe Jesus was born of a virgin till the nineteenth century?"

"Of course they did. But the Immaculate Conception means something entirely different from the Virgin Birth."

"These sophistries are beyond me. All right, explain the differences then, you little casuist."

She was beginning to explain when Nell returned from the kitchen.

"You two at it again?" she broke in. "Can't you ever keep off theology, Gerald? I believe you ought to have been a parson after all. Stop browbeating Clara and give me a drink."

"Clara was browbeating me," said Gerald. "I must say the Jesuits teach these kids their stuff."

"Whoever was browbeating who, you've brought her colour back."

Gerald poured her out a drink.

"Want one too, Clara?"

She shook her head.

"Come on, you don't have to abstain from all the pleasures of the flesh, even if it is Friday. Nell's insisted on having fish for supper on account of your scruples."

Clara said gratefully:

"That was sweet of you, Nell."

"It was Richard who reminded me. By the way, where *is* that boy?"

Clara said, without thinking.

"He'll be here very soon. He's only just managed to get a taxi."

Nell gave her an odd look.

"You said that as if you knew for certain."

"Well . . . I do. Actually, I'm rather surprised. Because he said he thought we'd better stop for a bit."

"What's this?" said Gerald. "The famous Crayshaw telepathy? Of course there's a perfectly rational explanation of it. Anyway, half the time it's lucky guesses or one takes the Crayshaws' word for it. I won't be convinced till some of you have tried it in properly controlled conditions. But Clara isn't a Crayshaw."

"Well, she's going to be," said Nell. She raised her glass. "Here's to the two of you." When she had drained it, she asked Clara: "Know who I ran into yesterday?"

"Someone I know?"

"Clive Heron. I thought he was looking slightly glum. Something warned me it would be more tactful not to mention I'd been seeing a good deal of you lately. I felt he was rather deliberately keeping off the subject of you."

179

"More likely he wasn't even thinking of me. We often don't see each other for months and months."

"I've never known old Clive bring a girl to a party before," said Nell. "And you did leave him pretty thoroughly in the lurch."

"It was he who went off without even saying goodbye," said Clara.

"Don't overdo the innocence, dear. I got a strong impression that night he was jealous. He arrived in tearing spirits and went off looking like death."

"You're being the innocent one, my good Nell," said Gerald. "That Heron chap isn't interested in women. Even in such an attractive piece as our Clara."

"I'm not sure you're right, Gerald," said Nell. "Oh, I know what everyone *thinks* about Clive. If he found the right woman . . . she'd have to be rather an unusual one, of course. I really had hopes when he turned up with Clara."

"They could hardly have been more well and truly dashed, could they?" asked Gerald with a grin.

"Poor old Clive," said Nell. "Well, I'm glad, for Richard's sake they were. But I'm sure you *were* that female, Clara."

"Which female?"

"The one he talked to me about once." She mimicked Clive's intonation with remarkable accuracy. "The only just conceivably *not* impossible she."

Footsteps sounded in the courtyard.

"Here comes the chap who blighted *that* dim hope," said Gerald. "Still it's nice for Clara to have something to fall back on."

Richard let himself in and stood surveying the three of them. He and Clara exchanged only the quickest glance but in that glance she knew that everything was all right. It was as if the wavering jet of a fountain had suddenly burst up straight and strong, balancing her heart like a light ball on its tip.

Gerald said:

"You're late, my boy." He winked. "Bus held up in the fog?"

Richard smiled.

"I stayed longer than I meant to at Angus's place – And it took me ages to find a taxi.'

Supper was a cheerful meal and they lingered over it for a considerable time. Though it was an effort for her to eat, Clara was not impatient for the meal to be over. She sat rather quietly while the other three talked and laughed, cutting her food into very small pieces to make it easier to swallow. Her security had returned so completely that she was happy merely to savour it. Her eyes rarely searched directly for Richard's. When they did, his were always quick to respond. Once again she felt her love well up and overflow to embrace not only Richard but Nell and Gerald. Looking at Moreton, she wondered how she could have found him even faintly dislikeable. She noticed how, even though he was in one of his aggressively humorous moods, his blue eyes followed Nell every time she went out to change the dishes, as if he could not bear her out of his sight. As for Nell herself, she felt a glow of admiration for this older woman who would one day be her sister. How much Nell must have suffered yet how gay and courageous she was. She loved the very lines which were beginning to mar the smoothness of her dark-skinned, rather Egyptian face. If Richard and herself were like Romeo and Juliet just as her mother said (and, for once, Clara had not reproved her being romantic), she could see those older lovers as Antony and Cleopatra.

When supper was over, they all went out into the tiny kitchen to wash up. Nell shooed her away from the sink, saying:

"Leave it to me. You've got a decent dress on." Gerald and Richard had already seized the only two drying-up cloths so Clara stood back, looking on from the open doorway. Suddenly she felt strangely detached from them, watching their movements as if watching a ballet. She was aware of an exquisite sense of timeless happiness. Something whispered in her head: "This is the perfect moment. Go *now*."

Feeling completely serene, she slipped away without their noticing, tiptoed across the studio and, closing the door very quietly, went out into the dark courtyard. She did not stop to think where she meant to go. She merely let her feet carry her, with slow even steps, wherever they wished. Of their own accord, they carried her down the narrow passage that led to the river. When the stones turned slippery under them, they moved on with the same, even, deliberate steps, taking her so accurately in the dark through the iron posts that her skirt barely brushed them. She gasped as the cold water came up round her ankles but did not pause in her slow, rhythmical walk. Suddenly, though she had heard no footsteps, someone grabbed her from behind and violently jerked her back.

"You little idiot," Richard's furious voice said in her ear. "What the hell do you think you're doing?" He dragged her back till she was out of reach of the water and turned her round to him. She could not see his face in the darkness but she knew from the savage grip of his arms that he was angry. She said mildly:

"I was only walking, Richard. I just felt like walking, that's all. Don't hold me so tight. You're hurting."

His grip relaxed a little. He said less angrily:

"I *told* you never to go down that passage at night alone. Giving me a fright like that! If I hadn't come running after you, you might have been drowned."

"I'm sorry," she said in the same mild voice. "I didn't go down there deliberately. I just found myself going down it."

"You're getting too absent-minded altogether for my comfort," he said, marching her along again in the crook of his arm. "Your feet must be soaking. We'd better go into the other studio and dry them."

She walked obediently beside him. Then she asked timidly:

"Oughtn't we to go back to Nell and Gerald first?"

"No. We don't want a lot of fuss and explaining – They were expecting us to go off on our own, anyway. They want to be alone, too. Gerald's in one of his difficult moods, as you saw."

She was relieved to hear that his voice sounded almost normal again. They crossed the courtyard in silence and he let her into the other studio. When he had turned on the light and the gasfire, he sat her in a chair and pulled off her soaking shoes and stockings. Then, he knelt in front of her, chafing her cold, wet feet. Looking down at his bent head she could see only his hair and the dark brows drawn together in a frown. At last the frown relaxed and he looked up at her kindly.

"Better now?"

She smiled and nodded.

"Quite dry and almost warm."

"What pretty feet you have," he said, bending down to kiss them. He stood up and lifted her out of the chair. "Now, my girl, you'd better lie down for a bit. I'll tuck you up warm in a rug. That must have given you a shock."

He laid her on the camp bed that Nell had put up for him and knelt beside her with his arm under her neck. She found that she was trembling a little.

"Cold? Shall I put a blanket over you too?"

"No, I'm perfectly all right."

All the same it was a relief to be lying down. She was not cold, but she felt numb and drowsy. She closed her eyes. After a while she heard him say:

"Darling, you will look after yourself next week while I'm away? I'm a little worried about you, you know."

She opened her eyes at the sound of his voice.

"Why? Because I was silly last night? I can't think what came over me. It won't happen again."

He kissed her and said gently:

"It wasn't exactly sensible wandering off down to the river like that, was it? You don't know what a fright you gave me. For one ghastly moment I thought you did it on purpose. . . ."

"But I told you I didn't. I just suddenly felt like going out of doors and I found myself walking down the passage."

He said doubtfully:

"I'm not sure that makes it any better."

She closed her eyes again, almost wishing he would not talk.

"Clara" he whispered. "You *are* all right? You're so awfully pale."

She smiled drowsily.

"Quite all right. A little sleepy."

"You *are* happy with me? There isn't anything worrying you?"

She turned and embraced him.

"Happy? Oh, Richard, I've never been so happy in my life. Don't you know that?"

He laid his forehead against her hair and muttered:

"I used to know it. But sometimes you seem to go off where I can't follow you. You won't be absent-minded about coming down to Peacocks will you?"

"Of course not. I'm so longing to be with you there."

He said in a tone of relief:

"Good. I'll send you a letter with the trains. There won't be much else in it. I can't say in words what I feel."

"Neither can I. But we don't have to, do we?"

"I'll send you a token. A jay's fly-feather. They take a bit of finding. But I'll find one all right."

"I've never given you anything. What would you like?"

"Don't give me anything yet."

"Why not?"

"Just a superstitious hunch. But I'd like you to promise me something."

"That's easy."

"You've got to keep it, mind."

"What is it?"

"Just to take most frightfully good care of yourself next week. I couldn't bear it if anything happened to you when I wasn't there."

"Why should anything happen?"

"Well, just take care that it doesn't. See?"

"I can't think why you're worrying so. I never felt better in my life."

He considered her face. "You look all right now. Perhaps I've been talking nonsense. All the same. . . . Sure you wouldn't rather I didn't go down to Peacocks tomorrow?"

"Of course you must go."

"Right. I will, then. I'm going by car. I could be back in three hours if you needed me for any reason."

She smiled and shook her head.

"Darling Richard, the next time I see you will be at Peacocks."

He kissed her gently.

"We've so little time left. Don't let's talk any more."

He stretched himself beside her on the narrow bed and folded her in his arms. She lay beside him in utter content, past thought or desire, aware only of being in the one right place for her. Without losing consciousness, she fell into a light, delicious sleep. When at last he roused her gently saying: "Darling, it's time I took you home", she could hardly bear to unseal her eyes. It was as if he had roused her from the quiet ecstasy of death.

184

CHAPTER SEVEN

THE NEXT morning, all Clara's gay confidence returned. She was aware indeed, of a new vigour, a sense of conscious power that was even more delightful than her former sense that everything was being made easy for her. Whatever danger might have threatened her and Richard in the last day or two had been safely averted. The crystal sphere had shuddered for a moment; now it poised and spun steadily in the sunlight again. All she had to do was to refrain from touching it. The more perfectly she kept her balance, the freer she left him. He must be bound to her only by the mysterious current between them. She must simply go on from day to day, doing each thing as it came to hand, in the light of her love that transmuted even the dullest task.

She sat down immediately after breakfast to tackle the advertising campaign. It was almost a pleasure to find that it presented one or two difficulties.

By the end of the morning she had overcome them and sketched out her rough drafts.

After lunch her father said:

"I suppose you haven't by any chance an hour or two to spare this afternoon, Clara? The last thing I want to do is to interrupt your work."

"I can easily finish that tomorrow or on Monday," she said. "Why? Is there something you want me to do?"

"I should be immensely grateful if you could help me out. It's one of those lectures I'm giving for those Saturday night classes for my scholarship boys. I've just looked out the one on the Cyclic Epic for tonight and find it's in a terrible mess. Besides, some interesting new stuff's come out since I wrote it. I want to insert some bits about that. If you could bear to let me dictate a revised version, it would save me no end of time."

"Of course I'll do it. Do me good to learn something about Cyclic Epics. Let's start straight away."

They went into the study. Her father settled her at his own desk and seated himself at the one opposite. Clara did not, however, learn anything about cyclic epics. As soon as her father began to dictate, she became a mere writing-machine. The words conveyed no meaning to her as she transcribed line after line in her small clear writing. At intervals, he would say "Stop me, if I'm going too fast," but she always shook her head. Her hand moved with tireless mechanical speed, keeping up with him almost word by word. Once he asked "Wouldn't you like a rest? Your hand must be aching, going at this rate." But, as before, she shook her head.

When he came to the end, he said:

"Wonderful, my dear. We've done the whole thing in just over two hours. However did you keep up that prodigious speed? Can I just glance through it?"

He took the manuscript and she saw him make a few corrections. Then he put away his pen and smiled across at her.

"Really, Clara, I congratulate you. Beautifully legible and amazingly accurate. In all those pages – Greek words and all – only one tiny slip."

"One? You made more than one correction."

"Only because it was a word that occurred several times. Rather an amusing slip, too."

"What was it?"

"Instead of 'cyclic epic' you invariably wrote 'sickly epic'."

There was a short interval before his teatime pupil was due. He made her sit in the big green armchair though she assured him she was not in the least tired.

"You're the one who's tired," she insisted. "It's absurd your having to work like this, even at week-ends."

He smiled at her.

"You forget that I shall have my Monday evening of wicked idleness."

"You ought to have every evening off," she declared. "Never mind. When Richard and I are married, you will."

"My dear, let's hope you and young Crayshaw will be able to get married long before I retire."

"Well, you needn't retire unless you wanted to. I haven't worked it all out. But if I were to allow you a thousand a year?"

He stared at her for a second, then laughed.

"My dear child, for a moment I thought you were serious."

"I am serious. Daddy. I can't do it just yet, of course. But it won't be so very long now."

He was still looking at her in a puzzled way when the doorbell rang. She jumped up and kissed him.

"There's your pupil. I'll be off now. Only don't tell Mother yet. It's a secret between you and me."

The next morning after she had gone, as usual, to early Mass with her father, she decided to go to High Mass with her mother as well. Armistice Day had fallen during the past week and they arrived to find that a solemn Requiem was being sung for all who had died in the war. In front of the altar was a catafalque guarded by four young men in uniform, standing with bowed heads and reversed arms.

As soon as Clara saw this, she realised it was not mere impulse that had decided her to go to Mass a second time. She had been intended to come to this soldiers' Requiem. The catafalque reminded her how easily Richard might have been one of those who had been killed. Along with her immense gratitude came sense of remorse. How lightly she had taken the deaths of all those young men. When had she thought of the ones she had personally known, however slightly, beyond an occasional, perfunctory prayer? The fact that she had been a schoolgirl when the war broke out was no excuse for her having shut it out of her mind. She had done worse: she had not merely refused to experience it, she had turned it into a game. When she was Charles Cressett's governess, she had invented for him and acted with him that toy warfare that mocked the cruel reality. It was in one of those very games that Charles had been killed. She was utterly unworthy to be a soldier's wife.

Suddenly, beyond the four bowed figures guarding the catafalque she saw a crowd of young men in torn and blood-stained uniforms. Their haggard faces were all turned reproachfully on her. She buried her own in her hands to shut them out, praying in utter abasement: "Forgive me . . . forgive me. Give me a chance to make up for my neglect. Put me to some test. Give me some share in your suffering. All my life I have been a coward." When, at last, she raised her head, the space in front of the altar was empty except for the catafalque and the four living men.

Gradually her mind grew calm again. She was able to follow the rest of the Mass lucidly and without distractions. But, at the end, when the priest came down from the altar to sprinkle the catafalque, she saw those other figures again. Once again their haggard faces were turned towards her but now they were smiling. An extraordinary peace descended on her. With it came a strange and indefinable sensation. It could not be called apprehension for there was no tinge of fear in it. Richard's words "Take special care of yourself" came into her head. They seemed to have acquired a new meaning. It was as if it were not just for his sake that she must be careful. She felt there was some other reason she could not yet discern, something connected with those soldiers she had seen during the Mass. Because of Richard they had a special claim on her. Perhaps there was something they wanted her to do for them? Whatever that strange, faint intimation meant, there was no need for her to probe. At the right moment, all would be made clear.

On the Monday morning, though she had not expected one so soon, there was a short note from Richard. It contained little beyond the time of the train he would meet the following Saturday and a reiteration, underlined, of "Take care of yourself." To her delight, he had enclosed the jay's feather. She could hardly bear not to pin the blue-green feather, brilliant as a jewel, to her dress. But, with the sense of making a small sacrificial act, she put it between the pages of her missal where they fell open, from yesterday, at the Mass for the Dead.

She spent the morning revising and copying out her advertising campaign. Then she sat down to write to Richard. She rejected all the passionate words and bright extravagant images that came into her head and wrote only:

"My dear love, I am glad you found the jay's feather so soon. I will never lose it. I am keeping my promise. There was a reason for your making me promise that. I do not know the whole reason yet but I shall. Perhaps quite soon. Nothing in the world would stop me from catching the 10.15 on Saturday. Only a few more days and I shall see you at Peacocks. I love you. Clara."

In the afternoon, when she came back from posting her letters, she saw that it was beginning to get foggy. It reminded her of the day she and Richard had driven through the fog. She was surprised to find how long ago that seemed. As she walked down Valetta Road, the fog seemed to thicken very suddenly, almost with every step she took. Even when she was indoors again, though it was no longer in her eyes and nostrils, a cloud of it seemed to have settled inside her head. She felt extraordinary sleepy. She went up to the drawing-room and tried to dispel the drowsiness and the mist in her head by strumming on the piano. Then she remembered that Wajid Ullah was probably working in the room overhead and stopped of her own accord. The idea of his creeping down and putting his pockmarked face round the door with a silky request to play more quietly was extraordinarily repellent. As she closed the piano-lid, a conviction formed in her hazy mind. For the next few hours she must speak only if it were absolutely necessary. At all costs she must allow no one to touch her. How fortunate that her grandmother was in bed with a cold and her mother out at a bridge party. Her father, too, would be going straight from the school to whatever secret place he would spend this particular Monday evening. She was secure of not being disturbed.

She lay down on the sofa, closed her eyes and let the drowsiness overwhelm her. She did not, however, go to sleep. Instead, she lay in a kind of passive stupor. She was perfectly conscious but incapable of the slightest movement. Nor was she aware of any passage of time or of any separate thoughts. Her whole mind and body seemed to be arrested in a cataleptic state in which the only thing she knew was that she was being mysteriously prepared for something and that it was imperative to make no attempt to disturb this strange experience.

She heard the door open and was aware, through her sealed eyelids, that the light had been turned on. The voice of Molly, the housemaid, said:

"Ah, there you are, Miss Clara. I've been looking all over the house for you. Lying there in the dark! You must have been sound asleep and not heard the gong."

Without opening her eyes, Clara forced herself to answer.

"I don't want any dinner, thank you, Molly."

"Now, come along, Miss Clara. Your mother and Mr. Ullah have been waiting ten minutes and more. You're not ill, are you? Open your eyes, do."

Clara tried to obey but her lids seemed glued to her eyeballs. Molly said anxiously:

"I've never known you sleep in the afternoon. And not wanting any dinner. I'm sure you're not well. I'll go and tell the mistress to come up."

"No, Molly, I'm perfectly all right," said Clara. She had managed to make her eyes come unstuck. "Tell Mother I'll be down in a moment."

"Very good, Miss Clara."

Molly gave her a doubtful glance and hurried away. It was an effort for Clara to get up from the sofa. She realised that she would have to go through this ordeal of sitting at the dinner-table with her mother and Wajid Ullah. It would be all right, provided she ate not a morsel and uttered not a word.

Her mother was sitting at the window end of the table with Ullah on her right. Clara took her place at the end opposite Isabel, with her back to the mahogany sideboard. When her mother spoke to her, she merely smiled without answering. Her mother began a desultory conversation with Ullah. With detached dislike, Clara watched the young Indian's pitted face and oily black eyes as he talked to her mother with that exaggerated courtesy that was so near insolence. Every now and then his white teeth flashed as he gave a giggle. Once Isabel addressed him as "Wajid". Clara was on the point of protesting when she remembered that she must not speak. To avoid being drawn into the conversation, she stared fixedly at her untouched plate. It was becoming more imperative for her not to speak. She could feel herself being slowly charged with a mysterious magnetic force. She must not speak but she could listen. Her mother and Ullah appeared to be talking the merest trivialities, about a play, about her father having overworked lately, about the fog which was so thick that it was seeping into the room through the heavy drawn curtains. Suddenly, she realised that all the words they used were a code language. What they were really doing was making an assignation. She must warn her father of the terrible danger that threatened him. But how, tonight, could she find him? Ullah wanted to be her mother's lover so as to give her small-pox. She was on the point of speaking when the magnetic currents began to run up and down her limbs with such force that she was aware of nothing else. She thought: "*Now* it is really beginning." She mastered a moment of panic by telling herself "Keep quiet. Let yourself go with it. No danger as long as you don't interrupt it. Something is possessing you, like a medium. Just let it *happen*." The currents became so intense that her whole body began to vibrate. These vibrations became so strong that they communicated themselves to the chair she was sitting on. It began to rock to and fro, with a gentle, insistent rhythm. She heard her mother's voice from a great distance:

"Clara, darling. Whatever are you doing?"

The chair's gentle rhythm changed to a rapid, violent one. Suddenly it gave a convulsive heave and flung itself backwards under her so that she fell with it, striking her head against the sideboard. She heard her mother give a little shriek. The next moment someone had pulled her to her feet. She opened her eyes and found herself in Wajid Ullah's arms. She struggled and clawed at his face, screaming: "Don't touch me! Don't touch me!" She fought, but he was surprisingly strong. He pinned her arms against her sides so that she could not move. Beyond him was her mother, making incoherent, wailing sounds. She heard Ullah say in a quiet, authoritative voice.

"Do not distress . . . do not distress. . . . My sister have such attacks. . . . Go at once and telephone doctor. I can hold her . . . I accustomed."

Clara stopped struggling. She shut her eyes and her mind went blank. She supposed she must have fainted for when she opened her eyes again she was sitting in an armchair by the fire. She looked round cautiously. She was still in the dining-room; the half-eaten meal was still on the table. There was no sign of her mother or Ullah. Yet she was sure she was not alone. The room was very foggy. There was a dull ache in the back of her head. Peering round painfully, she saw that a man was sitting only a few feet away from her in the armchair on the other side of the fire. A large, reddish, blue-eyed face was watching her intently. It took her a minute or so to realise that it was a face she knew, though she could not attach a name to it. She said:

"Hullo . . . how did *you* get here?"

"Well, so you've noticed me at last. You haven't forgotten me, have you, Clara?"

"I know your *face*," she said uncertainly.

"So I should hope. Considering we're very old friends indeed – Come along now, what's my name?"

It came to her.

"Doctor Mayfield."

He grinned.

"Splendid. Doctor Mayfield. Whom you've known since you were so high, haven't you?"

She said suspiciously:

"What are you doing here? Nobody's ill, are they?"

"Who said anyone was ill? Can't an old friend drop in for a chat? Well, how's the world treating you these days, Clara?"

Clara said, with sudden fury:

"It's a plot. Mother and that man. They want to get rid of me. That's why they've sent you in here to talk to me. To keep me quiet. But I won't be bribed."

"Steady on, now" said Doctor Mayfield, with an irritating smile. "You've given yourself a nasty bump on the head. Confuses one a bit. Did the same thing myself once, playing football for Guy's. Know what I did? Went round and round the Inner Circle twenty times without stopping. That was a silly thing to do, wasn't it?"

"Very," said Clara coldly. "Why are you treating me like an idiot? You can't deceive *me*."

"Who's trying to deceive you? And who's treating you like an idiot? We all know you're a very brainy young lady. Much too brainy to fall off a chair in the middle of dinner and bang your head against a sideboard without a very good reason. Now suppose you tell me exactly what happened." He leant forward and laid his hand on her knee.

Clara sprang to her feet and screamed:

"Don't touch me! Don't touch me! You'll be struck dead if you do."

The doctor stood up and caught her by the shoulder.

"I'll risk that. Now, Clara, take it easy. . . . Suppose we sit down again, shall we?"

His big, insolently smiling face loomed over her as he tried to force her back into the chair. He was a tall, heavily-built man. Clara sprang at him and slapped his face with such force that he staggered backwards and the imprint of her hand made white blotches on his red cheek.

"You little devil," he said, rubbing his cheek. "All right, young lady. We'll have to try something else."

He went quickly out of the room. The moment the door had closed behind him, Clara became calm and lucid. She realised she must act quickly. Her senses became preternaturally acute. She could hear Doctor Mayfield talking to her mother in the study next door. She heard him say "I'll just go back to my place and get an injection for her. Is there a key on the outside of the dining-room door? Good. Don't go in to her. She's rather excitable. My advice is, as soon as I've gone, lock her in. I'll be back in a quarter of an hour."

She waited to hear no more. In a flash, she was out of the room, had closed the door silently behind her and was running noiselessly up the stairs. From her bedroom she could hear their voices, her mother's high and tearful, the doctor's low and booming, though she could no longer distinguish the words. Her mind was taking lightning decisions but she felt astonishingly calm. Not only did she feel in the pocket of the fur coat she slipped on to make sure that her purse was in it, she took a minute or two to write a hurried note to her father. At all costs, he must not be worried. He must understand that she had good reason for her flight. She even told him where she was going. She slid the note in an envelope, wrote his name on it and added *Private and Confidential*. Then she stood, listening. It was all right. The voices were still going on in the study. She tiptoed down the stairs, left the note on the oak chest in the hall, and closed the front door behind her with hardly a sound.

Out in the street, the fog was so dense that she could hardly see a step ahead. She made her way carefully along the street, guiding herself by the railings. As she turned the corner, a taxi loomed out of the fog and she hailed it. She gave him the address of Nell's studio. The man said:

"That's somewhere Chelsea way by the river isn't it? It'll be worse than ever down there. I doubt if I can make it."

Clara said confidently:

"Please try, I don't mind how slowly you go. I can guide you. I know the way very well."

"More than I do. And in this pea-souper. . . . All right, if you're game to risk it, I am. But I don't guarantee to get you there. Jump in."

Once in the taxi, Clara felt perfectly safe. She knew that she would be able to direct him, however thick the fog. Her only concern was that, as they would have to creep along, she might not have enough money on her to pay him. She opened her purse and saw that there were two half-crowns in it. Normally it would have been twice as much as she needed. But would it be tonight? She prayed that the money would hold out and felt a reassurance that it would. When at last they reached the gateway to the courtyard, she jumped out and proffered him her two half-crowns.

"I can't see what it says on the meter. But it was terribly important for me to get here. This is all the money I have."

The man grinned at her.

"That's all right by me, Missie. Suppose *he's* waiting for you, eh?"

She smiled and said goodnight. In a moment the taxi had been swallowed up in the fog. She took a long time to cross the courtyard. Her mind was not so clear as it had been in the taxi. But at last she found the right studio and knocked urgently on the door.

CHAPTER EIGHT

BECAUSE of the fog, Claude Batchelor came straight home after his solitary dinner in Soho instead of going on to the Café Royal as he had intended. The moment he opened the door, Isabel appeared from the study and flung herself on him, sobbing.

"Oh, dearest, thank God, you've come."

"Isabel, whatever's the matter?"

She could only gasp, with her face buried in his shoulder:

"Clara. . . . She's run away. . . . She's ill. . . . We've searched the neighbourhood . . ."

He took her into the study and comforted her till she was calm enough to speak. When she had finished her story, his face was as pale as hers.

"The first thing to do is to find her" he said. "In this fog, anything might have happened to her. Have you telephoned the police?"

She nodded.

He sat down at his desk, clutching his head in his hands.

"If only I'd been here. If only I hadn't gone out in this insane way, not letting you know where to get hold of me – It's a judgement on me."

"Darling Claude, don't start blaming yourself – Thank heaven you're here now. Wait, there's something I forgot. She left a note for you. . . ."

"Why didn't you open it? It might give us a clue."

"Oh, Claude, I was so distracted. I didn't know what to do. Mayfield and I rushed out after her. I didn't see the note till I got back, and she's put 'Private and Confidential' on it." She began to cry again.

"Hush, Isabel . . . hush."

"It's in the hall. I'll get it."

She went out and fetched it. He put his arm round her, saying gently:

"We'll both read it, my dear."

He tore open the note. Together they read the scrawled, but legible lines:

"Darling Daddy,

I had to leave the house. So must you when you get this. The house is full of evil. It is not only the small-pox. Don't be worried to find me gone. I have gone to Nell Crayshaw. 3 Rivershore Studios. Chelsea Embankment. Your loving Clara."

"Thank God for that at least," Claude said. "If she was enough in her right mind to say where she was going . . ."

"But . . . dearest . . . that wild talk about the house being full of evil. . . ."

He said, straining after hope:

"You say she hit her head. . . . Doesn't concussion sometimes cause hallucinations? I must ring up Crayshaw's sister at once. When did Clara leave?"

"Nearly two hours ago."

"It's our one hope that she somehow managed to get there. You don't know the number?"

She shook her head. He began to search through the directory. His hand was shaking so much that it took him a long time to find the place.

He picked up the telephone and asked for the number. After a while, he said:

"It's ringing but no one's answering. Shall I hold on? Or try the police again?"

"Oh hold on," she implored. "They may not have heard it. . . ."

There was a long pause. At last, just as he had shaken his head and was about to replace the receiver, his face changed:

"Someone's answering," he said.

Isabel strained her ears in vain to catch what was being said the other end. Claude's almost monosyllabic questions and replies came at long intervals, and gave her little comfort except the knowledge that Clara was there. At last she heard Claude say:

"I'll get over to you as soon as possible, fog or no fog. Would you mind just giving me the directions again? Thank you. And thank you more than I can say for looking after her."

He hung up the receiver and immediately picked it up again and asked for Doctor Mayfield's number. As he waited for a reply, he gave her a hurried glance and said:

"I'll tell you everything when I've spoken to Mayfield. . . . Hullo? Is that you Mayfield? . . . Yes, thank God we've found her. . . . No . . . not reassuring, I fear. . . . This friend of hers says she can't make her understand anything. . . . I don't like to ask you to come out on such a filthy night . . . you will? . . . That's extraordinarily good of you. . . . Right. . . . I'll wait for you to pick me up. . . ."

He came and sat on the arm of the big green chair and drew Isabel's head on to his shoulder. He said, trying to keep his voice as steady as when he had spoken to the doctor:

"My dear . . . we must try not to lose our heads. It may not be as bad as it sounds. Till Mayfield's seen her, we can only guess. . . . These things always seem terrifying to the layman. . . ."

Isabel took his hand.

"Tell me everything Nell Crayshaw said."

"My dear . . . I don't want to upset you. Wouldn't you rather wait till Mayfield's seen her?"

"I want to know everything she told you" she said quietly.

"Well, if you insist. It seems Clara arrived there well over an hour ago. They . . . Miss Crayshaw kept saying 'we' and referring to someone called Gerald . . . were just sitting down rather late to their supper. They were very surprised to see Clara. Especially on such a foggy night."

"How did she find her way?"

"Apparently she picked up a taxi."

Isabel said hopefully: "Her mind must have been clear enough, then. How did she seem when she arrived?"

"Quite normal, even cheerful. She talked quite sensibly about being afraid of not having enough money on her for the fare – She gave no explanation why she had come to their place. Apparently her manner was a little excited. Nell said she had noticed that she had seemed a trifle over-excited lately and thought nothing of it." He broke off and said wretchedly. "I've noticed it myself. Odd, little things she said. Why only this very Saturday . . ."

"Oh, Claude . . ." Isabel broke in "We both thought that it was just that she was so happy about Richard." Her grip on his hand tightened. "If anything were to go wrong. . . . It would be too cruel . . . too tragic. . . ."

"My dear . . . I'm so afraid of distressing you. I'd rather not tell you any more."

"No . . . please, go on. I *must* know. I won't interrupt again. Every detail you can remember."

"Well, apparently Nell Crayshaw and this man Gerald, whoever he is, asked her to have some supper with them. Clara refused. She went and sat by the fire while they ate. She sat there without saying a word though she had been very talkative when she arrived. They asked her, even if she didn't want anything to eat, wouldn't she sit at the table with them? She said no and muttered something to the effect that it would be dangerous for her to move. They thought her manner strange but decided the best thing was to leave her alone and go on with their meal. Suddenly she asked for some bread and salt. Then she said . . . Nell Crayshaw was positive about this . . . 'Bread and salt is good against evil spirits.' Gerald then asked her if she thought they were evil spirits but she smiled and shook her head. She became rather insistent about the bread and salt so they gave her some. She ate a little and then sat for a long time saying nothing. They noticed she was looking very pale and seemed dazed. At last they suggested wouldn't she be better at home in bed? This man Gerald offered to go out, find a taxi and bring her back here. Nell said that, at that, she leapt to her feet and began to scream hysterically. When they tried to calm her, she fought like a wild-cat. It was as much as the two of them could do to hold her. Then, quite suddenly, she collapsed into a chair and began to cry. Nell tried to comfort her, but Clara did not seem to know who she was. She said her mood had changed completely. She was quite gentle, like a child. She even talked like a child. Nell said this frightened her more than the hysteria. She thought the best thing to do was to put Clara to bed in the other studio – apparently she rents two of them – and ring us up. However, as soon as she got her into the other one and undressed her, Clara became very obstinate and tried to run away. There was no bolt on the door and Nell dared not go back to the other studio where the telephone is in case she slipped out and wandered off in the fog. At last she persuaded her to go to bed. To her relief, Clara fell asleep.

"She dared not leave her alone, even to go across the courtyard to the other studio. She opened the window and called out to Gerald. He heard her and came over, saying he would sit by Clara while Nell telephoned us. But he had hardly arrived before Clara woke up and became so hysterical that it took the two of them to deal with her. She began to sing and rave as if she were delirious. She kept running over to the door and trying to get out. It was all the two of them could do to stop her. Nell said her strength was quite incredible. But at moments, she would become perfectly quiet and normal. She even recognised them and said 'Tell Richard not to worry'. But the next moment, the delirium and the violence would return. That was what was going on when I rang her up."

Isabel had begun to cry softly.

"The poor, poor child. . . . Oh, why doesn't Mayfield come?"

"He'll be here any minute," he said soothingly. "Try not to cry."

She dried her eyes.

"I'm sorry, dearest. It was just the shock. I'll go up and get a coat. I'm coming with you."

"Are you sure you can bear it?"

She was already on her feet.

"Of course I can. . . . My own child!"

The door bell rang. Claude started up.

"Thank heaven, there's Mayfield. Very well, get your coat while I tell him what I've just told you."

When Isabel returned to the study some minutes later, the doctor said to her:

"I think it would be better if you didn't come with us, Mrs. Batchelor. It'll only upset you . . . and it might upset Clara. She seemed to have got some wild notion about you when I saw her before. Hysterical girls often do about their mothers – My idea is to let your husband see her alone first. The fact that she left that note for him suggests that, whatever strange fancies she may have, she's not suspicious of him."

"But why . . . *why* should she have these strange fancies?" Isabel implored him. "You've known her since she was a child. . . . Clara's never been hysterical in her life . . . if anything she was too controlled. . . ."

"Controls have a way of breaking down, you know. After all you told me earlier on about how she's been ever since that abnormal marriage of hers. . . . First the apathy and depression . . . then this sudden emotional stimulus. . . . Perhaps this rather violent reaction isn't altogether surprising."

Claude said hopefully:

"You really think it may be only that . . . just a temporary nervous reaction?"

"My dear man, I can't give any opinion till I've seen her again. But a little burst of hysteria can look very alarming to the layman. Not to mention the effects of even mild concussion. Let's hope that this is nothing that sedatives and a few days' rest won't put right. If you're ready, Batchelor, we'd better be on our way. Thank heaven, this filthy fog seems to be clearing a little."

Claude said: "Right. My overcoat's in the hall."

Isabel murmured: "You're still wearing it, dearest."

He gave a painful smile.

"Of course . . . how idiotic of me."

She kissed him and begged:

"Let me come with you. I won't ask to see Clara."

Doctor Mayfield said with professional heartiness:

"Now, now Mrs. Batchelor. If you don't go straight up to bed, I shall have two patients in this family on my hands."

"I'll wait down here," she said quietly. "Will one of you telephone me when there's any news?"

When they had gone, she knelt for a long time beside the green armchair, with her face buried in her hands. Her prayer calmed her a little. She found that she was shivering with cold, in spite of the thick coat she had put on and the gas-fire which had been burning there ever since Dr. Mayfield's first visit. She went upstairs and fetched an eiderdown from her bedroom, and, wrapping it round her, huddled down in the great chair and closed her eyes. She must have fallen asleep for the whirr of the telephone bell startled her only as an irrelevant noise. Then she realised what it meant and leapt up, stumbling over the folds of the eiderdown, to grab the receiver. The voice was Claude's.

"Dearest . . . how is she?" she implored.

"Mayfield can't say anything definite yet." She could tell from the way he spoke that he was not alone. "He's with her now – Going to give her an injection."

"You've seen her? How did she seem? Did she know you?"

200

"I only saw her for a minute or two. She recognised me. She even said 'Why are you here, Daddy?'" There was a faint tremor in his voice.

"Surely that was a good sign?" Isabel said eagerly.

"Let's hope so. But I only stayed with her a moment. I'm afraid the sight of me upset her."

"Claude . . . does she seem very ill? To you, I mean? I know you don't want to say much with Richard's sister there – Just say yes or no. . . ."

After a pause before he answered:

"Frankly, my dear, yes. But remember my impressions mean nothing. We must wait and see what Mayfield says. . . ."

"Hasn't he *any* idea what it may be?"

"He says it's too early to tell – Try not to worry too much. The drug will put her to sleep. There might be a considerable improvement when she wakes up."

"Obviously she can't be moved tonight. Can we bring her back here tomorrow?"

There was another pause. Then Claude's voice said guardedly:

"He thinks probably better not. In fact, just to be on the safe side, he suggests putting her into a nursing-home for a few days. At all costs, she must have complete rest and quiet."

"But she could have that here. I'd look after her night and day."

"I know you would, my dear. But we must go by what Mayfield says. Forgive me if I ring off now. I can hear him coming across the courtyard."

"Oh, wait," she implored. "Let *me* speak to him. . . . I know you're keeping something back. . . . He'll tell me if you won't. . . ."

But it was too late. As she was speaking, she heard the click of the receiver and the line went dead.

CHAPTER NINE

WHEN SHE found herself lying in Richard's camp bed, she started up in a panic. Didn't they know that was the one place of all places where she must not be? She ran to the door, stumbling over the nightdress that was too long for her. (Why was she wearing a nightdress? Whose nightdress?) Two evil spirits, one male, one female, clutched her, trying to stop her from escaping. She fought with all her might but they dragged her back and forced her into the bed again. Over and over again, she started up and ran to the door. But each time the two evil spirits dragged her back in spite of her struggles until at last she was exhausted and lay quiet, with her eyes closed. When she opened them, there was no one in the room but Gerald and Nell. At least she thought they were Gerald and Nell but they looked very strange. There was blood on Gerald's forehead and Nell's black fringe hung in jagged peaks. They looked so funny that she had to smile. She asked:

"Is it really you, Nell?"

"Yes, Clara dear. And this is Gerald. You remember Gerald?"

"Of course." Then she asked anxiously: "Where's Richard?"

"He's gone down to Peacocks. Don't you remember?"

She thought for a moment. Then she remembered and leapt out of bed again.

"Nell," she cried. "I have to go to Peacocks too. Oh, where are my clothes? I shall miss the train. . . . I know I shall miss the train."

Nell said:

"Hush, dear. You haven't got to go to Peacocks till Saturday. There's plenty of time. Try and go to sleep."

She let Nell put her back to bed. Perhaps it was all right now the evil spirits had gone. She asked:

"Why am I here in Richard's bed?"

"You were so tired. We thought you'd like to stay the night."

Her eyelids came down suddenly like heavy blinds. She whispered:

"Tell Richard not to worry."

When she was able to open her eyes again, Nell was not there. Only Gerald was sitting by her bed. He said "Feeling better? You've had a little doze."

She wailed:

"Where's Nell? You shouldn't have let her go. Now she'll never come back."

He tried to stop her but she was out of bed and at the door before he caught her. She fought with him, screaming "You fool. . . . Let me go to her. . . . Don't you know what they're trying to do?" She screamed louder and louder trying to make him understand. Before she could make him realise that Nell had been tricked into going to the asylum to see her mad husband and they were going to lock her up there, the evil spirits reappeared and dragged her back to bed again. She shut her eyes and, to keep them at bay, sang with all her might, over and over again:

> "O Deus ego amo te
> Nec amo te ut salvas me
> Nec quia non amantes te
> Aeterno punis igne."

At last she felt it was safe to stop. She opened her eyes. They had gone. There was no one in the room at all. Then she saw the door slowly move on its hinges. Someone was coming in. Was it the evil ones again? She sat up and made the sign of the cross.

It was her father who came in. He looked just as usual except that he was wearing the brown habit of a monk. She asked: "Why are you here, Daddy?"

He smiled at her. She did not like the smile. He said "Clara, my dearest child." The voice did not sound like his. He came quite close up to the bed before she realised the truth. It was one of the evil spirits disguised as her father. He was going to try to kiss her. If this devil kissed her, she was lost for ever. She would never see Richard again. She whirled her arms and shrieked "Don't touch me. . . . Don't touch me. . . . I won't marry you. . . . I belong to Richard."

That drove him away. As the door shut after him, she lay back sobbing. "Richard . . . hold on . . . don't let me go . . . I *am* true . . . I will be true." For the first time, infinitely far away, she felt his presence. Silently, she called back "Don't be afraid. I can hold on, whatever they do."

Something tremendous was going to happen. A terrible ordeal to prepare her for her marriage. She must go through it bravely, asking for no mitigation, as a soldier's bride should. She saw the door slowly open again. At any moment the ordeal would begin.

This time it was Doctor Mayfield. He was carrying some small object concealed in one hand. Was it an instrument of torture?

He came and stood over her, smiling falsely, and asked:

"Well, Clara, do you know who I am?"

"Doctor Mayfield, of course." She was careful not to let him see how she hated his red face and false smile.

"Splendid, splendid! And you're not going to slap poor old Doctor Mayfield's face again? Shall we shake hands and make it up?"

His free hand slyly pulled one of hers from under the sheet. But she had seen what his other hand concealed. It was a hypodermic syringe. She tore her wrist away, imploring:

"No . . . no . . . I mustn't be drugged. Richard doesn't want me to be drugged. Please, please not that."

"Now, now," he said hypocritically. "Who's talking about drugs? Wouldn't you like to have a nice long sleep and dream about Richard?"

Her whole body was suddenly convulsed with such pain that her mind became confused. Why was it so essential she must not be drugged? Was it because she was in travail with Richard's child and, as a soldier's wife, she must not be spared any pang? When the doctor grabbed her arm again, the pain made it difficult to struggle with him. She fought as best she could but he was too strong for her. She felt the needle pierce her arm. In spite of her desperate effort to remain conscious, the heavy wave of the drug submerged her.

She was awakened by the distant noise of a car. Her mind was numb and drowsy but lucid. She was too exhausted to move her limbs, but she managed to raise her eyelids. Nell was sitting beside her.

"Nell," she said. "That car . . . I can still hear it?"

"What car, dear?"

"It's a long way away. . . . Listen, can't you hear it now?"

"I'm trying to, dear – But I can't yet."

"It's a very long way away still," said Clara and closed her eyes.

She lay in a stupor aware of nothing but the sound of the car. It was a long time before she realised it was Richard's car. Then she saw it quite clearly, driving very fast along the dark roads with its headlamps on. She could just make out his face, pale and concentrated, behind the steering wheel. His voice sounded in her head: "Hold on darling. I'm coming as fast as I can." At intervals she dozed off but in each conscious interval she saw and heard the car. Suddenly she saw some larger, heavier vehicle approaching from the other direction. She called out "Take care". But she was too late. The next moment she heard the crash of the collision and screamed.

She felt Nell's arm round her.

"Clara, what's the matter?"

She controlled herself and said:

"Wait . . . let me see what's happened."

After a minute or two, she said:

"Oh, thank God. He's not hurt."

"Who isn't hurt, dear?"

She opened her eyes and smiled at Nell's anxious face.

"Richard. It's all right. The car's smashed up but he's not hurt at all."

"You've had a bad dream. Try and go to sleep again."

She said quietly:

"No. It wasn't a dream. Richard started to drive back from Peacocks. That was his car I kept hearing. I saw it all happen. He ran into something. I couldn't see exactly what it was. But it's only his car that's smashed.

"Richard's quite safe, dear. So go back to sleep."

"Yes. Now I know he's safe. He'll have to come on by train now. You won't let them do anything to me till he comes, Nell?"

"No, dear. Of course not."

She slept. When she woke again, it was to the grey light of early morning. Her head had cleared; she felt sick and exhausted. She turned her head painfully and saw that the doctor was sitting beside her. She did not trust him but she no longer feared him.

He said:

"We're going to move you somewhere where you'll be more comfortable."

She did not protest. She knew what they were going to do. They were going to take her away and use her for some kind of experiment. Something to do with the war. She was willing to go. But when they lifted her out of bed, she cried out desperately:

"Richard. . . . Richard. . . . Oh, you're too late."

She was in a cab, with her head on a nurse's shoulder. Two men were sitting opposite her. One was a stranger. The other looked like Gerald Moreton. It was odd to be driving through the streets in broad daylight wearing only a nightdress that did not belong to her and the black imitation sealskin coat her father had given her. She was very sleepy. She kept trying to remember when she had last put that fur coat on but her mind was a blank.

They came to a tall house. Someone, Gerald perhaps, carried her up flights and flights of stairs. Now she was in a perfectly ordinary bedroom. An old nurse with a face she liked sat by the fire; a young one, very pink and white and self-conscious, stood near her. Clara wandered over to the window and looked out. A red bus went by. It was comforting to see the bus. She wanted to stand there and watch other buses going by. If she could see the numbers, she might be able to tell what road it was down there. But the young nurse took her by the elbow and led her away.

"I shouldn't look out of the window if I were you, dear," she said in a soft, hateful voice. "It's so ugly." Clara did not resist. Now she was puzzled and frightened; she wanted to explain something, but her head was too muddled. Presently she was in bed, alone but for the old nurse. Then she found that she was clutching a rosary. It was her father's old black one. She knew that her parents were downstairs, praying for her. Her throat was dry; a fearful weariness weighed her down. She was in her last agony. She must pray. As if the old nurse understood, she began 'Our Father' and 'Hail Mary'. Clara answered. They recited decade after decade in a mechanical rhythm. A cold sweat came out on Clara's forehead; all her limbs felt numb and bruised. Her strength was going out of her on the holy words. She was fighting the overpowering sleepiness that she knew was death. "Holy Mary, Mother of God", she forced out in beat after beat of sheer will-power. She lapsed at last. She was dead, but unable to leave the flesh. She waited; light, happy, disembodied.

Now she was a baby again. It was as if she had died and been reborn.

206

She was not in her own home but in Charles Cressett's night nursery at Maryhall. Yet she knew that she was still Clara. She lay very peacefully watching the nurse knitting under the green lamp. Her body was a baby's but her mind understood what had happened. She had been given a chance to live her life all over again. This new life would unfold perfectly day after day through a new childhood lapped in warmth and security. But just as she was savouring the bliss of this rebirth, the pleasant, firelit room and the old nurse vanished. She was standing alone in a dark crypt. Beside her, on a bier, was a glass-lidded coffin. In it, dressed as a First Communicant, lay a girl who had died at her convent-school. Instead of white flowers, Theresa wore a gilt paper crown on her head. As Clara watched the dead girl, a worm crawled out of her mouth. She screamed and woke out of the nightmare to find herself back in the firelit room. But she was no longer a baby and another nurse was sitting by the green lamp.

"You must be quiet, dear," said the woman.

There were whispers and footsteps outside.

"I hear she is wonderful," said a woman's voice.

"Yes," said another, "but all the conditions must be right, or it will be dangerous for her."

"How?"

"You must all dress as nurses," said the second voice, "then she thinks she is in a hospital. She lives through it again, or rather *they* do."

"Who . . . the sons?"

"Yes. The House of Mirrors is full of them."

One by one, women wearing nurses' veils and aprons tiptoed in and sat beside her bed. She knew quite well that they were not nurses; they were women whose sons had been killed in the war. Each time a woman came in, Clara went through a new agony. She became the dead boy. She spoke with his voice. She felt the pain of amputated limbs, of blinded eyes. She coughed up blood from lungs torn to rags by shrapnel. Over and over again, in trenches, in field hospitals, in German camps, she died a lingering death. Between the bouts of torture, the mothers, in their nurses' veils, would kiss her hands and sob out their gratitude.

"She must never speak of the House of Mirrors", one said to another.

And the other answered:

"She will forget when she wakes up. She is going to marry a soldier."

At last the ordeal was over. She lay back in the bed, too exhausted to open her eyes. Gradually she realised that, all through it, Richard had been in the room below. The horrors were over now. Any moment now he would be coming up to tell her that she had done everything that was needed. She had earned the right to marry him.

She heard the door open softly and knew that he had come in. She turned her head to look at him, but her eyelids were clamped down with leaden weights. She struggled desperately to speak to him but she could not manage even a whisper. She had gone dumb. Perhaps she had gone deaf too. She knew that he was speaking to her but she could not hear the words. He was close to her now but she could not get through to him nor he to her. At last, with a huge effort, she lifted her eyelids. He was standing close by her but she could not see him clearly. His face was a blur. The only thing she could see distinctly was the shepherd's plaid pattern of his suit. She strained her eyes to keep it in focus but, almost at once, that too began to blur. With her last remnant of consciousness she tried to force herself to keep aware of him, to implore him, in her agony of dumbness, to wait. But she could not get through to him. For one tiny flicker, her senses returned. She heard someone say:

"It's no use. She doesn't know you."

Before she could cry out "I do, I do," the darkness closed down.

Part Four

CHAPTER ONE

Months, perhaps years, later, she woke up in a small bare cell. The walls were whitewashed and dirty, and she was lying on a mattress on the floor, without sheets, with only rough, red-striped blankets over her. She was wearing a linen gown, like an old-fashioned nightshirt, and she was bitterly cold. In front of her was the blank yellow face of a heavy door without a handle of any kind. Going over to the door, she tried frantically to push it open. It was locked. She began to call out in panic and to beat on the door till her hands were red and swollen. She had forgotten her name. She did not know whether she were very young or very old. Had she died that night in Nell's studio? She could remember Nell and Richard, yet she knew that her memory of them was not quite right. Was this place a prison? If only, only her name would come back to her.

Suddenly the door opened. A young nurse whom she had never seen before stood there. As suddenly as the door had opened, Clara remembered her own name. She cried out: "It's come back – I'm Clara Batchelor. Ring up my father and tell him I'm here. The number is Hammersmith 2159."

The nurse did not answer, but she began to laugh. Slowly, mockingly, inch by inch, though Clara tried with all her strength to keep it open, she closed the door.

She lost herself again; this time completely. For months she was not even a human being; she was a horse. Ridden almost to death, beaten till she fell, she lay at last on the straw in her stable and waited for death. They buried her as she lay on her side, with outstretched head and legs. A child came and sowed turquoises round the outline of her body in the ground, and she rose up again as a horse of magic with a golden mane, and galloped across the sky. Again she woke on the mattress in her cell. She looked and saw that she had human hands and feet again, but she knew that she was still a horse.

She became a human being again. One day a nurse came in, put a coarse brown serge dressing-gown over her nightshirt and took her out of her cell. They went out into a long passage with a shiny waxed floor. There were more nurses there and several other women, all dressed in the same coarse brown dressing-gowns. The nurses all looked fresh and trim but the women were haggard and unkempt. Some of them were old and repellent and all had matted, untidy hair. The nurses formed the women up in a long line, pushing them back when they tried to break out of it. Her own nurse pushed her into the line too. She did not know what was going on at the top of the line. She thought it was some form of torture for she could hear the women ahead of her screaming. At last there was only one in front of her and she could see what was happening. One nurse held the woman down on a chair while another roughly dragged a comb through her tangled hair. Then she took a needle and thread and sewed it into a tight plait. But when her own turn came, they only dragged the comb unmercifully through hers. Someone said:

"It's too short to sew up. Lovely colour isn't it? My goodness, I'd give something to have natural waves like that. What a waste on one of them."

Then two nurses dragged her, one on each side, to an enormous room filled with baths. They dipped her into bath after bath of boiling water. Each bath was smaller than the last, with gold taps that came off in her hands when she tried to clutch them. There was something slightly wrong about everything in this strange bathroom. All the mugs were chipped. The chairs had only three legs. There were plates lying about with letters round the brim, but the letters never read the same twice running. After the hot baths, they ducked her, spluttering and choking, into an ice-cold one. A nurse took a bucket of cold water and splashed it over her, drenching her hair and half blinding her. She screamed, and nurses, dozens of them, crowded round the bath to laugh at her. "Oh Clara, you naughty, naughty girl," they giggled. They took her out and dried her and rubbed something on her eyes and nostrils that stung like fire. She had human limbs, but she was not human; she was a horse or a stag being prepared for the hunt. On the wall was a looking-glass, dim with steam.

"Look, Clara, look who's there," said the nurses.

She looked and saw a face in the glass, the face of a fairy horse or stag, sometimes with antlers, sometimes with a wild golden mane, but always with the same dark stony eyes and nostrils red as blood. She threw up her head and neighed and made a dash for the door. The nurses caught and dragged her along a passage. The passage was like a long room; it had a shiny wooden floor with double iron tracks in it like the tracks of a model railway. The nurses held her painfully by the armpits so that her feet only brushed the floor. The passage was like a musty old museum. There were wax flowers under cases and engravings of Queen Victoria and Balmoral. Suddenly the nurses opened a door in the wall, and there was her cell again. They threw her down on the mattress and went out, locking the door.

She went to sleep. She had a long nightmare about a girl who was lost in the dungeons under an old house on her wedding-day. Just as she was, in her white dress and wreath and veil, she fell into a trance and slept for thirty years. She woke up, thinking she had slept only a few hours, and found her way back to the house, and remembering her wedding, hurried to the chapel. There were lights and flowers and a young man standing at the altar. But as she walked up the aisle, people pushed her back, and she saw another bride going up before her. Up in her own room, she looked in the glass to see an old woman in a dirty satin dress with a dusty wreath on her head. She herself was the girl who had slept thirty years. They had shut her up here in the cell without a looking-glass so that she should not know how old she had grown.

Then she was Richard, endlessly climbing up the steps of a dark tower by the sea, knowing that she herself was imprisoned at the top. She came out of this dream suddenly to find herself being tortured in her own person. She was lying on her back with two nurses holding her down. A young man with a signet ring on his finger was bending over her, holding a funnel with a long tube attached. He forced the tube down her nose and began to pour some liquid into the funnel. There was a searing pain at the back of her nose, she choked and struggled, but they held her down ruthlessly. At last the man drew out the tube and dropped it coiling in a basin. The nurses released her and all three went out and shut the door.

This horror came at intervals for days. She grew to dread the opening of the door, which was nearly always followed by the procession of nurses and the young man with the basin and the funnel. Sometimes, instead of a signet ring, the young man wore one mounted with a white shield that had a red cross on it.

She was changed into a salmon. The salmon was suffocating in a dry, stone-floored cell behind iron bars. Just beyond the bars was the life-giving waterfall. It lay wriggling and gasping, scraping its scales on the stone floor, maddened by the noise of the water it could not reach.

Perhaps she died as a salmon as she had died as a horse, for she woke in a small six-sided room whose walls were all thick bulging panels of grey rubber. The door was rubber-padded too, with a small red window, shaped like an eye, deeply embedded in it. She was lying on the floor, and through the red, a face, stained red too, was watching her and laughing.

The rubber room was a compartment in a sinking ship, near the boiler room which would burst at any minute and scald her to death. Somehow she must get out. She flung herself against the rubber walls as if she could beat her way out by sheer force. The air was getting hotter. The rubber walls were already warm to touch. In a second her lungs would burst. At last the door opened. They were coming to rescue her. But it was the torturers who entered: the young man and the two nurses with the basin and funnel.

One day she found herself sitting on a heap of straw in a small room that was dusty and friendly, like an attic. She was a child of about twelve, dressed in an old blue pinafore. Her name was Clara. She sat patiently, with crossed legs and folded arms, making a spell to bring her brother Richard safe home. He was flying back to her in a white aeroplane with a green propeller. She could see his face quite clearly as he sat between the wings. He wore a fur cap like a cossack's pulled down to his black eyebrows, one of which was a little ragged. Enemies had put Clara in prison, but Richard would come to rescue her as he had always come before. She and Richard loved each other with a love far deeper and more subtle than any love between husband and wife. She knew at once if he were in pain or danger, even if he were a thousand miles away.

Richard came to her window and carried her away. They flew to Russia, and landed on a plain covered with snow. Then they drove for miles in a sledge until they came to a dark pine forest. They walked through the forest, hand in hand, Clara held close in Richard's great fur cape. But at last she was tired, dazed by the silence and the endless trees, all exactly alike. She wanted to lie down in the snow, to sleep.

Richard shook her: "Never go to sleep in the snow, Clara, or you will die."

But she was too tired to listen, and she lay down in the snow that was soft and strangely warm and fell into an exquisite dreamy torpor. And perhaps she did die in the snow as Richard had said, for the next thing she knew was that she was up in the clouds, following a beautiful Indian woman who sailed before her, and sifting snow down on the world through the holes in her blue pinafore.

She was sent back to the world. She was no longer a child. There was someone whom she must reach at all costs. He was a soldier. His name was Richard. She saw a huge, tiered wedding cake. On the top of it was a tiny figure in uniform, wearing a glengarry and tartan trews. The only way to reach him was to be turned into a mouse and gnaw patiently through tier after tier of the cake till she reached the top. She became a mouse. But when she began to gnaw, she found that the cake was made of painted tin. After working painfully for hours, she had only gnawed through an inch and her teeth were too blunt to bite any more.

She became a human being once more. She was no ordinary human being but Lord of the World. Whatever she ordered, came about. The walls of her prison turned to crystal. Beyond them was a garden full of larches and apple-trees, with peacocks strutting on the lawns. One of them had a blue jay's feather in its beak. She turned that peacock into a beautiful young man and the others into children lovelier than dreams. Then she tested her powers by ordering destruction. She changed the garden into a sea and summoned up a storm that blew great ships out of their courses as if they were paper boats. Only herself she could not command. She grew weary of making magic and longed only to sleep. But there was no one powerful enough to order her to sleep.

She raved, she prayed, but no sleep came. At last three old women appeared.

"You cannot sleep unless you die," they said.

She assented gladly. They took her to a beach and fettered her down on some stones, just under the bows of a huge ship that was about to be launched. One of the three gave a signal. Nothing could stop it now.

On it came, grinding the pebbles to dust, deafening her with noise It. passed, slowly, right over her body. She felt every bone crack; felt the intolerable weight on her shoulders; felt her skull split like a shell. But she could sleep now. She was free from the burden of having to will.

After this she was born and re-born with incredible swiftness as a woman, as an imp, as a dog, and finally as a flower. She was some name-less, tiny bell, growing in a stream, with a stalk as fine as hair and a human voice. The water flowing through her flower throat made her sing all day a little monotonous song, "Kulalla, kulalla, kullala, ripitalla, kulalla, kulalla, kulalla, kulla."

This happy flower life did not last long. She found herself a human being once more in a cell unlike any she remembered. She was lying on a mattress in what looked like a great wooden manger clamped to the floor. Over it was stretched a kind of stiff canvas apron, like a piece of sailcloth, fastened to the manger with studs and metal eyelets. At intervals the blank yellow door without a handle opened. Sometimes it was the two nurses and the young man with the funnel; sometimes the two nurses or even only one. When they unfastened the sailcloth and took her out of the manger as they sometimes did, she found she was wearing not a nightshirt but a curious white garment, very stiff and rough, that encased her legs and feet and came down over her hands. She was frightened of the nurses. Sometimes they were rough and called her "naughty girl": sometimes they were friendly and said "good girl". But she could not discover what it was that she did that made them say "naughty" or "good" though she was very anxious they should not be angry. They addressed her as "Clara". She did not know what her name was but she was sure it was not Clara. At first she sulked but soon she saw it pleased them if she answered to it like an animal.

Between the visitations of the nurses and the torture with the funnel, she dozed and dreamt. Or she lay quietly, content to watch, hour after hour, the play of pearly colours on the piece of sailcloth. Though she did not know who she was now, she could remember places and people from another world in which she had once lived. She found she knew several poems, both in English and French and enjoyed saying them over to herself. But if a word or a line had gone, she could only fill the gap with words she made up in a language of her own.

Among the people she remembered was the man who had been her father in that other life. She thought about him quite often: she had been very fond of him. She remembered a mother too: a very beautiful woman with big dark eyes. She remembered her coming up to the nursery to say goodnight, wearing an evening dress that sparkled with gold sequins. But a terrible punishment had fallen on her mother. She had taken a lover and caught small-pox from him. Her husband came home one night and found her face pitted with the marks of it and all her beauty gone. He knew then that she had been unfaithful to him and drove her out of the house on a night of thick fog. In the fog, her mother lost her way, wandered into the river and was drowned. Once her father's face was so vivid to her that she actually fancied he was sitting there beside the manger. She clearly saw not only his face but his shoulders in a grey tweed overcoat she recognised. Everything about that head and shoulders was familiar except the scarf he was wearing. The illusion was so complete that she said aloud:

"Daddy, you've got a new scarf."

But, as she said it, the face crumpled into a grimace which made it unrecognisable and, the next moment, it vanished.

One night there was a thunderstorm. She was terrified. The manger had become a little raft; when she put out her hand she could feel waves lapping right up to the brim. In that other life she had always been afraid of water lapping in the dark. She cried out: "Star of the Sea, pray for us." The Litany of Our Lady came back to her. She began to say it aloud, very slowly and distinctly, in Latin. She had just said "Vas insigne devotionis" when the door opened and a light shone in on the waves that surrounded her. In the doorway stood a nurse she had never seen before. The nurse was very young, with a gentle face, blue eyes and black hair. She knew at once that this girl was not really a nurse. Her name was Kathleen and she was Irish. She had disguised herself as a nurse so as to get into this nightmare place. The Irish girl said softly:

"Rosa Mystica."

"Turris Davidica" she herself replied.

"Turris eburnea."

"Domus aurea."

And thus, turn by turn, they completed the litany. Then the girl disguised as a nurse smiled and closed the door. But now it was light, the storm was over and the manger was no longer a raft on the sea but clamped as usual to the floor and surrounded by dingy yellow walls.

One day she discovered that the sailcloth and the stiff enveloping garment had gone. She was lying under coarse grey blankets and wearing the nightshirt once more. The change was as delicious as if she had been wrapped in silk and covered with swansdown. Her body felt as light as if, but for the weight of the blankets, it would have floated up to the ceiling. She found that she could stand up in the manger. For the first time she saw that there was a window high up in the wall behind it.

Through this window which was barred and covered with close wire netting she could see into a garden. This discovery gave her great pleasure. In the garden women and nurses were walking; they did not look like real people but oddly thin and bright, like figures cut out of coloured paper. And she could see birds flying across the sky, not real birds, but bird-shaped kites, lined with strips of white metal, that flew on wires. Only the clouds had thickness and depth and looked as clouds had looked in the other world. The clouds spoke to her sometimes. They wrote messages in white smoke on the blue. They would take shape after shape to amuse her, shapes of swans, of feathers, of charming ladies with fluffy white muffs and toques, of soldiers in white busbies.

Soon she became more daring. She leapt from the manger on to the high window-sill and crouched there like a cat. But one day she was so absorbed in watching the doll-like figures in the garden that she did not hear the cell-door open. Two nurses dragged her down from her perch. She fought with them. One slapped her and said:

"You know what happens to naughty girls. Do you want to go back to pads?"

The other said:

"The gymnastics they get up to! Almost like animals. She's been so quiet lately, too. Have to put the sheet on her."

They stripped her, forced her struggling limbs back into the heavy canvas garment and fastened her down under the sailcloth again. Exhausted, she fell asleep.

When she woke up again, a nurse was sitting beside her, holding a plate with some porridge in it and a spoon. The nurse kept spooning up bits of it and trying to make her eat. She did not want to eat, because she knew the porridge was poisoned, but the nurse forced a little between her teeth and she had to swallow it. The nurse smiled.

"There, that's a good girl."

Suddenly she noticed the plate the nurse was holding. It had letters printed round the rim. She could not make them all out because the nurse's hand covered part of them. But she could distinctly read the word HOSPITAL. Her mind suddenly became sharp. She asked:

"Is this place a hospital?"

"That's right, dear."

"What kind of a hospital?"

"Ah, that'd be telling," said the nurse slyly.

"Please, I must know. What *kind* of a hospital?"

"A hospital for girls who ask too many questions," said the nurse, thrusting the spoon into her open mouth. Now she knew for certain the porridge was poisoned. She spat it out and her mind went blank again.

CHAPTER TWO

ONE SUNDAY in April, Claude Batchelor returned later than usual from his weekly visit to the asylum. He let himself in so quietly that Isabel, who was waiting for him in the study as she did every Sunday afternoon, did not hear him. When he came into the room and she saw his face, she sprang up from her chair and ran to him.

"Dearest. . . . Is the news bad?"

He held her close, without answering. Then he moved stiffly and haltingly over to his desk and sat down, still not saying a word. Isabel stood, with her hand on his shoulder, anxiously watching his efforts to clench the quivering muscles of his face. He could not control them. With a choking cry, he buried his head in his hands and sobbed.

In all those months he had broken down like that only once: the day he had had to sign the certificate of insanity. Isabel was too shaken by his anguish to formulate any questions, even in her own mind. It was not till the loud, racking sobs ceased as abruptly as they had begun that she asked, with lips gone so dry that she could hardly shape the words:

"She's not dead?"

He lifted his marred face.

"No, thank God. Forgive me for frightening you like that."

"But what is it? . . . What have they said to you?"

"Just let me pull myself together." He fished out his handkerchief and blew his nose violently. Then he put her in the big green armchair and came and sat close to her. Taking her hand, he said:

"My love, we may have to face a rather dreadful possibility. But remember, it is only a possibility."

"Not that she will never get well?" she gripped his hand. "Oh Claude . . . I can't believe it . . . I *won't* believe it."

"No. They are fairly sure now that she will recover eventually."

"Oh, thank God . . . thank God. . . ."

"But, alas, it may not be for a long time."

"How long? A year? Two years even?"

Instead of answering, he leant forward and kissed her.

"If you can bear it, I would rather tell you exactly what he said. It was the head doctor I saw today. Brooke. I had a long talk with him."

"Yes?" she said, staring at him with sad expectancy. Much weeping had dulled her great brown eyes and permanently reddened the lids. "She's no better than she's been all these last weeks?"

He answered slowly:

"In some ways . . . from their point of view . . . there is an improvement. . . . No, wait, my dear. . . . This last violent phase seems to be passing. . . . I was even allowed to see her today. . . ." His face began to twitch again.

"My poor darling . . . how did she look?"

He swallowed hard and went on:

"Very pale and thin. Not, thank God, unhappy. She even smiled sometimes."

"But she still didn't know you?"

"Isabel . . . just for one flash, she did. She said, absolutely in her normal voice 'Daddy, you're wearing a new scarf.' His voice broke and tears came back into his eyes.

"Dearest . . . don't," she said, clasping his hand tight. "Surely that was a hopeful sign? . . . All these months . . . she's never recognised you."

"I thought it hopeful, too."

Ignoring the deadness of his voice, she went on eagerly:

"And the scarf. She was *right* about the scarf. It's the one I gave you for Christmas, and it was November that she was taken ill. She couldn't have seen it when she was well. Oh, darling, she's getting better."

"Hush, my dear. Try and be patient. I haven't told you all the doctor said."

"Very well. But I don't promise to believe it. Doctors aren't infallible."

"He would be the first to admit that. He kept stressing how little is really known about these things. There is some research going on, especially abroad, but so far they are only feeling their way – He impressed me as a remarkably honest man. I felt I could trust him to tell me the truth."

"How can he tell you the truth when he admitted no one knows it?"

"He has immense practical experience. And some facts are known. There are forms of . . . insanity which are recognisable. They know the symptoms . . . they have a fair idea of the course things will take. At first, just because her attack was so sudden and so violent, they thought she might recover, almost as suddenly, in a matter of months. There would have been a danger of its recurring but she might have had long intervals of being perfectly normal. . . ."

"To live with that horror always hanging over her? Could *anything* be worse than that?"

"Perhaps not. Perhaps not. At any rate, that is not what he thinks now."

"What *does* he think?"

He answered, speaking slowly and heavily again:

"That the symptoms are changing. There may possibly be a very marked improvement. What he fears is that she may develop a milder but more chronic form of mania. He has seen it happen before, in cases like hers. When she recovered . . . he says such patients nearly always do recover eventually . . . she would almost certainly be perfectly well for the rest of her life. . . ."

"She's still only twenty-two. What does he mean by the rest of her life?"

He took both her hands.

"My dearest . . . I don't know how to tell you. He can't be sure. . . . But he says the chances are that she may not come out till she is between forty-five and fifty."

She wrenched her hands out of his and covered her face. He moved them gently away. For a moment her eyes glared at him with a terrible bright blankness so like Clara's that he had to look away. She said on a high note:

"How can God be so cruel? Why didn't he let her die? I'd rather . . . far rather you'd told me she was dead."

"Hush, my love, hush." He gathered her in his arms. Her body was rigid and trembling. Then suddenly it went limp against him, and, to his relief, she wept.

He soothed her like a child, kissing her hair and wiping her face with his handkerchief. When at last she was quietened, he said:

"Lie back in the chair for a moment while I get you some whisky."

She lay with closed eyes, hearing him unfasten a cupboard, clink glass against glass, squirt a siphon. Her mind was numb. She could not remember why she had been weeping. She only knew she had lived through all this before, this lying back in a chair with burning eyelids, utterly spent, while a man moved about a room clinking glass, pouring out whisky. When, at last, she opened her eyes, she was half-dazed to find herself in the study. The man holding the glass to her lips was not Reynaud Callaghan but her husband, Claude.

She drank meekly. Her head cleared. She even made a wry mouth and said:

"How I hate the taste of whisky!"

"It will do you good. I've given you so little – See how much I've given myself."

Claude swallowed his in gulps. Faded patches of the old fresh pink came up in his cheeks. Isabel felt hers flush too: a reviving warmth ran down her back. She said:

"I don't wonder people take to drink."

Exhausted as she was, she suddenly felt inclined to talk. She became almost voluble. As if this were any other Sunday since the middle of last November, she began rehearsing over again every circumstance of Clara's breakdown; making all the old conjectures, stirring up all the old hopes as if somewhere there must be something they had overlooked, something they ought to have done, something they might still do. She said, for the hundredth time:

"If they'd left her in the nursing-home just a little longer. Instead of rushing her off to that dreadful place and making you certify her. Oh, I know Mayfield said it was the only thing to do. But how could he *know*? How could a stupid, commonplace man like that understand anyone as sensitive and imaginative as Clara? What she must have gone through in that terrible time with Archie. . . . And then that exquisite, idyllic happiness. . . . Wasn't it enough to unbalance her a little? . . . If they'd only waited . . . given her a moment's breathing space. . . ."

"My dear," he said, as he had said it so often before: "What else could we do? . . . We were in Mayfield's hands. . . . He thought it was the best place. . . . Remember, when he and I took her there, there was no shadow of doubt in any of *their* minds. . . ."

"A public asylum. Our darling child in a public asylum."

He said wearily.

"You know how terribly against the grain it went to send her there. If he thought a private home would have been better, I'd have sold what little I have, taken on any amount of extra work to pay the fees. But his argument seemed sound . . . still does seem sound. With a private home, there's always the suspicion they might want to keep them longer than strictly necessary, just because of the fees. And, if I were to die, who could go on paying them? Nazareth has the best record of all the public ones. They've got the best doctors. Mayfield's not the only one who's assured me of that. And, since they always have people waiting for admission, they *want* to discharge patients as soon as they reasonably can. Dearest, we've been into it all so often before."

"The fact remains she's been far, far worse since she went there. And the terrible things they do to her. This forcible feeding . . . oh, it's unbearable to think of."

"I wish I'd never told you about that, Isabel. But you dragged it out of me."

"It's what they did to those poor suffragettes in prison. I heard a woman who'd been forcibly fed speak once. I've never forgotten her description of it."

"It was only done as a last resort. She was starving herself to death. They don't think she knew what was happening."

"Don't tell me you can't feel pain, however deluded you are."

"Well, at least he thinks that will no longer be necessary. The nurse has managed, at last, to persuade her to eat a little. They've been very patient with her."

"Not as patient as I would be. . . . But they won't let me see her. Her own mother."

"Dearest, you know it only upsets you both."

"How can it upset her when she doesn't even recognise me?"

"Isabel, you know what happened the last time. Obviously it isn't you she sees or thinks she sees, but some terrifying hallucination."

"She doesn't know you yet she's not frightened when she sees you. Not since that dreadful night at Nell Crayshaw's. Why of me? In real life it was you she used to be frightened of. Never me."

"Isabel," he pleaded. "Don't remind me of that. If you knew how I'd searched my conscience, wondering if I were in any way respon sible. I I hadn't often been too harsh with her."

Her voice dropped its high, monotonous note of complaint . . .

"Dearest, of course it's not your fault. You mustn't let that terrible conscience of yours torment you. How could it be your fault?"

He sighed.

"I don't know. That first night, it seemed like a judgement on me."

"A judgement for what? There's not a better, more conscientious man in the world."

He shook his head.

"Only God knows how much evil there is in me. That was how *she* saw me that first night . . . as an evil spirit."

"She was obsessed with the idea of evil spirits. You even thought the poor child was possessed, and wanted to call in a priest. It wasn't till you gave her your rosary . . ."

"How often I've thought of that . . . that Catholic nurse telling us how she said the rosary aloud with her before her mind went altogether. They tell me even now, in there . . . they sometimes hear her praying. . . ."

"Why doesn't God hear her prayers? . . . and ours? Is there one single day we haven't prayed from the bottom of our hearts?"

He took her hand.

"My dear, we must be patient. Perhaps He will hear them. At least. He will give us strength to hear it."

"I haven't your resignation," she said. "I can't believe God could be so cruel. Wasn't it enough to strike her just when she had her first real chance of happiness? But to condemn her to this living death. Not to let her get well till she's almost an old woman.'. . ." Her voice rose. "I can't believe it. I won't believe it. I trust Richard more than any doctor. *He's* always been certain she'd get well."

"Dearest, how can he know? He wants to believe it. And he wants to comfort us."

"He has intuitions about her. Didn't he know she was ill that night? Didn't he start to drive back from Wiltshire to London? And she saw everything that was happening all those miles away . . . the accident . . . everything. That wasn't delusion. Richard told Nell that Clara was right in every detail."

"I know . . . I know, my dear. It was as if she had second sight. But in her abnormal state . . . I believe there are other instances . . ."

"It doesn't account for Richard's knowing something was wrong with her. He was as sane as you or I. No, there is some extraordinary bond between those two. They belong to each other. They can't be torn apart for ever."

He put his hand to his forehead and made no reply. After a while he said in a changed voice:

"Isabel. There's something I want to talk to you about. In the first shock, I could only think about Clara . . . and ourselves. . . . But there are others to whom this is going to be a terrible blow."

"Richard? He won't believe it. Any more than I do."

"Richard, yes. And also, Archie."

She said angrily:

"This eternal concern of yours for Archie. If anyone is to blame for her breakdown, he is."

"What right have we to say that? God knows it's what the poor boy feels himself. Don't you know how utterly wretched he's been ever since I had to tell him? Haven't you any pity for him?"

"Oh, I'm not saying he deliberately wrecked her life – But think of the change in her after three months of that ghastly marriage. Have you forgotten that morning you went to Chelsea? You told me – here in this very room – that she struck you as nearly out of her mind. . . ."

"Must we go over it all again? Does it make things any better for her – or us? I believe *she* would be sorry for Archie."

"She was always far too generous about that wretched boy. All right . . . he loved her in his feeble, selfish way. But how can you think of him in the same breath as Richard? That's *true* love. I think he'd have gone out of his own mind if it weren't for that wonderful confidence. . . ."

He said slowly:

"Yes. But I shall have to break this to him. He rang me up last night from his sister's place. He knows I was seeing the head doctor today."

"Need you tell him all you told me?"

"I promised faithfully."

"He won't believe it."

"I'm not so sure."

"Why? Claude, ever since he's been back in England, he's come to see us every time he was on leave. And every single time he's told us he was certain she'd be completely cured. He was sure it would be quite soon."

"Yes, poor boy. He's kept it up with us. Yet I've fancied lately that, in his own mind. . . . Remember there's already one tragedy of this kind in his own family."

"Nell's husband's case is entirely different. His brain was damaged. I never have . . . I never *will* believe that Clara is insane. Certainly not permanently insane."

"My dear . . . there's a terrible problem we all have to face. Even supposing our worst fears aren't justified . . . the cruel fact remains – Is it ever going to be right for Clara to risk marrying and having children?"

"Children . . . perhaps not. But if there were any real risk for her or for them, surely even the Church would allow . . ."

"No, my dear. That is out of the question."

"Oh, the Church is inhuman about marriage. If it weren't entirely run by men . . . if women were only allowed some say . . ."

"My dear, there are times when we all feel that the Church demands the impossible. When we're calmer, we remember *why* she demands it.

"I can't believe that God Himself would wish to keep those two apart. Two creatures made for each other – Aren't they to be allowed any human happiness . . .?"

"Isabel, my dear – What use are these wild speculations? You're only torturing yourself. We must . . . we *must* realise the facts. We can't let that boy wreck his life in impossible hopes. . . . It's only common justice."

"Justice," she said bitterly. "What justice is there in all this?"

"Oh my dear . . . that's something we can't understand." He put his arms round her. "We can only go on in the dark. Let me ring up Richard. He'll have been waiting in suspense all this time."

"What are you going to say to him?"

"Just what I said to you. Go into the next room, my dear. It would be too painful for you . . ."

"And him? To hear that on the telephone? Claude, you can't be so cruel. Ask him to come here and tell him yourself."

He said remorsefully:

"Yes. Of course. What a coward I am . . ."

"Would you like me to be there too?"

He hesitated.

"For my sake, yes. For his sake, no. . . . Men sometimes find it easier . . ."

Within an hour, Richard arrived. Claude was listening for his ring. When it came, he hurried at once to answer it. But before he reached the study door, he stopped and, on a sudden impulse, went to the mantelpiece, took down the two photographs of Clara as an obstinate child in a Hussar cap and as a demure, uncertain girl of sixteen and shut them in a drawer of his desk.

Two hours later, when Richard had gone, he took them out again and put them back in their old place. His eyes filled as he did so but he had no strength left to weep. He went and sat for a long time at his desk staring blankly at the rows of green-backed files in the bookcase and the dusty plaster cast of Athene. At last he took out the much-mended black rosary that had never left him since he picked it up from the floor by Clara's bed the day they had taken her from the nursing-home to the asylum. Pressing its cheap white metal crucifix against his forehead, he muttered over and over again in his mind:

"If it be Thy will. . . . If it be Thy will."

Then as the weary certainty came to him that he could live through another day and then another, he whispered aloud:

"If I have done wrong, punish me. But, oh my Lord, spare *her*."

CHAPTER THREE

GRADUALLY she became aware of certain changes. The most remarkable was that, whenever she was fully awake, she was always the same person. This person was called Clara. She was almost sure that, in the other life, her name had also been Clara. She wished she knew what she looked like but there was no looking-glass in her cell. The stiff garment and the sailcloth had gone: she no longer dreaded the opening of the door since the torturers with the funnel never appeared now.

Sometimes nurses came in and washed her. She grew interested in the body they washed and began to recognise certain features of it. If it was not the body she had had in the old life, it seemed definitely to belong to her. It was very thin, with hipbones that stuck out like knobs and shrunken, weak-looking legs. One day, as the nurse was washing her left arm, she noticed that about an inch of skin on the inner side was marked with small red blotches like a rash. In the other life, she had had a birthmark in the same place on her left arm. Her gaze moved down to the hand the nurse was washing. The bones stood out and the nails were discoloured and broken yet she could have sworn it was the hand she had had long ago.

One of the nurses said:

"What are you looking for, dear? Your wedding ring? Don't worry. It's put away safe. It kept falling off your finger."

"Wedding-ring?" she asked. "Am I married, then?"

"Must be, dear. You're down on the list as Mrs. Something-Something. Never can remember these double-barrelled names. We always call you Clara, don't we?"

"Yes. But who *is* Clara? And what am I doing here?"

"Never mind that now, dear. Give us your other hand like a good girl."

When they went out, they forgot to shut the door of the cell. She could hardly believe her good fortune. At first she was too delighted to have something new to look at, instead of the blank yellow surface of the door, to do more than stare contentedly. She could see a section of a passage and, in the far wall, a large window. The window gave on another wall, covered with a creeper that was just showing tiny shoots. Occasionally a nurse passed down the passage and, once, an untidy-looking woman in a brown dressing-gown. A similar brown dressing-gown hung on a peg in her cell. She was shivering with cold, even under the blankets. Very cautiously, she got out of the manger bed. The stone floor was like ice under her bare feet. As she put on the dressing-gown, she was seized with violent curiosity. She tiptoed out into the empty passage. At the far end it opened out into a kind of hall. In the hall was a fireplace in which was a beautiful leaping fire. There were women sitting round it; some in brown dressing-gowns, some in ordinary, but very ill-fitting clothes. Irresistibly drawn by the warmth and the flames, she padded silently down the passage and joined the women by the fire. They stared at her sullenly, but let her come close and hold out her hands to the blaze. But, just as her chilled body had begun to enjoy the heat, two nurses seized her under her armpits and dragged her away from the heavenly fire. They forced her back along the passage back into her cell and slammed the door on her.

There came another time when they left the cell door open. Remembering what had happened before, she resisted the tremendous temptation to go in search of the fire again. She contented herself with staring at the creeper on the wall beyond the window and was rewarded with a charming sight. Slowly, the tiny shoots lengthened and unfurled until they became green leaves. Then, suddenly, all the leaves began to dance, beating one against the other like thousands of miniature clapping hands. This made her very happy. She knew the leaves were dancing and clapping to encourage her.

A small space about her became solid and recognisable. In that space objects and people were always the same. There were two nurses who were quite distinct to her now whereas, before, there seemed to have been fifty different faces under starched caps and shapes in blue dresses and white aprons. Both were young and pretty: she liked one and feared the other. The one she liked had red hair and green eyes; the other was blue-eyed and fair. Once, when they were making up the manger bed, she heard them address each other as "Smith" and

"Jones". The red-haired one was Jones. She must try and remember that.

It was extraordinarily difficult to remember things. Words like 'before' and 'after' no longer had any meaning. There was only 'now'. Very occasionally there was a tiny thread of continuity, such as walking to the fire and being dragged away from it. But it always snapped off short and she would find herself in the middle of doing something without any idea how she had come to be doing it. Once she found herself standing on a rostrum in a room full of desks. At every desk a young man was sitting, with a notebook open in front of him. Beside her stood an elderly man with a beard, writing something on a blackboard. She snatched up a piece of chalk from the table in front of her and threw it at one of the young men. He laughed. Gradually all the rest of them began to laugh too and she joined in. The man at the blackboard turned round and said:

"That's enough, gentlemen. However, you have now observed that this patient's reactions are entirely different from those of the typical melancholic you saw a few minutes ago."

Often she found herself in a long tiled washroom with a row of basins at which other women were washing themselves. On the other side of the washroom was a row of lavatories unlike any she had ever seen. They had no doors to them and, instead of a chain, a thick brass rod hung down from the cistern. She so often found herself in this place that she came to recognise some of the other women who used it. Nearly all of them were middle-aged or old. Stripped to the waist, their shrivelled or pendulous breasts repelled her. But there was one quite young with a milk-white skin and firm round breasts. Clara always tried to take the basin next to the white-skinned girl. Sometimes they smiled at each other. Occasionally the girl gave a peculiar look and said, as if she were telling a secret:

"We're going to have lots of little sunny breezes today. And lovely sunny weather.

She never said anything else.

One day, in the washroom, a shaft of tempered sunlight came in through a high barred window at one end. There was a tree beyond the window, so that the light was tinged with green. The girl was standing full in the shaft so that her torso looked almost translucent. It was no longer white but touched with faint rose and green reflections

231

and dappled with moving shadows of leaves. Clara stared entranced at this beauty. It reminded her of something. She said:

"You look exactly like a Renoir."

The girl gave her a suspicious glance. For a moment, Clara thought she was going to be angry. But immediately she gave her usual smile and said confidingly:

"We're going to have *lots* of little sunny breezes. . . ."

Another thing that recurred was finding herself sitting up in the manger bed with a plate of food balanced on her knees. The food looked strangely unreal, like the painted cardboard food in dolls' teasets. The knives were blunt, too, like doll's knives. She usually ate the unreal, completely tasteless food because she wanted to see the pattern on the plates. She could see all the printed letters round the rim now. They read NAZARETH ROYAL HOSPITAL. When the centre of the plate was visible, it showed a picture of a rather handsome building with a pillared portico and a dome. The dome was like some dome she had seen before, but much more slender. She puzzled a great deal about the words and the picture. What and where could this hospital be? And why was she in it? One day it occurred to her that Nazareth was a misprint for Lazarus. Hadn't there been something called a Lazar House? Wasn't a Lazar House a place where lepers were segregated. But how could she have caught leprosy? Her mind became muddled and she gave up the effort to think.

Two things made it very hard to think consecutively. One was that, though she could now recognise certain sections of the place she was in, there was no way of connecting them together. They were like islands with a blank, featureless stretch of sea between them. How did one get from one to the other? It was the same with people; Smith, Jones and "Sunny Breezes" materialised and dematerialised. What happened to them in between? Even more confusing was the impossibility of establishing any sequence in time. For time behaved in the most extraordinary way. Sometimes it went at a tremendous pace, as when she saw the leaves of the creeper unfurl before her eyes like a slow motion film, or the nurses, instead of walking along the passage, sped by as fast as cars. Yet, often, it seemed to take her several hours to lift a spoon from her plate to her mouth.

Nevertheless, she continued to try desperately to piece things together, to find some connection between Clara *here* and Clara *there*. She was becoming slowly convinced that this extraordinary place not only existed but existed somewhere in the world she had once inhabited.

One day she was looking beyond the open door through the window when a bright idea struck her. Why had she never realised it before? She was in Looking-Glass Land. Of course everything was peculiar. Of course time behaved in this extraordinary way. She was so delighted at this discovery that she laughed out loud. At that moment Jones appeared in the open doorway. Jones said, smiling:

"You seem very cheery all of a sudden. That's a nice change. Going to tell me the joke?"

"I've discovered where I am. In the Looking-Glass."

"There's no looking-glasses in this ward, dear."

"I mean I've gone through. I'm like Alice Through the Looking-Glass."

"Who's she when she's at home?"

"A girl in a book. Not me. I'm Clara."

The red-haired nurse looked very pleased.

"Well, did you ever? You *are* coming on. Doctor B. will be ever so bucked. Ta-ta for now."

She smiled and hurried away. Later she came back with a bundle of old magazines.

"It was you mentioning books. Thought you might like to look at 'em to pass the time. They're old ones, so it doesn't matter if you mess them up."

Clara was very grateful for the magazines. She turned the pages and looked at the pictures. They reminded her of the other life. But soon they began to make her unhappy and confused. In one was a photograph of a dark, handsome young man in uniform who seemed to stare at her challengingly and ask: "Now who am I like?" She threw that magazine on the floor and picked up one called *Punch*. She read some of the words under the pictures but they did not seem to make much sense. Suddenly she notice something extraordinary . . . the date of the magazine. It was January 4th 1922. Another of those bright flashes came into her head. She was quite sure the year in the other life was 1921. If this place was in the same world, it should be 1921 here too.

But Jones had said these were *old* magazines. Was it a misprint? Then she grasped it. Here – in Looking-Glass Land – one could read things before they were written. Excitedly, she picked up the *Punch* again. Under a drawing she read:

> *Butler.* I'm afraid I shall 'ave to give notice, my Lady. Roulette and chemaing-de-fur I 'ave countenanced, but I cannot bear to see your guests stoopin' to 'put-and-take', which I understand is all the rage of the lower classes.

Of course she could not understand the meaning of such words as 'chemaing-de-fur' and 'put-and-take'. They belonged to the language of the future. Exhausted by her discoveries and by the effort of reading, she fell asleep.

She often stood up in the manger and looked out into the garden where the nurses and the women walked. They looked more like real people now. She came to recognise some of the women, especially one with a swarthy, cheerful face and a mass of short frizzy hair, who sometimes waved to her as she passed. One day, Jones came in and caught her waving back. Clara cowered down, terrified that this would mean some new punishment. But Jones only said:

"Keep on like this and we'll be getting *you* out in the garden one of these days."

The cell door was open all day now and only locked at night. Clara guessed now what the big keys that hung on Smith's waistbelt were for. At night she could hear the sound of grinding locks approaching all down the passage, sometimes followed by screams and the sound of fists beating on wood. One night, Smith came in looking cross and dishevelled. Clara implored:

"Please don't lock me in. I promise not to get out. *Please* . . ." She put out her hand and touched the key.

Smith said furiously:

"None of that, my lady. I've had enough trouble with you bitches for one day."

She rapped Clara hard on the knuckles with the great key. Clara cried out and pressed her hurt hand to her mouth.

"Oh God," said Smith. "Now I suppose you'll split on me."

Clara looked at her and saw that Smith's pert, pink and white face was frightened as well as angry. She said:

"I won't. I'll tell Jones I banged it on the door. People do bang on these doors."

Smith looked relieved.

"You've more sense than some of them," she said, as she went out. Clara fancied she locked the door less fiercely than usual.

One day, Smith and Jones came in carrying some clothes over their arms.

"Come on, Clara, we're going to dress you."

It felt very strange having clothes put on her. Stranger still, she seemed to recognise some of the clothes. There was a dark blue dress she was sure she had seen before. It hung on her thin body like a tent. She said:

"Where's the belt? It had a red belt."

"Well, it hasn't got one now," said Smith.

"But it *must* have some kind of belt. Look how loose it is."

"Miss Particular, aren't we, all of a sudden?"

Jones said kindly:

"Don't worry dear. No one'll notice. None of the other ladies have belts either."

"You and Smith have belts."

"That's enough of that. And we're *Nurse* Smith and *Nurse* Jones to you."

Jones said:

"Oh, Smithy, stop narking at her. Put your coat on, Clara dear. Look . . . a nice new coat."

Clara frowned.

"It's not my coat. I had a fur coat once."

Smith began to giggle.

"Oh, stop it, Smithy. Yes, dear, I'm sure you had. But it's too warm to wear it today. It's a lovely spring afternoon."

Clara put on the unfamiliar beige wool coat. Jones ran a comb through her hair.

"Lovely natural waves, you've got," she said kindly.

"Have I?"

"Yes, dear. Lucky you're a real blonde. You can't fool us with peroxide here. There. You look quite sweet."

"Almost human, if you didn't know," Smith said it under her breath, but Clara heard. She asked:

235

"Jones . . . I mean *Nurse* Jones . . . have I got leprosy?"

"Leprosy? What an idea! Of course not."

"Or . . . or small-pox?"

"Whatever next?"

"Promise?"

"I'll prove it." She bent forward and gave Clara a quick kiss. "There!"

"You make me sick sometimes, Jones," said Smith. "What's the good of being soft with them? Only leads to trouble."

Her legs were so weak that they had to support her, one on each side. They took her along the corridor, through the hall-like space where the grate was empty now, and out through a glass-topped door. To her disappointment, Clara found herself, not in the pleasant garden she could see from her cell, but in an asphalt yard surrounded by high brick walls. On one of the walls was chalked in big, sprawling letters:

> Baby
> Blood
> Murder

There was no green in the yard except a trampled patch of grass in the middle, surrounding a plane tree whose buds were barely visible. Under the tree was a broken bench. Smith and Jones led her to the bench and sat one on each side. Clara no longer wanted to talk. She was watching the other women walking round the asphalt yard, all in charge of nurses. She recognised some she had seen in the wash-room. 'Sunny Breezes' was there. She stood out from the others because she looked like a neat schoolgirl with her plaited hair and her trim dark blue coat. She walked with precision, as if at the head of the drill file, whereas the others loped or shambled. There were two faces she had not seen before. They were both terrifying. One belonged to an elderly woman who wore a hat and a tweed coat and skirt. It could hardly be called a face for the features were partly obliterated and the skin was red-glazed and puckered as if the flesh had been burnt away. The other face was that of a monster, half-human, half-animal. The human part was almost classically beautiful with a broad forehead under wiry black curls and great eyes that seemed to be carved out of green stone. But the mouth was hideously deformed. Two long yellow eye-teeth grew down over the lower lip, like the fangs of an old tiger. Suddenly, the creature, who was tall and strongly-built, caught sight of Clara and made a dash for her. Her nurses ran and pulled her back, but not before she had cuffed one and torn the other's cap off.

Smith said:

"That Micky playing up again. Bet she'll have to go back to pads."

Clara cowered against Jones's shoulder. Then she noticed something that made her forget her fear. Beyond one wall, she could see a high, slender dome like the one on the plates. There was a gilt spearhead at the apex that glittered in the sun. At the same moment, she heard the sound of a motor-horn beyond the walls. Something stirred in her mind. That car belonged to someone called Richard. He was looking for her, to carry her away from this dreadful place. But how could she let him know that she was so near, on the other side of the wall? She called despairingly: "Richard . . . I'm here . . . I'm here."

"Stop that now," said Smith.

The asphalt yard became another fixed point in her life. She learnt to associate it with the ringing of a bell and a voice calling: "Ladies for the garden, please." She joined the sad procession that trailed round and round the patch with the plane tree. Smith and Jones no longer held her arms: sometimes they let her walk alone. She liked this, for she could snatch a blade of grass as she passed. She knew now that it was useless to hope anything from the motor horns. He would never be allowed to pass through the walls. But he might have found another way to communicate with her. In the lines ruled on a blade of grass there might be a message, if she could only decipher it.

She spent much of her time wearing ordinary clothes now. They did not seem to mind if she wandered up and down the passage and even looked through the open doors of other cells. What strange-looking people there were in them. There was one who fascinated her. She was an old lady who wore very elaborate white draperies and a strange headdress like the Duchess's in Alice in Wonderland. The walls of her cell were covered with water-colours of garden-scenes. The old lady was often standing at a small easel, painting. She took no notice of Clara until, one day, she said rather severely:

"You should curtsy to me, you know."

Clara curtsied obediently. It seemed quite natural to do so. This person so obviously belonged to Looking-Glass Land.

"That's better," said the old lady more agreeably. "I see you are quite intelligent. You know a queen when you see one."

"I wasn't sure if you were a queen or a duchess."

"I am here incognito, of course. Just until my lawsuit is settled. My solicitors think it is safer for me. I have so many enemies who wish to defraud me of my rights. Of course I cannot mix with most of the people here. I am used to intelligent society."

After that Clara always curtsied when she passed the old lady's cell, whether the occupant acknowledged her existence or not.

CHAPTER FOUR

ONE DAY, she woke to find herself in entirely new surroundings. She was lying, not in the manger but in a real bed ... an ordinary iron bedstead that had not only blankets but coarse sheets. She stared about her in delight. It was almost like being in a tiny bedroom in the other world. The walls were painted blue and on them hung a small mirror. The floor was of stained boards and had a narrow strip of carpet on it. Best of all, there was a handle on the door. She got out of bed excitedly and put on her clothes which were lying neatly folded on a chair. It worried her more than ever that her dress had no belt. She thought of tying a stocking round her waist and then realised it would look even more absurd to go about wearing only one stocking than a loose-hanging dress. That was the sort of slovenly thing those dreadful women in the yard did. At all costs she must avoid looking like them. By the window (it was barred, but it looked otherwise like an ordinary window and gave out on the familiar garden) was a small low cupboard on which lay a brush and comb. The brush and comb were marked "Hughes–Follett". Since they obviously did not belong to her, she wondered if she dared to use them. But she had such a desire to make herself as neat as possible in honour of this wonderful room that she went to the mirror and began to brush and comb her hair. The face it reflected reminded her strongly of someone she knew, someone who might even once have been herself. The hair was thick and golden and wavy. It seemed more familiar than the face. She went on brushing it till it shone, trying to get used to this rather odd-looking face with the sharp, pointed chin and the neck that showed the collar-bones. The lips were almost as pale as the cheeks. In spite of its haggardness the face seemed strangely young, almost like a child's.

The door opened and a nurse whom Clara had never seen came in. She was fat and middle-aged, with a severe expression. Clara guiltily dropped the brush.

"So you've got yourself up and dressed, have you?" said the nurse. "Actually brushing your hair too. Good."

"I'm sorry I used this brush," Clara stammered. "You see I haven't one of my own."

"They're yours, all right. Can't you read?"

Some instinct warned Clara to make no comment. She said humbly: "What a lovely room. May I really stay in it?"

"As long as you behave yourself, yes. Now, do you think you can keep it tidy?"

"Oh yes," said Clara eagerly.

"Hmm. When I come back, let me see if you know how to make a bed."

The nurse went out. At first the task seemed impossible. The sheets and blankets tangled themselves into a shapeless mess. But she persevered with desperate concentration. Suddenly she remembered how one made a bed. She smoothed and tucked and folded slowly, but competently. Somewhere, a long time ago, she had done this every morning for critical eyes. She remembered a long row of white-curtained cubicles, and children in blue uniforms and black aprons making beds. The door clicked open with a sound so much like that of a nun's wooden 'signal' that she turned and said, without thinking:

"Are my corners all right today, Mother?"

The woman facing her wore, not a black habit but a nurse's uniform. She examined the bed.

"You've done that very nicely, Clara," she said. "You could give some of my nurses points. Your mother certainly taught you how to make a bed properly. But I'm not your mother, you know. I'm Sister Ware. Try and remember that."

"Yes, Sister Ware."

The room brought very definite changes in her life. Instead of having plates of food brought to her, she had her meals with other women at a long table in a big, bare dining-room. These women did not look so shabby and forlorn as the ones in the asphalt yard. When she tried to talk to them they answered, often very politely, but entirely at cross-purposes. The asphalt yard had vanished too, along with Smith and Jones and Micky and the woman with the burned face. She was sorry never to see Jones now. She did not like Sister Ware, though she made great efforts to please her But there were compensations. She did at last find herself in the real garden. It was summer there. Flowers were coming out; peonies and irises. There were daisies in the grass. No one seemed to mind if she wandered off by herself, provided she joined the line of other women when the bell rang. There were still gaps in time she could not account for but the recognisable islands had grown much larger.

One day, the door of her room opened and Sister Ware came in followed by a young man in a white jacket. Clara gave a start of terror when she saw his face. It was the young man who used to come in with the funnel and the basin.

"Now, don't be frightened, Clara," he said. "I see you recognise me."

She asked miserably:

"Is that going to begin again?"

"No, no, no. Not as long as you go on being so good. Sister Ware's very pleased with you. I just thought I'd drop in for a little chat. How nice and tidy your room is. Do you keep it tidy yourself?"

Sister Ware said:

"Yes, she does. Mislays her things sometimes, but pretty fair considering. She's improved a lot in Ward C."

"How would you like to have something to do? Some knitting, for example?"

"I don't know how to knit."

Sister Ware looked disapproving.

"I'm told you used to be very fond of reading. Would you like some nice books?"

"Thank you very much," said Clara meekly.

"How are you getting on with the other ladies? Made any friends?"

"I don't know what to talk to them about. They don't answer what I say."

"Dear, dear, that's very rude of them. Well, now is there anything you feel you *would* like?"

He looked so amiable that she faltered bravely:

"I couldn't go away from here, could I?"

"What, away from your nice room and Sister Ware? Don't you like it here?"

"I don't know," she said dully. She saw Sister Ware frowning and added hastily: "I mean, yes. It's very nice."

The young man said cheerfully:

"You'll see it can be nicer still if you go on being good. Lots of people would rather be here than anywhere else. We have good fun sometimes. Concerts, you know. And twice a year we have a dance. I bet you dance well. I'll book you as a partner for the next one. Doctor Bennett, my name is. Cheerio for now."

Sister Ware prompted reproachfully:

"Say, Goodbye, Doctor."

"Goodbye, Doctor."

When they had gone, she sat for a long time on her bed, trying to puzzle things out. Later, Sister Ware returned with a book.

"Don't read it all at once. You can't have another till next week."

The book was by someone called Dornford Yates. She began to read it without much enjoyment. But, as she was reading, a wonderful idea came to her. The next time Sister Ware came in, she said daringly:

"I suppose I couldn't have a pencil and some paper, could I?"

"I'll have to ask doctor about that."

"Please . . . he did ask me if there was anything I would like."

"Give some people an inch and they take an ell," said Sister Ware crossly. "You'll be asking for the moon next, I suppose." She went out, banging the door behind her.

Clara could not help crying a little. But, for the next few days, she made tremendous efforts to be "good". She noticed that some of the other women helped the nurses clear away the plates at mealtimes and she imitated them. The nurses seemed pleased. She heard one say to another "H.F.s coming on. She'll settle down all right."

She made more effort to talk to the other women. She was beginning to feel cut off and lonely. She noticed some of them giggled and chattered together quite happily. But, when she listened in to their conversations, they sounded almost meaningless. It was like listening to children talking. Each seemed to be talking aloud to herself and taking no notice of what the others said. Yet they seemed to have some sort of communication with each other. She began to wonder what was the difference between the women and the nurses. The nurses' chat was dull but easy to follow. And their faces looked different. There was something odd about the women's faces even though some of them were quite good-looking and had powdered cheeks and carefully arranged hair. It was something about their eyes, she decided. They had a sly, shallow look and they were always straying restlessly as if looking for something or someone. She wished she could find out what secret they all had in common and which she seemed unable to share. One afternoon, in the garden, she discovered what it was. Three of them came up to her, looking sly but friendly. One asked, with a giggle:

"Do you play croquet, dear?"

With astonishing confidence, Clara answered:

"Yes."

"Come on . . . we'll have a lovely game."

She went with them to a lawn she had not seen before. As soon as she saw the wide, bent hoops, she knew they were the wrong shape. The hoops at Paget's Fold were straight and narrow. Someone gave her an old mallet. She said firmly to the woman nearest her:

"You and I will be partners. Shall we take blue and black?"

"I'd rather be red."

"All right, we'll take red and yellow."

"No, dear. You have blue and I'll have red. I always have red. Up the rebels!"

In vain Clara tried to explain the rules of croquet. They had come back with absolute clarity. But it was hopeless. No one could understand. In the end she left them running gaily about the lawn, hitting any ball they saw and usually all playing at once.

Her first thought was. "Alice in Wonderland again. They might as well play with hedgehogs and flamingos." But the next moment, it came to her. These women were mad. All those women she saw at mealtimes were mad. No wonder she could make no contact with them. She was imprisoned in a place full of mad people.

She controlled her impulse to break into panic-stricken tears. She must think with all her might. She sat down on the grass, frowning with the effort. Croquet. A place called Paget's Fold. Who was it she used to play croquet with there? Her *father*! She could not remember when she had last thought about him. Perhaps he was still there in the world beyond the walls. How, how could she let him know where she was, since she did not know herself?

243

She stood up and began to pace up and down a path, not looking where she was going. Someone bumped into her.

"Hullo, all on your lonesome?"

It was Doctor Bennett.

"Yes. I was thinking."

"Were you now? And what were you thinking about?"

She was going to say "My father" but one had to be careful here. She smiled and said:

"Did Sister Ware ask you if I could have that pencil and paper?"

"So we'd like a pencil and paper? I daresay it might be managed. May one ask what you want to do with it?"

She said cautiously:

"Can people send letters from here?"

He gave her a considering look.

"Well, that depends. Who were you thinking of writing to?"

She decided to risk it.

"My father," she said.

"Well, well. And who is your father?"

It came to her as clearly as if she were reading it off his white coat.

"Claude Batchelor, 22 Valetta Road, W.14."

He asked gently:

"How long have you known that?"

"I've just remembered it." With sudden despondence, she added: "Perhaps he's dead."

"No, Clara. He's not dead."

"How do you know?" she asked, suspiciously.

"You must take my word for it. Come, come, we aren't enemies, you know. Would you like to write your father a note?"

She shook her head and began to cry a little.

"I haven't a stamp. . . . And where could I post it?"

"Now, now we're not going to be silly and cry, are we? I'll give you some paper and a pencil and a stamped envelope. You can come with me and I'll give you them now. I'm trusting you and you must trust me. If you write a nice, tidy letter, I'll see that it's posted.

She looked at his finger and saw he was wearing the signet ring, not the white shield with the red cross.

She said hesitantly:

244

"Very well. I'll trust you."

He took her into a room with a desk in it. Out of the desk-drawer he took three sheets of paper, a pencil and a stamped envelope.

"Now mind. If you spoil that envelope, you won't get another. And if you break the pencil, no one will give you a knife to sharpen it."

"Sister Ware. . . . Suppose she thinks I've stolen them?"

"I'll fix Sister Ware. Come on, I'll take you back to your room."

She could hardly wait to be left alone with her treasures. As soon as the door closed, she sat down, put a sheet of paper on the flat top of the cupboard and tried to write. But she had forgotten how to make letters. She took the Dornford Yates novel and began laboriously copying the print. It looked all wrong. She took another sheet, started at the left and tried to write cursively. But she could not do it. Then she realised her mistake. She was trying to write the wrong way round. In Looking-Glass Land one must use looking-glass writing. She began again at the right hand side and wrote backwards, reversing the letters. Her hand moved quickly and easily. She wrote a few sentences and held them up to the mirror on the wall. The writing was a little shaky but perfectly legible. Then it occurred to her that her father was on the other side of the looking-glass. It would be more sensible to write the way they did there.

She sat down again and stared at the third and last precious sheet. With a great effort she made her hand begin at the left. It was extraordinarily difficult to make the letters go that way. But she persevered, using all the concentration she could muster. Though it became a little easier after the first few words, she was tempted again and again to give up the task as hopeless. But, at last, she got to the end and read it through.

"Dearest Daddy,

I do not know where I am but I think it is Nazareth Royal Hospital. That is what it says on the plates. Please try and find me. I want so much to see you again. Please try hard. Perhaps you thought I was dead. I am alive but in a very strange place. Doctor Bennett (?) has promised to post this.

Your loving daughter,

Clara."

She sealed the envelope, addressed it carefully, and put the letter under her pillow. That night she could hardly sleep for fear the doctor should forget his promise.

In the morning he came in while she was still in bed. But someone else came in with him; an elderly man with a beard. Clara looked at the stranger and said:

"I've seen you before, I think."

"Have you indeed?" said the bearded man. "And where was that?"

"On a rostrum. Writing things on a blackboard."

The two men exchanged glances.

"Quite right," said the one with the beard. "My name is Doctor Brooke. We shall meet again. I've only come in to say goodbye. I'm going away on a holiday."

"Oh, you're *lucky*," she said, before she could stop herself.

He frowned, but he did not seem angry.

"Well, one never knows. Now I want you to be a very good girl while I'm away. You must do everything Doctor Bennett says."

She nodded gravely. They were moving towards the door. The bearded doctor had already gone out. She looked imploringly at Doctor Bennett. He had not said a word. Had he forgotten? Suddenly, he smiled: "Well, Clara, how about that letter?"

She snatched it from under the pillow and held it out to him. He scrutinised it carefully.

"Very nice . . . very nice indeed. I'll see that it goes."

As he went out, she heard him say:

"Just look at this, Sir. . . . Pretty good, eh? When you thought she'd never . . ."

The door closed before she could hear the rest. What . . . oh what was it that they thought she would never do?

CHAPTER FIVE

CLAUDE BATCHELOR walked down the brick path to meet the postman at the gate as he did every morning since he and Isabel had come down to Paget's Fold. They had been there for nearly a fortnight but, every single day, he had to fight down the memory of this time last year when Clara had been with them. He had grown used to her absence from Valetta Road. But here, where there was no work to distract him and where everything reminded him of their happiest days, the dull, accustomed ache flared up once more into anguish. Though the aunts were kinder than ever, their careful avoidance of Clara's name only made him more conscious of her absence. He longed for this travesty of a holiday to be over so that he could resume those fruitless Sunday visits to the asylum.

It was months since they had let him see her. As Doctor Brooke had foretold, that Sunday in April, she was, in many ways, much better. When the new phase was 'established', when she had settled into that twilight state that might go on till she was as old as he was now, they would let him see her again. Meanwhile they feared that, precisely because she might recognise him, it might over-excite her and bring on a relapse into the violence and delusions of the first attack. Though he could not see her, those visits to Nazareth brought him a faint consolation. At least, for a little while, he was under the same roof as Clara. Somewhere, in the dreary hinterland behind that ironically splendid façade, some part of her lived on. Taking down changes of clothes for her, though it tore his heart, reminded him at least that she still inhabited the same world. The red belt they had made him take back was still hidden in a drawer of his desk. He had not told Isabel that belts and cords were forbidden, any more than that the pretty, flimsy nightdresses it comforted her to make never reached Clara. There was a little pile of them locked away, along with a hand mirror and three bottles of scent, in a cupboard to which only he had the key. For Isabel seemed almost to have convinced herself that Clara was suffering from some

247

physical illness and he could not bear to remind her of the truth.

The morning walk to the gate to meet the postman had become a kind of substitute for the Sunday visits. There was always a chance there might be a note from Brooke or Bennett with the news of some slight change in her condition or a request to bring something for her next time he came. He had left them his holiday address, though they had assured him they were unlikely to need it as he would only be away three weeks.

On this brilliant August morning, the postman was later than usual. Isabel called from the window:

"Dearest . . . your breakfast's getting cold."

He was on the point of turning back to go indoors when he saw the postman coming across the green. He held out only one letter. It was the wrong shape for the Nazareth envelopes. Claude took it half-heartedly, merely noting it was something re-addressed from London in his mother's writing. When he glanced at it again, his hand shook so much that he could hardly tear it open. He took out a folded sheet. At first the writing jigged so wildly before his staring eyes that he could not read the words. When he had managed to read them, and take them in, he cried out:

"Isabel . . . Isabel. . . . Come here at once."

She came running down the brick path.

"Dearest . . . what is it?"

"You'll never guess. . . . Tell me I'm not dreaming. . . . This letter . . ."

"It's not? . . . But it *is*. . . . It's from Clara."

"From Clara herself. . . . Look, dearest. . . . Perfectly clear . . . perfectly reasonable. . . . Even the doctor's name. . . . Yes, dear child . . . quite right. . . ." He became incoherent in his joy. They clung together, half laughing, half crying.

"I must go up to London at once," he said. "This very moment. They *must* let me see her after this. . . . They might even. . . . No. . . . I must be reasonable. . . . Oh, Isabel, was there ever such a glorious morning?"

She kissed him.

"I always knew she'd get better."

"We mustn't hope too much. . . . But, oh, I can't *help* hoping. . . ."

It was she who made him come in and eat some breakfast, reminding him that there was no train from Bellhurst for another two hours. He could hardly eat in his excitement. He called the aunts to hear the news. They put on their steel-rimmed spectacles and read the letter, looking a little dazed.

"Her writing was always so clear," said Aunt Sophy. "I could almost read it without my spectacles. It hasn't changed."

Her faded blue eyes brimmed over.

Aunt Leah said tremulously:

"Now, Sophy, dear. . . . This is good news, you know . . ."

But when the first exultation had died down, Claude's face clouded over.

"Shall we take a turn round the garden, Isabel? There's plenty of time before I need leave. I want your advice."

They walked up the grass path towards the orchard.

"Why are you looking so worried, Claude? After this wonderful, wonderful sign. . . . If she's well enough to write a letter . . ."

"I know . . . I know. The doctors never hinted at such an improvement as that. . . ."

"Then why do you sigh like that? When she's remembered you of her own accord. When she longs to *see* you . . ."

"If they let me see her. . . ."

"They wouldn't be so heartless as to stop you – Surely . . . now that her memory's obviously coming back. . . ."

"That's just it, Isabel. How much does she remember?"

"She doesn't want to see *me*. . . . Perhaps it's only the first glimmerings. . . . Even so, Oh, Claude . . . if there'd been just one word."

He put his arm round her.

"I know how you must feel, my dear. But perhaps the less she remembers the better."

"Even her own mother? Oh, Claude, why?"

"Dearest . . . mightn't every memory make her suffer more? I was too overjoyed at first to think what this might mean to her. Suppose she asks me today to take her home? How can I bring myself to tell her it's impossible?"

"It will be possible one day. Perhaps quite soon. I *know* she's going to get well."

"Isabel . . . we *daren't* hope. . . . How can I help being obsessed with the same idea? . . . But we mustn't let ourselves. . . ."

"*I've* never given up hope. I've always believed – like Richard – that she'd recover. Recover completely."

"Richard," he said heavily. "That's what's troubling me most of all. Suppose she asks about *him* . . . wants to see him, even?"

"Poor darling child. . . . You can only say he loves her and that, as soon as she's better. . . . Why . . . it might be just the incentive she needs to get competely well. . . ."

"Isabel," he said slowly. "Supposing I'm not justified in saying that. . . . We haven't seen Richard for a long time. . . ."

She stared at him.

"What do you mean? It's true he hasn't written. . . . But he never did write. He always came to see us when he was on leave from Plymouth. The regiment may have gone back to Ireland . . . abroad even. I agree he ought to have let us know."

He said, more slowly still:

"He's still at Plymouth. I heard from him about three weeks ago."

"You never told me."

"I didn't want to upset you."

"Was it such a very sad letter? All the more wonderful for him when he hears *this*. I'll write as soon as you've gone. . . . No, before. . . . You can post the letter in London. It'll get there sooner."

"Wait, Isabel. There's something I have to tell you about Richard. I'm afraid it will come as a great shock."

He told his story quietly, calming her fierce, incredulous interruptions. When he had finished, she was in angry tears.

"I can't believe it," she sobbed. "Of him. . . . Or of you. He *did* love her. . . . If you hadn't dashed all his hopes. What *right* had you? . . . Why, here, in this very orchard. . . . The little larch tree he brought from his home and planted for her. . . . Only this very spring."

"Dearest, I implore you . . . I *had* to tell him what I believed to be the truth. What else, in fairness, could I do?"

"He shouldn't have believed you. Even if he did . . . how *could* he go back to this girl as if Clara had never existed? . . . I wonder the creature herself hadn't more pride than to take him. . . . Perhaps he never even told her. . . . Of course he didn't. . . . The coward . . . the liar.

Oh, what a fool I've been. *You're* not to blame. He's rotten to the core."

"Isabel, you're far too harsh. Richard's neither a coward nor a liar. He did tell her. What's more he told her, just as he told me, that he could never feel for anyone again as he felt for Clara."

"She must be despicable too. Snatching up another girl's leavings...."

"Isabel... Isabel....She'd cared for him long before.... She put his happiness before hers. Because he loved Clara, she wanted her to recover.... Yes... to marry him."

"No doubt she *said* so. Clever minx. Was he so blind as not to see through that? Oh, the weak-minded *fool*. Thank heavens, he'll suffer too. He's got the sort of wife he deserves."

"You know nothing about her."

"Don't tell me you've met her... that she's taken you in too?"

"I've never met her, Isabel.... I've known of her existence for some time. In those first terrible months, when Richard was nearly beside himself... when he could think of nothing but Clara... he said he seemed to bring nothing but misery wherever he went.... But, as long as there was any hope of Clara's recovery... Isabel... I know that girl's sincere.... She's a Catholic.... She made a pilgrimage to Lourdes to pray that Clara might be cured.... Cured to marry the man she loved herself."

"Very saintly, no doubt," said Isabel with scorn. "Pity she couldn't wait to see whether her prayers were answered. Or that *he* couldn't."

"My dear... have any of us as much faith... or strength... as we'd like to have? I didn't know about it at the time... it was long ago, when the delusions were at their worst. If I *had* known... and month after month had gone by with no sign of Clara's getting better ... would I still have expected a miracle? As for Richard... he wasn't a Catholic.... He'd hoped against hope for a natural recovery. But after that dreadful Sunday night..."

She said, still with bitterness, but more calmly:

"I went on hoping. Mothers are more faithful than lovers. After all *she's* suffered...." Her eyes filled again. "Oh what a cruel world for her to come back to...."

He took her in his arms.

"My dearest... I can hardly bear to remind you.... But it may be a long, long time before there is any question of her coming back."

CHAPTER SIX

EVER SINCE she had given Doctor Bennett the letter, Clara had realised that it was of the utmost importance to hold on to her new awareness. There was the possibility that her father might write back. It would be unendurable if a letter came during one of her blank spells. She might lose it or never even know it had come.

By forcing herself to attend vigilantly to every detail, she managed to piece together the run of a whole day without once finding herself unable to account for how she came to be in a particular place or doing a particular thing. By the time she had done this for four successive days, it had become habitual. This awareness brought perplexities of a new kind. For one thing, she had never realised how long and monotonous a day could be. Now, when she woke, she knew what the routine would be . . . tidying her room, wandering about the ward outside, turning over magazines, lining up with the other women waiting for the bell and the call of "Ladies for the garden". At mealtimes she listened to the bird-like, meaningless twitter, feeling more and more isolated. If, for some reason, she was condemned to live among mad women, would it not be wiser to try and enter into their world? She began to study them, not only what they said, but their glances and gestures. If she learnt their language, she could make some kind of contact to appease her loneliness. Some of them seemed ready enough to be friendly. Alone in her room she began to imitate certain gestures they repeated, their darting looks, their irrelevant scowls and giggles. Soon, she saw how much easier it would be to slip into their ways than to keep up this tremendous effort of piecing things together in logical sequence.

Trying out these looks and gestures was rather soothing; it dulled the new sharp edge of her mind, as if she were a little drunk. If there were no sign from her father, why not gently relapse to a state where no more effort was needed? She felt she could easily become so like the rest that she would not even have to make the effort of acting.

Four endless days and not a sign. If only she knew what day of the week she had given Doctor Bennett the letter. But how could one know what any day was here? She did not even know the month, except that it was high summer . . . July or possibly August. There was nothing to distinguish one day from another. Not knowing where she had started was like sewing with an unknotted thread. Suppose she assumed that the first day had been Saturday? The fourth day would have been the first when she could hope for any reply. The fifth day passed, more slowly and wearily than any of the others. Agonising doubts began to assail her. He had received her letter but he could not find her. No one was allowed to know where Nazareth Royal Hospital was. Doctor Bennett had forgotten to post the letter. Worst of all, he had never meant to post it. The whole thing had been a cruel trick. She became more and more convinced that this was the real explanation.

It was on the afternoon of the sixth day, as she was lining up for the garden file, that she saw Doctor Bennett appear from a door in the passage. He smiled and beckoned to her but she pretended not to notice. She was not going to trust that lying smile again. He came up to her, took her arm and drew her away from the others.

"Don't look so frightened, Clara. I have a very pleasant surprise for you."

She asked, with wild hope:

"A letter?"

"Something better than that. Come in here."

He took her through the door from which he had appeared. Someone was standing on the far side of the room. She took one look and ran into his outstretched arms.

"Daddy . . . it's really you. . . . Oh, Daddy, Daddy."

She heard the doctor's voice say:

"I'll leave you two together. I'll be back in a quarter of an hour. Then we'll have our little talk."

At first the two of them could only look at each other, then kiss and laugh and kiss again. It was Clara who recovered her sobriety first.

"Then you *did* get my letter?"

"Indeed I did, dearest child. I couldn't believe my eyes – It reached me at Paget's Fold this morning. I came up straight away. . . ."

"Paget's Fold . . . I never thought of that. . . . Is it the summer holidays then? What day is it today?"

"August the fourth."

"However did you find me so quickly?"

He said, with a touch of hesitation:

"Well, my dear . . . I knew where you were."

"You mean you've known all along?"

"Yes. . . . Let's sit down, shall we? You mustn't get overtired or upset. . . . You see, you've been ill."

"But I feel perfectly well."

"You're much, much better, thank God."

"Oh, Daddy, there are so many things I want to ask you."

"Very well, my dear. But take it easily. What is it you want to know?"

"This place. It's a hospital, I know. But such a peculiar one. How do I come to be in it?"

"You were too ill to remember coming. My darling, you've been very ill indeed."

"How long?"

"A long time. . . . Many, many months – If you knew how wonderful it was to see you looking better! Your Mother will be so happy when I tell her."

"Mother . . . where *is* Mother?"

"Down at the cottage. We read your letter together. You can't think how excited we were to see your very own writing. She sends you her fondest love."

"Oh, give mine to her. . . . And the aunts . . . they're still alive?"

"Yes, indeed. And Granny too. She sent your letter on. She must have recognised your writing. How she must have wondered what was in the letter."

Clara laughed.

"Poor Granny. She must have been dying to open it and see. Curiosity's her ruling passion, isn't it?"

Her father laughed too.

"Well, she likes to be in on things. And I haven't had time to tell her yet. I came straight here from the station. I couldn't wait."

"From Victoria?"

"Yes."

She thought for a moment.

"Is this place in London?"

"Yes. Just over the river . . . on the Surrey side."

"Have you ever been here before?"

It was his turn to look thoughtful. He said, after a pause:

"Yes, dear. Very often."

"Have you seen me ever?"

"Sometimes, dear. You weren't always well enough to see me."

"Funny," she mused. "I thought I saw *you* once. Long, long ago. When I was down in the manger. But you had a scarf I didn't know. A black and white one."

"I have a black and white one. It was your mother's Christmas present."

"Christmas!" she said. "Has there been a Christmas then? Where was I at Christmas?"

"You were here, dear."

She knitted her brows.

"How extraordinary not to remember. . . . Wait. . . . You said it was August . . . I must have had a birthday too."

"Yes . . . dear child."

"How old am I now?"

"Twenty-three."

"Twenty-three," she said. "Fancy being twenty-three . . . and not knowing it. How long have I been here? Oh, Daddy it seems forever. If only I could tell you the extraordinary things that have been happening. . . . If only I could sort it all out. . . ."

"Don't try, dear. You mustn't tire your head."

"Have I had brain fever or something?"

"Something of the kind, yes. Try not to think about having been ill. Think about getting better."

"Oh, Daddy . . . aren't I better enough? Can't I come home now? I don't think I can *bear* being here any longer. Please, please take me home with you."

He put his arms round her. . . .

"Dearest, dearest child. One day, we hope. . . . But the doctor thinks you're not quite well enough yet. . . . There, there, don't cry. . . . If you cry, the doctor will say it's bad for you to see me. . . ."

She checked her tears.

"Anything but that. I'll be good. I promise I'll be good. Only don't go away and never come back."

The door opened and the doctor came in. He had a file of papers under his arm.

"Oh, Doctor Bennett . . . please don't take him away," she implored.

"There, there Clara. I'm not going to take your father away. I just want to borrow him for a few minutes. Will you be a good girl and wait outside the door."

She stood up obediently.

"Yes. But promise you won't take him away without my seeing him again?"

"I promise. And I keep my promises, don't I?"

"Yes. So far."

It seemed hours that she waited outside. It was torture to be separated from her father by that door. At any moment the bright, empty ward would be filled again with the nurses and the crazy women. Sister Ware might pounce on her, ask her what she was doing, and send her back to her room. She might never see him again. At last, just when she had given up hope, when she could hear the approaching twitter of the procession returning from the garden, the door opened and Doctor Bennett called her in.

The first time she had gone into that room, she had been aware of nothing but her father. Now she noticed that it contained a desk with some papers strewn on it. Her father was sitting in a chair against the wall. He looked anxious, she thought. He smiled at her when she entered, but the smile seemed strained. To her dismay, the doctor did not go out and leave them alone. Instead, he sat down at the desk and motioned Clara to take the chair on the other side. She glanced nervously from his face to her father's.

"Don't look so worried, Clara. I only want to have a little talk to you. Would you like your father to stay or to come back when we've finished?"

"Oh, stay, *please*."

"Very well. Mr. Batchelor, would you mind moving your chair farther back where she can't see you? I want her answers to be quite spontaneous."

Doctor Bennett clasped his hands before him on the desk and leant forward, looking searchingly into Clara's face.

"Now, Clara, I'm going to ask you one or two questions. Not difficult ones . . . but I want you to think carefully before you answer."

"Yes?"

"To begin with, you know you've been ill, don't you?"

"Yes."

"And that when people are ill, they often have to stay in hospital quite a long time?"

"Yes."

"Now . . . I want you to be quite frank with me . . . you're getting rather tired of being in this particular hospital, aren't you?"

"I'm afraid I am, yes," she said cautiously.

"Can you give me any definite reason why? For example, how do you get on with the nurses?"

"Quite well, I think. If I do what I'm told."

"How about the other patients?"

She hesitated.

"Well . . . it's rather hard to get on with *them*. I do try. But they don't seem to understand what I say. And what *they* say doesn't always make sense."

"I see. Now, when you talk to the nurses or to me nowadays . . . do *we* seem to talk sensibly?"

"Oh, yes. . . . And when I talked to Daddy . . ."

"So you feel *you're* like me and your father and the other ladies in the ward are different in some way?"

"I'm afraid I do, yes."

"Could you tell me what you think makes them different?"

"I know what I think. But I don't like to say it.'

"Come, come . . . you can say it to *me*."

"I'm not sure . . . I'd rather not. . . . You see, you're a doctor. . . ."

"What's that got to do with it? No . . . no . . . don't look round at your father . . . I'm asking you the questions."

"Yes. But I'm so frightened of giving the wrong answers."

He said more gently:

"Why, Clara?"

"Because I think you're trying to find out something. Whether I'm mad or not. . . ." Her lips began to tremble. "It seems to me that those women are mad. . . . But people say . . . don't they? . . . They say . . ."

"Now . . . now . . . don't cry. . . ."

She heard her father make an inarticulate noise but forced herself not to look round. The doctor raised his hand. . . .

"It's all right, Mr. Batchelor. Well, Clara? *What* do people say?"

She rallied herself.

"That mad people think everyone is mad but themselves."

"But you've just said your father and I and the nurses seem all right. So you don't think everyone's mad."

"No."

He pulled a piece of paper towards him and began to write on it. There was a good deal written on it already. At the top were two words in block capitals, that were easy to read upside down.

"Hughes-Follett," she said. "That's my name."

He pulled the paper nearer him.

"Yes, Clara. But it's rude to try and read what people are writing, isn't it? It might be something private."

"I'm sorry," she said, and stared down at her hands.

After a minute or two, he spoke again.

"Clara. . . . Come along, it's all right to look at *me*. . . . Now how would you like to go somewhere else? A very nice place . . . out in the country?"

She burst out . . . she could not help it:

"Oh please . . . *please* mayn't I go home?"

"Well . . . not yet, I'm afraid. . . . Some day not too far off. . . . Maybe even in six months. If you go on as well as you've been doing lately. It all depends on you "

". . . Six whole more *months* . . . I couldn't bear it."

"Now, Clara, be reasonable. . . . We're delighted with the progress you've made. . . . But only a week or two ago, you were still far from yourself, you know. Listen, let me tell you about this place in the country. You'll have far more freedom – You can have your own books and things – They'll even let nurse take you to a cinema sometimes."

"There'll still be nurses. . . . And . . . and those women."

"Oh, it'll all be quite different from here. A thoroughly cheery atmosphere. They play tennis – Some of them even play a remarkably good game of bridge. You'll be able to get on with *them* all right."

She said slowly:

"That's just what I'm afraid of."

"Now whatever do you mean by that?"

"I was beginning to here. It's so awfully lonely . . . having to be with the same people always and not being able to talk to them. They seem to understand each other in a sort of way. I've been trying to be like them . . . deliberately . . . copying their gestures . . . the sort of way they talk. . . . It was beginning to work. . . . And in time . . ." she glanced at him, afraid she was talking too much. But he did not look angry. Instead he prompted her:

"Go on. . . . And in time . . .?"

"I might get really like them. Just from being so bored. And *stay* like them. For ever. It's so hard keeping it up all by oneself."

There was a silence. She could see that Doctor Bennett was exchanging glances over her head with her father. She gathered a little courage.

"Please . . . please . . . if you'd let me go home. . . . With ordinary things round me. . . . And Daddy and Mother. . . . It would be so much easier to keep things clear in my head. Why can't Daddy take me with him?"

She turned desperately round to him: "Don't you want me home?"

"My dear . . . of course . . . of course. . . ."

"Then why don't you just take me?"

"Clara . . . I can't. Not yet. I'm not allowed to."

"Why? I'm not a prisoner, am I?"

Doctor Bennett intervened. He said softly:

"Now, Clara, don't get excited. . . . Listen. . . . Do you think we're keeping you here against your will?"

Something in that soft voice made her suspect a trap. She did not answer at once. This was the test question. Everything depended on how she answered it. She searched wildly for the right answer, but she perceived that either alternative was fatal. Instead of replying, she burst into tears. Her father started forward and put his arm round her.

"There . . . my dear, dear child. Try not to cry. Can't you tell *me* if you can't tell the doctor?"

"What's the good," she sobbed. "If I say yes, he'll think I'm mad. And if I say no, he'll think I don't want to go home."

Through her tears, she heard Doctor Bennett say:

"You know, Mr. Batchelor, that strikes me as an extraordinarily reasonable answer. I wonder if I dare. . . . What do you think?"

"That's not a fair question. . . . You know only too well what I think . . . what I long for you to say. But we're both entirely in your hands."

Clara sat up, clasping her father's arm. He was there . . . he was her ally. She blinked back her tears and managed to say: "Dearest Daddy. . . . It's just as bad for you, isn't it?"

The doctor bit his fountain pen and surveyed them thoughtfully. At last he said:

"The pair of you. . . . You almost convince me. . . . But, no, I don't think I dare. . . . After all, I'm only second-in-command. . . . Dr. Brooke's on holiday. . . . If anything went wrong, I might be in danger of losing my job."

"Yes. . . . I understand that," her father said. "One couldn't expect you to take such a risk. Perhaps, you think . . . just as an experiment . . . for a few days even . . . there would be a risk for her too?"

They seemed to have forgotten Clara's presence. She listened in a mute agony of hope.

The doctor went on frowning and biting his pen. The sun flashed on his signet ring and struck coloured rays from it.

"It would be a big responsibility for you, too."

"I'd willingly undertake that. Her mother and I. . . . We wouldn't let her out of our sight."

"Well, she's certainly improved beyond all expectation. A return to normal surroundings *might* be a good thing. But you realise there's no question of decertifying her yet. This may be only a flash in the pan. The very utmost I'm empowered to do is to let her out for a short time on parole. But Brooke will be back in a fortnight. . . . Hadn't we better wait till he's had another look at her?"

Her father sighed.

"I suppose. . . . If you think that best. . . ."

Clara clutched his hand. She stared imploringly at the doctor but did not say a word. At last he remembered her existence and looked at her.

"And what does Clara think?"

"Oh – As if you didn't *know*. . . ."

He gave her a long look. She looked back steadily, beseechingly. Suddenly he smiled.

"I'll take a chance on it. You can take her back with you to the country for a fortnight. No excitement, mind. And in bed by ten at the earliest. Bring her back here at three o'clock a fortnight from today to report. I can trust you?"

"Of course . . . of course."

"And you, Clara? You'll be a good girl and not make a fuss about coming back to see me and Doctor Brooke?"

"I promise," she said.

He smiled and stood up, holding out his hand.

"Good. Now be off, the pair of you."

Clara and her father blinked at each other. Her father said:

"You mean . . . we can go now . . . this minute?"

"As soon as you've signed this paper. Clara, go and ask Sister Ware for your coat. Need any other things?"

"We've everything she wants at home."

"Good. I'm sure you don't want to hang about more than necessary. Wait a moment, Clara . . . I'd better give you a chit for Sister." He scribbled a few lines on a piece of paper and put them in an envelope. "Say nothing . . . just give her this. And don't say a word to any of the others. It might upset them. They're not as lucky as you."

"Oh, poor things," Clara said remorsefully. "I'm so happy . . . I'd forgotten. . . ."

"Well, perhaps they'll be lucky one day. See you in a fortnight."

She had one moment of panic, back in the ward without the protection of her father and the doctor. Sister Ware looked disapproving as she read the note. She muttered under her breath:

"Hmm. Very irregular. I wonder what Dr. Brooke will say to this – *I* haven't even been consulted."

She marched off without a word to Clara and returned with the coat.

"Here," she said ungraciously. "Now be off with you. I don't want my other ladies upset."

Clara put on the coat and said meekly:

"Thank you. Goodbye, Sister Ware."

"Oh, don't think you're leaving us for ever. There's many goes out on parole. I'll say orryvoir. And you'll be lucky if it *is* orryvoir. If you don't behave, I won't have you back in Ward C."

But not even Sister Ware could spoil the joy of finding her father waiting for her in the room with the desk. They did not stop to kiss. She could feel he was as frightened as she that something would happen to stop their getting away. Holding her hand tight, he hurried her so fast down staircases and along unfamiliar passages that she could hardly keep up with him. She was amazed how easily he threaded his way through the great labyrinth of a building she could never piece together. Through a window, she caught a flying glimpse of the asphalt yard with the plane tree now in full leaf. It existed then: it was not just something she had imagined. She almost wanted to stop and investigate: to try and identify other places; the washroom, the cell with the manger-bed, even the terrible room with the convex rubber walls. She longed to know what had been real and what had been dream or nightmare.

"How do you know your way so well, Daddy? I could never find mine," she panted excitedly. "Have you been here very often, then?"

"Almost every week, my dear. But let's forget all that now."

Sometimes a nurse gave them a curious glance but no one stopped them till they came out into a great circular vestibule with a parquet floor and white walls garlanded with gilt mouldings. Just as they were reaching the double doors that were flung open, showing a vista of pillars and steps, a man in uniform appeared from a glass cage, demanding:

"Passes, please."

Her father handed him two things that looked like tickets: the uniformed man scrutinised them and gave them back to him.

"Right, Sir. Don't forget these when you bring her back, on the eighteenth."

They ran down the step hand in hand, like children escaping from school, and did not pause for breath till they reached an iron gate at the end of an avenue. Beyond it, buses and trams were racing past. Clara was nearly deafened with the noise. Her father waved his free arm shouting frantically "Taxi! Taxi".

One came at last. As it turned and threaded its way through the traffic, Clara looked back. There was the façade she had seen on the plates – the pillared portico and the slender dome rising behind it.

"It's beautiful from the front," she said. "You'd never guess from the back. No grey stone *there* . . . beastly browny-yellow brick. But, from here, it looks like some famous building, doesn't it?"

Her father said wonderingly:

"Beautiful? I suppose it is. I'm afraid I shall loathe anything Wren built to the end of my life. Here's our taxi. . . . Jump in."

As the door slammed on them, they hugged and kissed each other like reunited lovers. He was even more wildly gay than she was.

"We're free. . . . We've escaped. . . . Dear child . . . you'll have to restrain me. . . . Otherwise they'll have to put *me* away. . . . My blessed, darling girl. . . ."

He broke off his babble of joy for a moment as they passed a huge church:

"Look, Clara. St. George's Cathedral. How often I've gone in on a Sunday after going *there*. . . . I'd almost like to go in now with you. Ah, well . . . perhaps better get you straight home. It's absurd . . . I can't help feeling they're pursuing us and we shan't be safe till we're back on our own side of the Thames."

"It might have been the other side of the *sea*. Or in another world altogether. You actually used to come there and I never knew. How often?"

"Every Sunday except these last two."

She laughed.

"Fancy . . . just as you used to at the convent."

"You look hardly older than you did at school." He stroked her hair. "Thank God, it's golden, still."

CHAPTER SEVEN

As THE taxi approached West Kensington, her father said:

"I really must collect my wits. Your Granny doesn't even know I'm in London. Let alone who's with me."

Clara laughed.

"I say, won't Mother be jealous! To think Granny will see me before she does. . . . You'll have to break it to Granny gently, I suppose. . . . Look, why not stop the taxi at the end of Valetta Road? Then you can smuggle me in quietly. You know how deaf she is. Anyway, she's probably up in her room. She usually is between tea-time and dinner-time."

"Fancy your remembering that," he said fondly.

"Oh, things are coming back with a rush. I can't cope with them all. The old streets . . . even the colours of front doors. . . . Except that it's summer now. . . ." She broke off and said "Fog. . . . There was a fog. . . ." She asked anxiously:

"Daddy . . . that Indian student . . . Wajid someone . . . he'd had small-pox. . . . Is *he* still there?"

"No, dear, he left long ago."

"I'm glad . . . I'd have been rather embarrassed . . . I had some sort of row with him, didn't I?"

Her father stopped the taxi.

"We're so near, we might as well get out now."

As they turned into Valetta Road, she said:

"Daddy, I don't want Granny to see me like this. Let me go up to my room and tidy up. And change into some other clothes. I won't feel really myself till I've got out of *these*. You can break it to her while I'm changing."

Alone in her old bedroom, her first impulse was not, after all, to tear off the clothes she had worn in the asylum. She went straight to the wardrobe glass and studied her full-length reflection. *There* she had never been able to see more than her head and shoulders. She took off the hated beige coat which had never seemed to belong to her any more than the uniform brown serge dressing-gown. The old navy dress that hung so loose on the body whose thinness she approved had had its place in her real life. She felt a sudden affection for it, as if it were a loyal friend who had followed her into exile. If she could find its belt, she might even keep it on. She began to rummage through drawers in search of the scarlet belt.

She became so fascinated in discovering things she remembered and things she had forgotten she possessed that, soon, it seemed no more astonishing to be back in that room than if she had just returned from school after a particularly long and dreary term. Presently, she gave up the search for the missing belt and sat down on the bed with its faded Indian cotton bedspread. The springs sagged so violently that she realised that there was not even a mattress underneath. Then she grasped that this was a very different homecoming. Perhaps they had never expected her to return at all. She pressed her knuckles to her temples, trying to remember when she had last slept in that bed. What had she been doing before *it* happened? Who had taken her to Nazareth? She had a confused memory of driving somewhere in a taxi, wearing a fur coat over a nightdress. She brushed it aside. It was something *before* that she wanted to recover. Something desperately important in the real world . . . a *person*. Before she could recover this vital missing piece, her father knocked on the door:

"Nearly ready, dear?"

"Give me five minutes," she called back.

She hurriedly changed into the first dress she pulled out of the wardrobe, went to the dressing table and combed her hair. Her brushes were still there; their silver backs tarnished. There was a bowl with a little powder and a worn puff still in it. She fluffed some powder over her face. It smelt delicious after the smell of hospital soap which still clung to her hands. The scent was not only delicious – it brought her so much nearer to what she was trying to track down that she could hardly bear to leave the bedroom to go downstairs.

Dinner with her father and her grandmother fell curiously flat. She managed not to comment on the fact that her grandmother was now wearing a white wig instead of the curled chestnut one she had known from childhood. After the first tearful, excited greeting, old Mrs.

Batchelor seemed more bewildered than happy. She kept staring at Clara and then hastily averting her eyes. Even her father seemed to be suffering from a reaction after his wild spirits of the drive home. Her grandmother did little more than keep repeating how nice it would be for Clara to get down to Paget's Fold tomorrow and that she hoped the weather would stay so wonderfully fine. Every time the maid came in, there was an awkward silence, followed by more comments on the weather, the state of the croquet lawn or the best train for them to take in the morning. On Molly's first entrance in, Clara said:

"How nice to see you again, Molly."

The girl turned fiery red.

"Very pleased, I'm sure, Miss Clara. Such a surprise. We didn't even know the Master. . . . And Cook on her holiday too. . . . I hope there's enough to go round, Sir. No time to make a pudding even."

The conversation flagged so desperately that, in the effort to keep it going, Clara had to give up searching for the missing piece. She began to ask for news of people in whom she was not particularly interested, merely to prove that she remembered their existence. At each "How is . . .?" or "Where is . . . ?" she fancied her father looked apprehensive until she mentioned the name.

When she had run through various acquaintances, she remembered someone whom she really wanted to hear about.

"Goodness, I'd almost forgotten . . ." she began, then broke off: "No, I don't suppose you'd know. . . . You'd be hardly likely to have seen *him*."

"Seen whom?" her father asked faintly. This time he looked really frightened.

"Clive Heron. I don't suppose you even remember him. You've probably forgotten his existence. I think he's only been here once."

Her father's face relaxed as he answered volubly:

"Heron? Most certainly, I remember. Tall, thin, red-haired man in the . . . let's see . . . Home Office, wasn't it. A most amusing man. . . . Very intelligent. Extraordinarily likeable chap altogether. No, my dear . . . I haven't set eyes on him. Wait now . . . I'm sure someone told me he'd rung up to inquire after you?"

"Rung up? But Clive loathes telephoning. Actually rung up *here*? . . . I can hardly believe it."

"Not here, I think. Some mutual friend I fancy. . . ."

"I wonder who. We've hardly any mutual friends. . . . Let me think . . ."

Her father said hurriedly:

"I've probably got it wrong. . . . Mistaken the name. So many people inquired. . . . Shall we have coffee in the study?"

To her relief, her grandmother announced that she was going straight up to bed.

"I'm getting an old lady now, dear," she said. "I daresay you noticed my hair had gone white but were too polite to say so. You always had such nice manners, like your Daddy. At my age, even a pleasant surprise can be quite a shock. And I'm sure you and Daddy must have a lot to talk about after all this time."

In her gratitude, Clara gave her quite a demonstrative goodnight kiss. Her grandmother's flabby cheek made her think again, as she used to as a child, that it was like kissing a poached egg.

Once she was sitting in the big green chair in the study, with her father at his usual place at his desk, stuffing his burned-down pipe, her joy returned.

"Oh, Daddy . . . it's so wonderful to be back in this room. I can't believe a single thing in it's changed. Do you know, I remember the last time I was in it."

"Do you, my dear?"

"Yes . . . I was sitting where you are now and you were dictating one of your lectures. . . . Wait . . . it was a Saturday afternoon . . . I don't believe it was long before I was . . . all right, darling . . . ill."

"It was only two days. . . . Don't let's talk about your having been ill. . . . Ah, I've just remembered something pleasant. I've got twenty-five pounds for you. A cheque came, so I cashed it for you."

"How exciting. . . . A present?"

"No . . . you earned it."

"I earned it? . . . Wait a minute. . . . I remember writing some advertising copy. . . . I believe it was *after* that lecture. . . . Was it?"

"Actually, it was, yes. But don't cudgel your memory."

"Two days," she said, with interest. "Well . . . if they've paid me. I must have been in my right mind when I wrote it. I say . . . it must have happened very suddenly."

267

"Yes. Dear child . . . just to please me . . . will you stop talking about the past?"

"Very well. How wonderful to have all that money. I shall buy some new clothes tomorrow. Heaven knows I need them."

"Won't the old ones do, just for the country? Your mother's expecting us by the first train – I've sent her a telegram – She'll be so disappointed if we're late."

"Very well. I'll wait till we get back. Oh – I'd almost forgotten. I'm not officially free yet, am I?"

"I'd almost forgotten myself. . . . To see you now. . . . No one could believe. . . . Please God, in a fortnight you'll be home for good."

Clara hardly heard him. Something had caught her attention.

"Daddy, there *is* something new in the study. That photograph. . . . I hardly realised it *was* Mother at first. She looks so much older. . . ."

"Well . . . after what she's been through since last November. . . . She'll look as young as ever, as soon as she sets eyes on you."

Clara thought, with interest. "November, was it? When the fog came down. . . . A *fog?* . . ." She said aloud. "Older . . . older . . . but in a way, *more* beautiful. I've seen her with that face before. . . . It's a wonderful photograph. Who took it?"

He did not answer at once. Perhaps he had not heard. The next moment, she was straining eagerly for the answer herself.

"Wasn't it Nell something . . . Nell . . . Nell . . . Nell . . . *Crayshaw?*" Something lit up in her brain. She said excitedly:

"Daddy . . . I've found it . . . the missing piece. . . . Darling! You must tell me one thing about the past. . . . It's most desperately important. Nell had a brother. . . . Oh, was he real? Or did I once just see a photograph? . . . Richard his name was. . . . Did I really know him?"

"Yes . . . my dear . . . you did. . . ."

"Tell me . . . oh, was *this* something I imagined? Or was it real? Oh, Daddy . . . tell me. . . ."

"My child . . . don't look so distressed. What is it you want me to tell you?"

"Richard and I? Were we going to be married one day. . .? Oh, I know it couldn't be for a long time – I *know* I'm still married to Archie. Poor Archie . . . I haven't given him a thought. He did love me . . .

that was real.... But Richard ... did he.... Oh, did he? Or was I having delusions? Women have them, don't they ... about men wanting to marry them? ... Lots of them did *there*...."

"Hush ... darling ... listen.... It was no delusion. Richard ..."

"Have you seen him?" she broke in. "Does he know where I've been all this time?"

"Yes, Clara," her father answered slowly. "I've seen him many times. He was very, very unhappy about you."

"Where is he now? When did you last see him?"

"Well ... not for some time."

"You don't think he's forgotten me?"

"No, no. Wherever he is, I am sure he hasn't forgotten you."

"Why do you sound so miserable? Why do you look away like that? Is there something you're afraid to tell me? Daddy ... he's not dead, is he?"

Her father looked at her again.

"No, my dear. He's not dead."

"Oh, it's so wonderful to find that it was all true. He's alive.... He hasn't forgotten me.... In there, I used to think about him all the time at first.... I used to see him even ... and, in the asphalt yard, when I heard a motor horn I used to think it was Richard trying to find me. ... How extraordinary that during all the last part, I forgot all about *him*.... It wasn't till after I'd got home.... Oh, I must write at once and tell him I've come back.... You've got his address?"

"Yes.... But, Clara, one moment.... Wouldn't it be better to wait a little?"

"Why?"

"I hate to remind you on our very first evening.... But, in a fortnight, we have to report to the hospital. Please God, then you'll be home for good with no conditions.... Wouldn't you yourself rather wait till you're absolutely free?"

She said, with a sigh.

"You don't know how hard it is to wait.... Still, perhaps you're right.... After what he saw happen to Nell.... It might be kinder to *him* not to tell him till they let me out for good.... Perhaps they told him I was incurable, like John. Perhaps he's given up hope.... Do you think that was why he stopped coming to see you?"

"Dear child . . . there were times when we were all tempted to despair."

"Then it will be all the more wonderful when I *can* tell him? . . . Daddy, stop looking so sad. . . . What is it? . . . Wait. . . . I think I know. It's all coming back now. . . . I'm still married to Archie. . . . You didn't want to have to remind me of something else . . . the nullity suit. . . . It was only just beginning. . . . Oh, to think of all the time I've wasted in there. . . . Nearly a whole year. . . . The Civil part might have been settled by now. . . . And then there's Rome." She wrung her hands. . . . "Oh, Daddy, it may be years before we can get married. . . ."

He sighed.

"My child, you will have to be patient. . . . But you're so young . . . you've all your life ahead. . . ."

"Oh, I don't know how to wait. . . . After all, I'm twenty-three. . . . And I've lost nine whole months of my life. . . ."

"Clara . . . can't you be grateful that it wasn't much longer? Must you begin to worry about the future so soon? Can't you just rejoice in this wonderful thing that's happened today? If you knew what it means to me . . . to your mother. . . ."

She went over to him and kissed him remorsefully.

"Dearest Daddy. . . . I'm sorry. You must have been unhappy, too. Of course, I rejoice. . . . But we know and he doesn't. . . . It's just that it won't be quite perfect till he does too."

CHAPTER EIGHT

IT WAS bliss at first to be back at Paget's Fold. But, after the first joy of seeing her mother and the old aunts and the place she had loved so much, Clara began to grow secretly restless. As each hot, lazy day went by, her restlessness increased. She concealed her impatience, so as not to spoil everyone's delight in her return, but there were times when the hours seemed to drag as slowly as they had done in that last week in Nazareth. The two worlds were quite distinct to her now. She was not even frightened of the interview ahead. Something told her that, when they saw her again, they would know as well as she did that she no longer belonged to the world beyond the glass. There were moments when she almost wished she did. She had forgotten two tortures of the world this side: boredom and suspense. Beyond the glass, however agonising the nightmare experiences, they had had a peculiar intensity. If some had been terrifying, others had been exquisite. When those experiences had ceased, she had been as passive as a child until the tremendous, absorbing effort of willing herself back to consciousness. Here, for all the kindness and love about her, she felt frustrated and only half alive. Her days were regulated to a routine of meals and walks and games of croquet; to conversations which always edged away from the only two things that really interested her: Richard and her memories of Nazareth.

Whenever she tried to tell them about anything that happened *there*, they looked so pained that she had to give it up. Once Isabel said:

"Darling . . . it's so bad for you even to think of these dreadful things – Can't you try to forget? Don't you ever think of what Daddy and I went through during that appalling time?"

"I'm sorry. Yes. . . . I expect it was horrible for you. . . . But some of it was pretty bad for me. . . ."

"My poor pet. . . . Still you were unconscious, mercifully, most of the time. Daddy and I had to live through each awful day. . . . That Sunday . . . only last April . . . when they thought you mightn't get

271

well for years and years. . . . *I* never believed it. But poor Daddy did. He broke down and cried like a child."

"How awful," said Clara with a shudder. But she knew, with the cold clarity that was becoming her permanent state, that she shuddered, not with sympathy but with distaste. There was only one point left where she could feel intensely and that point was daily becoming more painfully inflamed by her enforced silence. Soon, she no longer wanted to talk about Richard. She dared not, even yet, envisage the hope of seeing him. All she wanted was to be alone, so that she could think about him and try and reconstruct everything she could remember of their three weeks together.

After a week at Paget's Fold, she could look back, almost with amusement, to her parents' obvious distress the first time she went into the orchard and saw the little larch, no bigger than a Christmas tree. Why had they been so frightened? Did they think the remembrance of her love would turn her brain again? Didn't they know that the thought of Richard was the only thing that kept her alive, still able to feel and suffer and hope? Without it, she would have sunk back into an apathy in which she hardly cared whether she were here at Paget's Fold or back in Ward C.

When she saw the tree, she had merely said:

"Did Richard send that? From Peacocks?"

They told her, yes. They told her he had planted it himself. She had answered coldly, with no pity for their anxious, tender faces. "Thanks. I only wanted to make sure."

She began to long more and more to return to London. Paget's Fold was beginning to be haunted with disturbing thoughts. That day she and Richard had driven down here, something had gone wrong. What was it? There were gaps in that day that, try as she might, she could not fill. She could remember more and more of what she had been through in the asylum but those last days with Richard remained a curious dazzle of brilliant light and utter darkness. Was it possible she had been going out of her mind then and that he had known it? Desperately, she tried their old game, crying in her mind.

"Richard . . . Richard. . . . Wherever you are . . ."

But she did not feel his answering call. Was he deliberately avoiding her? Did he fear her . . . even hate her? In an unguarded moment, her mother had told her about his driving up from Peacocks the night she had been taken ill. Had he ever seen her in the asylum? Had she terrified or repelled him as Micky and the others had repelled her?

She became convinced that something was being kept from her. If her parents knew the truth, as she now suspected they did, they would not tell her. Who . . . oh who . . . both knew and would have the honesty to tell?

The agony of her suspense made her sullen and irritable. In the second week, her father began to look at her with increasing anxiety. He asked her one day:

"Are you sleeping all right, my dear? Not overdoing things? You wouldn't like a day in bed?"

She was going to answer crossly but the sight of his face touched her.

"I'm quite all right, Daddy dear."

"You're not worrying about the interview next week?"

"No . . . not that. . . . But there's something I awfully want to do."

"Yes?" he said, rather apprehensively.

"If I mayn't write to Richard, can't I at least write to Nell?"

He hesitated before answering.

"Well . . . just at the moment, she's on holiday."

"How do you know?" she pounced. "Have you heard from her, then?"

He said hastily:

"I wrote to her . . . to say you were so much better. . . . She's been so kind . . . I thought she would like to know."

"And she answered. Did she say anything about Richard?"

"Er . . . only to say she agreed with me that it would be better not to tell him just yet."

"Till I'm decertified, you mean?"

He sighed.

"I hoped you didn't know. . . . But we had no alternative. . . . Can't you think of it, as we do, as an acute nervous breakdown?"

"I'd rather call a spade a spade. After all, Richard knows the facts. . . ." She added suspiciously. "Or doesn't he? . . . Is that it?"

"Oh, he knows, my dear. We couldn't conceal it from him. But there's no reason why anyone outside the immediate family need ever know. Please God, this time next week, we can all forget it ever happened."

She was a little reassured. He included Richard in 'the immediate family'.

She kissed him, mollified.

"Poor Daddy, don't worry. *That* will be all right. Sometimes I forget it means a lot to you too."

"It means more than anything in the whole world," he said.

The day they had to report at Nazareth came at last. On the way up in the train, her spirits were almost as high as his on the day they had driven away in the taxi. She was thinking only that, at last, she would be able to write to Richard. Her father was obviously anxious though he did his best to conceal it. He kept on saying:

"The doctors can't say you don't look well. You look splendid. At the worst, it can only be a question of weeks."

The interview, in which Doctor Brooke took the leading part, did not last long. The moment she came into the room, the bearded doctor said:

"Well, well, so this is really the young woman I saw before?"

He asked her a few questions to which she replied confidently. She did not feel in the least afraid of either of them. It was almost impossible to connect these obviously routine enquiries with the agonised tension of that other inquisition.

At last, he turned to Dr. Bennett.

"Well, your rather rash experiment seems to have been successful. I admit I was somewhat sceptical but results appear to have justified it. Let's hope they are permanent. Yes . . . I think we can quite safely give this patient her discharge."

She heard her father's deep sigh of relief.

"I can't tell you how grateful I am, Doctor Brooke. And to you too Doctor Bennett. I'm sure she couldn't have been in better hands. I'm thankful we were advised to send her to Nazareth."

"Well, we fancy we have as good a record as any. Pity so many people are prejudiced against us. Partly snobbery . . . the idea of having a relative in a public institution. And partly our name . . . there's still a stigma attached to the idea of a Nazarite . . . though that old term's never used now." He turned to Clara, who had been listening with faint resentment. "Well, Mrs. Hughes-Follett . . . so you can go out and begin a normal life again and forget you were ever here. But you'll

274

have to take things easy for the next six months. . . . Bed at ten, no overworking of that brain of yours . . . no gadding about and getting over-excited."

Clara said sullenly:

"I thought I was supposed to be well."

His face became stern.

"Look here, young lady. You're very lucky to be getting your discharge so soon. If it had been left to me, you'd have spent the next six months in our convalescent home. Remember, I can still change my mind."

"Oh please no. I'm sorry. I'll do everything you say."

"Hmm. That's better. You can say goodbye to me now and Dr. Bennett will take you to the office to collect your things. Your father and I have a few little matters to settle up."

She went out, feeling as if she had been dismissed from a head-master's study.

Outside, Dr. Bennett smiled at her.

"You didn't seem awfully grateful to the Head. In fact, you jolly nearly got on his wrong side."

"You're the one I'm grateful to," she said. "If it hadn't been for you, I might still be here."

He looked pleased.

"Well, I'm glad I took the risk. Now I suppose you hope you'll never set eyes on any of us again. No one else you'd like to say goodbye to? Sister Ware?"

"Do I have to?"

He laughed.

"No. She's a bit of a tartar, isn't she? Still, she has to be."

"I would like to say goodbye to Nurse Jones?"

"What, the red-haired one in Ward J. Fancy your remembering her. She'll be pleased. Suppose I just give her a message? Ward J isn't an awfully pleasant place, you know. I don't want to upset you."

"I'd like to see it again. It helps me to remember."

"You're an odd girl. Don't you want to forget it all?"

She shook her head.

"No. My family won't let me talk about it. But I think about it. Some day, perhaps, I'll be able to piece it all together."

"All right, then. I'll take you down there. You've got a knack of getting your own way, haven't you?"

Once again she found herself in the ward on the ground floor. It hung together now . . . the long, narrow corridor, the wide space with the fireplace, the glass-topped door giving on to the asphalt yard. The dreary procession of nurses and patients was walking round it. She recognised Micky and the woman with the burnt face and forced herself not to feel sick. Nurse Jones was on duty in the narrow passage, sitting, with her back to them, by the window that looked on to the wall with the creeper. Facing her was a row of doors, all shut but one. Through that one open door Clara saw the old lady in the white draperies and the strange headdress, busy at her easel.

"I remember her," she whispered. "My cell was the one next door to hers."

The doctor whispered back:

"She's very clever. Had pictures in the Academy when she was young. She's been here fifteen years. We're all quite fond of her." He said aloud:

"How's Your Majesty today?"

"Tolerably well, thank you. Who's this young person with you? Doesn't she know who I am?"

Clara curtseyed.

"That's better, my dear. You may go now, both of you. I'm busy with my painting."

The doctor went up to Nurse Jones and tapped her on the shoulder. She jumped up and turned round.

"Well . . . if it isn't our Clara! My goodness, what a difference!"

"She's come to say goodbye. . . . She's leaving us."

"Well, isn't that wonderful? I thought as much when I saw her with a hat on. Fancy you remembering Jones."

"You were sweet to me," said Clara.

Jones kissed her.

"There . . . isn't that nice? We miss you, dear. I bet you won't miss us, though. You used to sing like a lark sometimes. Quite a pleasure to hear you."

"Sing?" asked Clara with interest. "But I always wanted to be able to sing. I'm sure I can't now."

Doctor Bennett said rather severely:

276

"Say goodbye, Clara. We've still got to go to the office."

"Well, cheerio, Clara, dear. See you in the great big world some day, perhaps. Remember Smith?"

"Yes."

"She won't half be furious. I had a bet with her. Five bob that you'd be out within the year. She's lost. God bless and lots of luck."

At the office, she asked the doctor:

"Did I really sing quite well?"

"Yes. Very well indeed."

"How extraordinary."

"Hmm. It's remarkable what people *can* do when the brakes are off."

At the office, the nurse in charge said:

"It'll take some time to pack her things. Will you wait or shall we post them on?"

"I don't want anything I had here," said Clara. "Please keep them."

"That's against the rules. I'll post them on. You'd better take your wedding-ring though."

She fumbled in a pigeon-hole and produced a small packet. Clara opened it and there was Archie's ring.

"Thank you," she said, slipping it in her pocket.

"Sign the receipt, please."

Suddenly Clara remembered something else.

"Nurse . . . didn't I have a fur coat? . . . a black one. . . . Not real sealskin. But almost new. Perhaps I could just take *that* with me."

"I'll look at your list," said the nurse. She opened an index file and took out a card. After a minute she said in an embarrassed voice, glancing not at Clara, but at Doctor Bennett. "That's correct. But I'm afraid there was a bit of a mishap." She showed the card to the doctor. "Wouldn't be much good to her now, I'm afraid."

"All right, nurse. We'll forget about the coat, shall we, Clara? Your father will be getting impatient."

As they were approaching the room where she had been interviewed, she said to Doctor Bennett.

"It doesn't matter. . . . Except that Daddy gave it to me. . . . But what *did* happen to my coat?"

"What an inquisitive young woman you are. Do you really want to know?"

"Yes, I do."

"When you arrived here you were in pretty bad shape, you know. The fact is, before we could put it safely away, you tore it to shreds."

She stopped and stared at him.

"*I* did? Tore a fur coat? . . . why, that's *leather*. I'm frightfully feeble with my hands. I can hardly tear *cardboard*. . . . However could I have been capable?"

"Well, Clara. . . . As I told you just now, people develop some strange capacities when the brakes are off."

CHAPTER NINE

WHEN THEY returned to Valetta Road where she was to stay the night, Clara said:

"Daddy, I don't want to go back to Paget's Fold. Now that your holiday's finished I'd rather stay on in London with you."

"But my dear, the country air and peace is so much better for you. And your mother will be so disappointed not to have your company for her last two weeks."

"I'm sorry. But I'm getting awfully restless down there."

"All the same, I'm sure it's better for you. Doctor Brooke thought it might be a good idea for you to be altogether out of London for a time. He suggested you might get some sort of outdoor work . . . on a farm, perhaps. That would give you something to do without tiring your brain."

"There's nothing I should loathe more, Daddy. I'm no longer a certified lunatic. Have I got to go on being treated like one? Am I never going to be allowed to decide anything for myself again?"

"Come, my dear, there's no need to get angry. You heard yourself what they said. You've got to go quietly. But no one's going to force you to do anything you don't want to do. It's very unkind of you to talk like that."

"I'm sorry. I didn't mean to be unkind. But London's so much easier to get to – Suppose Richard manages to get leave when he's heard from me – I don't want him to waste any of it in travelling."

"Well, my dear . . . I'm afraid you can't count on his getting leave. . . . And, I confess, at the moment, I haven't his address. . . . I believe his unit has been moved since I saw him."

"Then I shall ring up Nell. She's sure to know. . . . Oh, I know you said she was away. But I'll ring up on the off-chance."

Before he could say any more, she picked up the receiver and asked for Nell's number.

"I remember it, you see," she said triumphantly, while she waited for a reply.... "Ah, you see, she *is* back. Nell.... Hullo, Nell ... who do you think this is? It's Clara."

Nell's voice said at the other end:

"Clara ... what a wonderful surprise ... I thought you were in the country."

"Daddy and I have just come back from the hospital. Everything's all right. I've got a clean bill. I don't ever have to go back."

"That's splendid news, dear. I'm so glad."

"Nell ... I want most awfully to see you."

"Yes ... we must meet some day. Actually, I'll be out of town for a bit. And I expect you'll be going back to the country for some time, won't you? Give me a ring when you come back. Well, goodbye for the moment, dear, and tremendous congratulations."

"Please, Nell, don't ring off. I want to see you today ... before you go. It's something very important."

Nell said slowly.

"Well, Clara, I don't know.... Actually I've got a frightful lot of things to do...."

"I promise I won't stay long. If I came over right away? Please, Nell...."

"Well, perhaps ... Clara ... is your father there? He must be frightfully pleased."

"Yes. He's here in this very room. He knows why I want to see you...."

"All right ... in that case, come over now."

"Oh *thank* you ... Nell.... Oh, just one thing ..."

"Yes?"

"Is Gerald there?"

"No ... he's out at the moment."

"Good. I'd rather like to see you alone ... this first time. I'll be over in twenty minutes ... less ..."

Half an hour later she was talking to Nell in her studio. At first, she had felt strangely shy being in that room again. She suspected she might have behaved rather strangely the last time she had been there. She devoted the first minutes to proving that now, at least, she was perfectly normal. She asked Nell about her work and congratulated her on the photograph of Isabel. Gradually Nell's manner, which had been friendly but constrained, began to thaw.

"Let's make some tea, shall we? G. won't be back for ages."

As Clara helped her in that once familiar kitchen, Nell suddenly smiled and said:

"You must ring poor old Clive Heron, and tell him the good news. He's been in quite a state about your having been ill. Rang me up at least once a month. Quite sensational for him. You know how he loathes 'phoning anyone."

"Ah . . . it was *you* then. Why didn't Daddy tell me? He pretended he'd forgotten who it was. He even said he must have muddled Clive up with someone else. Nell, I'm getting sick of all these mysteries. That's why I so much wanted to see you today."

A look of fear came into Nell's green eyes.

"What mysteries, Clara?"

Clara looked steadily at the face that was both like and unlike another face.

"First and foremost about Richard. Daddy made me promise not to write to him till I'd been . . . been decertified. Well, I could just see the point of that. Then today . . . when I was really free at last, he pretended he didn't know his address. And when I suggested asking you for it, he made every excuse to stop me."

Nell said faintly:

"Do you want so very much to write to Richard?"

"Why . . . of course. Nell . . . you look so strange. Is there some reason why I shouldn't? . . . Do you mean he doesn't *want* to hear from me?"

Nell grabbed a cigarette and lit it."

"Clara, dear . . . he'll be very, very glad to know you're well again. That I'm sure of."

They seemed to have changed parts. It was Clara now who felt assured and self-possessed while Nell seemed to be growing every moment more diffident.

Clara pressed her:

"I think there's something everyone's trying to keep back from me. Whatever it is, I believe Daddy knows and I'm quite sure you do."

Nell said miserably:

"Your father . . . I thought, perhaps, from the way you talked on the phone . . . I daresay, this last week or two, everything's slipped his mind except that things should go right today. . . ." She rallied her voice to a false cheerfulness. "And they *did* go right. It's simply too marvellous. You look splendid. A bit thin . . . but *I* think it suits you."

"So you said that last night I was here with Richard. Before he went down to Peacocks. Remember?"

"Did I? I'm sure I did if you say so. It's amazing how your memory's come back. You always did have a frightfully good brain. I expect that's why you got well sooner than anyone hoped."

"Nell, if I'm well, I'm well enough to be told the truth. I can't explain to Daddy that what I can't stand is not knowing. That's why I came to you. You've always been honest with me."

Nell frowned and puffed at her cigarette.

"It's nice of you to say that. . . . But sometimes it's jolly hard to be honest."

"Why? Because you're afraid of hurting someone? Or because it's not always easy to know what the truth is?"

"Both, sometimes," said Nell, still frowning.

"I understand that. Nell . . . look here, I don't want to talk about that place because it might hurt *you*. But I don't want to forget it, as Daddy thinks I should. You see . . . it was real, in its way. And it's desperately important for me now to know what's real and what isn't."

Nell's face softened.

"Poor kid. . . . You've certainly been through it, haven't you? It's changed you. You're more grown-up."

"Am I? Nell, will you tell me this much? How much did I imagine about me and Richard? *Before*, I mean? Suppose, already, I was beginning to have delusions . . . ? Perhaps he didn't love me as much as I thought?"

Nell answered slowly:

"You certainly didn't imagine he was in love with you. I've never seen him like that about any girl. After all, one knows one's own brother pretty well. No, there was something between you two that was almost uncanny."

"The game, you mean? And his coming back the night I was ill and my seeing the car and the accident. . . ."

"So you know about that?"

"Mother let it out by mistake. Perhaps she was exaggerating. She's apt to, you know, sometimes."

"No, she wasn't exaggerating. I was with you at the time. When Richard got here, his story confirmed yours in every detail. Even Gerald was convinced. And you know what an old sceptic *he* is."

"I certainly do." The relief of being able to talk about Richard almost naturally was so great that she laughed. But, the next moment, she was serious again.

"You say he *was* in love with me. . . . My going mad . . . was that so repulsive for him that. . . ?" Her face contracted. "But the larch tree . . . Nell . . . that was months *after*. . . ."

"Yes . . . dear. No . . . no . . . he was just terribly unhappy . . . Clara, I'll be frank with you. . . . I couldn't bear to see him going through what I'd been through. You know about John. You'll think it beastly of me but I tried to persuade him to forget you. He wouldn't listen to me. He was absolutely convinced you'd get better. But when, last April, your father had to tell him they thought there wasn't a hope . . . at least not till you were round about fifty. . . . Dear, do you really want me to go on?"

"Yes," said Clara, summoning up all her strength. . . . "Wait . . . Nell. . . . I don't think you have to tell me. I think I know." She paused. Her lips had gone so dry that she had to run her tongue over them before she could whisper:

"Kathleen?"

Nell nodded. Then she came across and knelt by her chair.

"Sure you're all right dear? Shall I get you a drink?"

"No . . . I'll be all right in a minute."

The room steadied itself. When Nell's face was in focus again, she said:

"They're married? I think I knew it. . . . It's queer . . . I believe I saw her in *there*. . . . There was a thunderstorm. . . . We said prayers together. . . ."

Nell was holding a glass to her lips. She refused at first, then drank the brandy obediently. After a moment she said:

"Thank you. I'm all right now. It was just the shock."

"I should think so, dear. You took it magnificently."

"It's a relief to know. I think I'll go now."

"Not for a minute or two. Just get steadied up. I'll come back with you, shall I?"

"No, thank you, Nell. I want to be alone for a bit. Before I see Daddy again. . . . There's so much he didn't tell me. . . . That about being fifty. . . . I can't face him just yet . . . I'll go for a walk. . . ."

"Good idea. Just sit quiet for a little first."

They sat in silence for some minutes. Then Nell said gently:

"Your religion means a lot to you, doesn't it, Clara?"

"It did once. Even in *there*, it did sometimes. And in that queer place I was in before. More like an ordinary house: you could see buses going past the window. But since I've been back . . . it's seemed awfully remote. Everything has . . . except wanting to know about Richard. Well, now I know. There's nothing more to know."

"There's one thing . . ." said Nell. "It might even be a sort of comfort."

Clara smiled painfully. "I doubt it. But you may as well tell me."

"He's become a Catholic. Gerald and I aren't religious, as you know. We weren't awfully pleased about it. But, if it's the least little help to you . . . why, even G. would be delighted."

"A Catholic? . . . It's hard to take in. I've got such an awful lot to take in . . . I don't even feel anything much . . . Kathleen. . . . Of course she'd want him to be a Catholic. . . ."

"Certainly, she wanted it. But I don't think she expected it. He was thinking about it before there was any question of their marrying. I believe it had something to do with you. . . ."

"I can't take that in either," she said. "Some day perhaps. . . . At the moment, I just feel numb."

"Poor child, no wonder . . . you've had about enough for one day."

"Yes . . . perhaps . . . I daresay I'll work it all out in time . . . I think I'll go now.

They both stood up. Nell kissed her and said, almost with her old roughness.

"You've got guts. Life won't get you down. One of these days, you'll get some sort of real happiness too. I have, you know. I could have sworn I never would."

"I wonder," said Clara. She gave a rather strained smile. "Funny, the only time in my life I should have been really happy was when I was on the point of going out of my mind. That would amuse Clive Heron."

"Would it? You understand him much better than I do. He told me once you were the only person who *did* understand him."

"We're both mad in a way, I suppose. I'm very fond of him. . . . But I don't think I could bear ever to see him again. . . . *He* brought me here that night. . . ." Her voice faltered: "Oh . . . if Richard had only trusted me. . . . If he'd only told me himself . . . given me some sign. . . ." The tears came into her eyes. "He won't even want to know I'm better. . . . There's no point in writing to him now. . . ."

"Clara," Nell said urgently. "There's something I'd forgotten. . . . He left me something for you. Something I was to give you when you came back . . . however long it was. . . . He said you'd understand what it meant."

She went to a drawer and took out a small red silk purse. Clara watched her in silence.

"I know just when he bought it," Nell went on. "It was the morning after that awful Sunday night your father told him. . . . He went off early to catch his train . . . he couldn't bear to be even with me and Gerald. Afterwards he told me he went into Westminster Cathedral on the way. . . . He'd been there once with you. . . . There was a shop opposite that sells statues and crucifixes and so on. . . . He wanted something Catholics used often. . . ."

The red purse was lying in Clara's palm now. She did not open it. She knew from the feel of it that it was a rosary. She could not say anything, not even a word of thanks to Nell. She felt Nell's kiss on her cheek and, a moment later, she was standing alone in the courtyard.

She stood for a while, clenching her wet eyelids together and clutching the little red purse. Then she became conscious of the faint sluck, sluck of the river. She remembered the narrow stone passage. A quiet, urgent impulse came over her to walk down it; to walk on and on with her eyes shut until it would be impossible to return. But, even more urgently, she felt the small weight pressing against her palm like a detaining hand. She forced herself to open her eyes. For a moment, she was no longer alone in the courtyard. She whispered, knowing that he heard:

"Richard . . . I'll hold on. . . . Go in peace."

Virago

If you would like to know more about Virago books, write to us
at Ely House, 37 Dover Street, London W 1X 4HS for a full
catalogue.

Please send a stamped addressed envelope

VIRAGO
Advisory Group

Andrea Adam	Zoë Fairbairns
Carol Adams	Carolyn Faulder
Sally Alexander	Germaine Greer
Anita Bennett	Jane Gregory
Liz Calder	Suzanne Lowry
Bea Campbell	Jean McCrindle
Angela Carter	Cathy Porter
Mary Chamberlain	Alison Rimmer
Anna Coote	Elaine Showalter (USA)
Jane Cousins	Spare Rib Collective
Jill Craigie	Mary Stott
Anna Davin	Rosalie Swedlin
Rosalind Delmar	Margaret Walters
Christine Downer (Australia)	Elizabeth Wilson
Barbara Wynn	

Book
Tokens

Give them
the pleasure of choosing
Book Tokens can be bought
and exchanged at most
bookshops